TROUBLED LEGACY

Phil Moncur

Phil Moncur

authorHOUSE®

AuthorHouse™ *UK Ltd.*
500 Avebury Boulevard
Central Milton Keynes, MK9 2BE
www.authorhouse.co.uk
Phone: 08001974150

© 2009 Phil Moncur. All rights reserved.

No part of this book may be reproduced, stored in a retrieval system, or transmitted by any means without the written permission of the author.

First published by AuthorHouse 12/4/2009

ISBN: 978-1-4490-5438-0 (sc)

Printed in the United States of America
Bloomington, Indiana

This book is printed on acid-free paper.

CHAPTER ONE

Despite the fact that she led three separate lives, Natalie Robertson was lonely. If only, she thought, it was not quite so important for her to keep all three lives quite separate from each other there might have been a possibility of some sort of relationship with someone, but the reality was far too complicated. One day, perhaps in a year or so, things might be different, but, at present, the greater part of her day to day existence was something to be endured rather than enjoyed.

Natalie was seated in front of her dressing table mirror wearing only her underwear. Although she had just taken a shower, her fair skin was covered in a thin film of perspiration as she contemplated the task of preparing herself to take on a fourth persona. The still, muggy air, heated by the late August afternoon sunshine and tainted with diesel fumes from the nearby railway station, permeated every corner of her eighth floor city centre flat. In the mirror the girl stared absently at her shoulder length mid-brown hair, deep blue eyes and perfect features. People said that Natalie was beautiful. Experience had taught her that men found her attractive; she had lost count of the number of times she had been told that if only she was taller she could have been a model. The image that stared back at her, though, did not strike her as being in any way attractive; she knew what lay beneath the surface all too well.

The French doors onto her tiny balcony were flung wide open, allowing the disjointed voice of the station announcer to filter into the solitary bedroom that she had shared with no one at all for the past three years and Natalie roused herself from her lethargic introspection and began to rifle through the top drawer of her dressing table. She took out a creased brown envelope, extracted a single sheet of paper, crumpled it into a ball and threw it across the room, narrowly missing the waste paper bin.

From Monday to Friday Natalie spent the daytime working as a mortgage approvals supervisor for the Northern Counties Bank in their Leeds headquarters, a ten minute walk across the city from her apartment. She had started work there at the age of eighteen. From humble beginnings in the call centre she had been promoted twice during her six years with the bank and had survived the staffing reductions caused by the credit crunch. Natalie, her managers had told her, possessed good people skills. What they actually meant was that she had the ability to persuade customers to borrow just that little bit more than they had first intended and then add icing to the cake by convincing them of the need to take out expensive insurance cover to ease their consciences at having taken on such a substantial debt. This she did with absolutely no compunction, as Natalie Robertson was almost completely amoral. That was evidenced in the way she had come to buy her flat "off plan" almost four years previously. Although she could have applied to her own employers for a subsidised mortgage she knew that her income was insufficient to meet their borrowing criteria. Using her knowledge that income checks were normally only perfunctory in the financial services industry's haste to sell mortgages, she had made a few judicious transfers from her meagre savings into her current account in order to "doctor" the two bank statements required. She then claimed to have an additional annual income of ten thousand pounds from a trust fund. As Natalie had anticipated the mortgage was granted within a matter of days and, together with her boyfriend; a final year art student from Leeds Metropolitan University, she had moved into the flat as soon as it was complete.

At first Natalie had anticipated that she would only struggle to meet the mortgage payments for a few months; until her partner graduated and got a job. A third class degree in modern art however, failed to open the door to paid employment and Matt had seemed content to spend his job seeker's allowance and a substantial amount of Natalie's income on fine wines, soft drugs and a party lifestyle. When Matt walked out on her in February 2006 Natalie found herself with several thousand pounds worth of debt on her credit and store cards and three months in arrears with her mortgage payments. Drastic action had proved necessary.

Since that time, on two or three evenings each week, Natalie Robertson metamorphosed into "Kelly" a high class "escort" who took internet bookings for clandestine encounters with wealthy businessmen in Manchester hotels. Described on her website as "34B", "a perfect size ten" and "five foot six tall", Kelly charged two hundred and fifty pounds for the first hour of her company and two hundred pounds for each hour thereafter. The fast and frequent train service between Leeds and Manchester, which carried on into the early hours of the morning, meant that, even if she travelled by taxi at both ends, her overheads worked out at less than fifty pounds per visit; the rest was tax-free profit. Although both Kelly and Natalie shared the same deep blue eyes and "perfect size ten" body, Kelly had long auburn hair and wore heavy make-up, exotic underwear, designer dresses and three inch heels; while Natalie was more often than not seen in smart casuals and comfortable shoes. By the autumn of 2006, apart from the balance of her mortgage, Natalie Robertson had become debt free and, because she was able to use cash for most of her day to day living expenses, her bank balance was rising rapidly.

Ironically, it had been an unintentional parting gift from Matt which lit the touch-paper of Natalie's third existence. In the acrimony of their parting he had left a jumble of discarded clothing, toiletries and paperwork in the bottom of his wardrobe. Amongst this detritus Natalie had discovered a gift voucher for a flying lesson in a light aircraft which Matt's parents had sent to him as a Christmas present. Feeling in need of a distraction she had appropriated the voucher with no hesitation and booked the lesson for herself. On a glorious spring day Natalie had taken the controls of a two seat Robin HR200 low wing monoplane trainer over the Vale of York and, under the watchful eye of her instructor, had flown it back to within a mile of touchdown at Leeds Bradford Airport. From that day she was hooked. At first, while she was clearing her debts, Natalie managed only one or two flying lessons each month; travelling to and from the airport by bus. In January 2007 though, she translated some of her savings into a five year old Ford Fiesta and began to spend most of her weekends at the Multiflight Flying School at Leeds Bradford Airport, flying twice a day if the weather permitted and occupying a corner of the cafe-bar studying for her pilot's examinations or chatting with likeminded enthusiasts if it did not. Dressing in trainers, jeans and loose fitting tops did little to detract from her appeal to the opposite sex, but within a matter of weeks, the predominantly male clientele had learned that "Nat", good company though she was, politely but firmly rebutted any advances that might be made. Within a year she had gained her Private Pilot's License and had graduated onto a four seat Piper Warrior in which she quickly added a Night Flying Rating and an Instrument Flying Qualification to her repertoire. Her burning ambition was to train as an airline pilot and she had passed the first batch of theoretical examinations for her Commercial License a few months previously and was undertaking a distance learning course for the second element. She had done her research and discovered that the best option for her flying training would be to take a residential course in the USA which would cost her the equivalent of thirty thousand pounds. Adding a further twelve thousand for food and accommodation and ten thousand more to keep up with the mortgage repayments on her flat brought her target to fifty two thousand pounds. That morning she had checked the balances in her current account, deposit account, ISA and the cash box she kept in a kitchen cupboard. She had twenty seven thousand eight hundred and nine pounds; more than half the total. The offer of five thousand pounds for one night's work had been just too tempting to resist.

Keeping her three lives separate was very important to Natalie. When she was Kelly she left the flat wearing a calf-length raincoat whatever the weather with the auburn wig in her bag. The transformation took place in the ladies' toilets at Manchester Piccadilly railway station both before and after her assignments. Her work colleagues had long since stopped trying to involve her in their social lives and she had little fear of meeting any of them in either the Manchester railway station or hotels that Kelly frequented. Her deepest dread, though, was to be recognised by someone from the flying school while in her role of escort.

Working as Kelly, Natalie had quickly developed the ability to maintain a mental and emotional detachment from what she was doing. While a small number of clients made energetic and bizarre sexual demands of her, she had found that the majority of her regulars wanted nothing more than entertaining conversation and relatively straightforward sex. It was not unusual for the first half of a three hour booking to involve a good meal in the hotel restaurant followed by twenty minutes of frenetic sexual activity and a further hour or so of quiet conversation. Only on half a dozen occasions had she been subject to what she thought of as abuse. In each case she had refused to meet the man concerned again. The client of the previous Saturday, however, had proved to be an exception to her rule.

"Barry", as he had called himself, had booked her by e-mail for two hours. The hotel he was staying at was not one of the salubrious city centre establishments that Natalie was familiar with but the down-market Travelodge at the corner of Deansgate and Blackfriars Road. She had arrived five minutes early in a taxi and, as instructed, went straight past the reception desk and climbed the staircase, following the signs for room 304. "Barry" was a thickset and powerful man in his late thirties with tattooed arms, hooded eyes and cropped black hair. There had been few preliminaries. No sooner had the door closed behind her than he had slapped a wad of cash on the dressing table and ordered her to strip. The sex was rough and painful; with only Natalie's strong mental detachment from what was being done to "Kelly" preventing her from crying out. It was over in a matter of minutes. Taking the man's obvious disinterest after the act as her cue for dismissal, she cleaned herself up and dressed in the bathroom. Returning to the bedroom, Natalie found Barry fully dressed. She picked up the banknotes from the dressing table and counted them carefully.

'There's five hundred here,' she said, 'that's fifty over the odds.'

'Keep it,' he replied.

With the cash stowed in the bottom of her bag, Natalie moved towards the door.

'Do yer fancy making ten times that?' asked Barry.

'Er, no thanks,' replied Natalie, not daring to imagine what might be required of her for five thousand pounds.

The man moved quickly towards her and gripped her tightly by the wrist.

'Just 'ear me out,' he said dragging her towards the bed and pulling her down to sit beside him. Natalie felt in her bag with her free hand, gripping the can of pepper spray that she kept for just such a situation, but before she had time to act Barry gripped her other arm and forced the can from her grip.

'I'm not going to hurt yer, yer stupid tart,' he snarled. 'Just listen will yer.'

With no alternative, Natalie let her arms go limp and the man in turn slightly relaxed his grip on her. 'All yer 'ave to do is pick up a nerd. That should be easy enough now, shouldn't it? Five thousand in cash for one night's work; now, if I let go of yer are yer going to hear me out?'

Natalie nodded and Barry let go of her wrists. Determined not to show any trace of fear she held his gaze as he outlined what he wanted her to do.

A certain man would be staying at the Midland Hotel the following Friday evening he explained. The man concerned would have details of a revolutionary new type of 3-D video games device in his possession. Barry's employer wanted access to this information and needed the man to be kept away from his room while the files on his laptop and the papers in his briefcase were copied. Natalie's job would be to persuade him to go with her to her room, have sex with him and then inject him with a powerful sedative to render him unconscious before stealing his wallet. When he woke up with a used condom in the bed beside him he would assume that the seduction had been a ploy to steal his money and credit cards. When he returned to his room he would find his laptop and papers exactly as he had left them. It was most unlikely, Barry told her, that he would even report the matter to the police. He would most probably just tell his bank that he had lost his wallet.

With little thought as to the rights and wrongs of the matter Natalie quickly assessed the potential risks of the venture against the benefit of gaining five thousand pounds towards her target. Her experience of the darker side of human nature had taught her that Barry was probably correct in his assertion that the victim would be reluctant to tell anyone the full story of what had happened in order to preserve his pride and dignity.

The risks were small and the potential reward was great. She agreed to the proposition.

Barry crossed the room and extracted a large brown envelope from a canvas holdall. He slid out a thin sheaf of documents, a grainy photograph and a small plastic box.

'This is Simon Fenton,' he said, ''e's your target.'

Natalie looked at the picture, which appeared to be a passport photograph very much enlarged. It showed a man who looked to be in his early thirties with grey eyes, brown hair and a neat beard and moustache.

'Nor a very good picture, I'm afraid,' said Barry, 'but good enough for yer to recognise him.' Also in the envelope was a copy of an e-mail confirming the reservation of and payment for an "Executive Double" room at the Midland Hotel the following Friday in the name of Samantha Evans and a page of handwritten notes.

'The notes are yer cover story,' explained Barry. 'Yer work for a PR firm in York. You're a secretary travelling with your lady boss on a trip to negotiate a big deal to re-brand Manchester City Council. Yer boss closed it that afternoon and is being wined and dined by the top knobs while you've been left on yer own so you're a bit pissed off. There's also a fake address for yer to use when you register. Simon Fenton, believe it or not, started off 'is workin' life as a bloody vicar before he went into electronics. 'E might be a bit prudish at first, so don't make yer move on 'im too strong. 'E'll also know that what e's doing in Manchester is a big deal and 'e might 'ave a cover story of 'is own, so don't be surprised if 'e spins yer a yarn 'cos he's not likely to tell you that he's carrying the stuff that could spark off a big do in 'ow we play video games forever until e's sold it to the 'ighest bidder.'

Barry snapped open the plastic box to reveal two syringes containing a colourless liquid.

'Yer give him one shot of this. It should send 'im drowsy right away and off to sleep within a few seconds. If anything goes wrong, or 'e doesn't drop off quickly enough like there's a spare.'

Natalie took the box from him and picked up one of the syringes, 'How do I know this is what you say it is?' she asked.

Barry snatched the syringe and box from her, returned the syringe to the box and snapped it shut. 'Because I say so,' he snapped, 'and because of the five big ones you're going to be paid. Right, on yer instructions sheet is my mobile. You call me as soon as 'e's in the land of nod. Stay in the room with 'im and I'll come and find yer when I've copied 'is stuff. I'll give yer five hundred now and the rest then, OK?'

Natalie nodded her assent.

'Right, fuck off now. Learn yer story and be in the foyer of the Midland from five next Friday. I'll be in the bar, but don't let on yer know me. How you get 'im laid is up to yer. Don't let me down, though or y'll live to regret it.'

He took hold of Natalie's wrist once again and jerked her to her feet. Silently, Natalie packed the photograph, paper and plastic box into her bag. Barry produced another roll of banknotes from his pocket and tossed them to her.

'Remember,' he said, 'Friday at five. Don't cross me tart. Yer wouldn't want me for an enemy.'

Slipping the roll of cash into her bag, Natalie walked unsteadily to the door without daring to look back.

For the next couple of days she managed to relegate any disturbing thoughts to the back of her mind. She would do her best. After all five thousand pounds was well worth a bit of a risk. If things did not go as planned she would just disappear into the night. A new name, wig and website and she would be back in business in no time.

The brown envelope, which had been waiting for her on her doormat when she got home on Thursday evening, though, had scuppered any thought of an easy way out. The envelope contained a print out of the homepage of "Kelly's" website. In the margin someone had written "Don't let me down – I know where you live." For the first time in many years Natalie Robertson had been truly frightened.

CHAPTER TWO

Simon Fenton was sitting at a rickety circular aluminium table outside the Pumpkin Coffee Shop next to the main entrance of Norwich railway station nursing a large latté in a cardboard cup. With more than half an hour to wait for his connection, time hung heavily on his hands and he took the letter from his pocket and spread it out on the table. The envelope had arrived along with a scattering of birthday cards the previous Wednesday. Since the death of his wife on that very day two years ago he had taken little joy in the celebration of birthdays and, at first, the letter had remained unopened on the hall table in his small two-bedroomed house on the outskirts of the small Norfolk town of Wroxham. It was not until the following morning that he opened the mail. Birthday cards from a couple of friends; one from his former in-laws and one, very obviously not in the old lady's own hand, from his grandmother in her nursing home in South Cumbria. The long white envelope had contained only a single sheet. He read it again. Mr Fenton, it instructed, should contact a Mr. Baldwin of Green, Arbuthnott and Harris, Solicitors, at their Manchester office where he may well hear news that would be to his advantage. For twenty four hours he had done nothing, half suspecting some form of scam, but eventually curiosity had got the better of him. A quick check on the internet found the firm listed in a number of business directories and their own website seemed to be authentic. During his lunch break he had taken the plunge and dialled the number. After a series of questions to establish that he actually was the Simon Fenton, born in August 1975 in Barrow in Furness he received the news that he was a beneficiary of the estate of the late Michael Charles Duckworth; a name he could not recall ever hearing before. It transpired that he was required to attend a meeting with Mr Baldwin and to bring with him his passport, birth certificate and driving license as proof of his identity. Expenses would be met from the estate. Mr Baldwin refused to discuss the details of the legacy over the telephone, but intimated that the sum involved would certainly make a visit to Manchester worthwhile. Eventually they had agreed a late afternoon appointment on the Friday before the August Bank Holiday. Simon had arranged to take a day of his annual leave from his job in the office of a firm of agricultural merchants and, deciding that the round trip to Manchester was too great a challenge for his twelve year old Mini Cooper, he had booked advance purchase train tickets. The solicitors had reserved him a room at the Midland Hotel for the Friday night as the last suitable train departed Manchester at only an hour and a half after the time of his appointment.

More intrigued than excited, Simon had plumbed the depths of his memory for a Michael Charles Duckworth. His father had been killed five months before he was born by the IRA while serving with the RAF Regiment in Northern Ireland and his mother had died the day she had given birth to him following what his grandmother had always referred to as "complications". Brought up by his maternal grandparents, Simon could recall little contact with his father's family although there had been cards and presents for Christmas and birthdays until his early teens. Michael Duckworth, he surmised was most probably related to his father in some way.

Roused from his thoughts by an announcement that the nine fifty seven to Liverpool was now ready for boarding at platform 3B, Simon stood up, picked up his small canvas holdall and checked the departure screen. As he walked along the platform he caught sight of his reflection in the carriage windows. His dark brown hair, he noticed, was getting a little long and his beard could really do with a trim. At the age of thirty four he recognised that he was clearly no slave to fashion. Dressed in a slightly shabby tweed jacket over an open necked shirt and black cord trousers, he resembled the prematurely aged eccentric that he knew he was rapidly becoming. It had been different during his time with Sophie. For ten short years he had been drawn out of his innate reserve by her sheer energy and almost overwhelming beauty. Since her death and his subsequent descent into disillusionment Simon accepted that his less than demanding job, contentment with his own company and growing obsession with crime thrillers and transport magazines increasingly marked him out from his generation. Simon Fenton was becoming old before his time and was not particularly troubled by the fact.

Settled into a window seat he watched the suburbs of the city gradually fade into the flat featureless East Anglian countryside as the train gathered speed. Simon began to read a railway magazine which he had bought from the W H Smith bookstall at Norwich station, but the heat of the sun through the window gradually overcame the best efforts of the train's air conditioning and he felt his eyelids becoming heavy. By the time the train began to slow down for its first station stop at Thetford he has slipped into a light sleep.

Two hours later, awake and hungry, Simon bought a sandwich and drink from the on-board trolley as the train rattled through the familiar countryside on its approach to Nottingham. Nottingham; where his relationship with Sophie had blossomed from simply "going out" into full blown romance. Nottingham; where he had asked her to marry him and been filled with relief and ecstasy when she had agreed. Nottingham; where his faith in God had been nurtured and developed as he studied theology and prepared for his ordination at St. John's College. The train pulled slowly into the railway station and Simon's carriage came to a halt adjacent to the staircase leading to the concourse, bringing back more poignant memories of Sophie. Upon that very spot there had been so many emotional partings and reunions as she had departed and arrived for weekends during her two years while she completed her training contract in Norwich. He realised that he had succeeded in almost erasing memories of Sophie from his consciousness for almost two months, but they now came flooding back in a torrent. They had been in the same year at the University of East Anglia, although he had not met her until the beginning of his fourth term there. An announcement over the public address system informed passengers that the train would be delayed slightly pending the arrival of a driver, but Simon was barely aware of the fact as his pent up memories followed one another into the miasma of his overburdened mind.

The first year of his degree course in modern history had passed without incident. Living in halls of residence, Simon had spread his time between a largely unremarkable social life, enough academic study to satisfy both himself and his lecturers and periods of near reclusiveness in his room with Radio Four, crime thrillers and the occasional transport magazine. He had briefly dated two young women, but the relationships had not developed into anything serious. It was during the summer vacation at the end of the year that his grandfather had died unexpectedly from a heart attack just nine months before he had been due to retire. Upon his return to university, Simon discovered the few friendships he had made during his first year to be no more than superficial as he slowly came to terms with his grief. For several weeks the young man withdrew into deep introspection as he contemplated the big questions of life. It was purely by chance that he noticed the advertisement on the history department notice board. "Life after death: fact or fable" a debate was to be hosted by the University Christian Union that evening. The case for eternal life was to be put by the University Chaplain while the case against was to be expounded by the Professor of Philosophy. Intrigued, Simon made the effort to attend and slipped into the room, sitting alongside a tall thin young man on the back row. He was slightly disappointed by what he considered the predictable rhetoric of the debate and was not surprised with the outcome of the vote which was three to one in favour of the hosts' beliefs. Just as he was about to leave, the tall thin man asked him if he fancied a pint. Simon, suspecting that an attempt to convert him to Christianity might be in the offing, was inclined to decline the invitation, but his lonely room held little attraction and he found himself agreeing to join his new acquaintance in the pub across the road. The young man introduced himself as Andrew Watkins and, to Simon's surprise, made no mention of the debate they had attended as they consumed two glasses of warm beer. Instead, Simon found himself doing most of the talking; Andrew Watkins was a good listener. They agreed to meet for coffee the following afternoon and so began a friendship that led Simon slowly but surely towards a faith that he had not been in any way seeking. Not once did Andrew instigate a conversation on spiritual matters, but Simon found himself increasingly intrigued by Andrew's faith, which he described as a relationship and not a religion, whenever Simon raised the matter. Within a couple of weeks Andrew had introduced Simon to several members of the Christian Union and, in mid November, having been invited by his new friends to a special service in the Chapel, Simon responded to an invitation to be prayed for and so began his journey into the Christian Faith. The next day he attended his first Christian Union meeting and encountered Sophie Drake for the first time. At five foot one, the top of her head barely reached his shoulder, but what she lacked in stature she more than made up for in sheer energy and the force of her personality. Petite and vivacious with dark eyes and an olive skin, Sophie had instantly adopted Simon's spiritual development as her own pet project. The daughter of a local clergyman and his Greek wife, Sophie lived at the family home in Great Yarmouth and commuted to and from the university in an elderly Vauxhall Astra. She insisted that he attended her father's church the following Sunday and drove into Norwich to collect him. After the service she had taken him home for Sunday lunch before driving him back as the November darkness fell across the flat and featureless landscape. That set the pattern for the rest of term. He would see her at the weekly Christian Union meeting, two or three times a week for coffee and every Sunday she would collect him in the morning and return him in the evening. Simon was aware that he was developing a powerful attraction to the girl but, fearful of damaging a valuable friendship and mindful of the significance of the emerging walk with his God, did not dare to make any verbal or physical expressions of his feelings for her. When they parted for the Christmas holidays he took the risk of giving her a ten pound book token as a gift, along with a box of chocolates for her family. In return she had given him a small leather bound Bible.

To his astonishment, Sophie telephoned him at home almost every day during the holiday. Without his grandfather Simon and his grandmother had spent a rather lonely Christmas together and he had forsaken the fragile remnants of his pre-university social life in order to keep the old lady company. The calls from Sophie were a welcome if slightly perplexing distraction from shared memories of Christmas past and the predictable diet of festive television. The day after his return to Norwich for the new term he had plucked up the courage to ask Sophie out. Within the week they were officially an item and Simon continued his assimilation into both the church and Sophie's family. His faith in God grew in parallel with his love for Sophie as the spring and summer terms flew by. As became their sincere Christian faith the couple remained chaste but were rarely apart. In the summer Simon and his grandmother spent a happy holiday in Great Yarmouth with the Drakes and when Sophie's father had first suggested that Simon might consider training for ordained ministry within the church it had seemed the natural thing to Simon to begin the process of testing the call. Just after Easter in his final year at University he had been invited to attend a Selection Conference at Ely and, shortly afterwards, it was confirmed that he would begin a three year course of theological training in Nottingham the following September. Sophie was delighted as she had already secured a place at the Nottingham Law School in order to complete her qualification as a solicitor. She had also been offered a two year training contract by a prestigious firm of commercial lawyers in Norwich. With their futures seemingly assured, Simon and Sophie had spent the summer helping out on a series of Christian Camps for young people in the Lake District before moving to Nottingham; Simon into residential accommodation at the college and Sophie into a nearby bedsit.

The train started with a jerk and roused Simon from his contemplation. He checked his watch. Twenty-eight minutes late; there was still plenty of time to keep his appointment in Manchester if there were no more delays. The sunshine of the morning faded behind hazy clouds, but the train's air conditioning continued to struggle. The guard passed along the carriage opening small windows with a large key. The relative coolness of the breeze ruffed Simon's hair as his thoughts returned to that long gone period of happiness. As the end of Sophie's year at Law School approached they had both contemplated the future with dismay. In Norwich Sophie would be working long hours and many weekends as she completed her on the job training while Simon continued with his course in Nottingham. They had become engaged in Nottingham Ice Rink less than twenty four hours before Sophie's parents had arrived to take her home for the last time.

The next two years had been difficult in more ways than one. As she had anticipated, Sophie's workload was very high and there were few opportunities for them to spend time together. The occasional snatched weekend and holiday times when Simon had stayed with Sophie's family were characterised by Sophie's fatigue and their shared frustration. A mutual yearning for intimacy stretched the limits of their self-imposed celibacy and there were one or two very close shaves. They were finally married just two weeks after Simon's ordination and, following a ten day honeymoon in Greece, they settled down as a married couple in a semi-detached house in the small market town where Simon was to serve his curacy. Having completed her training Sophie had been offered a permanent job as a junior solicitor by her firm. Initially her workload was more reasonable and the curate and his wife spent their spare time alternating between sharing in the work of the parish and making passionate love to one another. They had decided that Sophie would work for a couple of years to build up a "nest egg" and then they would start a family. By Christmas 2001, with savings of over thirty thousand pounds, Sophie gleefully flushed her contraceptive pills down the lavatory and they embarked upon a frenzy of lovemaking which left Simon both exhausted and exhilarated. Eighteen months later Simon had moved on to become Vicar of a small parish comprised mainly of a council estate on the outskirts of Norwich. Sophie had still not conceived and their lovemaking had subsided into a more systematic activity regulated by theories of ovulation and temperature graphs. Twelve months later with Sophie still not pregnant Simon had acquiesced to medical tests which showed that there was no biological reason why they should not have a child. That was when the rows had started. Sophie was successful in her work, often needing to spend several days away in London or occasionally European cities on business. Her immediate superior, a recently divorced junior partner named Alan Greenly, acted as her mentor and suggested that she had the potential to become a partner within five years. Simon, working over fifty hours a week to sustain and grow his congregation, came to accept that his wife had her own life to lead and their lovemaking gradually faded from the pre-planned program to occasional bouts of guilt induced duty. In May 2004, after returning from a week-long business trip to Rome, Sophie moved into the spare bedroom and rebutted all Simon's efforts to entice her back to his bed. By the time of her death in 2005 they had not made love for over a year.

Staring through the window into the middle distance as the urban sprawl of Nottingham faded into open countryside, Simon felt his eyes becoming moist as the painful memories of the fateful day forced their way into his consciousness. Sophie had told him that she had to go to London for a series of meetings which would probably take two or three days. He had dropped her off at the railway station on his way to a Clergy

Chapter meeting. His last view of her was as she walked across the station forecourt, wearing a tailored suit and carrying a leather holdall in one hand and her briefcase in the other. It had been nine thirty in the evening when the policeman had called. Simon had just returned from a visiting a young couple who had inquired about having their new baby baptised. At first he had been absolutely certain that there had been some mistake. How could his wife possibly have died in a road accident near Stratford upon Avon when she was staying in London? As the further details emerged, however, the story gradually became more plausible and distressing. A dark blue BMW registered to a Mr. Alan Greenly had collided head on with a Transit van while overtaking a lorry at high speed. Mr. Greenly and his passenger had been killed instantly. The female passenger had been carrying a driving licence and several credit cards in the name of Sophie Fenton. Two awful truths collided head on with Simon Fenton in an instant. The first was that his wife was dead and the second was that she had not gone to London on business, but had been going somewhere quite different with her boss.

CHAPTER THREE

Natalie finished applying her subdued make up and turned her attention to the creation of an appropriate look for "Samantha". She decided to leave her hair as it was; swept back in a neat pony tail. Rifling through her wardrobe she selected her outfit with care; taking out and discarding a number of items before putting on a tight knee-length plain navy skirt and a white cotton shirt with a thin blue vertical stripe over her lacy white cotton bra and briefs. In the late summer heat she decided to leave her legs bare and wriggled her feet into a pair of blue sandals with a small heel. Looking far more like Natalie than she was entirely comfortable with, she completed the outfit with a matching plain navy jacket and laid out her raincoat on the bed. In the bottom of her wardrobe was a large shoulder bag in which she kept a number of items purchased from the Ann Summers shop, her can of pepper spray and some other paraphernalia which she made use of in her clandestine work. No, Samantha would certainly not have anything of that nature in her possession on a business trip, she thought, and instead she chose a smart blue leather handbag into which she transferred her purse, mobile phone, keys and the folded up photograph of her quarry. She also packed a small holdall with a change of underwear, a pair of jeans and three cotton t-shirts, together with a few toiletry items and some make up.

Natalie closed the balcony doors, picked up her bags, folded her raincoat and put it into the holdall and set out on her mission. The short walk to the railway station took her less than ten minutes. She purchased her ticket, bought a magazine at the W H Smith bookstall, passed through the ticket barrier and checked the time on the large digital clock on the platform; two fifteen. Her instructions required her to be at the hotel by five. With trains every fifteen minutes and a journey time of around an hour she had plenty of time in hand. Natalie climbed the stairs onto the wide over-bridge, bought herself a skinny latté at the Starbuck's coffee stand and settled down at a table with her magazine. Experience had taught her that the trains which went through to Manchester Airport were often the most crowded and those which terminated at Piccadilly were usually the least busy. The next service terminating at Piccadilly departed at two forty and a few minutes before it was due she left her temporary refuge and steeled herself for the ordeal ahead.

The train arrived in Manchester on time and, upon leaving its air-conditioned comfort, the oppressive humidity of the afternoon hit Natalie like the open door of a furnace. Eschewing the fifteen-minute walk to the Midland Hotel, she took a taxi, checked in and threw off her clothes in the cool comfort of her room. Enough time for a quick shower and to prepare herself once again for her task, she thought. Half an hour later, still with time in hand before she was required to station herself in the reception area, Natalie developed a bout of severe anxiety. It was not that she had developed any scruples as to the right and wrong of what she was about to do. No, it was much more a case of the fear of failure. What if Simon Fenton rebuffed her advances? What if he saw through her subterfuge and called her bluff? What if he spotted the syringe and fought her off? For several minutes she contemplated slipping out of the hotel and making her escape. Frightened as she was by Barry's threats and the fact that he knew where she lived it was always possible that he would not come after her. No, he would find her and hurt her, of that she was convinced. Her only hope then would be to run away and begin a new life somewhere else. For a few minutes the thought of leaving her past behind seemed attractive. No more dull days in the bank. Certainly the prospect of not having to sell her body to whoever could afford it had some appeal. Her dream of becoming an airline pilot, however, held that promise too and, grasping her hands together to still their trembling, Natalie checked her appearance in the mirror one last time and stepped out into the corridor, closing the door firmly behind her.

She spotted Barry as soon as she stepped out of the lift into reception. Dressed in a crumpled suit that was at least a size too small for him he was seated at on a cream sofa close to the door. He caught her eye briefly as she walked across the foyer and gave a half smile before she looked away. With heavy legs Natalie chose an identical sofa opposite of the reception desk with a view of the door. Avoiding looking at Barry, she picked up a discarded newspaper and settled down to await the arrival of her prey. Leafing through the paper, she digested the news that, following a minor heart attack while on holiday in Jersey earlier in the month, the Prime Minister had announced that he had decided to stand down before the new session of Parliament. The coming Party Conference was to be the first round in the fight to replace him. The Chancellor had already announced that he would not be standing, so the press speculation was that either Eddie Duggan, the Home Secretary, or Tom Atkins, the Secretary of State for Children, Schools and families would be his logical successor. There was also the possibility of a strong challenge from the left wing of the party from Helen Bancroft, a former Treasury Minister who had resigned in protest at the Government's handling of the economic crisis of 2009 and a possible outsider was Ellen Westcliffe, an up and coming youngster who had been unexpectedly been promoted to Health Secretary just a few months ago. Although not particularly interested in politics, Natalie found the news a welcome distraction from her anxiety as she briefly scanned the faces of everyone who entered the foyer.

After what seemed like an eternity she looked up as yet another figure entered from the street and recognised the face from the photograph. He was taller than she had anticipated, but with his unkempt appearance and straggly beard she was in no doubt that he was the computer nerd that she was stalking. Apparently startled by the grandeur of his surroundings he stood still at the top of the entrance steps and turned his head from side to side before making his way slowly to the reception desk. Natalie watched as he began the check in procedure then she stood up and walked slowly over to stand behind him.

'Would you like someone to take your bag?' asked the young receptionist, gesturing to the small holdall that he had put down at his feet.

'No thanks,' he replied, 'it's not heavy. Can I ask, what time is dinner served?'

'The Restaurant is open now Sir,' replied the receptionist, 'would you like to book a table?'

'Yes, I suppose so', he replied, glancing at his watch, 'Seven thirty, OK?'

'Seven thirty in the Restaurant, Sir, enjoy your stay.'

The man picked up his bag and walked slowly towards the lift.

'Yes Miss, how may I help you?' The receptionist smiled at Natalie.

'Oh, it's alright, I was just going to ask about the restaurant, but I heard you telling that gentleman,' she replied, turning briskly to follow Simon Fenton towards the lift. As she caught up with him the lift door slid opened and she followed him inside.

CHAPTER FOUR

Simon Fenton had been relieved when he was startled from his melancholy reflections by the voice of the guard over the train's PA system. The train had drawn to a halt alongside a large B&Q store.

'Ladies and gentlemen, I am sorry to inform you that due to a signal failure our arrival in Sheffield will be delayed by approximately fifteen; one, five, minutes.' Simon checked his watch. The extra delay would make the train around forty-five minutes late arriving at Manchester Oxford Road. He pulled a crumpled Google Map from his pocket and studied it carefully. Still enough time for him to check into his hotel and freshen up before his four thirty appointment. The train remained where it was, however for almost thirty minutes and when it did finally crawl into Sheffield railway station there was a further ten minute delay before it moved off again in the reverse direction on the last leg of its journey. Anxiety about being on time for his appointment had driven the unpleasant replay of the darkest hours of his life from his mind. He contemplated calling the solicitors' office on his mobile phone, but decided that if he went straight there from the station he would probably make it with a few minutes to spare.

There were no more delays. Simon passed the remainder of the journey reading his magazine and the train eventually drew into Oxford Road station just a few minutes after four o'clock. In the warm humidity of the station approach Simon consulted his map and set off at a brisk pace towards St. Peter's Square. Passing the entrance to the Midland Hotel he continued along Mosley Street and into the warren of narrow roadways until he located the office of Green, Arbuthnott and Harris. Upon entering the building almost five minutes late for his appointment he was directed straight to Mr. Baldwin's office on the first floor. The solicitor looked up from his desk as Simon entered. He was younger than Simon had expected, fresh faced and wearing a sharp suit, Mr. Baldwin rose to shake hands with his visitor, brushing aside Simon's apology for being late.

'It doesn't matter,' he said, 'you're my last appointment today so we can take as long as we like. Now would you like a coffee?'

Five minutes later the solicitor returned with the drinks. Mr. Baldwin began proceedings by asking for Simon's passport driving license, and birth certificate, which he photocopied on a small copier situated behind his desk.

'Well,' he said, 'handing back the documents, 'there's no doubt you are the Simon Fenton in question. The address on the driving licence tallies with the information given us by our client.'

'That's as may be,' replied Simon, 'but I've been wracking my brain and I've absolutely no idea who Michael Charles Duckworth might have been.'

'From a legal point of view there's absolutely no need for you to know,' replied the solicitor, 'but I can certainly understand your curiosity.' He opened a buff coloured file which was on his desk. 'Michael Duckworth was born in Stockport on April 11th 1950.' He announced, consulting the file. 'Latterly he lived at 22 Chester Green Lane in Derby and it seems that he was married in 1979 and divorced six years later. He had no children and was employed by Cross Country Trains at their depot outside Burton on Trent. Does that ring any bells?'

'No, none at all,' replied Simon.

'He died on May 2nd this year in Derby City Hospital after being seriously injured in a hit and run road accident,' continued Baldwin, 'I can tell you that he made his will here in April and that you are the only beneficiary. I've taken the liberty of having the house valued. It's a two-bedroomed terraced property and should fetch in the region of a hundred and thirty thousand pounds. He had a current account, a savings account and a Cash ISA which added up to just under thirty eight thousand pounds. There was a car, an eight year old Ford Focus, but its tax and MOT expired in June so I used my discretion as executor and sent it to auction. It raised a further eight hundred and fifty. After our fees and disbursements you stand to inherit around thirty four thousand pounds. I can arrange to sell the house on your behalf if you'd like me to. In the meantime I've had the house cleaned, left all the services connected and the council tax and water rates are paid up until March next year. The furniture is still in situ, but there's nothing special so I suppose it wouldn't bring in more than six or eight hundred from a house clearance. I've a cheque here made out to you for thirty thousand. You'll get the balance when things are finally settled. Do you know what you'd like to do about the house or would you like more time to think about it?'

For several seconds Simon sat staring over the solicitor's shoulder at the buildings visible through the window.

'I don't think I want to make any decisions at the moment...' he answered, 'all this take quite a bit of thinking about. I just can't take it all in. I still have no idea at all who he was.'

'I'm sorry, but there is one more thing I need to trouble you with,' said Mr. Baldwin, with an apologetic smile, 'but my instructions are very clear.' The solicitor shuffled papers in his file and extracted two large brown wax-sealed envelopes and a small key in a transparent plastic bag. 'I have here two envelopes. I was instructed to give you the first one and give you time to read the contents. After that you are to decide whether or not you want to take the other one and the key. If you choose not to take them I am instructed to destroy the second envelope in the shredder and to throw away the key. This is an unusual request, but I do have to comply with it. Here, take the first letter. I'll leave you alone for a few minutes. You can tell me when I come back whether you want the second envelope or whether we put it in the shredder.'

The solicitor handed Simon the sealed envelope and picked up the remaining papers from his desk and left Simon sitting in a perplexed silence. After a few seconds he slowly broke the seal, extracted two pages covered with untidy handwriting and began to read.

Dear Simon

I don't suppose you will remember me, but I came to visit you a couple of times when you were very small. I know it will sound melodramatic, but I deliberately broke off contact with you before you were five because I thought my visits might put you at risk. Your grandparents were very kind to me and I remember you as a rather serious but clever little lad.

I was a friend of your dad. I was with him when he was killed and had served with him for nearly two years before that. He was a fine and brave man. I expect that you will have been told that he died during a shoot-out with the Provisional IRA. That's the truth, but it wasn't an IRA bullet that killed him. The man who killed him has also killed at least three other people and, by the time you read this will have almost certainly killed me as well. The murderer is a powerful man and very dangerous with it. If you want to find out about how he killed your dad you will almost certainly put yourself in danger. People who ask certain questions about him tend to end up dead. That's why I want you to have a choice.

If you think that sleeping dogs are best left alone you are very welcome to my house and money. I have no one else to leave it to anyway. I have followed your life from a safe distance and I know that you have already suffered another tragedy as well as losing both your parents before you had the chance to know them. I hope that what I leave you will, in some small way, help you out.

On the other hand, if you do want to know more about your dad and the monster who killed him then take the second envelope. There's a key that should come with it. Remember that once you start investigating your dad's death you will be putting yourself in very great danger so don't do it lightly. Even if you do read the other letter (do it somewhere where you can be on your own, Simon) you can always destroy it straight away, but don't tell a soul about in until you have all the evidence you need. Even then don't go to the police. They can't be trusted in this. Take it to the newspapers and ask them to hide you away until it's sorted.

Yours affectionately

Michael

Simon was stunned by the unexpected revelation about how his father had died. Although the details were never discussed, his grandparents had told him that his father had been shot by the IRA in an exchange of fire with an RAF Regiment patrol in Northern Ireland. The IRA had been trying to land drugs from a small boat in a bay just to the north of a Radar Station in County Down when they had been surprised by the RAF men. All of the terrorists had been killed in the battle and Simon had always thought of his father as a hero. Now it seemed that there was more to the story than he had thought. In truth, Simon had not thought a great deal about his parents for many years. Having known them only from fading photographs, the reality of being brought up by his maternal grandmother and grandfather had kept them at the back rather than the front of his mind. There had been cards and presents from his father's parents in London when he was younger, but they had never sought him out, or he them. Still in a state of shock he was startled by the sound of the door opening signalling the return of Mr. Baldwin.

'Well, Mr. Fenton, what's the verdict; take or shred?' He held out the second envelope and the key.

'Er, I'll take them,' replied Simon, unsure of how he had come to make the decision. Fifteen minutes later he was back out on the street, having signed several papers without bothering to read them, with a cheque for thirty thousand pounds in his wallet, a set of keys for a house he had never seen in his holdall and two brown envelopes and a small key in his inside jacket pocket. He had also been given a copy of the will. The heat-seared streets were busy with workers leaving their offices for the bank holiday weekend and Simon had to retreat into a doorway on several occasions get his bearings. Eventually, a few minutes after six o'clock, he arrived back at the Midland Hotel, checked in and entered the lift in search of room 411. A pretty girl followed him into the lift momentarily distracting him from his thoughts with a warm smile. She asked him if he had stayed in the hotel before and responded to his polite answer with a friendly prattle about being there on business before they parted company on the fourth floor. Deep in thought Simon unlocked the door of his room, threw his holdall and jacket on the bed, opened the second envelope and began to read.

Phil Moncur

Dear Simon

I don't know whether or not you reading this is a good thing or not. I fear that you may be on the brink of danger. You may be risking your life if you act on what I am about to tell you so this is not the full story. This letter will tell you how to get it, though.

When our patrol took on the Provos that night I can tell you that your dad survived the fight. Only one of us Rocks was hit by the IRA and he lived to tell the tale. It was drugs that the bad guys were landing. We caught them in a cross-fire and all of them were down within a minute or so. Your dad was killed by one of our own because he wouldn't go along with stealing half the drugs and a bagful of cash that we got hold of.

I'm not going to tell you any more than that for now. Covering up what happened has already cost too many lives and the man responsible is so powerful that you may already be being watched. He is in politics now, and very near the top. No one would believe anything without proof. For what its worth my advice is to go back to your normal life for at least a few months before you follow up what I am going to tell you. Remember it may not be safe to go to the police. The newspapers would be a better bet when you have all the evidence. I know now that I should have done that, but by the time I realised just what I had to do it was too late. They have been watching my every move and I am afraid that they will do away with me and, as you may find out, I don't have all the evidence with me. It is all hidden and no one would believe me without it. I am afraid that if I make an attempt to get it they will get me before I can do anything with it. There are certain papers which they are very keen to destroy – that's why I'm afraid you will be on a bit of a goose chase if you decide to try and avenge your dad.

You can still decide to forget all this and just take what I have left you. Your life would be much safer if you did, but, knowing that you are John's son I suspect that you might well have a go. With this letter you will have been given a key. That will open a safe deposit box at the bank on the corner of the street where your grandfather ate fish and chips with Shirley Bassey and a street named after a flower. I'm sorry to be so cryptic, but I can't risk this letter falling into the wrong hands. You will need a copy of my will and proof of identity to get access to the box.

Whatever you decide be assured of my very best wishes.

Good Luck

Michael

For several minutes Simon stared blankly at the paper in front of him. The cryptic clue was no problem to him. All through his childhood his grandfather had boasted about the day when he had been an office junior in a Glasgow theatre and the teenage star had been top of the bill. Bored and lonely in a strange city she had sneaked away from her entourage and enlisted the young man's help in organising an illicit escape. They had walked the length of Sauchihall Street and back eating fish suppers before returning to the theatre to face the minor wrath of both the theatre manager and Miss Bassey's chaperone. All he had to do was to Google a street map of Glasgow and locate an intersection with a street named after a flower. Almost without realising it Simon was forced to admit that he was hooked. He would take the old man's advice and return home to give the matter some more thought, but the fuse had been well and ignited. Perplexing as it was, the unexpected information about his father's death seemed to offer the glimmer of a sense of purpose to his life that had been lacking since he had walked away from the church after Sophie's death. Apart from a grandmother who no longer recognised him he had no ties; nothing to hold him back. With unaccustomed determination he undressed and stood under a tepid shower, washing away both the fatigue of the day and a modicum of the lassitude that had become a major component in his life over that past two years. Refreshed and dressed in a clean shirt and underwear, Simon impulsively folded the both letters and the key into one envelope and put it in his trouser pocket before emerging from his room in search of a meal.

The restaurant was quiet. Only three businessmen dining alone and two couples were seated when he arrived. The waiter explained that this was common on the Friday before a bank holiday as most business people had departed for the long weekend and few of the expected leisure visitors arrived early enough to eat before eight thirty. He showed Simon to a table for two on the opposite wall to the door and took his order for a cold beer, leaving him to examine the menu. Unable to decide between the bruschetta and the prawn salad he was mildly irritated by the shadow of a figure standing next to him falling on the menu. Could the waiter not see that he had not yet decided? Simon looked up. It was not the waiter. Standing opposite him was the girl he vaguely remembered from lift. She was smiling down at him. He noticed that she had lovely deep blue eyes.

'I'm sorry to bother you,' she said, 'but would you mind if I joined you? I've been on my own all afternoon and I could certainly do with a bit of company.'

CHAPTER FIVE

Despite her best efforts, Natalie had to concede that her attempt to engage Simon Fenton in conversation in the hotel lift could hardly have been deemed successful. Apart from a perfunctory admission that he had not stayed in the hotel before, he seemed to have paid little attention to either her conversation or forced smile. Indeed she had been unable to hold him in eye contact for more than a second or so. He appeared, she concluded, to be preoccupied with something or other. Anyway, she knew when and where he would be eating. That would be her next opportunity.

She spent a long hour sitting in her room with the flat screen TV providing moving wallpaper while she rehearsed the details of her next move. Time passed slowly as uncertainty and the very real fear of failure nibbled at her fragile self-confidence. Strange as it was, although Natalie, Kelly or even Nat could cope with almost any situation they might find themselves in, Samantha felt vulnerable and nervous. Eventually the hands on her watch showed it to be half past seven and, with a last check of her appearance in the mirror, Natalie left the room, locked the door behind her and descended in the lift to the ground floor. Once there she sought out the Derby Restaurant. From the doorway she spotted Simon Fenton sitting on the opposite side of the room studying the menu.

'Table for one madam?' inquired a waiter who had spotted her hesitating in the doorway.

'No thanks,' she replied,' I've spotted a friend over there. I'll just pop over and join him.'

Consciously fixing a smile onto her face she walked directly over to where the man was sitting. As she reached his table he looked up, a slight frown of irritation evident in his features. Clutching tightly to her handbag to prevent her hands from shaking she met his gaze.

'I'm sorry to bother you,' she said, 'but would you mind if I joined you. I've been on my own all afternoon and I could certainly do with a bit of company.'

Flustered by both the unexpected interruption and the undoubted attractiveness of the interrupter, Simon was momentarily lost for words. Averting his eyes from hers he muttered a reply,

'Er..., yes..., please sit down.' He gestured to the chair opposite and half stood up as she pulled it out from the table.

'I'm Samantha,' she announced as she sat down, holding out her hand, 'but most people call me Sam.'

'Simon', he said, taking her hand briefly in his, 'pleased to meet you.'

'I'm sorry if you wanted to be on your own,' she continued, 'I'll go away if you want me to, but I'm having a pretty rotten day and you've got a friendly face.'

Treated to the full allure of a smile that reached the corners of her eyes, Simon found himself drawn into the engaging aura of the girl's presence.

'No, I'm on my own too, please stay,' he replied, 'what brings you to Manchester on a Friday night?'

Giving him the full benefit of the practiced charm gleaned from both of her paid professions, Natalie began to expound the well rehearsed story. Her boss, she told him, had disappeared in mid afternoon with two copies of a fiercely negotiated contract with the City Council in her briefcase and the promise that, as soon as the ink was dry on them, she and "Sam" would be on their way back across the Pennines to York. Half an hour later, she claimed, there had been a call on her mobile informing her that her boss was going to be wined and dined by a senior council officer in celebration of the contract and that "Sam" should book the rooms for another night.

'She told me to just get on and have a good time,' complained Natalie, 'but I don't know anyone here and I'm not really a party animal. I don't fancy being the girl alone in a club or anything, so I decided just to stay here and watch TV. It's pretty boring being on your own, though, so when I came down for dinner and saw you I thought I'd take a chance on a bit of intelligent company.'

The waiter returned with Simon's beer and went away with an order for dry white wine for the lady. Simon was relieved that the girl had made the running in terms of their conversation and had limited himself to brief questions and affirmations. The intervention of the waiter, however, had signalled a pause in proceedings and Natalie handed the baton to Simon.

'How about you?' she asked, 'Are you here on business?'

'No, not really,' he replied, uncertain how open he should be with a stranger, albeit a rather attractive one, about the tumultuous nature of his legacy. Undecided as to how far discretion would be preferable to honesty in the light of the contents of Michael Duckworth's letters, he chose to steer a middle course, an aversion to deliberate deceit still lingering deep within hid psyche from his previous way of life.

'It's personal actually; I had a letter from a solicitor. It seems that I've inherited a house and a bit of money from an old family friend that I can't even remember meeting.'

'Wow,' Natalie replied, smiling inwardly at his bare faced deception, 'that's amazing. Nothing like that ever happens to me.'

'Not to me either,' Simon continued, 'my life is usually completely boring.

There was an awkward silence as Natalie struggled mentally to find another line of conversation. Get him talking about himself, she thought; just find the right questions to get him going. From her clandestine life as Kelly she had learned that a man's favourite topic for conversation was usually himself. All she had to do was to find the key to unlock the door and it would all come tumbling out. Then all she would have to do would be to smile and make the occasional comment. Her dilemma was that he was obviously lying about the reason for his visit and might well find it difficult to elaborate on the lie. If she asked him about his work he would probably not admit to being a technology geek. He would be forced to tell more lies and then would not feel comfortable talking to her. Unless rapport could be established she would have to rely solely on her physical charms to get him into her room and, with her characteristic low self-esteem coming into play, Natalie felt a momentary pang of fear. She picked up the menu and held it in front of her.

The lapse in conversation gave Simon time to pause for thought. While her eyes were on the menu he took in her shiny brown hair, which was neatly tied back into a pony tail, her small features and flawless complexion. The two top buttons of her shirt were undone, revealing a generous expanse of cleavage and just a glimpse of the white lace of her bra. For a moment he felt like the hero of one of his thriller novels; a kind of James Bond figure. Within a matter of a couple of hours he had been presented with unexpected wealth, an intriguing and possibly dangerous mission and now the company of a beautiful woman. The absurdity of the situation amused him. Straight-laced, sad Simon, he thought, was well and truly out of his depth. For a moment he contemplated feigning illness and retreating to his room, but a return to self-imposed introspection held no attraction for him. The letters from Michael Duckworth, he realised, actually had jolted him out of the blandness of life that he had chosen to embrace since Sophie's had died. The company of an attractive young woman, he decided, could do him no harm. Talking to Samantha would be a pleasant way to spend the next hour or so. The solitude of his hotel room would come soon enough. In the meantime he would try and practice some of the social skills that seemed to have been lacking in his life for some time.

The hiatus was interrupted by the arrival of the waiter with Natalie's wine and to take their food order. Simon ordered the prawn salad, followed by pan-fried cod while Natalie chose duck and chicken terrine followed by chicken Caesar salad.

'So,' began Simon, 'what do you do when you're not at work, Sam?'

Troubled Legacy

Still preoccupied with how to steer the conversation so that he did most of the talking, Natalie's answer was on her lips before she had thought it out.

'I fly light aeroplanes,' she said, regretting her honesty as soon as the words left her mouth.

'Isn't that terribly expensive?' asked Simon.

'Well,' continued Natalie, taking the chance to partially redeem the situation, 'I was a bit fed up when my boyfriend left me a couple of years ago. Now that there's no one else but me I can spend my money how I like.'

Pleased to have communicated both her singleness and availability, Natalie once more realised that her answer had been essentially truthful. Sam, it appeared was turning out to be too much like Natalie for comfort.

'How long did it take you to lean?' inquired Simon.

'Around a year', she replied, 'it cost me just a bit less than seven thousand pounds. I know that's a lot of money, but you could spend more on a car or an exotic holiday.'

'And what was it like the first time you flew one on your own?'

'It was amazing,' she replied, her eyes sparkling with enthusiasm at the memory, 'I went solo after fifteen hours training. It was on a Saturday afternoon in early March. It was a calm, still day and the sun had been shining in the morning, but it had clouded over a bit by then. I did an hour of circuits with my instructor just before lunch and I had another hour booked at three. The CFI, sorry, Chief Flying Instructor, turned up instead of my usual instructor. He told me that Henry had been needed for another job. I had no idea that it was my final check. We did two circuits then he told me to do one on my own. It was amazing; scary and exciting all at once. I hadn't time to do much thinking though. It all happened so quickly, calling Air Traffic for permission to take off, lining up and doing the checks, full throttle, keep her straight, sixty knots and pull back, check temperatures and pressures at three hundred feet, flaps up, landing light off then turn crosswind. Then it was downwind checks and calling on the radio. You get a minute or so to think after that and there I was; heading towards Otley, the airfield on my left and no one in the seat beside me. I think it was probably the best moment in my life. Then you have to turn onto left base and things get busy again; carb. heat on, throttle back to fifteen hundred, two stages of flap and trim for seventy knots in the descent. Turn onto final, get permission to land, full flap and hold her at seventy, keeping on the glide-path with the throttle. Chop the power over the threshold, round out and hold her off until she stops flying.'

Seeing Simon's half smile brought a flush of embarrassment to Natalie's cheeks.

'Oh, sorry,' she said, 'I got a bit carried away didn't I?'

The half smile turned into a grin.

'Don't worry about it,' replied Simon, 'it's interesting and you're obviously passionate about your flying. When were you last in the air?'

The waiter arrived with their starters providing a brief interruption, but no sooner had he left than Natalie continued; the sparkle still evident in her eyes.

'It was last Sunday,' she began, suddenly recalling that it had been the day before her fateful encounter with Barry. A brief frown crossed her face before she took up the story again. 'I'd booked the Warrior for the day. Leeds to Campbeltown and back; that's on the Mull of Kyntyre. Two and a quarter hours each way. Anyway it was a beautiful day. I don't know if you remember, but a cold front had gone through before dawn and the sky was clear with visibility of over fifty K's. By the time I'd reached five thousand feet over the Pennines you could see the North Sea on the right and all the Irish Sea on the left. You'd think it might be lonely on a long flight like that, but there's always something to do; navigation, engine and fuel checks and then there's the scenery. Everything looks so different from above; cleaner somehow and you feel as if nothing can get at you or touch you......'

Feeling suddenly foolish, she hesitated. Samantha had almost become Natalie and there was a job to be done.

Troubled Legacy

'Sorry' she said again, 'you must think I'm awfully boring. You've listened to me long enough. Tell me what you do when you're not at work.' Natalie picked up her knife and fork and Simon followed her lead.

'Nothing like you,' he said with a broad grin, 'I read a lot actually, not proper literature or anything; crime novels and thrillers.' He almost went on to talk about his interest in transport, but a touch of what he had to acknowledge was most probably vanity held him back. He was reluctant to be judged an anorak by a pretty girl. Not that he was interested in her in that way, though. Anyway she was way out of his league. Still, for the first time in years he began to contemplate the possibility that he might one day be in a league of sorts once again. Since he had firmly and none too politely rebuffed the fairly transparent advances of two lonely single Christian women the year after Sophie's death he had closed his mind to romance completely. Once bitten twice shy had been his mantra. Now that the letters from Michel Duckworth had begun to turn his life around, though, might it not also be the time to dare to think again?'

'How about films?' Sam's next question roused him from his thoughts.

'Oh sometimes,' he said as he finished his starter, 'I used go with a friend to Norwich every few weeks, but he's moved to London. I don't think I've seen a film for over a year, apart from on TV of course.'

With a little gentle fishing, Natalie established some common ground surrounding films and TV and the conversation stayed safe and general while she finished her starter and the main courses arrived. As he began to eat his fish, Natalie made a quick appraisal. Until meeting him she had not thought of Simon Fenton as a person. In the same way that Kelly's clients did not connect directly with Natalie, but remained a mere matter of business, she had supposed that Simon Fenton would fit neatly into the same mould. Having met him as Samantha, however, things were not going to plan. She was rather enjoying his company. There was no physical attraction though. While he was not exactly ugly, his unkempt hair and straggly beard were a distinct turn off. He was carrying a few surplus pounds and his dress sense was appalling. Kelly had got into bed with much worse, though. As the banal chatter continued she began to turn her mind to the task in hand. He seemed to be absorbing her ready smiles and, on more than one occasion she had noticed him glancing at her cleavage. She toyed with moving on to verbal flirting and occasional innuendo, but feared that such a move might break the growing rapport between them. With the main courses finished Natalie decided that she needed to prolong their time together in the public areas of the hotel before she made her move. A drink in the bar seemed to be the next move. Yes, a couple of drinks would relax his inhibitions and give her the chance to touch his hand and brush her breasts against his arm. Then moving on to her room would be a more natural progression. Perhaps she could ask him to have a look at her fictitious laptop or something as an excuse. Once she had him behind closed doors she would pull him towards her and kiss him she decided. It was then that she remembered. She had no condoms with her; her stock was in the shoulder bag that was still in the bottom of her wardrobe at home. A used condom was what Barry had said he required and, anyway, there was no way she was going to have unprotected sex anyway.

'Simon' she said, giving him another glowing smile, 'I just need to pop to the loo. I don't want a sweet, but could you order me a cappuccino, I'll be back in a minute or two.'

Natalie walked slowly across the restaurant. Simon found his eyes drawn to her. From the back he noticed her shapely calves, neat bottom, narrow waist and the way her pony tail swayed gently from side to side as she walked. Way out of my league, he thought, dismissing an uncomfortable pang of desire from his mind. Even though he had drifted from the regular practice of his Christian faith, the teachings of Christ still held some sway in his life. Both Simon and the Bible concurred that casual sex was not an option and the girl certainly didn't seem to be in the market for courtship. He would not be seeing her again. Better to enjoy her company for the evening and move on.

The piped music in the ladies' toilet complemented the salubrious decor and freshly laundered handtowels. Even so, there, on the wall adjacent to the door was the ubiquitous condom machine. Natalie fished in her purse for three pound coins and began feeding them into the slot. Each one, however, dropped straight through. She tried with the two other pound coins in her purse but with the same result. Reluctantly she concluded that the machine was out of order. She walked briskly across the reception area to the bar and entered the ladies' toilets there only to find a laminated "out of order" sign affixed to the first machine's twin. Slowly she made her way back towards the restaurant. Simon Fenton, she concluded was highly unlikely to be carrying condoms. He was simply not the sort. Close to panic she decided on a brazen solution and ducked smartly into the gents' toilets next to the restaurant. Once again there was the luxurious ambience of a first class hotel, but the expected vending machine was clearly visible on the wall beside the door. The four urinals and two cubicles were deserted. Natalie quickly fed three coins into the machine, which obligingly disgorged a twin pack of the required items. Just as she was slipping the packet into her bag, though, she heard voices immediately behind the door. Instinctively she stepped into the nearest cubicle. Inside, a narrow ledge ran alongside the wall on her right. Two people were by then coming through the door and, fearing that slamming the door behind her would draw their attention, she swung her bottom onto the ledge and drew her feet up from the floor behind the still ajar cubicle door. In a moment of panic she recognised one of the voices as Barry's. The sound of footsteps passed along the small room and back.

'Good, no one here.' reported a voice that did not belong to Barry, 'now, lean against the door and keep it that way for a couple of minutes.'

'OK Chief,' replied Barry.

'Right, just to make sure you've got it all sorted run me through where we're up to,' said the other voice, which Natalie identified as having a London accent.

''E's in the dining room with the tart,' reported Barry, 'I looked in on 'em ten minutes ago and it seemed like they was gettin' on like a 'ouse on fire. She gets 'im in 'er room and shags him silly, then pumps in the juice. Once 'e's under she calls me and then we go in.'

'Then what, just so we're clear,' asked the Londoner.

'I jump 'er, tie 'er 'ands and knock 'er about a bit,' continued Barry, 'then I strangle 'er to make it like 'e's done it. We leave 'er body on the bed and 'av im away down the back stairs. I've got a nicked Volvo estate on false plates with a disabled badge out back waitin'.

Natalie's stomach churned in terror as she listened to the description of her own impending fate.

'What about the CCTV?'

'Simple, chief,' Barry continued, 'The security guy's gonna be busy between eleven an' midnight. There's no camera in the corridor anyway, but there's this fifty quid tart from Piccadilly what lost 'er way last night and dropped into 'is office to chat 'im up. E's on a promise tonight. She'll keep 'im busy in the linen room. Spot on eleven 'is recorder gets a pint of sugary coffee in it an' is control unit shorts out. Even when it's fixed e'll find the camera on the back is out with a loose wire.'

Natalie realised that she had almost stopped breathing as the full horror of her predicament began to grow on her. There was a creak from the toilet door as someone attempted to enter.

'Out of order, mate,' said Barry, aggressively, 'you'll 'ave to use the ones by the bar.'

The door closed again and the conversation resumed.

'OK, you know where to take him?' asked the Londoner.

'Right, I take 'im to the car park at Torside on the B6114 'an wait for yer there. If yer've got what you need from 'is room OK, if not I give 'im the treatment till e' tells us what yer want to know, then I pump 'im full of 'eroin and dump 'im in't reservoir.'

'Right, give me your room key. You keep an eye on them and come up when they're in her room.'

'What about my other twenty five grand?' asked Barry.

'In my briefcase,' said the Londoner, 'you get it when you deliver.'

The door creaked open and closed again. Natalie lowered herself gently to the floor and closed and locked the cubicle door. She sat down on the toilet seat and let her head slump into her hands. She had got into something that was way out of her depth. Petrified, she tried desperately to force her brain to think rationally. Escape. That was the answer. She would simply walk out through the front door. Yes, Barry knew how to find her, so going home was a non-starter, but staying alive was more important. She could start again somewhere else; anything she just had to get away. Sod the geek. He would have to take his chances. Fear had made her legs and arms numb. Natalie rose unsteadily to her feet and opened the cubicle door. Tentatively she pulled the toilet door open, glancing furtively around it before emerging. The coast was clear. She slipped along the corridor and into the foyer – where the first thing she saw was Barry sitting on one of the leather sofas. He spotted her right away and walked briskly up to her.

'What's this then?' he asked, 'not thinking o' leaving was yer?'

Her mouth dry, Natalie struggled to speak,

'No, er... I just turned the wrong way out of the toilet,' she replied.

'Right then, come wi' me, I'll show yer the way back,' he said, taking her roughly by the arm and turning her around.

There was no chance of escape. As they arrived at the dining room doorway Barry patted her bottom.

'In yer go,' he said, 'do yer stuff then. I'll be right behind yer.'

Natalie walked hesitantly through the door and towards Simon, who smiled broadly at her. As she reached her chair she glanced back over her shoulder. To her horror Barry had followed her into the restaurant and was pulling out a chair from under a table on the opposite side of the room from where he would be able to see her, but she would not be able to see him without turning right round.

'I thought you weren't coming back,' said Simon, still smiling, 'your coffee's probably cold by now.'

Natalie sat rigid in her chair, trying frantically to think of her next move.

'Are you all right?' asked Simon, noticing her glazed expression.

Summoning all her courage, Natalie forced herself to smile and meet his gaze. She reached out across the table and rested two fingers on the back of his hand.

'Whatever you do, please, please, keep smiling', she said, 'we're both in serious danger. I'll tell you about it, but please don't look over my shoulder when I start, just look as if we're happily chatting, please, Simon, I'm scared and so should you be. Please help me. Nod your head if you understand.'

Feeling the girl's hand trembling on the back of his own, Simon slowly nodded his head once, forcing himself to smile. 'Danger' there was that word again. He had no comprehension of what was actually going on, but some kind of sixth sense sent a shiver down his spine. Samantha was clearly very frightened of something.

'There's a man sitting behind me,' Natalie continued, 'who's planning to hurt us both.' She decided to deliberately understate the threat, thinking that to tell him that they were both intended to become murder victims might sound too melodramatic. 'He's watching me and if I don't do exactly what I'm told he'll hurt me.'

'OK, I see him,' said Simon, 'so what do you have to do?'

'I'll tell you later,' she replied, playing for time to come up with a plausible story. She had decided that she needed to get Simon to come to her room and then find an excuse to leave him on his own while she made herself scarce. 'For now can you just get the bill?'

Perplexed, Simon agreed, once again nodding his head.

'Oh, thank you,' whispered Natalie, 'please could you just do what I ask for the next ten minutes or so, please?'

'OK,' replied Simon, 'you're the boss,' uncertain as to whether Samantha was neurotic or genuinely in trouble, he acquiesced. There was also the disturbing thought at the back of his mind that, in the light of what he had learned that afternoon, he might be in some way the cause of her predicament.

The waiter duly appeared and Simon asked for the bill.

'Keep talking,' said Natalie.

Simon spoke quietly, but rather incoherently about how he would do his best to help and asked what she wanted him to do next.

'Look,' she replied, 'I'm not exactly sure, but just follow my lead and do what I say, OK?'

They were interrupted by the return of the waiter. Simon signed the bill and asked it to be charged to his room. The waiter left. Natalie took a deep breath.

'Simon, I'm going to stand up in a minute. I want you to stand up as well and hold my hand. Then we're going to walk out of here, into the lift and go to my room.'

Her tone left no opening for a flippant reply and, all of a sudden, her cold fear transmitted itself to Simon. He reached across the table and squeezed her hand gently.

'Right Sam,' he said quietly, 'we hold hands, smile and go. I understand.'

With the briefest of nods, Natalie pushed herself upright. Simon followed her lead and accepted the hand she offered him. Doing their best not to let their faces betray them, the couple set off across the room. Natalie leaned towards Simon and whispered into his ear. 'Thanks for this; I'll explain in a minute.'

He half turned towards her,

'I hope so,' she replied as they passed through the doorway and walked hand in hand towards the lift.

CHAPTER SIX

As the lift doors closed behind them Natalie let go of Simon's hand.

'Just a couple more minutes,' she said, 'then I'll explain.'

Simon shrugged his shoulders, unsure what was happening to him. The lift stopped on the fourth floor and the doors opened. Natalie once again took hold of his hand and led him along the corridor. Approaching her room, she noticed that the door of the room opposite was propped open by a holdall. A sickeningly familiar voice with a London accent could be heard from within.

'OK..... both together?....I'll keep an eye...'

Not daring to look into the room with the open door Natalie fumbled in her bag for the key card and, her hand visibly trembling she slid the card through the lock, pushed the door open, pulled Simon into the room behind her and closed the door firmly behind them. Once again she released his hand. Throwing herself onto the bed she beat her hands into the softness of the mattress.

'Shit, shit, fuck, fuck, shit!' she muttered, burying her head into a pillow.

Simon turned the chair in front of the dressing table towards the bed and lowered himself gently into it.

'Is anyone going to tell me just what's going on?' he asked gently.

Natalie made no reply. With her escape route effectively cut off by the cockney in the room opposite she was rapidly trying to think of a way out. She could always go ahead with the plan and try and get away when the two men arrived. Perhaps she could stab one of them with the spare syringe? She didn't fancy her chances against two of them though. She would need the geek's help. How much should she tell him? From what she's learned about him so far he didn't seem as if he would fall for a cock and bull story. Still he didn't have to know it all, did he? Or should she come clean? No, he would probably despise her for what she had set out to do to him, why should he help her? From his point of view she would probably seem like one of the bad guys if she told him everything. No there had to be a way of enlisting his help without giving too much away. Perhaps she could portray Barry as a jealous ex-lover or something. No, that in wouldn't be enough to justify going on the attack when he walked in. Oh, shit! In despair, she began to sob gently into the pillow. Shit, she thought, Natalie Robertson didn't cry. Natalie was smart and in control. So why was she crying now? What had she done to deserve this?

Natalie felt a hand on her shoulder. The geek was sitting on the bed beside her.

'Sam,' he said, 'do you want to tell me what's going on?'

She rolled over and pulled away from him. Levering herself into a sitting position with her back against the wall she wiped the back of her hand across her face, smudging her mascara into dark lines.

'I'm not who you think I am', she sobbed. 'I'm a fucking prostitute, that's who I am and now they're going to kill us both.'

'Who?' asked Simon, 'who is going to kill us?'

'Oh, shit, Barry and his mate. The bastard watching my door from the room opposite and the sod who put me up to it. I heard them in the toilet. They're going to strangle me and I don't know what the fuck to do. Me! I'm so bloody good at keeping things separate and now they're all mixed up and they're going to kill us.'

'Just calm down,' said Simon, 'and tell me just what's going on.'

Natalie wiped her eyes again and Simon passed her the box of tissues from the top of the bedside cabinet. Still unable to fabricate a plausible story, the truth began to spill from her mouth.

'I'm supposed to get you into bed with me and drug you,' she said, 'I was supposed to pick you up, keep you out of your room while they copied your papers and the files on your laptop. I was supposed to have sex with you then inject you.' She pulled the twin syringes from her bag.

'Look! One shot of this is supposed to put you out for hours. He said I had to steal your wallet and you would be too embarrassed to report it. He said you wouldn't even know they'd copied your stuff. He said he was going to give me five bloody grand, but he was lying.'

'Just a minute,' interrupted Simon, 'what stuff?'

'You don't have to pretend,' she said, 'I know you're some kind of computer geek. I know you've invented 3D games machine or something. That's what they're after.'

'Sam, I'm not a computer geek, 'said Simon, 'I haven't invented anything. If they told you that they were lying. I was given some papers this afternoon though. That might be what they're after. All this might be my fault, not yours.'

Simon's first impression had been of that she had become hysterical over some kind of misunderstanding, but, as her story had unfolded, it began to dawn on him that the letters from Michael Duckworth might well be the cause of the problem.

'Go on, he said, 'tell me what you heard.'

Natalie blew her nose. She had regained a little of her composure, but her face remained deathly white.

'I realised I'd come without my condoms,' she said, 'a bit fucking stupid for a tart eh? Oh, by the way did you really used to be a vicar like they said; only here I am swearing like a trooper.'

'Yes, I did,' he replied, 'but I don't mind, Sam. Carry on.'

'Anyway I tried the ladies but the machines were knackered so I went in the gents. That's when they came in. I hid in one of the cubicles; sitting on a shelf. The door was part open, but they couldn't see me. Barry and this cockney bugger. The cockney's the boss. He asked Barry to go over the plan. I was supposed to phone Barry when we've done it; when I'd given you the sleeping stuff. Barry told the cockney bloke that he was going to tie my hands, knock me about and strangle me. Then they were going to cart you off somewhere beside a reservoir, find out what you knew, pump you full of heroin and chuck you in the reservoir. Honest, they're going to kill us. The boss is watching from the room across the way so we can't get away. They really are going to kill us.'

For what seemed like an eternity Simon struggled to make sense of what he was being told. Although it sounded far fetched, Samantha seemed to be more or less coherent and what she was saying had a ring of plausibility. Incredulous as it seemed, Simon Fenton actually seemed to be in a situation from one of his crime thrillers! The girl's fear was certainly real. It was quite possible that what she said was true.

'Oh, and another thing,' she continued,' they've fixed for the CCTV to be off between eleven and midnight so they can get you out into a car.'

'Right,' he said, looking at his watch, 'it's ten past nine. You don't have to call until after eleven. That gives us nearly two hours to come up with a plan.'

Just then a muffled beeping sound emerged from Natalie's bag. She withdrew her mobile 'phone.

'Shit, oh sorry', she said, turning the display towards Simon.

"Slow down not B4 eleven" It read.

'Well that confirms the time, anyway,' said Simon. 'Now, what if we just burst through the door and run for it in opposite directions?'

'Or what if one of us left and went to the bar or somewhere... he'd probably follow them, the other could get away,' suggested Natalie.

'But what if they're both in the room?' asked Simon, 'that wouldn't work.'

'Oh shit,' muttered Natalie, throwing her bag to the floor in frustration, 'even if we get away they know where I live. Barry will come after me won't he? I'll have to go on the run, shit, shit, shit.'

'I suspect that they know where I live too,' commented Simon.

Five minutes passed. Simon sat back in the chair and put his feet up on the bottom of the bed while Natalie walked over to stare out of the window into the gathering darkness.

'What about the police?' asked Simon, 'we could dial nine, nine, nine.'

'And tell them what exactly?' countered Natalie, 'that we think two men might just want to murder us because I overheard a conversation in the gents' loo. They'd never believe us.'

'What we need to do,' said Simon, 'is to get a couple of coppers into the room and....' His voice tailed off, remembering Simon Duckworth's warning about not trusting the police.

'What if I said you were trying to rape me?' asked Natalie, 'sorry, but that would bring them wouldn't it. They'd have to come. We could play along, you know I could tear my top and cry a bit and they'd arrest you and take me in as well. Then we could come clean, I promise I would, as soon as we were at the police station. Even if they didn't believe us, I mean even if they did me for lying we'd be alive.'

'That just might work,' mumbled Simon, trying hard to think of an alternative plan that would get them out without involving the police. At the back of his mind was the fear that someone was trying to stop him following the leads about his father's death; that and the fact that he was not certain that he could trust the girl. He would end up in a cell and, as a perceived victim; she would have every chance to slip away leaving him at the mercy of the police.

Again there was a long silence. Natalie checked her watch.

'It's nearly half nine,' she said, 'we'd better come up with something soon.'

'OK, then,' conceded Simon, 'call nine, nine, nine. Say I conned you into letting me into your room and I've tried to rape you.'

'Yes,' agreed Natalie, 'I'll say I've locked myself in the bathroom and you're hammering on the door. With my face the way it is they'll have no problem believing me.'

She tore at the front of her shirt, ripping off two buttons to reveal a white lacy bra. Simon looked away and Natalie coloured up in embarrassment. Strange, she thought, how an hour ago she would have had no compunction about him seeing her naked, but in the changes circumstances revealing her underwear seemed somehow sordid. Natalie retrieved her phone and dialled the number. In a suitably tremulous voice she asked the operator for the police and told her tale quite convincingly. Simon was unnerved at her competence in deceit. In his time in the church he had met many different types of people from all sorts of backgrounds, but Samantha was quite unlike anyone he had ever come across. The germ of an idea began to form at the back of his mind.

Natalie threw the handset against the wall, picked it up again and terminated the call.

'That's that then,' she said, 'I'll keep an eye out on the street. When they come I'll slip into the loo and lock the door. You just look a bit sheepish when they get here.'

Natalie once again took station by the window. After what seemed an age, she turned towards Simon,

'Yes!' she exclaimed they're here.'

Simon moved to stand behind her. A police car with its blue lights flashing had pulled up at the kerb and two policemen stepped outside and moved towards the hotel entrance. Natalie stepped away from the window and into the bathroom while Simon continued to stare out of the window while he awaited the fateful knock on the door. Nothing happened. Five minutes passed, ten, and then Simon watched in horror as the two policemen returned to their car and drove off. Natalie's 'phone beeped again disturbing the silence.

'Sam,' he called, 'they've gone and your 'phone's gone off again.

Natalie returned to the room and picked up her telephone.

'Oh fuck!' she exclaimed, 'oh fucking shit.'

She passed the handset to Simon.

He read the text message;

"Stop pissing me about. Just shag him and give him the stuff. Eleven."

Simon looked at her thoughtfully. Feisty and quick witted, he thought, they might just have a chance.

'Look, Sam, we can't escape, but maybe we could fight back. We know they intend to do us harm so how if we jump them. We've got the knock out stuff. Maybe we could get them in here and inject them. Then we'd have a chance.'

Natalie looked Simon up and down.

'Well I don't want to be funny, but you're not exactly in fighting trim are you? Barry's a big bugger and his mate might be as well. Do you really think they'd let us get close enough to stick a needle into them?' She remembered the pepper spray that she usually carried. Some use it was to her when she really needed it. Along with the other tools of her clandestine trade she had left in her apartment.

'We could always hit them with something,' suggested Simon.

'Like what?' retorted Natalie gesturing around the room, 'do you see any baseball bats or stuff?'

Simon looked around. There were not even any of the once ubiquitous table lamps on the bedside cabinets; just light fittings fixed to the wall.

'Well?' goaded Natalie, 'any more bright ideas?'

Simon sat down on the bed.

'I still think we ought to try,' he said, 'do we really have any choice?'

Natalie slumped down beside him.

'Champagne!' she exclaimed moments later, 'champagne! We order it from room service you could do anyone a bit of no good if you laid a full bottle of that on his head.'

'Brilliant,' affirmed Simon, 'go on order it. It's your room.'

'I'll just get one for now. If they're watching they'll see the waiter and thing we're getting it on, she said, reaching across Simon for the room telephone. We'll order the second in about twenty minutes; then we'll hide behind the door, one on each side and let them have it when they come in. Inject them while they're down and run for it.'

Natalie ordered a bottle of Champagne from room service. Suddenly conscious that her exposed bra was no more than six inches from Simon's eyes as she replaced the receiver, she coloured up again. I'll just put a clean t-shirt on,' she said, retrieving her holdall and disappearing once more into the bathroom.

Eleven o'clock came and passed. Each holding a full bottle of champagne by the neck Simon and Natalie rehearsed standing one each side of the door.

'Ready?' asked Simon.

'Ready.' replied Natalie, putting down her bottle and picking up her telephone. Simon noticed her hands trembling as she dialled the number

'Hello,' she said, '....yes, he's out cold.....yes we did....no, no I fucking didn't enjoy it.....'

She pressed a button to end the call.

'Shit!' she exclaimed 'he wants me to send him a picture. Quick, get your shirt off and get on the bed.'

Simon put down his bottle and pulled his shirt over his head as Natalie took him by the arm and manoeuvred him onto the bed.

'Close your eyes,' she said. There was a beep from her telephone.

'Now get up,' she shouted, 'they're coming.'

No sooner had they resumed their stations on each side of the door than someone knocked. Natalie reached out for the handle and slowly began to open the door. With a violent thump the door handle was wrenched from her grasp as Barry shoulder charged his way into the room, followed immediately by a tall thin man in a blue pin-stripe suit. Both men were wearing latex gloves. The door swung fully open, knocking Simon back against the wall. Natalie swung her bottle high and brought it down with an almighty crash on the back of Barry's head as he rushed into the room. Although the bottle remained intact Barry crumpled to the ground and Natalie jumped on his back, retrieving the syringe from the bed on her way down.

Unbalanced by the door, Simon flailed with his bottle towards the taller man, making contact with his shoulder. The tall man staggered sideways as Simon hefted the bottle for another attempt. The man regained his balance and stepped back, away from Simon; from behind his back he produced a small automatic pistol with a silencer attached and pointed it towards his adversary. At that moment Natalie leapt at him like an angry tiger, with one hand grasping the gun and the other his lower arm. She forced his arm upwards and he turned towards her. Taking advantage of the distraction Simon swung again with his bottle, this time connecting with the side of his adversary's head. The man stumbled, giving Natalie the chance to force his gun arm towards the floor. Simon closed in, raising the bottle for another blow, but the man sidestepped, forcing Natalie to step closer to him. She held on grimly and the gun became trapped between their bodies. Letting the bottle fall to the floor, Simon retrieved the syringe from his trouser pocket and began to remove the protective cover. At that moment there was a dull thud and Natalie began to scream.

The tall man crumpled to the floor and Natalie recoiled in horror, her white T-shirt red with blood. She fell backwards onto the floor, her back against the wall and held her hands to her stomach. The man lay still, his arms and legs akimbo, a dark red stain spreading rapidly over his shirt and jacket. Natalie drew her knees up under her chin and wrapped her arms around her legs, sobbing gently while Simon stood transfixed; the syringe in his hand.

'Samantha,' he spluttered, 'are you all right?'

The girl continued sobbing, her eyes staring vacantly into space.

'Sam, are you hurt?' he continued, taking a step towards her. He reached out and touched her on the shoulder. She shrugged him off and shook her head.

'No....I thought....oh god...is he dead?' she mumbled, still sobbing.

Simon stepped over to the tall man, who now lay in a small pool of blood, and felt for a pulse on the side of his neck.

'I think he is?' he said, 'oh shit what have I got you in to?'

For a few moments the tableau remained as if set in stone. Then Simon closed the door, took his shirt from the dressing table and pulled it over his head before returning to sit on the floor beside Natalie. He put his hand on top of hers and, this time, she let it rest there.

'I've killed him haven't I?' she asked through her sobs.

'No,' replied Simon firmly, 'It's not your fault. 'He was trying to kill us; me, he was going to shoot me and you stopped him.'

'Oh fuck,' continued Natalie, 'what are we going to do?'

Simon stood up and retrieved a box of tissues from the bedside table.

'Here, blow your nose,' he said gently, 'I think this is all because of me, It's not your fault Sam, and you're just an innocent bystander. I'll explain it. It will be all right.'

Natalie made an effort to regain her composure, but the tears would not stop. She pulled herself up from the floor, retrieved her bag and disappeared into the bathroom. With the sound of running water in the background Simon steeled himself and examined the gunman more closely.

There was no doubt that he was dead. He had no pulse and was clearly not breathing. Simon gingerly eased a wallet from his jacket pocket. He sat down on the dressing table stool and began to examine the contents as Natalie returned wearing a clean blue t-shirt.

'Oh shit!' he exclaimed, extracting an identity card from the wallet, 'he is the police. It's right; they are part of this, look.' He held the card towards Natalie. 'He's Detective Inspector Andrew Gilroy of the Metropolitan Police. Oh shit, I was just going to call them but we'd better not, had we?'

Natalie stared at the card. 'I don't know what you're on about,' she said, vacantly.

'Look, Samantha,' continued Simon, 'I don't know what they told you about me, but I'm not an inventor. I was given a letter this afternoon that warned me I might be in danger and it seems like it was right.'

'I'm not Samantha,' muttered Natalie, 'I was going to get you to have sex with me and drug you. I'm not exactly an innocent bystander am I? Oh fuck, what are we going to do now?'

'Listen, you can just walk away if you want. I'll do my best to get rid of the evidence. Just go. Get off out of here. Go home and put it behind you. Go on, I'll clean up the best I can. It looks like I'll have to go on the run for a bit while I try and unravel all this, but there's no need for you to be involved. Just go.'

Natalie stood rooted to the spot. 'But they've got my DNA and finger prints, she said, I was arrested once so they'll be on to me for sure; oh shit what can I do?'

To his surprise, Simon realised that his brain was working on overdrive as he grappled to make sense of the bizarre and potentially terrifying situation. He had found the sudden adrenaline rush was stimulating and he rapidly began to assess the options.

'Look,' he said, 'for the time being I think we would be better off sticking together. First of all we need to get away from here. Then I'll explain what I think is going on. You can make your mind up after that whether you want to go and try your luck with the police or run for it or just go home and keep your head down.'

Natalie looked blankly at him.

'Whatever,' she replied compliantly.

'Right,' said Simon, 'pack up what you need in your bag. Get all your stuff. We can't dispose of all the evidence of being here, but take your other t-shirt and we'll dump it later.'

Natalie retreated into the bathroom and emerged wearing a clean t-shirt and carrying her bag. She picked up a few items from the dressing table and bedside cabinet.

'I've got the messy shirt in a plastic bag,' she reported.

'OK, let's just have a look in their room, shall we – see what we can learn.'

Simon moved to open the door.

'What about Barry?' asked Natalie, 'should we give him the other dose of knock out stuff? That might give us more time to get away.'

'Good girl,' commented Simon, picking up the discarded syringe and injecting its contents into Barry's arm. They turned their backs on the scene of carnage, pulling the door closed behind them. Simon slipped a "do not disturb" sign over the door handle and then unlocked the door of the room opposite with a key card he had taken from the dead policeman's wallet. He pulled Natalie gently into the room behind him and closed the door. On the bed, beside a pornographic magazine, were a black leather brief case and a shabby overnight bag. The bag contained a few items of clothing and more magazines. The brief case was locked. Simon picked it up.

'Come on,' he said, taking an uncharacteristic lead, 'come to my room and we'll get my stuff.'

He led the way along the corridor and once again drew Natalie along behind him. Closing the door firmly he turned his attention to the brief case. Simon pulled a bunch of keys from the pocket of his jacket, which lay draped across the back of a chair and, after a brief struggle, managed to open the case by levering the locks apart with the strong brass fob attached to the bunch of keys the solicitor had given him only a few hours previously.

'Wow!' he exclaimed, holding up a wad of twenty pound notes, it's full of cash.' Simon sorted the notes into piles on his bed while Natalie stood staring absently out of the window.

'There must be twenty or thirty thousand here,' he reported. 'This might come in handy.'

Noticing the girl's pallid face and apparent disinterest he put a hand on her shoulder and turned her to face him.

'You can still just walk away from this,' he said, holding her gaze, 'you can take your chance, just give me ten minutes start and call the police, or do your own thing if you'd rather, but I feel a bit responsible for what's happened so I'll help you if you want me to. Is that OK with you?' Natalie gave the briefest of nods and turned away. She felt numb and completely deflated. Out of control; that was it, Natalie was way out of her depth and was had absolutely no idea what to do. Going to the police was not an option. She had killed the man after all. She was a murderer; or at best, a man slaughterer. If she went to the police it would all come out. They would soon find out that she was a prostitute and they would never believe that she had been set up to seduce a man for money. The story just wasn't plausible. If she went on the run where would she go? They would soon find her. If only she hadn't been arrested when she'd been caught with Matt's joints in her bag, she thought. They'd let her go without charging her when he'd admitted they were his, but her fingerprints and DNA would be forever on record. They would soon find her prints or DNA and that would be that. She watched idly as the geek began to pack his bag and stuff in the wads of cash. She'd go along with him for a while anyway. She had no ideas of her own and he seemed to know what he was doing. Perhaps he wasn't a geek after all. Perhaps she'd stumbled into something much more sinister.

Troubled Legacy

'Come on then.' Natalie was disturbed from her train of thought by Simon shaking her gently by the shoulder. 'Come on, Sam, it's nearly half eleven. We need to get going.'

Natalie compliantly followed him along the corridor as he commented quietly on what he was going to attempt. 'The hotel CCTV isn't working. Not if Barry did what you heard him say he would. There's lots of CCTV outside though, so we'll have to try and lay a false trail for a bit.' Simon pondered the source of his knowledge. Detective novels could have unexpected benefits he mused as he continued. 'We need to get to Piccadilly station before all the trains stop,' he said as they descended in the lift, 'then we'll see how far we can get. There's CCTV in some of the trains, but if we keep chopping and changing our trail gets harder and harder to follow. They probably won't start looking for us until sometime tomorrow morning so we need to drop off the radar before then.' He led her through the foyer and out into the sticky humidity of the street. Friday night revellers thronged the pavements, many obviously the worse for drink. Natalie linked arms with him, suddenly grateful for the human contact.

'Look, a tram,' Simon exclaimed as the vehicle ratted towards the tram stop in St. Peter's Square. Simon increased his pace, dragging Natalie along behind him onto the low platform as the tram drew to a halt. They ducked through the doors just as they began to close and sat alongside each other on a narrow seat as it began to move off. Five minutes later the tram disgorged its human cargo into the grey concrete cavern below Piccadilly railway station. Simon led Natalie, who had again linked arms with him, up the stairs into the station concourse. She had not spoken a word since leaving the hotel. There were a few people milling around, but the train departure boards indicated that most of the late evening services had long departed. A train for Manchester Airport was shown as due to leave at twenty three fifty four from platform thirteen. Simon checked his watch.

'Twelve minutes,' he said, 'come on we'll need tickets.'

Natalie nodded and, letting go of his arm, followed him to ticket machine. Armed with two single tickets, Simon set off briskly, leading the way through the main part of the station towards the footbridge that gave access to the through platforms. As they descended towards platform thirteen the train drew in. Simon found an empty bay of seats in the front carriage and sat down. Natalie took the seat on the opposite side of the small table and stared vacantly out of the window. Simon's mind was whirling with ideas, the adrenaline still coursing through his veins. It seemed almost as if the last few hours had brought him back to life; resurrected his spirit in some strange way, he mused with a faint smile. For the first time since Sophie's death there seemed to be something urgent that he needed to deal with. No time to drift with the flow. Michael Duckworth had given him a mission in life. A dangerous and frightening one it might be, but vindicating his father's death seemed somehow a worthy cause. He was surprised to realise that he did not actually care all that much for his own safety. His next task was to duck beneath the inevitability of the UK's twenty-first century surveillance society and get himself to Glasgow to collect the next instalment of the story. The girl was a worry, though; obviously in shock and feeling an unreasonable burden of guilt for the policeman's death. A strongly rooted but half remembered instinct told him that she probably had a deeply underlying need for some form of absolution. He was also aware of a growing sense of responsibility for her safety and welfare. When his mission was complete he would hand himself in to the police and do his best to keep her out of trouble, but he feared that he would not be able to get her completely exonerated. It was all due to him, he reasoned, it was him they had been after, she was just an innocent pawn. Looking at her pale face and blank expression he felt a surge of compassion. When she had first interrupted him at his table in the restaurant he had been drawn to her beauty. With a pang of guilt he realised that her mission to entice him into her bed might well have succeeded had events not intervened. With her tear-streaked face and unkempt clothing she still held a degree of physical fascination for him, but with sudden clarity he recognised her as a young and very vulnerable fellow human being. If he was to accept the responsibility he felt for bringing great trouble upon him there would be no place for any romantic involvement. Anyway, as if a looker like her would be the remotest bit interested in him! Simon's thoughts returned to evading the web of CCTV and finding a way to Glasgow.

Natalie felt numb. It was as is if it was all happening to someone else. Things seemed beyond either her control or comprehension. She stared at the lights in the windows of the houses the train passed as it trundled it's was through the night. Behind each curtain, she thought, there would be people going about their everyday lives. Sitting in front of the television; making a late-night drink; getting ready for bed; scenes of normality. The thought made her ache with envy. Even if she could get back to her flat undetected she would just have to wait in an agony of fear for the knock on the door that would signal her imminent incarceration. There was no doubt about it. She had killed a man. She had set out to help to do harm to someone whom she had known all along had done nothing whatsoever to deserve it; an innocent man. Although she had a sense that the man whose death she felt the burden of responsibility for was far from innocent, the law almost certainly wouldn't see things that way. She knew that. And now this truly innocent man was doing her thinking for her and even worse, she was passively letting him. Her, Natalie Robertson; self contained and always in control. Natalie Robertson who always took care of number one; who was in total charge of her own destiny was following a stranger who she hardly knew like a little lap dog. God! She had even linked arms with him more than once and been glad of the warmth of his skin next to hers.

CHAPTER SEVEN

The train began to slow down and the garish lights of the airport station came into sight as it drew into the platform. Simon stood up and took his holdall down from the overhead rack. Natalie made no move. She continued to stare out of the windows as the thin trickle of passengers made their way past the window.

'Sam,' Simon shook her gently by the shoulder, 'Sam, come on, it's time to get off.'

Natalie levered herself slowly from the seat, avoiding Simon's eyes. She scooped up her bag from the seat beside her and silently followed him as he followed the sparse gaggle of late night passengers. Aware that they were trapped by the web of CCTV Simon led her along the platform, up an escalator and along the long corridor suspended above the car park, following the signs for Terminal 2. The Mancunian Restaurant in the Arrivals Area was still open as a number of flights had been delayed by thunderstorms in northern Spain and a trickle of arrivals was expected throughout the night. Simon steered Natalie in, found seats at a vacant table and ordered two coffees. Natalie remained compliant, but silent. The drinks arrived and Simon touched her arm. Natalie looked up at him.

'Sam,' he began, 'try and drink some. It will do you good.'

'I told you, I'm not Sam. You don't know who I am.'

'Well, whoever you are, you look as if you could do with a strong coffee,' he half smiled, 'you've had a hell of a shock.'

Natalie looked at him quizzically.

'Are you allowed to say hell of a shock?' she asked, 'being a vicar and that.... Anyway, Mr. Vicar if you still know any prayers now might be a good time! Look, there's a sign that says "Prayer Room" over there,' she gestured towards the sign, 'how about you pop over and get this mess sorted out?' The corners of her mouth turned up in the faintest glimmer of a wry smile.

'How about "Oh God, please get me out of this"?' he offered, 'anyway, I'm not a vicar, not now.'

'It's not funny,' retorted Natalie in a quiet voice, 'we're in deep shit. At least I am anyway. I've killed a bloody copper.'

'It was self defence from where I was standing,' he said, 'If you want to turn yourself in I'll back you up, but I need a few days first.'

'No, I don't want to turn myself in,' she muttered, 'I just want to go home, but I can't, can I? They know who I am. I just don't bloody well know what to do.'

She picked up her coffee and took a sip.

'Listen,' Simon continued, 'there's some stuff I need to do. Something to do with why all this has happened, I think. If I can just follow up a trail I might just be able to sort this mess out, but I might not be able to either. It's me the bad guys want, you know, not you. Can't you just get away for a bit, stay with family or something and lay low?'

'I haven't got any family, she replied, 'not that I can go to anyway, I suppose I could go to a hotel or something, book in under a false name and stay in my room, but when would it be safe to come out? Oh god, what a fucking mess.'

A cleaner was hovering uncomfortably close, waiting to clear their table as all the other customers had left.

'Come on,' whispered Simon, 'we'd better move before she hears what we're saying.'

He led her up the escalator into the departure lounge where, despite the next flight not being due to depart until six ten the next morning, a smattering of couples and families were sat in small huddles on the uncomfortable vinyl seats. Simon steered Natalie into a corner and they sat down next to each other.

'If you want to go, just say the word,' he continued, but if you want us to do this together I'd be glad of your help.'

Natalie looked at him, deep in thought. To acknowledge that she either wanted to help or needed help from anyone was an alien thought to her. Since the incident in her hotel room, however, she had let him take the lead; this peculiar quietly-spoken stranger. Every instinct screamed at her to just get up and walk away, yet she had know idea were to walk to. On the few occasions in her life when she had placed her trust in another human being they had always let her down but, amidst her confusion, worry and fear she sensed something in Simon Fenton that seemed different; some kind of steadiness, perhaps reliability was the word she was looking for. Strange to think that such an obviously boring and uninspiring man could be the only one who could help her now. Even stranger that he did not seem to mind in the least that was her had led him into the nightmarish situation in the first place. A tear trickled down her cheek as she nodded her head.

'Yes,' she whispered, 'yes, I'd like to help.'

'Good, girl,' he replied, 'now I need to do some planning. Just you stay right here. Don't go anywhere. I need to find some stuff out. I'll be half an hour or so. Look after my bag, will you?'

Simon stretched out his arm across her shoulders and gave her the briefest of hugs before standing up and striding purposefully across the departure lounge. He examined the departure displays carefully before retracing his steps to the railway station where he collected a small bundle of timetables and leaflets. Seeking temporary sanctuary in a cubicle in the gents' toilets he leafed through his booty and began to scribble notes and annotations on the side of a railway timetable.

When he returned to the departure lounge Natalie was almost asleep, her head propped up against their bags on the seat next to her. Simon's return roused her into wakefulness and she looked at him quizzically.

'First we have to lay some red herrings,' he said, 'then we'll have to split up for a bit and meet up later on. What we both need to do is to disappear from CCTV at about the same time in two different places and then meet up where they can't see us. Now, I don't suppose you have your passport or a note of your passport number with you do you?'

Natalie shook her head. 'Not my passport,' she replied, 'it's in my flat, but I've got a note of the number in my purse.'

'That's better than nothing,' replied Simon, 'how about a driving license?'

'Yes, I've got that,' she answered.

'Right,' he said, 'put your bag on the seat between us, that's right, next to mine.'

Masking the bags with his body he retrieved a roll of cash from his holdall and slipped it into Natalie's bag.

'Now, switch off your mobile and slip that into my bag. They'll be able to trace it so I need to make sure it ends up somewhere we aren't.'

Natalie did as he asked her.

'Come on then,' he replied, 'let's start laying some false trails.'

He led her to the Thomas Cook desk, which was still open. There a sleepy girl sold them two tickets for a late afternoon flight to Corfu. Simon paid in cash from his holdall as she entered their names, addresses and passport numbers into her computer. He noticed that she booked the ticket in the name of Natalie Robertson. From there they began a grand tour of the almost deserted airport complex, pausing at a Clare's Accessories boutique where, at Simon's bidding, Natalie purchased two baseball caps; one black and one white together with a floppy sun hat. Simon slipped the black cap into his bag, leaving the other two for Natalie. From there they sought out the British Airways desk where he used his credit card to buy tickets for an evening flight to London Heathrow. Their next port of call was the railway station booking office where, again using cash, Natalie purchased a return ticket to Leeds while Simon bought a single to London. As soon as they left the ticket window Simon held out his hand towards her. She gave him the ticket, which he appeared to study alongside his own. After a few seconds he swapped the tickets in his hand and gave the one that he had bought to Natalie. They then sought out the WH Smith bookshop where Simon bought a notebook and a collection of newspapers and magazines.

They returned to the departure lounge and regained their seats at the top of the escalator. Natalie looked quizzically at Simon.

'What was the point of all that, then?' she asked.

'To confuse the enemy,' he replied, 'when they start to look for us; when they find the body and put two and two together, they'll track us here by CCTV. The air tickets will keep them occupied chasing their tails while we get away. They'll track us for a bit on CCTV, but when we disappear they'll probably start looking in the wrong places at first. We need to buy time, a week or so if we can.'

'What's it all about, really?' asked Natalie, yawning.

'I'll tell you tomorrow,' he replied, 'or rather later on today. I'm going to the loo again. I'll write out a list of instructions for you to follow and slip them in a paper. I don't want them to spot what we're doing on camera and there's no CCTV in the loo. Do you trust me, Sam? If this is going to work you'll have to do what I tell you. Will you?'

Natalie nodded sleepily and Simon left her with her head once again resting on the bags while he sought the cover of the gents' toilet. When he returned Natalie was fast asleep. He sat down beside her and made a desultory effort at reading a newspaper. After a while Natalie made a low moaning sound in her sleep and wriggled in her seat, turning towards him and resting her head on his shoulder. He made no effort to move her. From the corner of his eye he noticed how terribly young and vulnerable she looked. He wondered whether or not involving her in his plans was the right thing to do. With a sigh he resigned himself to whatever the future might hold. He would do his best for the girl. It wasn't as if the way she looked made any difference, was it? He would do the same for anyone, he eventually convinced himself.

As the check in desks began to open for the early morning flights the departure lounge became increasingly crowded and the hubbub of noise woke Natalie at just before five. The awful memory of what had happened the evening before slowly began to permeate her consciousness, then she realised that her head was resting on Simon Fenton's shoulder. She jerked herself upright with a start, rousing Simon from a light doze.

'What...I mean where, I mean...oh shit!' she spluttered.

'Good morning to you too,' grinned Simon.

Natalie shook her head slowly from side to side and rubbed her eyes. Had she really agreed to rely on this man to help her out of the mess she was in? With his unkempt hair and scruffy beard she decided he looked like a teddy bear. How could she take a teddy bear seriously? Would it be better just to stand up and walk away? With a sickening lurch from her stomach she realised that she still had no plan; no options; no hope. He was the only chance she could contemplate. She forced herself to smile back at him.

'Morning,' she replied groggily as she pushed herself up from the discomfort of her seat and staggered sleepily towards the escalator leading to the ladies toilets in the arrivals hall below. Ten minutes later, with all traces of make-up gone and the benefit of cold water to wash away her fatigue she returned. Simon handed her a newspaper.

'Before you read your instructions,' he began, 'a few things to think of. In a while we're going to act as if we are having a row. You're going to storm off and leave me. They'll watch it on TV, but they won't hear anything, so when you go don't look back. Just do what it says on your sheet. Just trust me, Sam. Now have a look in the paper and tell me anything you don't understand.'

'I'm not Sam,' she said under her breath. Simon appeared not to have heard her and continued speaking.

'Now, listen, just a few pointers. First, you're going to travel by train. As you get on the train put on your white baseball cap. Don't look up. Avoid looking for the cameras. Keep your head down and read a magazine. Pretend to anyway. Later on you'll have to change your appearance. That means switch the baseball cap for your sun hat and change any clothes you can. OK?'

Natalie nodded.

'Then when you get where you're going you'll need to change more drastically, but keep out of the town centre until you do. Stay in the suburbs. Get your hair dyed in one place and cut in another and buy some different clothes. Then you can go into town. Buy some more stuff there, but go to the chain stores, not the expensive shops. Stay in crowds if you can. It doesn't matter if you're on CCTV because they won't know which town to look in and even if they do you'll look so different by then they probably won't pick you up. OK?'

Natalie nodded again.

'Now have a look in the paper and tell me if there's anything you don't understand.'

Natalie opened the newspaper. Inside was a page from a notebook covered with scrawly writing. She read:

When we do the row thing stomp off and get on the 5.37 train to Middlesbrough. Sit in the front coach and keep your head down. Show the London ticket if you need to, they'll just tell you to change at Piccadilly.

Get off the train at Manchester Piccadilly. Buy a FREEDOM OF THE NORTH WEST SEVEN DAY ROVER ticket – this covers all the journeys and will make you hard to keep track of.

Get the 6.33 train to Barrow in Furness. Keep your head down and get off at SILVERDALE at 7.51.

Silverdale is in the middle of nowhere. There's no CCTV. Walk out of the station and out into the countryside for about ten minutes. Find somewhere to change how you look and come back to the station.

Troubled Legacy

Wait on the same platform you got off at for the 9.18 to Barrow in Furness. Read a paper or something. Try not to talk to anyone. This should be a local train with no CCTV.

Get off at ROOSE (9.59) – again no CCTV. It's a suburb of Barrow.

Turn right out of the station and right again. Follow a big wide road for about ten minutes. There are shops and stuff. Get your hair sorted and get some different clothes if you can.

Buy a street map and head for the town centre. Buy some holiday type stuff and a rucksack to pack it in. Pack it up in a public loo.

Find your way to the corner of Blake Street and Holker Street (Not far from the main railway station).

On the corner there's a shelter made out of an old boat. Wait there for me. I'll try to get there by four. If I don't turn up by five I'm sorry, but they'll have caught me and you'll be on your own.

Simon watched as she read.

'Is that alright?' he asked.

'Mm,' nodded Natalie, re-reading the list, 'just a minute....yes, I think so. Yes, I don't know where any of these places are, but yes, it seems OK.'

'Right,' replied Simon, looking at his watch, 'twenty five past five. Time to go; are you ready for a row?'

He stood up abruptly. Natalie rose beside him, a scowl on her face. Simon laid a hand on her shoulder which she pushed aggressively away. Simon took a step back while Natalie put her hands on her hips. A few nearby onlookers turned towards them.

'Piss off,' hissed Natalie, 'just leave me alone.

'But Samantha,' retorted Simon.

'No!' cried Natalie. 'It's off, don't you understand? I don't want to be with you.'

She snatched up her holdall and turned abruptly away and strode briskly in the direction of the railway station. Simon took a few steps after her and then turned to retrieve his own bag before following slowly after the girl. He made no effort to catch her up. He watched her merge with the growing mass of holidaymakers, her pony tail swaying gently from side to side as she disappeared from view.

He wondered if he would ever see her again.

CHAPTER EIGHT

The couch in Detective Chief Superintendant Jimmy Bell's in office was lumpy and the faded leather beneath him was slick with perspiration as he rolled over in the twilight between sleep and wakefulness. Jimmy Bell was a worried man. A breeze stirred the papers on his desk beside the open window and a wave of anxiety jolted him into full consciousness. He got up from the couch and tottered along the short corridor to the toilet where he made use of the facilities and splashed cold water over his face before returning to his office. He checked the mobile telephone on his desk then straightened up and stared absently out of the window along Queen Anne Gate towards the green expanse of St. James' Park. There had been no call from Andy Gilroy. He had heard nothing since ten thirty the previous evening. The operation should have been over hours ago. Something must have gone wrong. He redialled Gilroy's number yet again, but the ring tone clicked into voicemail as it had done since he began calling just after midnight. He sighed and checked his watch. Six fifteen. He would have to call the man he always referred to as the Governor. It just couldn't be put off any longer.

Bell had been in charge of the Independent Criminal Intelligence Section of the Metropolitan Police for just over a year; its second commanding officer in its two year existence. ICIS had been set up with wide jurisdiction by the previous Home Secretary as to supplement the work of the Serious and Organised Crime Authority and to work independently from the rest of the UK police forces to tackle organised crime; particularly where there was the possibility of police corruption. Reporting only to the

Metropolitan Police Commissioner and the Home Secretary, its small staff had a wide remit and a generous budget to adopt unorthodox tactics in order to bring organised crime rings to justice. Based on the third floor of the London Transport building at fifty-five Broadway, well away from any routine contact with the occupants of nearby New Scotland Yard, the four police officers had a small administrative staff of five. In the first year of operations a people trafficking ring in South London, a drugs distribution network in Newcastle and a pyramid property syndicating scam based in Brighton had been rolled up by their local forces under the close supervision of one or more of the three Detective inspectors that formed the core of the ICIS team. Highly paid informants were the prime source of intelligence gathering. In return for substantial payouts and immunity from prosecution, highly placed criminals had shopped their bosses. In two of the cases, mid-ranking local police officers had been found complicit in the criminal activity.

The original head of ICIS had earned his promotion and had been appointed Assistant Chief Constable of the North Yorkshire Force. Jimmy Bell an experienced London detective had succeeded him on the recommendation of the new Home Secretary. Following Bell's appointment two of the three Detective Inspectors on the team had also secured promotion and the third had taken early retirement, enabling Bell to bring in his own men. ICIS had continued to be successful with the exposure and arrest of criminal gangs in East London, Birmingham and Merseyside. Once again police corruption had been discovered in two of the operations.

That was not quite the full story though as Jimmy Bell and all three of his Detective Inspectors were corrupt themselves. The operation in East London had resulted in a "reward" of two hundred and fifty thousand pounds to share between the four of them from a rival gangland boss. While the Birmingham operation had been legitimate, the winding up of the vice-ring in Merseyside had been played out to the advantage of a rival gang of Ukrainians who showed their appreciation to the ICIS officers with a further two hundred thousand pounds in cash. Although more than one member of the administrative staff had reservations about the legitimacy of some of what was going on they kept them to themselves,

Jimmy Bell's imposing presence and liberal interpretation of conditions of employment had proved more than enough to keep them all in line.

The operation that Andy Gilroy was currently engaged in was not legitimate police work. The Governor made sure that the piper was paid, but always called the tune. He would be far from happy when he received Bell's telephone call. By seven o'clock Bell knew that he could delay no longer. After one more attempt to contact Gilroy he took a second mobile phone from his briefcase and made the call.

'Morning, Gov, its Jimmy. I think we may have a problem.'

Bell quickly relayed the details.

'Yes, she got him to her room alright. Then it looks like she tried to bottle it – called the local plods and said he was trying to rape her. Locked herself in the bathroom or something. Anyway Andy intercepted the uniforms and sent them on their way and the muscle leant on her by sending a text message. Ten minutes later they were ordering champagne so they must have been getting along OK by then. Andy called at half ten; said he'd be in touch in a couple of hours when they got the geezer out to the reservoir, but I've heard nothing. I've been calling every hour, but no reply.'

Jimmy Bell grimaced as the man on the other end of the telephone made his feelings about the competence of the ICIS Team known.

'Might just be that they're out of phone coverage,' he suggested, 'but after all this time it's not looking good. I daren't call the local plods after Andy bumped them last night. We'll just have to sit tight.'

Having agreed to call and update the Governor at three o'clock, after his important engagement, Bell disconnected the call. He turned to the keyboard of his computer and began to trawl the internet for local news from the Manchester area.

CHAPTER NINE

Simon Fenton stood on the upper level of the railway station at Manchester Airport, pretending to read a large timetable on the wall beside the booking office. From the corner of his eye he watched the figures on a digital clock move silently, but relentlessly towards five thirty seven. At exactly five thirty five he set off, down the staircase and onto the platform where the five thirty seven train to Middlesbrough was due to depart. At five thirty six and fifteen seconds he stepped onto the train through the door nearest the back as the guard looked up and down the platform and blew his whistle. Simon tilted his face towards the floor and took a seat at the rear of the train, facing forwards. Because of the high seat backs the CCTV camera at the far end of the carriage would not get a clear shot of him and the one above him and to his left would only see the back of his head. Although he expected that the airport security cameras would have caught him entering the train he was determined not to make the job of tracking him easy. He took a magazine from his bag and pretended to read it.

After a short journey the train drew into Manchester Piccadilly and Simon glanced furtively out of the window, hoping to catch a glance of the girl. He was disappointed however. She was not amongst the trickle of passengers passing along the platform. Within minutes the train started off again in the reverse direction and Simon once more sought the anonymity afforded by hiding behind his magazine while he retrieved Natalie's mobile phone from his holdall. He switched it on, but the low-battery warning flashed. He shrugged his shoulders and slipped it down between the seat back and cushion even though the false trail he had hoped it would lay was now unlikely to be a very long one. Despite an underlying gut-wrenching anxiety, he found that the adrenaline was still coursing through his veins as he rehearsed his next move in his mind.

At six twenty six precisely he stepped off the train into the already warm morning and found himself on platform eight of Huddersfield railway station. Conscious of the all seeing eye of CCTV he walked steadily down the steps into the subway, emerging into the booking hall where he surrendered his ticket and made his way across the station forecourt past a large bronze statue of Harold Wilson. He followed the road straight ahead of him down a gentle slope, crossed the wide dual carriageway at the bottom and turned left, sensing that to be the most direct route away from the town centre and its array of surveillance cameras. He passed through a collection of car dealerships into a shabby agglomeration of derelict land and poorly maintained industrial units mixed with unkempt Victorian terraces and a motley collection of shops. Turning right into a side street his confidence grew and he quickly scanned through three hundred and sixty degrees, confirming the absence of CCTV coverage. It was time to begin to put his plan into action. At that time on a Saturday morning the streets were empty. It took him less than five minutes to achieve his first goal. A shabby house that was clearly unoccupied engaged his interest. On closer inspection it proved to be an even better prospect than he had dared hope for. Protruding from the letter box was a handful of envelopes. Feigning an interest in peering in through the glass panel in the door he shielded the letterbox with his body while he pulled out the envelopes. Glancing downward he saw that three of them were circulars addressed to "The Occupier" but the other two named the occupant as a Mr. William Beavis. He had struck pure gold at his first attempt. Simon pocketed the letters and continued on his way, emerging a few minutes later at a crossroads where he found a newsagent's shop. There he bought a copy of the previous day's local newspaper and a street map. Standing outside he located his position on the map and navigated further away from the town centre towards a large supermarket shown on the map. On the way he spotted small parade of shops which contained a greasy spoon cafe and an old fashioned barber's shop. He hid himself inside the cafe and, passing the time with a chipped mug of scalding hot tea and a rather suspect bacon sandwich, he began to scan through the advertisements in the paper, drawing rings round those that showed promise. A second cup of tea helped pass even more time and, eventually, a thickset man wearing a short-sleeved black t-shirt revealing multiple tattoos on his arms arrived to open the barber's shop next door. Ten minutes later Simon emerged from the barber's with a grade two haircut and his beard trimmed to match. Wearing the black baseball cap, he strode purposefully towards the supermarket which turned out to be a large ASDA store. There he bought a number of items, including a pair of light brown cargo trousers, an olive green polo shirt, a pre-pay mobile phone, a battery powered emergency phone charger, some shaving gel, a razor a small mirror and a plastic food container. These he took into the gents' toilet where, as the sole occupant, he filled the plastic container with hot water before secreting himself in a cubicle. When he emerged he was clean shaven for the first time in more than ten years and dressed in the type of clothes more typical for a man of his age.

Using his new mobile phone, Simon made a short call before hailing a mini-cab which was idling in the car park close to the door. Twenty minutes later he parted with two thousand one hundred and fifty pounds, a hundred and ninety less than the asking price, in exchange for a dark blue seven year old Ford Mondeo diesel with ninety two thousand miles on the clock, three months MOT, five months road tax and a broken radio. On the DVLA transfer document he wrote the name William Beavis and the address on the letter he had taken from the empty house. With the money handed over and counted and the paperwork complete he was just leaving the house when he spotted the trailer in the garden. He glanced at the rear end of the car he had just bought and noticed that it had a tow-bar fitted. His mind went into overdrive as the possibilities flashed into his mind. When he drove off he was also in possession of the trailer number plate, which matched that of the car and Simon Fenton felt rather pleased with himself. He had worked out exactly how he would lie low while he planned his next move. If the girl played along their cover would be nigh on perfect.

His first stop was at a dowdy insurance broker's on the edge of town where he again used the name and address from the empty house and some totally fictitious personal details to purchase a third party insurance policy for the car. At four hundred and eighty pounds it was far from a bargain, but the knowledge that the policy would be registered on the

DVLA database together with the change of ownership details reassured him that four hundred and eighty pounds was quite a small price to pay for relative anonymity. Sitting in the car outside Simon re-examined the newspaper, drawing circles round several other advertisements.

After making another telephone call he studied his street map and set out on a short journey to the other side of town. The object of his interest was parked on the drive of a stone-built bungalow. The advertisement had described it as a 1996 Swift Rapide 440 in excellent condition for its age; complete with awning and all accessories. The large white touring caravan had obviously been cleaned and polished recently. An elderly gentleman answered Simon's knock at the door. He explained that, since the death of his wife the previous December, the caravan had been unused. While showing Simon what had obviously been his pride and joy, the elderly man regaled him with nostalgic tales of holidays spent in the caravan with his wife and their two grandchildren. Within minutes Simon realised that it was exactly what he was looking for. The phrase "fully equipped" was absolutely right; from a full propane gas bottle to cutlery and crockery the caravan was indeed ready to go. Eventually Simon, conscious that time was passing quickly, interrupted the flow of reminiscence and agreed to pay the asking price of three thousand five hundred pounds, influenced partly by his compassion for the still grieving vendor. He left a deposit of a thousand pounds and claimed that he needed to visit the bank to withdraw the balance. Just before he left he obtained the address of the nearest caravan dealer from the old man. Instead of the bank, Simon paid a short visit to the caravan dealership where he bought a pair of sleeping bags and a variety of other items from the leisure shop. He also purchased a twelve month instant membership of The Caravan Club. The pervading smell of chemical toilet fluid in the shop reminded Simon of the caravan holidays he had spent with his grandparents as a boy. He allowed himself a brief moment of reminiscence before loading his purchases into the car boot and making yet more telephone calls to the owners of tiny members' only caravan sites in north-west Cumbria. Being a bank holiday weekend finding a vacant pitch proved difficult, but, on his sixth attempt, he managed to reserve a pitch at a farm located on the coast between Maryport and Silloth.

By two fifteen, with the caravan hitched securely behind and the car's tank full of fuel, Simon drove out of Huddersfield, under the M62 and down the hill towards Halifax. In order to avoid the car and caravan being registered by any automatic number plate recognition cameras he had decided to avoid using motorways. With a journey of a hundred miles ahead of him he realised that it would certainly be later than four o'clock when he arrived at the rendezvous. He wondered if the girl would be there waiting for him.

CHAPTER TEN

The man known to Natalie as "Barry" blinked his eyes rapidly as the sun streaming through the hotel room window fell upon his face. His arms and legs felt like lead and his head hurt. He lay still for several minutes as the events of the previous evening forced their way through the fuzzy miasma of his half-drugged brain. He groaned softly and tried to push himself into a sitting position, but his limbs seemed reluctant to work properly. He rolled slowly over onto his stomach, wincing at the throbbing pain that erupted in his head. As the field of his still blurred vision changed he became aware of someone else lying on the floor beside him. Recognition dawned and he finally succeeded in pushing himself up and rolling sideways until his back made contact with the wall. Sitting upright he rubbed his eyes. His companion of the previous evening was sprawled on the floor in a large pool of blood. The policeman was most certainly dead. "Barry" knew that at once. He had seen dead men before.

He made a tentative exploration of his head with both hands. There was no blood, but he located a large and tender lump above his left ear. Looking around he spotted the two discarded syringes on the floor close to where he had been lying and an automatic pistol with a silencer attached next to the body on the floor. A sick feeling erupted in the pit of his stomach as he realised that not only had his mission failed, but that his only benefactor and lifeline was dead. He took several deep breaths as his mind and body slowly began to function properly and tried to think his way out of what looked pretty much like a complete disaster.

Six weeks ago he had really been someone; a man who commanded respect; a respect born out of fear perhaps, but respect nonetheless. Wayne Stevens, for that was his real name, had been one of a small group of "enforcers" working for Dean Driscoll; a Liverpool-based villain who controlled half a dozen brothelsand three lap dancing clubs while masterminding a people smuggling operation using small cargo ships plying between the Baltic and the Mersey. He also ran a useful sideline in money laundering. It was Wayne, often with one or more of his three colleagues who provided the muscle to persuade anyone who fell out of line that it was in their best interests do what Mr. Driscoll wanted or to pay him what they owed him. He had worked his way up into a position of trust in the organisation over a period of ten years, starting out as a bouncer at one of the lap dancing clubs. Officially that had still been his job until six weeks ago. He had drawn a salary of a little over fifteen thousand pounds a year, paying tax and National Insurance like any other employee. He had, however received around the same again, tax free, in cash, for his other services to Mr. Driscoll. At first it had been a matter of a bit of slapping about and threatening. Very occasionally a leg or arm had needed to be broken or a face cut and scarred. That was until the Ukrainians had moved in eighteen months previously, then it had got really nasty as rival brothels and clubs began to appear on Driscoll's patch. Wayne and his colleagues had paid several visits to the new establishments, causing damage to fixtures and fittings and to the staff working there. The Ukrainians had retaliated in kind and eventually an uneasy truce had prevailed while both sides licked their wounds and plotted their next moves. Mr. Driscoll had made the first play. In return for a bonus of ten thousand pounds, Wayne had cut the throat of the manager of one of the Ukrainian-owned clubs in a dark alley as he was on his way home in the early hours of the morning. Three weeks later one of Driscoll's massage parlours had caught fire. Staff and clients trying to escape had found the rear door barred by battens of wood screwed into the door frame from the outside. Three of Driscoll's girls and two punters had died. In retaliation Wayne and his three colleagues, armed with knives and baseball bats had paid a surprise visit to a similar establishment belonging to their rivals. The staff had been herded into one room while the terrified punters were ejected from the premises. The two male 'minders' had been left dying in pools of blood while all five of the girls on duty were allowed to live, but with ugly disfiguring scars on both cheeks.

Then Tony Flynn, Driscoll's second in command, disappeared from his plush detached house on the Wirral. His wife and teenage daughter were found bruised and tied up in their bedrooms, but of Flynn there was no trace. The police were called in but could offer little help. The wife and daughter could only say that four men in dark clothing wearing balaclava masks had been the perpetrators. Although the police had their suspicions, Flynn had always fronted as a legitimate business man and there was widespread public sympathy for the family but, despite an appeal on the "Crimewatch" television show, the Merseyside CID made no progress with their enquiries. Tony Flynn's body was washed up on the Welsh shore of the Dee estuary six weeks after his disappearance. The cause of death, however, was not found to be drowning; his throat had been cut.

Driscoll's response was to send Wayne Stevens and his colleagues on a kidnap mission of their own. Their target was the Ukrainian gang leader's twenty one year old son. They snatched him on his way home from the cinema with his girlfriend, who they left wailing in the dark street as the boy was bundled into the back of a stolen Transit van. They took him to a disused factory in Croxteth where he was imprisoned in a derelict office with his hands and feet manacled. Photographs were taken and sent to his father together with a proposal that, in return for his release, the Ukrainians should close one of their clubs and two brothels. So long as that took place a truce would be declared.

Twelve hours later a gunman took a pot shop at Dean Driscoll as he left his office. The gunman missed his target and fled on a motorcycle. Driscoll ordered Wayne to cut off the boy's little fingers and post them to his father. The Ukrainians capitulated. Driscoll was still furious about the attempt on his life and ordered Wayne to break the boy's legs and dump him outside the Royal Liverpool Hospital. Wayne had complied, but, as the lad had struggled to escape his blows, the baseball bat had caught him squarely on the lower spine and had left him paralysed from the waist downwards. Members of both gangs awaited the next move with a mixture of dread and alarm.

In the event nothing happened for almost three weeks. Then it was the police who had intervened. Every senior member of Driscoll's organisation received an early morning call from armed police at four in the morning on the second Monday of July. Wayne's visitors were three men, dressed in civilian clothing. They smashed open the door and burst into his house brandishing automatic pistols. His current partner, a twenty year old lap dancer from Dublin with a cocaine addiction who worked in one of Driscoll's clubs had cowered in a corner of the bedroom as Wayne had tried to retrieve the revolver he kept in his bedside cabinet, but he had not been quick enough. Two of the men fell on him and handcuffed his hands behind his back while the other stood back, covering them with his pistol. After they had been allowed to dress, Wayne and his girlfriend were held in the living room by one of the policemen while the other two searched the house. Within minutes they had unearthed his small armoury of weapons, a substantial amount of cocaine and over ten thousand pounds in cash. The couple were then bundled into the back of an unmarked car and driven off by a tall man into the dawn. The other two policemen left separately.

Instead of the short journey to the local police station he had expected, Wayne found himself being driven out of the city on the M62 motorway. After thirty five minutes or so the car turned onto the M60 then southwards into rural Cheshire. The car eventually drew up outside a run-down semi-detached house on a council estate on the edge of Warrington. The houses next door both had boarded up windows and all three gardens were overgrown and unkempt. The policeman got out and opened the back door. He helped Wayne and the girl out of the car and freed their hands.

'Now you have to make a choice, Stevens,' the man said, 'we can turn around and take you to visit some very angry Ukrainians in Liverpool or you can do a job for us. Do as you're told and you'll be free to go wherever you want in a couple of weeks. You can have your money back and thirty thousand beside. Make your choice.'

It was no choice at all really. There was no doubt as to his fate at the hand of the Ukrainians.

'OK,' Wayne had replied, 'I'll do as you say.'

Troubled Legacy

The three of them had gone into the house, which was as shabby on the inside as it was on the outside. The policeman, who had never given his name, set out the task. Wayne and the girl were to stay in the house. They were not to go outside at all. Food and drink would be delivered every few days by a supermarket delivery service and the tall man produced a small tobacco tin containing cocaine from his pocket. In return, Wayne was to await his instructions. To ensure compliance both Wayne and the girl were fitted with electronic tags before the policeman left.

The call to action had come a week later. The tall policeman returned unannounced late one evening. He had brought Wayne's stash of money, a mobile phone, a blurred photograph of a man with a beard and a few sheets of paper. Wayne's task was to meet a high class prostitute at a Travelodge in Manchester and offer her money to set up a honey-trap for the man in the photograph. If she refused he was to use whatever measures he thought necessary to persuade her to comply. The man was to be drugged and abducted. Wayne would strangle the girl and dispose of the man's body when the requisite information had been extracted from him. Wayne would get to keep his own cash and an additional thirty thousand. All the necessary hotel bookings had been made, but it was up to Wayne to make all the other arrangements. The policeman removed Wayne's tag and promised to do the same for his girlfriend as soon as the job was over. Wayne and his partner would then be free to leave and begin a new life wherever they pleased.

As the strength returned to his limbs, Wayne Stevens realised that the deal was now most certainly off. He stood up rather unsteadily and checked the time on his watch. Seven fifteen. He made a brief search of the room but found nothing of interest. He picked up the gun and tucked it in the waistband of his trousers, slipped out of the room. Pulling the door shut behind him, he pushed at the door of the room opposite, which had been booked in his pseudonym, but found it firmly locked. So much for his thirty grand, he thought. He crept quietly down the stairs and out of the hotel. Locating the parked Volvo estate he threaded his way through the early morning traffic out of the city and back to a virtually empty car park at a DIY superstore on the outskirts of Warrington. There he abandoned the car and set off on foot towards the shabby council house.

Phil Moncur

He still had most of his ten thousand pounds, but it would probably be wise to lie low for a bit before breaking the tag from his girlfriend's leg and making a run for it. When they discovered the body of the dead copper, he mused, the shit would certainly hit the fan.

CHAPTER ELEVEN

The train was standing in the platform with its doors open as Natalie reached the foot of the staircase. Following her instructions she sought out the front carriage, which was almost deserted and chose a window seat. The back of the seat in front of her partially masked her from the view of anyone entering the carriage and, she hoped from the all-seeing eye of CCTV. Pulling a magazine from her bag she laid it down on the narrow shelf-like table that folded down from the seat back in front of her and pretended to read. After a few minutes the train jerked into life and moved off into the early morning twilight. No ticket collector disturbed her during the short journey into the centre of Manchester and, wearing the white baseball cap, she merged with the trickle of passengers heading for the main concourse. Risking a brief glance up at the departure board she noted that the Barrow train would depart from platform fourteen in just under half an hour.

Only two windows were open at the booking office and there was a short queue. Natalie took a quick glance inside the newspaper to refresh her memory of the name of the ticket. When her turn came she was served by a pimply young man who paid little attention to his customer as he typed the details into his computer. In a matter of seconds the ticket emerged from the issuing machine with a whirring noise and she handed over the payment without a word. Armed with her ticket she followed the familiar route towards platform fourteen. With twenty minutes before her train, she felt conspicuous as she ascended the escalator and entered the small mezzanine above the through platforms. The refuge of the ladies toilet beckoned and, ensconced in a cubicle, she took a few deep breaths before rummaging in her bag. Her first move was to count the money Simon had slipped into her bag. She had broken the seal on one of the bundles in order to extract the notes to pay for her ticket. The two intact bundles each contained a thousand pounds in twenties. In total she had two thousand nine hundred and twenty in her bag. Together with the forty odd pounds remaining in her purse that was almost three thousand pounds. Perhaps, she thought, she would be able to withdraw her savings from the bank before the police caught on. That would make a total of thirty thousand pounds. Could she start a new life on that she wondered? Would it be possible to change her identity? What about a job? She would need a National Insurance Number for that, or could she go into the cash rich sex-trade full time? She shuddered with revulsion at the thought. While it had been a means to a positive end, selling her body had seemed to be some kind of almost neutral transaction, but the memory of a time when sex with strangers had been necessary in order to survive was an uncomfortable one. Without income she thought that thirty thousand might keep her alive for a year, maybe two if she was frugal, but she would need to be constantly looking over her shoulder. Again she flirted with the idea of turning herself in. Although unlikely, a jury just might believe her. But that would be the end of her dream, even if she got off with it in the end the media would get into the act. Even if she sold her story to the newspapers for a small fortune airlines didn't make a habit of employing murder suspects as pilots. Slipping around half of the loose notes into her purse, she stuffed the remainder of the money back into her bag and stood up. It still looked as if going along with what the Teddy Bear wanted was the only viable option. She emerged from her sanctuary, bought herself a large latté from the coffee stall and took the escalator down to platform fourteen.

In her dream, Natalie was flying her usual Piper Warrior but she did not recognise the land below her and she could not match up any features on the ground with her map. None of the navigation aids seemed to be working and the radio was dead. Sitting beside her, in the right hand seat, was a dead policeman, his head lolling from side to side as the aeroplane rose and fell in the gentle air currents. The lower half of his body was covered in blood, a pool of which had collected on the cockpit floor between the rudder pedals. In desperation she rummaged in the flight bag on the back seat and pulled out a flight manual. Instead of giving details of airfields, though, it contained railway timetables. Natalie felt the onset of panic. The engine spluttered and faltered. Reaching down to the switch on the left hand side of the cockpit she selected the other fuel tank. The engine picked up, but lost power again and after a few seconds it cut out completely. She lowered the nose and scanned the ground on either side for a field long enough to land in as she lowered the nose and trimmed the aircraft for its best gliding speed of seventy knots. Still unable to restart the engine, she chose a field about a mile to the left of her current position and began to plan her approach. She tried the radio one last time, making the internationally recognised MAYDAY call. Through her headphones came an unexpected response,

'Land at Silverdale, Sam, land at Silverdale,' the voice was disjointed, but somehow she perceived that it belonged to the only person who could help her, even if she didn't particularly like him.

'I'm sick of bloody telling you', she replied, 'my name's not Sam, its....'

Someone was gently shaking her shoulder. The dream faded as dreadful reality resumed.

'Could I see your ticket please?' asked the ticket inspector.

Natalie showed her ticket to the inspector, her heart fluttering both because of the fading fear from the dream and because of her almost instinctive desire to avoid drawing attention to herself. After a perfunctory glance the man moved on along the carriage. Natalie noted with a degree of relief that he also had to wake up two other passengers. In a renewed flash of panic she was afraid that she had slept for too long and missed her stop, but a quick check of her watch and the list of instructions inside the newspaper reassured her. It was not yet half past seven. More than twenty minutes before the train was due to stop at Silverdale. The train paused briefly in the stations at Lancaster and Carnforth before the information screen, which Natalie could just see between the high seat backs in front of her, announced that the next stop was Silverdale. There were a few people waiting on the platform as the train drew in but, to Natalie's relief, she was the only passenger to alight from the train. She left the station through a narrow gateway and turned left along a deserted road. At the road junction next to a railway bridge she kept to the right, having noticed woodland in that direction. Presently she began climbing a hill until the road was bordered by woodland on both sides. On her left was a stone wall with a large gap in it, giving easy access to the dense undergrowth. After a brief look all around to make certain that no one was in sight, she slipped through the gap and carried on walking across the spongy and uneven ground, making erratic progress through the trees until she could no longer see the road. Off to her right Natalie saw sunlight rippling on water and turned in that direction until she stood on the bank of a small circular pond in a clearing. Taking a broken branch in her hand she tested the depth of the murky water. The branch penetrated to a depth of three feet or so in the middle.

Natalie wriggled out of her skirt and pulled her t-shirt over her head. Taking a furtive glance all around, she quickly changed into her spare underwear before pulling on her jeans and a black t-shirt. She laid her raincoat over a branch and set about transferring the bundles of cash into her handbag. All of her discarded clothing she stuffed into her holdall alongside her navy jacket and the plastic bag containing the bloodstained shirt. She added a number of large stones from the ground close to the tree-line and used the broken branch to slowly lower the holdall into the deepest part of the pond. Natalie sighed as the bag sank below the surface and sat down slowly on a large flat stone in the shade of a tree and began to brush her hair. It had taken her less than fifteen minutes to get from the station to the pond. She decided it would be safer to wait where she was until fifteen, no better be safe than sorry, twenty minutes before her next train was due. Sitting on the trunk of a fallen tree in the shade of the canopy of branches on a warm summer morning, she could hear the singing of what sounded like a million birds. Natalie had always been a city girl and the countryside was a novelty. As she sat in her patient idyll she almost forgot the severity of her predicament. Time passed, however, and the imperative of continuing her journey levered her from her repose as the hands on her watch moved inexorably towards nine o'clock. Despite the warmth of the day she put on her raincoat, picked up her handbag and the newspaper and retraced her steps. No sooner had she joined the small knot of waiting passengers at Silverdale station than the train arrived. It was moderately busy and as it rattled and swayed along the track she watched the sandbanks and rippling waves of a wide estuary pass the window. At each wayside station more people joined the little train and Natalie was squashed against the window for the last twenty minutes or so of her journey by the corpulent bulk of an elderly woman who seemed to fall asleep as soon as her bottom hit the seat.

The train pulled into Roose on time and Natalie squeezed her way past a cluster of passengers standing in the doorway. The sun had disappeared behind a bank of hazy cloud but the air was still warm and humid. As instructed she turned right after leaving the platform, then right at the top of the slope along the wide tree-lined road that Simon had described. There was a fair amount of passing traffic, but few pedestrians. The promised shops materialised in front of her and, among them, she located a small hairdressing salon. Both chairs were occupied, but a smiling plump hairdresser beckoned her in and promised that she would not be long. In the event, Natalie had to wait the best part of twenty minutes before the plump girl finished blow drying her customer's hair and beckoned Natalie into the chair.

'I'd like a quick trim and to go blonde,' instructed Natalie, 'I've just split up with my boyfriend and I'm ready for a bit of cheering up.'

Off the top of her head she concocted a story about splitting with her boyfriend in Yorkshire and coming to spend a couple of weeks with an old school friend who had moved to Barrow recently because of her job in a bank. The hairdresser showed little real interest and prattled on about the lack of romance in her own life as she trimmed the loose ends from Natalie's hair and began to apply the dye. By half past ten she emerged with blonde hair and paid a visit to an adjoining clothes shop. In a nearby public convenience she exchanged her jeans and t-shirt for a pale blue sundress and then located a newsagent where she bought a street map. Five minutes later she dumped a plastic bag containing her discarded clothing into a litter bin as she strode briskly along another wide avenue in the direction of the town centre. As the wide road passed through a scatter of outlying shops she spotted a second hair salon. Here there was a vacant chair and a gangly teenage girl washed her newly dried hair before an older woman began to cut it shorter. The salon also offered a fifteen minute express "Fake Bake" spray-tan service and Natalie took advantage of the offer. Once again she spun a variation on her original yarn about being dumped by her boyfriend and staying with a friend. By twelve thirty Natalie had changed her appearance drastically. Her small features were framed by blonde hair that fell to just below her jaw-line at the front, but gradually feathered upwards towards the back of her neck. Her face, arms and legs had a healthy brown glow and the transformation was completed when she bought a short white cotton jacket, pair of black lycra calf-length leggings and a short light blue top and changed into them in the ladies' toilet in Debenhams. Following her instructions she also bought a medium sized rucksack and began to shop in earnest. She visited Marks and Spencer, JD Sports, Topshop and New Look, collating the sorts of collection of clothing that a woman of her age might take on holiday. She visited Superdrug where she purchased an assortment of toiletries and make-up together with a pair of weak reading glasses. In a crowded Specsavers outlet she sneakily substituted her new reading glasses for a pair of designer spectacles with plain glass lenses while trying on a number of styles and parading them to and from a mirror. From a stall in the indoor market she obtained a long blonde wig and some hair grips and finally, as a last indulgence, a pair of rather expensive designer sunglasses that caught her eye in the window of an upmarket optician. The burst of activity had pushed her worries to the back of her mind and, sipping a cool milkshake and nibbling a deli roll in MacDonald's at the conclusion of her retail expedition she was surprised to discover that it was almost three o'clock. She checked her map and set out on the last lap of her journey. She walked away from the town centre, map in hand, along Dalton Road. She crossed Abbey Road into Hartington Street then, following her map closely, she took the fourth right into Blake Street. There, right at the end, she found the upturned boat seat, just as Simon had described it. Although still very warm, a blustery breeze was swirling litter around on the paved area surrounding the seat and Natalie sought shelter under the cover of the prow of the boat. She checked the time; three thirty. As four o'clock approached she began to check out every car that drove past. Four fifteen and she felt her eyelids becoming heavy. Four Thirty; she was struggling to stay awake in the heat and humidity. Four forty five; anxiety began to gnaw at her, helping her to stay awake. Where was he? Had he been picked up by the police or had he been stringing her along; using her as some kind of decoy? Five o'clock came and still no Teddy Bear. Stupid man she thought; or perhaps it was her that had been stupid for allowing herself to trust a man in the first place. Natalie was angry and upset. She was also very tired. As the fog of despair descended upon her she rested her head against the side of the boat. She was on her own, then, but what should she do? It just wasn't bloody fair. Her mind was in turmoil and fatigue seemed to permeate every fibre of her being. As large raindrops began to fall all around her Natalie Robertson closed her eyes and drifted of into a sound and dreamless sleep.

CHAPTER TWELVE

Detective Chief Superintendent Bell's three o'clock telephone call was every bit as unpleasant as he had anticipated. He had been contacted by a Detective Chief Inspector from the Greater Manchester force just after eleven thirty and informed that one of his officers had been found shot dead in a Manchester hotel room. Bell had told the caller that Detective Inspector Gilroy had been involved in an undercover operation involving a major drug distribution network and had asked for more details. Gilroy's body, it transpired, had been found in a room registered to a Samantha Evans who had checked in earlier in the day. Ms. Evans had been seen having dinner with a Mr. Simon Fenton in the restaurant the previous evening and appeared to have gone back to the room with the gentleman. There had been a major failure of the hotel's CCTV system just before eleven and it had not been restored until five the next morning. Simon Fenton and Samantha Evans had left without checking out as had a Mr Barry Clough who was registered in the room opposite. A team of twenty officers and fifteen civilian staff were currently engaged in scrolling through the city's CCTV recordings from eleven onwards. They had already spotted the couple leaving the hotel and taking a tram. Footage from CCTV cameras on the tram itself and of each stop it had made was currently being studied. Thinking quickly, Bell had offered to fax a photograph of Wayne Stevens, a man who he claimed was a major player in the drug ring who had recently evaded capture. He asked to be kept informed of all developments. He had then immediately contacted Gerry Jewel, another of his Detective Inspectors and ordered him to Manchester to offer his assistance and to fabricate a cover story about Inspector Gilroy's fictitious undercover operation..

The Governor was not best pleased at the news and gruffly demanded a full review of the operation. With a deep intake of breath Bell began to tell the tale.

'It's bad, Guv', he said, 'Gilroy's dead; shot in the tom's hotel room. The local plods are on to our man and the girl. They've also got CCTV of the muscle legging it this morning.'

'I don't pay you to fucking fail,' replied the man on the other end of the telephone, 'now run the whole operation past me again and tell me what you're going to do about it.'

Jimmy Bell began to tap his fingers impatiently on his desk as he prepared to go over the well worn narrative.

'We got a line on our man through the solicitors,' he began, 'and that was after we leant on the undertakers to tell us where they sent the bill for the fat bugger's funeral. Andy Gilroy organised a tap on the office phone and, lo and behold, our man rang up to confirm his ID and make an appointment. Andy had been keeping the heavy on ice after the Liverpool job; you know the one the Ukrainians would gladly cut into little pieces. Once we found out that our bloke would be staying overnight Andy set up the muscle to meet a posh tart from Leeds and lean on her to pick up Fenton in the hotel. She was supposed to shag him stupid and dope him. Then the muscle was going to knock her about a bit, tie her up and strangle her. With our man's DNA all over the shop he'd be squarely in the frame. Andy and the muscle were going to get him up into the hills, find out where the papers were and make it look like he'd taken an overdose of the hard stuff and fallen in a reservoir. Andy would pick up the papers and tip off the Ukrainians where to find their man. You'd get the papers and no loose ends.'

'So what went bloody wrong, then?' asked the man.

'I don't know, Guv,' answered the Detective Chief Superintendent, 'from what the Manchester plods tell me our guy and the tart left together about half eleven and disappeared onto a late-night tram heading for the city centre. They're trying to trail them by CCTV. They could have put their heads together and jumped Andy and the muscle. I've sent Gerry up to Manchester to keep an eye on things. He'll tip me the wink if they get a positive lead. I take it you'd rather we get to them before the locals?'

'You've got it right,' replied the Governor, 'The girl needs to disappear smartly. She knows too much. You need a long chat with our man before anything happens to him. The last thing we need is the local boys reeling them in. We don't know what tale they'll have to tell, so don't leak them too much information. Send Paul Cavendish to Leeds to check out the tart's place before the locals cotton on to her then keep him out of sight until we get a lead. He'll need to get to them first, or to whichever one pops up first. I can't see them sticking together, can you?'

'Not too likely, Guv. He must know that she was in on it. We'll check out his contacts and put a tap on them. If he gets in touch with any of his cronies we'll know straight away. The Manchester plods might cotton on eventually, but we won't tell them anything we don't have to and Gerry will keep us in the loop.'

'What a bloody mess, Bell, 'responded the other man, 'you'd better pull this one out of the hat if you want to stay in your cushy job.'

'Right, Gov,' acknowledged Jimmy Bell, feeling a rush of adrenaline coursing through his veins, 'what about the muscle?'

'Oh, feed him to the Ukrainians. He knows far too much.' Was the reply, 'Now call me when you're on to something; otherwise call me at eleven tonight with an update.'

The man disconnected the call, leaving Bell holding a dead telephone. Grimly he hit the end call button and threw himself down on the battered leather sofa. It was a good job he was single again, he reflected. He might not see his home again for quite a while at this rate. It was probably just as well that his wife had walked out on him the Christmas before last, taking their two boys with her.

CHAPTER THIRTEEN

The journey from Huddersfield to Barrow in Furness was taking much longer than Simon had anticipated. Towing a caravan was unfamiliar to him and it took a while for him to become accustomed to the sluggish acceleration and the slightly wider line that he had to take when turning tight corners. Having incurred the wrath of a number of fellow road users he was irritable and frustrated by the time he dropped down into Keighley an hour and a quarter after into his journey. Bank holiday traffic in Ilkley delayed him still further and at his estimated arrival time of four o'clock he was no further than the Settle by-pass. With his confidence in towing the caravan gradually increasing he began to increase his speed on the more favourable stretches of road but, mindful of the need not to draw any unnecessary attention he dared not force the pace too much. He was also becoming very tired. Despite having the air conditioning set to low the temperature inside the car was no more than cool and he felt his eyes growing heavy. Between crossing the M6 motorway and turning onto the A590 he momentarily closed his eyes in the prelude to sleep. Only the alarming snaking and swaying of the caravan behind him roused him and he regained control just in time. By five o'clock he was approaching Ulverston. Convinced that the girl would have given up on him by then he was sorely tempted to find a lay-by or car park and rest, but hope triumphed over adversity and he pressed on towards his destination. From the outskirts of Dalton-in-Furness he forsook the modern by-pass and followed the old route through the small town's narrow streets as large drops of rain began to fall intermittently on the windscreen. He drove over Mill Brow Hill before approaching Barrow on the tree-lined Abbey Road; the familiar streetscape bringing back poignant memories of his childhood. After crossing the railway bridge next to the old post office he turned right into Holker Street at the traffic lights and pulled up beside the ornamental upturned boat at the end of Blake Street, fully expecting to find no one there.

As he drew to a halt he grimaced in disappointment. There was someone sitting in the shelter, but it was not the girl he had been expecting to find. The person sitting with her head against the side of the boat was much younger; a slightly built blonde girl wearing a white jacket over a blue top and a pair of black leggings. Simon rubbed his eyes and took another look. No it couldn't be. It just might be. He opened the car door and stepped out into the warm rain. He walked tentatively towards her, noticing that there was a rucksack on the floor beside her. Recognition dawned and, with it, came a peculiar flood of relief. She had waited for him.

As he drew closer he observed that she was fast asleep. He shook her gently by the shoulder.

'Sam,' he said, 'wake up it's me.'

Natalie opened her eyes. For a moment she did not recognise the man who was shaking her by the shoulder and was gripped by panic. A second look brought recognition and, with it, anger. Forcing herself unsteadily to her feet she punched him on the left shoulder.

'You bastard,' she hissed, 'I thought you weren't going to come.'

Natalie pushed him away from her, and stood squarely in front of him.

'You might have cut your hair and shaved your scruffy beard, but you're still a bloody teddy bear,' she ranted.

The hands that had forced Simon away then took hold of his shirt just under each shoulder and she pulled him back towards her and buried her head in his chest.

'Oh you bastard, she sobbed, 'you great big teddy bear bastard. I thought you'd gone and let me down, but you haven't, have you?'

Simon felt the dampness of her tears through the thin material of his shirt as he tentatively put his arms round her shoulders in reassurance. The smell of her hair filled his nostrils and, as the large gentle raindrops continued to fall in the quiet northern street, Simon held her close and let her cry.

'Come on,' he said after a minute or so, 'we'd better get going.'

Natalie looked up and then over his shoulder.

'Oh, bloody hell', she exclaimed, 'not a bloody caravan. You don't expect me to go camping do you?'

The hiatus well and truly broken, Simon picked up her rucksack and tossed it onto the back seat of the car.

'It's that or nothing, he grinned, 'now get in.'

Natalie complied and Simon drove off while she wiped her eyes with a tissue from her handbag.

'Where are we going?' she asked.

'Camping,' he relied flippantly, whether Samantha likes it or not.'

'I keep on telling you, that's not my name,' Natalie replied, 'It's Natalie, my real name, if there's anything real about me that is.'

'What do you mean by real?' asked Simon.

'Oh, nothing,' she replied, 'you wouldn't understand.'

Rebuffed, Simon drove on in silence as they turned onto the main route eastwards, passing a series of small industrial units. The rain became heavier as they turned off onto a narrower road signposted Askam and Millom.

'You look tired,' commented Natalie, 'when did you last eat?'

'I had a bacon butty at about eight this morning,' he said, 'but nothing since, I'm starving.'

'Find a shop, then' ordered Natalie, 'You need to eat.'

Simon turned left onto a narrower road and drew up beside a small SPAR shop in the centre of a village. Natalie swung her door open and made a run for the shop doorway through the now torrential rain. She emerged with two large carrier bags which she placed on the floor in front of the back seat before regaining the shelter of the car. Reaching behind her, she produced a cheese roll, a bar of milk chocolate and a can of cola.

'That should keep you going for a bit,' she said, 'I've got some bread and butter and milk and stuff as well, oh, and a packet of Fruit and Fibre. I hope you like it 'cos I'm not going back out in this.' She gestured at the rain, still falling in torrents and overflowing the guttering above the shop front.

'Thanks, Sam..er I mean Natalie,' answered Simon, 'I didn't think about what we were going to eat.'

'Where are we going anyway?' she asked as they drove off.

Simon began to tell her about his day. She listened with growing fascination as he explained how he had managed to get hold of the car and caravan and how he had attempted to cover his tracks. He produced the Caravan Club Sites Book from his door bin and passed it to her.

'That's where we're going,' he said, 'there, where the page is folded over...the one with the ring round it.'

'Maryport? Where's that?'

'On the coast between Workington and Carlisle,' he replied, 'in the back of beyond. No one will think to look for us in a caravan. I hope not anyway. How about you? How was your day?'

She recounted her journey, transformation and shopping expedition as they travelled along the winding coastal road. Presently the rhythmic sweep on the windscreen wipers and the undulating rumble from the diesel engine began to have a soporific effect and Natalie's head began to fall lower and lower. Simon was also very tired, having slept very little the previous night and not at all since boarding the train at Manchester Airport. He felt his eyes growing increasingly heavy and found the car veering onto the wrong side of the road more than once. He waited for a straight stretch of road and pulled into the kerb. Once again he shook the girl's shoulder to rouse her from her sleep.

'Could you drive for a bit?' he asked his sleepy companion.

Natalie glanced anxiously over her shoulder at the caravan and in front at the narrow winding road.

'Er..well, no I don't think I could drive this...I mean I've got a little car, but I don't think I could tow a caravan. What's up?'

'I'm all in,' replied Simon, 'I nearly dropped off twice. I just can't stay awake.'

'How far is it?' asked Natalie.

'More than an hour,' answered Simon, 'If you can't drive you'll have to talk to me. Keep me awake.'

'Talk? What about?' asked the girl irritably.

'About you, probably,' answered Simon, rising to the irritation in her voice, 'that's what women are good at isn't it?'

Natalie turned her head to look away from him. Simon sighed and began to drive again.

'What you mean is how did a nice girl like me end up on shagging men for money, don't you?' she said, her voice edged with sarcasm.

'No,' retorted Simon, 'not unless you really want to tell me about it that is.'

'Oh fuck off Mr. Holier than thou vicar. If you really want to know then I'll tell you. I'll tell you in all the gory detail. Get off on that will you?'

Simon made no reply, realising that whatever he said next would almost certainly be the wrong thing.

The rain continued unabated as they passed through a small town.

'I was born in Oldham,' Natalie began in a quiet voice, 'I never knew my dad. My mum told me later that he was a rich bloke, who didn't want to know her after she fell pregnant with me, but she never did tell me his name and it's not on my birth certificate. The first I can remember is that we lived in a grey house with a big garden, Mum, me and Uncle Paul. I liked Uncle Paul he used to pick me up and swing me around when he came home from work. We went to the seaside in his car and he was always saying silly things. I thought my Mum was very pretty in those days, she smelled of flowers and washing up liquid. That's where I started school, Oldham, but by then Mum and Uncle Paul weren't getting on. They were shouting all the time and Mum slept a lot. Now I know that she was drinking, but I didn't then. Anyway we left Uncle Paul after a bit, me and Mum. Next we went to live in a council house in Halifax. Uncle Tim moved in with us soon after. Mum was good looking and never seemed to have any trouble getting boyfriends. They just didn't stay very long that's all. The school in Halifax wasn't bad. I always liked school; until I was a lot older anyway. I didn't like Uncle Tim, much though; he didn't seem as if he liked me either. We stayed there until I was half way through Year Two. Then Mum and Uncle Tim fell out and he left us. I thought that was great, but Mum said we were short of money. We moved to Elland; to a flat in a tower block and I started at the Church School. That was OK too; I stayed at that school for more than three years. We had two different flats and there were four more uncles, but other people in the flats seemed to be the same. Then mum got ill. She was in hospital for six weeks and I was taken into care while she got better. I know now that she was an alcoholic and she went in to dry out, but they didn't tell me that then. My foster parents were nice enough but there were three older kids there. I didn't like it. Then my mum came back. She was lots better; pretty again. She hooked up with Michael. I was too old to fall for that uncle stuff again. We moved in with him in Batley; a nice house with a garden. It was great at first. Another new school, though. I always seemed to get on all right at school. It wasn't as if I was dead bright or anything and I didn't have loads of friends, but I think the teachers liked me. Anyway I got Level Fives in my SATs. By the time I started high school my mum was drinking again. My first secondary school was a bit naff. All girls and right bitchy, but I didn't stay long 'cos Michael chucked us out. We went to a B and B at first, not far away and I had to stay at the school. Then we rented a house in Bradford and I had to change schools again. That's hard when you're eleven. I mean I'd got used to being the "new girl" by then; everyone's all over you at first then, after a couple of weeks they don't want to know you – you just don't fit in. Anyway I got on all right with my work and that and I just kept myself to myself. Then, by the time I was thirteen the boys, especially the older ones started hanging round me. I didn't ever have much to do with boys before then. They were always into football and fighting and stuff, but these were different. They kept on pestering me to go out with them or to do stuff I didn't want to.'

Natalie fell silent and Simon glanced over at her. She was sitting with her knees drawn up in front of her. She had her arms folded round her knees and her head was bowed.

'Go on, Natalie,' he said softly, 'what happened?'

'No. You'll think I'm really cheap. I mean you probably think I am already, but it's not as if I started it; not really.'

'You don't have to tell me anything, you know,' continued Simon, 'let's talk about something else if you want to.'

Natalie fell silent again for a minute or so before she continued,

'There was this one lad, Thomas Miller; he was in the year above me. I fancied him a bit and he talked me into meeting him in the park one night. It was just before Easter and it was getting dark. He kissed me and I went along with it. Then he took me into the bushes. We kissed a bit more then he started touching me. I let him take my top off; and then my bra. As soon as he'd got them the bastard shouted out and ran off with them. Half a dozen of his mates were waiting for him and they were all on at me to come out and show them what I'd got. I just sat down and cried, trying to cover myself up. Eventually I think he felt sorry for me 'cos he brought my stuff back, but it was all over school the next day. I ran off at break and didn't go back all week. That's when I decided that I was never going to trust a lad again. I did, though, twice more and then I regretted it both times. When I went back to school I acted like a hard little bitch. One of the lads from the park said stuff and I kicked him in the balls. Another one tried to grab me from behind so I bust his nose. They left me alone after that. It was OK for a bit. A couple of other girls let on that he'd done the same to them and I got a bit of respect for standing up to them. The next time I got in with a lad it was the start of it all; the sex for sale stuff.'

The rain had eased off into a faint drizzle and they drove through the almost deserted streets of a small town.

'I was fifteen,' said Natalie, 'and we'd moved house again, but I was still at the same school. Mum had taken up with a bloke called Liam; quite a bit younger than her. She was off the booze for a bit and things weren't too bad. Anyway, this lad was nearly seventeen and in the lower sixth. His name was John Darrow, Johnnie everyone called him. He wasn't like the others; he was a bit of a loner; quiet like, but I thought he was gorgeous. He lived near us and he sometimes used to walk to school with me. I think he waited for me on purpose. We used to chat about all sorts and he took me to the pictures a couple of times. We kissed and that and it was going OK. After a bit of petting and stuff we started to talk about doing it. He wasn't pushy; said it didn't matter if we waited until we were both ready, but I told him we'd do it on his seventeenth birthday as a sort of present. My mum had a cleaning job in the mornings and Liam worked for the council as a plumber so we planned that we'd skip school and he'd sneak into our house. We were both a bit scared. He'd brought some condoms, but it took us ages of kissing and stuff to get going; in my bedroom, that's where we were.......Anyway we eventually got going and then.... and then......'

Natalie began to cry in earnest and Simon squeezed her shoulder.

'Shh, there's no need to talk about it,' he said, 'I'm sorry I asked you to...you know, tell me about your life.'

Natalie shrugged his hand off and sobbed gently. The rawness of the long-submerged memories stung her, but she was also irritated with the man beside her. She had told him more than she had ever told anyone else about her formative years and that, somehow, seemed to make her even more upset. Sensing the awkwardness of the moment Simon had the good sense to say nothing as they passed through another built up area. He noticed a large Tesco Superstore beside the road and, glancing at the now quiet girl, he wondered whether to suggest they stop and do some shopping. She was staring fixedly ahead though and he remained silent.

The road threaded its way through an extensive sea-side wind-farm. The massive turbines rose high into the rapidly darkening overcast, dwarfing the car and caravan as the fugitives followed the grey ribbon of tarmac northwards. As they approached Maryport Simon took the risk of re-opening communication.

'Nat, could you read out the directions from the book, please?' he asked, risking a glance at her.

Natalie picked up the book from the door pocket and thumbed through it, eventually locating the turned down page. She calmly read out the instructions, struggling to interpret the peculiar abbreviations. Ten minutes later they drew up outside a cramped farmyard about half a mile to the south of the village of Allonby. Natalie, who seemed to have regained some of her composure, slipped out of the car and opened the gate and Simon drove in. He got out and located the farmhouse door as Natalie returned to her seat. Upon his return he announced that he had paid for seven nights and drove cautiously along a bumpy track towards the dull grey waters of the Solway Firth, still just visible in the fading twilight of the day. The site was a small level field adjacent to a rocky beach. There were two other caravans already sited and Simon pulled up beside a small board indicating pitch number four. With Natalie's help he unhitched the caravan from the car and manoeuvred it backwards towards the low stone wall marking the edge of the field. He suggested that Natalie returned to the car to shelter from the fine drizzle and then began the half-forgotten process of levelling the caravan and connecting mains electricity, the waste container and a full fresh water tank. He then disappeared inside the caravan and cajoled the water pump into life. Emerging with the awning in a large bag which he pushed underneath the caravan, he gestured for Natalie to join him and she retrieved her rucksack and stepped into the cramped interior of the place of refuge. At the front of the caravan were two long parallel bench seats, long enough to double as twin beds, upholstered in a dark red fabric. Between them, at the very front was a small chest of drawers with a top that Simon had folded out to form a small table. On the far side from the door was a tiny wardrobe, which Natalie discovered contained a larger folded up table. Next to the wardrobe was a microscopic bathroom containing a toilet, washbasin and an overhead shower. At the very back of the caravan was a miniature version of the seats at the front with a square table between them and, to the left of the doorway was a kitchen area with an oven, hob and refrigerator. This was all new to Natalie and she was fascinated by the proliferation of gadgets and the clever use of space. She could hear Simon outside doing something under the bathroom window. With a flash of anxiety she realised that she had not fathomed out the sleeping arrangements. Would they both sleep on the front parallel benches she wondered, suddenly embarrassed at the prospect of their physical proximity.

Simon burst in through the door with his arms full of sleeping bags, two large beach towels, the shopping from the car and his own holdall. Natalie sat down on one of the front seats as he began to busy himself inside. To her relief he detached the small rear table and slid it between the seats, covering the bare wood with the upholstered seat backs to form a narrow bed.

'There,' he said, 'laying out a sleeping bag, 'that's your room, look.' He drew a curtain across from the rear of the bathroom area which screened off the little bed before opening it again. 'Up here are your lockers,' He opened two small lockers above the bed which Natalie had not noticed, 'and you can put the rest of your stuff in the wardrobe.'

Natalie busied herself stowing away her things as Simon filled an old fashioned kettle and lit the gas burner beneath it. He discovered a tin of tuna amongst the shopping and began to prepare a simple meal of tuna sandwiches. By the time Natalie had finished her unpacking he had made two cups of tea and two plates of sandwiches and put them on the folding table. For a moment Natalie felt a girlish impulse to show him the things she had bought on her shopping expedition, but the memory of what had happened in the hotel room forced its way into the forefront of her mind and she sat down on the opposite bench to Simon and they ate their meal in silence.

CHAPTER FOURTEEN

The food revived them both. Natalie kicked off her sandals and curled up into the front corner of the seat, her back against a large cushion while Simon sat on the opposite seat, his back against the wall of the wardrobe. Natalie looked quizzically into his eyes, unsure of what came next. He smiled back at her and she dropped her head to avoid his gaze.

'Liam walked in on us,' she said, keeping her eyes averted, 'both of us stark naked and in he walked. He'd come back for something and he must have heard us. He went ballistic, called Johnnie a pervert and me a dirty little slut. He told us to get dressed and went downstairs. Johnny took off and I went to face the music, but he didn't say anything. Just gave me a black look and went off back to work. I was scared all day of what Mum would do when she found out, but he didn't tell her. Mum was drinking a fair bit again and she often used to flake out after tea. That night, while she was legless, he came into my room; told me again that I was a dirty little slut. He threatened to tell Mum unless I did what he told me to. He said that if I wanted sex I should have it with a real man and not a boy. He pulled my nightdress off over my head and he did it to me. I just lay there and let him because I was scared he'd tell mum. I could have fought him off, but I just lay there and let him. It was awful. It hurt like hell and I just let him....I let him...I didn't even bloody struggle.'

Simon reached out to her, but she shuffled herself further into the corner.

'The next morning he came back. I thought he was going to do it again, but he stood by the door and told me that he was sorry; a moment of weakness, that's what he called it. He said if we both kept our secrets from Mum everything would be all right. Then he gave me twenty quid. That's the first time I got paid for selling my body. School was awful. I felt as if everyone could tell what I'd done with Liam. Poor Johnnie, he couldn't even look at me. He cut me dead. I suppose he must have known deep down that I was soiled goods or something.'

Natalie looked up and saw that Simon was looking at her with an expression of deep concern. He gestured towards the empty mugs and the kettle. Natalie nodded her head and he busied himself making more tea. For some strange reason now that she had begun to tell her story she was somehow unable to stop herself. Why she was telling all her inmost secrets to this strange man she had no idea. Perhaps it was because he knew not to interrupt, she thought; or perhaps it was a means of escape from her anguished memories of the struggle in the hotel room. She knew that she would not be able to rest now until he knew it all.

Once Simon had made the tea Natalie resumed her head down posture and carried on.

'Liam kept well away for weeks,' she muttered,' then he did it again. He'd had a bit to drink and Mum was dead to the world as usual. He came in to my room one night and tried to kiss me. I wriggled away, but he was too strong for me so I just let him again. It didn't hurt so much this time; it was as if it was someone else doing it with him and not me. Then, the next morning there he was; all sorry, or so he said, and twenty pounds to keep quiet. For more than a year that's how it was; every three of four weeks. I just got my head down and started revising like mad for my exams. The shame of it, I suppose, but I didn't feel much like a teenager. I expect that's why I got decent GCSEs: three 'A's and five 'B's. I got a Saturday job in Boots and stayed on into the sixth form. I got a bit cocky with him after I got my GCSEs. I told him I wanted fifty quid to keep quiet and he paid up right enough. Proper little tart wasn't I?' Natalie glanced up at Simon, who smiled weakly. Unable to maintain eye contact, Natalie dropped her head again.

'I tried to pluck up the courage to tell Mum once or twice, but she was in a bad way. I suppose I was scared she'd not believe me, or think I was leading him on or something. School work was my refuge, really, I was working dead hard and I wanted to go to university. I don't suppose it would ever have happened, though. Mum never had any money; she drank it as soon as it arrived. Anyway, I did tell her in the end...and that was probably the worst thing I could have done. It was the week after my seventeenth birthday. As usual Mum was on another planet. He came back pissed one Saturday night; him and his mate. He told me that for a birthday treat they were both going to have me and I would get paid double. I tried to struggle good and proper that night, but each of them held me down while the other did it. I was covered in bruises the next morning. There was a hundred quid on my dressing table and I stayed in my room all day. I heard him go out in his van after teatime and I went and told Mum. She was quite well gone, but she knew well enough what I was saying. Said she'd make him stop and that she'd call the police if he did it again, but she was well pissed and I wasn't sure if she'd remember. I was up early the next morning and off to school before either of them got up. All day I was hoping that when I got home she'd have chucked him out, but it didn't work out like that....oh shit, I'm crying again......sorry, I mean....'

Simon reached up into an overhead locker and brought out a toilet roll which he passed to her. She blew her nose noisily, but kept her head down and avoided his gaze.

'Natalie,' he said gently, 'you don't have to tell me all this. I know it's hurting. Just stop. I really don't have to know.'

She looked up briefly and blinked back her tears.

'Y..y..yes you bloody well do,' she stammered, 'you asked and I'm going to tell you. All of it, you bloody nosey parker teddy bear vicar who isn't...who isn't either a teddy bear or a vicar any more....and you're just going to listen until I'm finished.'

Their eyes met briefly. Simon smiled and gestured for her to continue.

'They'd bloody gone and done a moonlight while I was at school,' she said, 'most of the furniture was still there, but all the other stuff had gone. They'd left me my clothes and bedding, but he'd found my little stash of money; nearly three hundred quid in a shoe box on the top of my wardrobe. I was left with nothing; no money and lots of red bills I couldn't pay. My own bloody mother had chosen a bloody paedo over me and gone off and left me. Bastards, both of them! I kept on going to school for a bit; then I asked at Boots about going full time, but they didn't want me. The landlord was getting stroppy and the electric people threatened to cut it off so I decided that if I had already made money from being shagged by men I could probably make some more. There was no way I was going into care. I was fed up with being pissed about by other people so I decided to look after number one. After all it's not as if anyone else cares is it?

I spotted an advert in the free paper and went to work in a massage parlour in Keighley. One to midnight four days a week. Told them I was nineteen. Compared to Liam and his mate it was easy. Punters paid fifty quid for half an hour and I got to keep half. I had to pretend I liked the bastards, but somewhere deep inside it wasn't really me so that was easy after a bit. I could make two hundred quid a night and the bills got paid. Funny thing, though, I kept my Saturday job at Boots all along. It was as if it kept me sane; something that was the real me. Natalie Robertson who worked in Boots and not 'Sexy Suzy' the fifty quid tart.'

Natalie's voice had risen as she recounted her story. She looked up at Simon briefly and noticed that he was looking intently at her.

'I did it for nearly a year,' she said, 'got fucked forty times a week for money. Most of the punters were nasty smelly bastards. Some knocked me about a bit, but we had a panic button and a minder on call if they got too rough. One or two were quite sweet. There was one old chap who'd lost his wife to cancer. He came once a fortnight and always paid for an hour. Sometimes he didn't want sex at all, just to talk. He told me that he had a music shop in Otley. It was him who helped me to get out in the end. I told him how much I hated what I was doing and he asked me why I didn't get a proper job. He said he'd give me a reference, a proper one, not about being a prostitute. I saw an advert for telesales in the Northern Counties Bank in Leeds and applied for it. I gave the music man and the manager of Boots for references. I had an interview and I got the job. It was less money than I was getting and I had to pay tax and stuff, but it was proper, not dirty. I moved out of the old place and got a room in a student house in Headingley with three girls: trainee teachers. I got along with them alright, but we didn't have all that much in common. They were right party animals, but I was determined to get on in the bank; and I did.'

Natalie stopped abruptly and looked up at Simon through her moist eyes. Simon, fighting his fatigue, recognised that to interrupt her flow might cause her irreparable harm. Instincts and insights from his prior life told him that Natalie was almost certainly pouring out the whole story for the first time in her life; brought on no doubt by the trauma caused by the events of the previous evening.

'What happened next?' he prompted.

Maintaining eye contact she continued.

'It was one of the best times of my life. I was earning quite a bit of commission and doing something I was good at. I could talk the customers into buying all sorts of insurances and stuff as well as their loans or credit cards. After a bit they transferred me to the mortgage department. I was just nineteen; the youngest in the team by four years. I took driving lessons and passed my test. I even started going out with the girls sometimes. That's when I met Matt and it all started to go wrong again. I didn't know that at the time. I suppose he was my first real boyfriend; my only real boyfriend, come to that. He lived in the house opposite. He was an art student in his last year at Leeds Met. I met him a couple of times at parties. He was nice to me; he didn't look down on me for not being a student like some did. He told me about his paintings – offered to show them to me. He was a good artist; abstracts and stuff were what he did. We got together after a bit. I told him that my Mum had chucked me out, but I never told him what I'd done; the sex and that. When we made love it felt different. He was gentle and kind. I didn't realise until then why people talked about having sex as making love; not that I ever told him that. Perhaps I should have done, perhaps I should have told him everything, but I was frightened of losing him.

I was doing well at work and earning quite a bit. There were these new flats going up in the city centre; next to the railway station. I got invited to the launch with the rest of the mortgage team and I fell in love with the idea of us having our own place. I worked the system and got a big mortgage from another bank. We moved in as soon as the flat was finished. I still live there. Matt was always a bit on the wild side, smoking weed and drinking a lot, but I thought he would calm down when there were just the two of us. It was a real struggle with money 'cos I'd borrowed more than I could afford. Even after I got promoted again we hade no spare cash at all, but Matt was due to graduate and it would have been OK when he started earning; only he never did.'

Natalie's eyes fell again as she continued in a quieter voice.

'We moved in the Friday before Spring Bank Holiday. Matt got his degree; a third, in the summer but he didn't bother trying to find a job. By Christmas I owed six grand on credit and store cards and the mortgage was in arrears. By then we were rowing fairly regularly. He was still on the weed and some nights he would go out with his mates and not come back until the next day. I knew then he was just using me, but I kidded myself that I was in love with him. He was still nice to me sometimes. He finally left me on Valentines Day. He'd been out all night again and when I got back from work the next day all his stuff was gone. He left me a note saying that he was no good for me and I'd be better on my own. I cried for three days, called in sick for the rest of the week, and I thought my life was over. Then I met Melanie again.

I knew her from my time at the massage parlour. She was a few years older than me and, not like most of the girls, she wasn't doing it to feed a habit. We got on OK. She was a single mum with two kids; twins they were. Her bloke had walked out on her and she left her kids with her mum while she worked; told her mum she was working at a call centre. Anyway, I met up with her again in the cafe in Debenhams the next Saturday. I was just wandering round the shops trying to forget about my troubles and there she was. I just poured it all out to her. We were there hours. She told me that she was still on the game, but working what she called the "top end". She was an escort with her own website and charged a fortune to posh blokes in their hotels. She said she could put me in touch with a photographer and a web designer. I maxed out my credit card and went for it; bought some decent clothes and a wig and stuff. Cost me over a grand to get set up, but I got that back within a fortnight. I just switched myself off from what I was doing; pretended it was someone else; "Kelly", that's what I call myself. I had no choice, did I? No one else was going to look out for me so I had to look after number one. I was only going to do it for a few months; just until I was out of debt, but then I got my big break; a real purpose and I had to carry on a bit longer to pay for it.'

Natalie looked up again and observed that Simon was listening attentively. He gave her a brief smile as she warmed to her theme.

'Flying; Matt had left a voucher for a flying lesson at Leeds Bradford. I took it; an hour in a Robin HR200. The instructor let me fly it and said I was a natural. It was awesome. I was hooked straight away. I just had to learn to fly. I used the extra money I made and took the course. It was the best thing that I ever did. Before long I knew exactly what I wanted to do with my life. I'm going to be an airline pilot. I've been saving for more than a year. I need another twenty three grand and I can start. The best way is to do the course in the US; Florida.'

Simon noticed the sparkle in her eyes fade as she looked away once again.

'That's how I came to be involved in this,' she said quietly, 'Barry offered me five grand to have sex with you and drug you. That would have brought getting off the game and going to Florida a few weeks closer. You probably think I'm a right slapper, don't you? Five grand for a quick shag and off into the night; that was the plan. So, Mr Bloody Vicar, what do you think of that?' Her voice was rising again. 'What do you think of me now? What does your bloody god think of me? Are you happy now you know what a selfish cow I am? Don't come up to your standards do I? Are you regretting being with me now? Should have walked away when you had the chance, shouldn't you? Bet you're really sorry you ever met........'

Natalie buried her head in her hands and began to cry again. Deep within Simon stirred an impulse to pronounce the absolution that he discerned that she was desperately seeking, but he lacked both the words and the conviction to do so. Instead he rose from his seat and crossed the tiny gap between the sofas to sit beside her. He slipped his left arm around her shoulder and gently pulled her head against his chest and, for the second time that day, he held Natalie Robertson close while her tears dampened the fabric of his shirt.

Eventually the tears subsided but Natalie was reluctant to move. She sensed some sort of unspoken companionship and acceptance passing to her from this perplexing man through the damp warmth where her face was snuggled into his chest. Looking down at her short fair hair, Simon was perturbed by his feelings for her. He felt a deep compassion for her and a sincere desire to do all that he could to help her. He also could not avoid the fact that he found her physically very attractive; uncomfortably so. He lifted her head gently.

'Nat,' he said quietly, 'I'm glad you told me all that. I know how much it must have cost you. Now, I'm going to go for a bit of a walk while you get ready for bed. I don't know what to say about all the stuff you've told me; except that I believe that we, all of us, matter because of who we are and not because of whatever we might have done or not done. None of us are perfect; we've all got things in our pasts that we don't like to think about.'

He squeezed her shoulder gently as he eased himself up from the seat and smiled as he stepped out into the night. Natalie retreated to the bathroom, and changed into her nightclothes before wriggling into her sleeping bag and pulling the curtain across to screen her miniscule bedroom from the rest of the caravan.

Simon ambled slowly through the gap in the hedge and onto the rocky foreshore, his mind reeling from the torrents of emotion the girl had released. For the first time in many months he felt a heartfelt desire to commune with his God, but the words would not come. As he stared out at the waves breaking unevenly on the rocks in the dim and diffused moonlight that penetrated a thin layer of high clouds he tried to come to grips with the turmoil in his mind. He was a wanted man on a mission to vindicate his dead father with a disturbingly attractive and emotionally fragile girl in tow. Such was the stuff of the novels he was so keen on. This was real though, Natalie had opened up her entire life to him; shown him a degree of trust he knew that he far from deserved. He would not let her down, he vowed to himself; he would put the attraction he felt for her completely aside. She was part of this now, he would not only do whatever he had to do to follow the trail left by Michael Duckworth; he would do his level best to make sure that Natalie Robertson realised her ambition to fly airliners and could put all the pain of the past behind her. He had over a hundred thousand pounds in savings, plus what he had been left by Michael Duckworth, she would never have to sell her body again, he resolved. As soon as this adventure was over he would see to it that she could follow her dream.

In the cocoon of her sleeping bag Natalie lay awake. She heard Simon return and listened while he pottered about, getting himself ready for bed. Presently the sound of rhythmic breathing told her that he was asleep. No wonder he had dropped off so quickly, she thought, he must have been totally exhausted. She wondered why she had told him so much. At first it had been an angry reaction to him asking her to keep him awake while he was driving, then, later, she had deliberately set out to shock him, but the words had kept on tumbling out of her mouth. She had told him far more than she had ever told any other human being. Well, he certainly knew it all now, she thought, the whole sordid lot. She wondered what he thought of her: not that it really mattered, of course, but nonetheless his opinion of her perturbed her as a collection of random thoughts began to pursue each other round and round in her head, keeping her awake. She liked the way he had started to call her "Nat" she decided. He was certainly a good listener as well. Perhaps he had looked a bit like a teddy bear with his long hair and beard. His new clean shaven look suited him she concluded. And she felt good and safe when he held her close to his chest. What a pity she had told him all about her, though, he would probably despise her now. Just as well, really because if she trusted him too much he would surely let her down just like all the others. Oh sod you, Mr. Vicar, she thought as she rolled over and snuggled her head into the cushion. Within seconds she too was sound asleep.

CHAPTER FIFTEEN

Wayne Stevens had got back to his erstwhile prison at lunchtime, badly shaken and increasingly angry. His girlfriend was waiting for him in the kitchen of the house still in her dressing gown. High from her recent fix she had made an amorous advance as soon as he came through the door, but he shrugged her off. He busied himself in packing their few belongings before sitting down in front of the television set to await nightfall. They had to get out quickly, he had decided. London would probably be the best place; you could easily disappear in London. Colleen could get a job in one of the clubs and he would lie low. He would steal a car that night and they would dump it near a tube station early in the morning.

When he slipped out into the darkness just after midnight he did not notice the white Transit van parked a hundred yards down the road. He strode briskly toward the main road, oblivious to the van which began to move slowly after him.

Wayne's body was not discovered until dawn the next morning. As the sun came up a man walking his dog spotted it on waste ground beside the Manchester Ship Canal. The police were called. Wayne had been shot in each kneecap and elbow before the coup de grace had been administered with a bullet through his forehead. Forensics would show that the same gun as had been used to kill Detective Inspector Gilroy had been used. It was found later on in the day under a bush less than fifty yards from the body.

Colleen Rourke waited for her man to return until lunchtime the following day. When he failed to appear she replenished her cocaine level, threw a handful of clothes into a small shoulder bag together with Wayne's stash of crumpled cash and her remaining supply of white powder. She broke the plastic tag from her leg and set off walking towards the town centre. At Bank Quay railway station she purchased a single ticket to Holyhead. She would get there in time to catch the overnight ferry to Dublin.

The Governor had called Jimmy Bell on his unofficial mobile phone at an awkward moment. The Detective Chief Superintendent had made a brief foray home from his office to freshen up and change his clothes. It was the hour before dawn; he had just stepped out of the shower when the strident ring tone summoned his dripping naked form back to his bedroom. There was little good news to report. Paul Cavendish had checked out the girl's flat and had taken away a crumpled printout of her web-page. She appeared not to have returned there from Manchester. Cavendish had then driven over to Manchester to be on hand if there were any developments. Detective Inspector Jewel had reported that the man and girl had travelled to the airport together where they had bought both air and rail tickets. The girl had booked her flights in her real name, giving the locals a real lead. Later on there had appeared to have been some sort of altercation between them. She had stormed off onto a Middlesbrough train, but had got off at Piccadilly. CCTV had tracked her onto a train for Barrow-in-Furness, but the train's own CCTV had proved defective. CCTV pictures from the stations the train had stopped at were being followed up, but several of its calling points had no CCTV coverage. The train conductor had been interviewed and seemed to think that she was on the train between Preston and Lancaster, but might have got off at Lancaster. To make things worse the CCTV at Lancaster station was also out of order. The man had also ended up on the same train, but in a different carriage. He had not got off at Piccadilly, but had been picked up by CCTV in Huddersfield where he had last been seen heading out of the town centre along Bradford Road. Since then there had been no trace. The airport police had waited in vain for them to check in for the flights they had booked. Enlarged CCTV images from the airport had been made available to the media, but too late to make it into the Sunday papers.

The Governor was less than impressed. Demanding a further update by late afternoon he disconnected the call. The palms of Jimmy Bell's hands were sweating as he drove back into Westminster. He and the Governor went back a long way. He knew that the consequences of failing his patron would be dire.

CHAPTER SIXTEEN

Simon woke to the sound of Natalie bumping about in the caravan's tiny bathroom. Daylight streamed through the thin curtains, bathing the interior in a pale orange colourwash. Still feeling exhausted, he lay still as she emerged. She was wearing a short tight-fitting white vest and a pair of brief running shorts. She had her back to him as she filled the kettle and lit the gas burner under it. There was a gap of about two inches between the hem of her top and the waistband of her shorts towards which he found his eyes drawn in fascination. With a flush of shame he felt his body begin to respond to the visual stimulus and he rolled over, turning to face the wall.

'Oh, good morning,' she said brightly, 'I'm going for a run, I'm just making you a cup of coffee before I go.'

Simon rolled back over in his sleeping bag and wriggled himself awkwardly into a sitting position. He was rewarded with a smile that lit up his world. Oh, shit, he thought, doing the right thing by this girl and for the right reasons was going to be a lot harder than he had thought. Still he would do his best. After all, it wasn't as if she could ever possibly fancy someone like him, was it?

'Thanks,' he said as she brought the mug over to him and put it on the top of the folding table, giving him another bitter-sweet eyeful of her bare midriff.

Natalie, fit from her thrice weekly visits to the gym that she convinced herself were necessary to keep her toned for her role as "Kelly", jogged through the farmyard and turned right along the narrow road along which they had travelled the previous evening. She had not intended to run for more than a mile or so, but she began to find the release of endorphins into her bloodstream cathartic and maintained her pace for more than twenty minutes before pausing briefly outside a low bungalow with a sign outside proclaiming it to be Maryport Golf Club. From there she noticed the beginning of a long promenade beside the sea and, after a short rest she started to jog along the promenade, gradually increasing her pace until, breathless and with aching legs she reached Maryport harbour. Throwing herself onto a seat overlooking the marina she put her head between her legs and gulped in huge draughts of air as her pulse rate gradually subsided. Her exertions had driven the twin qualms about her present predicament and her growing obsession with the man she called Mr. Vicar from her mind. As she felt the perspiration cool on her body in the gentle breeze her thoughts once again turned to her dilemma. OK, so he wasn't a teddy bear, still a bit of a geek, though; but quite a nice one. Anyway she was on the run from a murder charge. Well, actually it probably wasn't murder, but manslaughter was bad enough. It still looked like sticking with him was her best plan. He seemed to have some idea what was going on. She would ask him when she got back. Then she would make her mind up. If she thought he had a plan which would get her off she would stick with him. If she wasn't convinced she could always split. She could probably get the bag full of cash from him when she went; wait until he was asleep or something. After all she had to look after number one, didn't she? Lost in her thoughts, she got up from the seat and began to jog and walk alternately back towards the caravan. However hard she tried to pretend otherwise though, the prospect of walking away from Simon Fenton sent an uncomfortable shiver down her spine. Having bared her soul to him the previous evening it was almost as if she had handed over some part of her that would be almost impossible to take back.

Almost as soon as Natalie had closed the door behind her Simon got out of bed and took a shower. Dressed in the clothes he had bought the previous day he sought a distraction from his troubled thoughts about Natalie and emerged into the overcast day. A warm westerly breeze was blowing in from the sea. He emptied the waste container and replenished the water supply before retrieving the awning from underneath the caravan and beginning to lay out the jumble of poles on the grass beside the caravan. The occupants of the two other caravans on the site, who appeared to know one another, gave him a cheery wave as they loaded coats and bags into their cars and set off for a day out. Puzzling out the intricate design of the awning frame kept him occupied for some time. With a wry grin he recalled the frequent heated exchanges between his grandparents as they had struggled to erect their caravan awning on numerous occasions during his childhood and adolescence. By the time Natalie returned he had succeeded in attaching the canvas of the awning to the channel on the side of the caravan and had put together the frame within it. He was busy hammering tent pegs into the ground as she jogged into the field. He looked up and was again rewarded with a smile.

'I need a shower,' she gasped, slightly breathless, and disappeared through the door. Simon finished pegging down the canvas and sat on the caravan step, reluctant to infringe her privacy. Presently she emerged, dressed in tight-fitting jeans and a baggy t-shirt.

'I've put some toast on,' she announced, 'come and have some breakfast.' Over tea, toast and cereals they chatted about nothing in particular, both apparently relieved that the deep conversation of the previous evening was a thing of the past.

'We need to go shopping,' Natalie announced, 'I really need a hair dryer and we could do with some proper food and stuff.'

'Right,' replied Simon, 'I need a few things too, like a toothbrush for example. I spotted a Tesco a few miles back yesterday. Shall we go now?'

They joined the Sunday lunchtime throng of shoppers at the Tesco Superstore on the northern outskirts of Workington. In addition to Natalie's hairdryer and an assortment of foodstuffs, toiletries and general domestic items, Simon picked up a pair of pre-pay mobile 'phones and two twenty pound top-ups, a small DAB radio and an up to date road atlas. Natalie helped him choose some casual clothes and, following her advice he had to agree that the items he put into the shopping trolley were certainly very different from anything he would have chosen himself. Finally they took advantage of an end of season promotion and selected a matching pair of metal framed sun-lounger chairs for the price of one. When they emerged from the store and began to pack their purchases into the car it began to rain. On the way to the exit Simon pulled into the filling station and topped up the car with diesel. He also bought a selection of Sunday newspapers. As they drove back Natalie anxiously scanned the papers.

'They know who we are,' she announced softly, 'but they still think I'm Samantha Evans. They seem to know a bit more about you. We're supposed to be armed and dangerous. There are no photographs though so it looks like we're safe for a little bit longer.

'There's a picture of Barry, though. He must have got away before they found the body,' she continued, 'they don't say much about it all really, just that the copper was on an undercover operation and that drugs are involved.'

'There's more to it than that,' said Simon thoughtfully, 'we can't be sure what they really know, or who knows it. I know that some of the police are probably out to get me, but it won't be all of them. I just don't know who to trust.'

'What's really going on?' asked Natalie, 'you promised you would tell me.'

Simon began to relate how, completely out of the blue, a letter from a Manchester solicitor had disturbed the equilibrium of his unexciting, but relaxed, lifestyle as an office manager in Norfolk. He told her about his meeting with the solicitor and of the strange letters he had inherited along with thirty odd thousand pounds and a house in Derby from someone he did not know. Touching briefly on his father's death, purportedly at the hands of the IRA, he went on to tell her about his next step: a visit to Glasgow to collect the contents of a safe deposit box.

'The letters are in my bag; on the back seat,' he gestured over his shoulders, 'have a look if you want to, Nat.'

She unfastened her seatbelt and reached across, pulling the holdall through the gap between the seats. Delving in, amongst the bundles of cash and a few personal items she retrieved the letters and began to read them. A lumbering tractor pulling a trailer load of hay delayed their arrival back at the caravan and Natalie finished reading just in time to open the farmyard gate. Closing it behind the car she waved Simon off and followed on foot, deep in thought. At least she knew what it was all about. He had been telling the truth and everything that Barry had told her was a lie. She also thought that, by telling her the truth and showing her the letters, Simon had put his trust in her. Something that, if he had known her better he might not have done. But he did know her, didn't he? She had told him the lot last night and still he had trusted her. That didn't make sense; he knew all about her and he still treated her like an equal. He seemed to be quite happy to have her around. Perplexed and strangely moved she joined him in unloading the car and transferring the contents into the caravan.

They argued briefly over who should cook the meal. In the end Simon forced the issue and began to brown some cubes of chicken in a small frying pan while he boiled up a pan of water for the pasta. He extracted the folding table from the wardrobe and asked Natalie to set it up in the awning with the sun-loungers. By the time Simon had combined the pasta and chicken with sauce from jar in a Pyrex dish and placed it in the oven to bake along with a stick of garlic bread Natalie has set the table in the awning and opened a bottle of white wine. The rain continued unabated and the walls of the awning began to ripple in the strengthening breeze as Simon served up the meal. Sitting at opposite ends of the rectangular table they ate in a comfortable silence. The wind loosened a few of the awning pegs and Simon made running repairs as Natalie went inside and filled the kettle. The rain had steadily increased and was hammering noisily down on the metal roof of the caravan by the time he returned and closed the door behind him, Natalie had made two mugs of coffee and was busy washing the pots as Simon switched on the radio for the four o'clock news.

An airliner had burst into flames after making an emergency landing at Luton following an engine problem. Eleven people had been killed and seventeen hurt. The alleged murder of Detective Inspector Gilroy had been demoted to second place. The three suspects were now known to be Simon Fenton (34) an office manager from Wroxham in Norfolk, Natalie Robertson; also known as Samantha Evans, (24) a mortgage adviser from Leeds and Wayne Stevens (38) of no fixed abode. Mr. Fenton and Miss

Robertson had been tracked by CCTV to Manchester Airport, but had left by train separately and were not believed to be travelling together. Simon Fenton had last been seen in Huddersfield early on Saturday morning; Natalie Robertson was thought to be somewhere in north-west Lancashire, possibly in the Lancaster area and Wayne Stevens was last seen driving a stolen Volvo estate westbound along the M62 between Manchester and Warrington. Descriptions of all three suspects followed and members of the public were asked to report all sightings to the local "Crimestoppers" number.

Simon switched off the radio.

'Well, at the moment, I think we're a couple of steps ahead,' he said.

'What will you do now,' Natalie asked; 'are we off to Glasgow in the morning?'

'No, it's a bank holiday,' replied Simon. 'I need to think it out. They might be looking out for us in Glasgow. I don't really want to use the car too much after tomorrow. Not unless we have to, because either the bloke I bought it off might recognise me or the DVLA might throw up the false address I gave. I think it would be better if I went to Glasgow on my own; by train. I've put you in enough danger, Nat.'

'But I want to help,' protested Natalie, 'I'm in this now, up to my neck.'

'I know,' reassured Simon, but I think it would be less conspicuous if I went on my own. I promise you, Natalie Robertson, I won't abandon you to the wolves. I'm getting to like having you around.'

Natalie coloured up and looked away. Simon, shocked at how naturally the last sentence had tumbled from his lips, also felt an acute embarrassment and quickly busied himself in drying the pots and putting them away. Still reluctant to face the girl, he then made another coffee for them both before settling back on the opposite seat.

'So,' Natalie began, 'how about you, then? You found out everything about me last night. Even stuff I've never told anyone else.' Her voice faltered slightly at the memory. 'If you really are getting to like having me around, even after you know what I'm really like, are you going to tell me who you are, Simon Fenton, thirty four?'

Simon made no reply. Natalie Robertson, he thought was not only very attractive, she was also rather astute. While he was aware that there was some sort of growing chemistry between the two of them he was both afraid and reluctant to let his imagination run away with itself. It was only circumstances that had thrown them together; nothing more. They were lumbered with each other and would almost certainly never have chosen to spend time in each others company if they had not been forced together. He harboured no romantic illusions. They had died with Sophie. Still, Natalie was proving to a good friend, perhaps the best one he had made since leaving the church. She had trusted him to help her get away from the trouble they were both in and she had trusted him with her deepest hurts and closest secrets. In the pale light of the late afternoon, to the accompaniment of the irregular rhythm of rain falling on the caravan roof, he took a deep breath and began to speak.

'My dad died six months before I was born,' he began, 'He was in the RAF Regiment. I'd always been told that he'd been killed fighting the IRA, but you know about that now. My mum died the day after I was born. I was brought up by my grandparents; on my mum's side. I don't ever remember seeing my dad's parents, even though they sent me cards and presents until I was thirteen. I suppose that with six surviving children and over a dozen grandchildren they just didn't have enough time. Granny and Grandad were all I had; my mum had been their only child. Grandad married Granny in Scotland. They were very young. He had just been made assistant manager of the Palace Theatre in Glasgow and Granny worked there as an usherette. They came south to live in Barrow-in-Furness when Grandad got the job of managing the theatre there, but it closed before I was born and he was working in the booking office at the railway station by then. He ended up as stationmaster. We lived in a Victorian terrace on Chatsworth Street; just round the corner from where I met up with you yesterday. Grandad had a free pass on the railway, so he used to take me on long train trips since before I can remember. Granny worked in a tobacconist in the town, just up from Woolworths. We had a caravan when I got older and, every summer we would go away to Yorkshire or Wales or somewhere. We even went over to France on a ferry, once.'

Natalie listened attentively as he recounted stories from his childhood and adolescence. As he explained some of the eccentricities and embarrassments of being brought up by people of a generation out of touch with the majority of the parents of his peers she began to make some sense of the mild eccentricities exhibited by the man himself.

The story moved on to his move away to university in Norwich and the unexpected death of his grandfather and Natalie realised that he had some sort of gift of storytelling that both kept her interest and gave her a penetrating insight into the make up of this rather intense man. She nodded from time to time and asked the occasional question as he began to explain how he had come to faith in his second year. The pace and pitch of his voiced changed slightly as he spoke of his introduction to Sophie and Natalie became aware that the story he was recounting had now moved from the realm of general description into something altogether more significant. With a mixture of intrigue and apprehension she smiled in encouragement as Simon adjusted the cushion behind his head. He gave a half smile in return and steeled himself for the ordeal. He would hold nothing back, he decided as, for the first time ever. He prepared to tell a fellow human being the full story of how losing Sophie had changed his life beyond recognition. Incongruous as it seemed, this girl, this bruised and damaged young woman who had set out to do him harm, yet had ended up saving his life seemed to have wormed her way into the core of his very being.

He described his courtship of Sophie and how the influence of her and her family had helped him draw close to God. When he spoke of his spiritual journey Natalie became uncomfortable. Such matters were completely unfamiliar to her; half forgotten snippets from school assemblies and RE lessons tumbled into her mind, but she could made no connection between them and Simon's obvious sincerity. He went on to talk about the frantic excitement of being engaged to Sophie and the heady mix of trepidation and anticipation as he had approached his ordination. He was good with words, Natalie realised; although he used a number of unfamiliar words as he described his curacy and move into parish ministry alongside the early days of his marriage to Sophie he used them in a way that made them intelligible to her. As the story moved on to their failure to have a child and the early signs of a breakdown in the marriage, Simon's anguish began to become apparent in both his facial expression and the tone of his voice. Once or twice he seemed to stumble over some of his words and Natalie noticed that he had started to wring his hands together.

'Simon,' she interrupted, 'you can stop now. It's just me being nosey. It's like you said to me yesterday, you don't have to tell me any of this.'

Halted in his flow, Simon paused. Natalie reached over to the refrigerator and extracted the half-full wine bottle, looking quizzically at him. He nodded and she poured it out into two glasses.

'Actually, I want to tell you,' said Simon, 'It still hurts, Nat, but I want you to know it all.'

'But it's really none of my business is it?' she replied, 'It's between you and Sophie. Even if you're not together any more I don't think she'd like it if you told me all the gory details.'

'No, Nat, we're not together; she died, and I want to tell you about it,' he said softly.

He told her about Sophie's hectic work schedule; about her self-imposed celibacy in the spare bedroom; about the strange pretence of normality they had maintained for the outside world and finally, with tears trickling from his moist grey eyes, about her final fateful journey with Alan Greenly.

'Are you sure?' Natalie asked, passing him the box of tissues, 'are you sure it was like that; they couldn't have been on a business trip after all. Perhaps her plans got changed or something?'

'I tried to pretend that at first,' he replied, 'I tried to convince myself that I'd misheard where she was going or that something had come up. But later; after the accident investigators had finished with it, they gave me her luggage. There was underwear and stuff in it that told its own story.'

Simon stopped talking and averted his gaze from her. Natalie felt the colour rising in her cheeks fearing that she had pushed him too far; that by taking him back to what was so obviously a place of deep anguish she might have burst the bubble of the mutual trust that had been growing between them.

'Is that why you gave up being a vicar?' she asked, her voice barely a whisper. Simon shook his head, but still kept looking through the window into the gathering dusk.

'No, I was angry with God for sure, but that wasn't it....I mean shit happens doesn't it. It doesn't say anywhere in the Bible that bad things don't happen to you if you believe......but I expected to feel that God was close to me in it all, but I just couldn't seem to find him any more...... At first I thought I would get over it; not Sophie, but not being close to God. I thought I'd just wake up one day and there He would be, but it didn't happen.....'

The tears were again flowing freely as he contemplated his two lost loves.

'Tim Baxter, the Suffragan, that's the Assistant Bishop, was good to me. He's been promoted to Bishop of Carlisle and he thoroughly deserves it. Anyway he made me take three months off; time to begin to heal, he said; time to come to terms with it. I told him that I just couldn't connect with God, but that didn't seem to bother him; he let me talk for hours and popped in every couple of days. After a month I thought things might get better one day, but they didn't; they just got worse..........it was the bloody inquest that put the lid on it.'

Again Simon lapsed into silence. For several minutes neither Simon nor Natalie dared to look anywhere but out of opposite windows. Eventually, Natalie found the courage to make the next move. She turned to look at him.

'What happened next, Simon,' she said softly, 'do you still want to tell me?'

For a moment he made no reply. Then, hesitantly he began.

'The inquest was in Stratford......two days before the Coroner's Officer came to see me. He rang up, but wouldn't say what it was about....he said that he needed to ask me something....I had no idea what it was about, I mean I'd not been involved in anything like that...except when Grandad died, but that was different......He came after lunch; not that I was eating much then....anyway he wanted to ask me about the post mortem report. I didn't know what he was on about.....She'd died from multiple injuries, he said, she wouldn't have suffered.....then he told me.....he asked me if I wanted it read out....he said how sorry he was at my double loss. You see Sophie was three months pregnant when she died.'

CHAPTER SEVENTEEN

Simon stared sightlessly out into the darkness. Aware that she had precipitated what appeared to be an emotional crisis in the life of her companion, Natalie hesitated. His distress and anguish was written plainly on his face. She slowly got to her feet and removed the empty wine glass gently from his grip as he sat immobile on the bench seat. Putting the glass down on the draining board she sat down beside him and took his hand in hers.

'It's all right, Simon,' she said, squeezing his hand gently, 'It's all right.'

She felt the pressure on her hand returned, but he continued to stare out into the darkness.

'She was having someone else's baby,' he continued softly, 'and she hadn't even told me. That's why I gave up my parish. I just couldn't face telling people that God would never let them down when he's let that happen to me. I know that bad stuff happens all the time and I've got a few of the answers in my head from all the training and Bible stuff, but nothing prepares you for that. Anyway, they didn't read that bit out at the inquest; about her being pregnant, and the verdict was accidental death. Everyone was really nice to me, especially Sophie' parents, but that made it even harder. I think they must have known that things weren't working out between us and I'm pretty sure they had their suspicions about why she was on her way to Stratford, but I didn't tell anyone about the lies she'd told me about where she was going. When somebody dies no one wants to think badly of them do they? People thought it was just that Sophie had died in a tragic accident and that was what had knocked me off course. But it wasn't; it was that she had been cheating on me and that she was having someone else's baby. I never did work out when she was going to tell me and what her long term plans were and that made it worse somehow. After a few weeks I knew I'd never be able to carry on in the church. You find out who your friends really are at times like that. Tim Baxter was great. It was like he really cared. I think he guessed quite a bit about Sophie and me not getting on. He said I could take as much time as I wanted, but I knew straight away that I wasn't going to carry on. Just a couple of others made the effort after a few weeks. Kynpham Johal was a good mate. He's been a student, doing journalism, when I was a curate and he's got a job on the local rag and came to live in my parish. We're still in touch. Then there was Andy Carr. We were curates in next door parishes and we got along really well. He's vicar of West Wroxham now. I suppose that's one of the reasons I moved there. He never talks to me about the God stuff, you know, but he's always dropping round; him and his wife Jane. They drag me round for Sunday lunch every now and then. Just occasionally I go to his church. I haven't lost every bit of my faith, Nat, but I just can't join it up with the rest of my life any more. Would you believe that, apart from those three… and Sophie's family, but I've sort of deliberately kept them at arms length, no-one else has bothered with me from my church days.'

'How about your Granny?' asked Natalie, 'what did you tell her?'

'That's what made it even worse,' continued Simon, 'I think it was Sophie dying that tipped her over the edge. She'd been getting a bit forgetful and stuff for a while. When she came down for the funeral she kept forgetting why she was there; kept asking where Sophie was. She just seemed to get more and more confused after that. I went back home with her and found that she hadn't been looking after herself properly. I took her to see her doctor and eventually they diagnosed Alzheimer's. She had to go into a home and sell the house. It's a nice one; Abbeyfields beside a small tarn just outside Dalton. At first she could remember some things quite well, but she's gone downhill now. I go over by train every couple of months; travel up on Saturday and put up in a little hotel. I spend Saturday evening and Sunday morning with her before I set off back, but she doesn't know who I am any more.......Anyway, Sophie had a life insurance policy for a hundred and fifty thousand pounds and her pension scheme paid out the best part of another hundred thousand so I suddenly found myself well off. I saw an advert for a job in Wroxham; at an agricultural merchants. Office manager they called it, the pay wasn't so hot, but that didn't matter. The firm was owned by two elderly brothers and the office had been run by one of their wives until she had a stroke. They took on an office junior, a seventeen year old called Sharon, but it was far too much to expect a youngster to sort everything out. She's still there, Sharon I mean; she's pretty good at it now. It's a friendly enough place to work in; it was just what I needed. I used some of Sophie's money to buy a little house there and that's what I do now...I mean I did until this mess came along. I don't know how it all will end.'

Natalie glanced downwards at their entwined hands. Simon's story had somehow penetrated her thick veneer of self-sufficiency and had moved her in a way that he had never before experienced. She snuggled her head into his neck and they sat close together in silence for what seemed to both of them to be a long time. For Natalie the moment seemed to be loaded with significance, but she could not articulate or understand why. She had felt a deep empathy with the man whose warm body was uncomfortably, or perhaps too comfortably, nestled against her own. Finally daring to move she lifted her head. Simon turned to look at her and their eyes met. At the last second her courage failed her, or perhaps it was her common sense that had prevailed.

'How about some tea and cake?' she asked rising from the seat.

Simon was aware that, in the depth of the anguish of his memories, he had made a significant connection with this pretty blonde girl. For a moment he had thought that she had been going to kiss him. He was glad that she hadn't though, that might have spoiled the moment. Then the absurd reality of the situation hit him. They were on the run from he knew not who or what. It was only the strangeness of circumstance that had thrown them together and a consequence of their shared boredom and frustration with inactivity that had brought them almost to the point of intimacy. In any other place and at any other time a girl like this wouldn't have given him a second glance. He felt deeply sorry for the quirks of life that had driven her to prostitution and was filled with compassion for the way her lifestyle had eroded her self-esteem. He recognised that her more recent enterprise in the murky world of the sex industry was motivated not by greed as she had suggested, but because of a deep need for her to hold on to a dream of a better life. He also experienced a welling up of relief when he realised that his body had not reacted at all to her intimate proximity. A deep friendship; that was what was on the cards, here. A deep friendship the like of which he had never known before.

Natalie brewed the tea and cut up the cake they had bought earlier and set the small meal on the folding table, retreating to the safety of the seat opposite as Simon wriggled forwards to take his seat at the table. With the thin plywood of the table safely demarcating their personal space normal relations were slowly resumed.

'I need to find out train times for Glasgow on Tuesday,' Simon announced, 'I don't want to use the mobiles from here – just in case. I think we'd better go out somewhere in the morning. I could do with some internet access as well.'

'How about a disguise?' asked Natalie, 'you could do with looking different when you go into the city; perhaps you should get a suit and dress up as a businessman?'

Both relieved of the burden of soul-searching conversation they began to plan a shopping trip to Carlisle the following day. They would leave the car at Maryport station and travel in by train. Natalie would wear her long blonde wig and plain glass spectacles with one of her new outfits while Simon would just have to manage with the clothes he had bought at Tesco and a pair of sunglasses.

Presently Natalie yawned and that was the cue for bedtime. To avoid awkwardness Simon suggested that he take care of emptying the waste and topping up the water container while she got ready for bed. By the time he had finished the curtain at the back of the caravan was closed.

From the cocoon of her sleeping bag Natalie listened once again to the sound of Simon getting ready for bed. The edge of the curtain barely overlapped with the rear wall of the bathroom and she had to fight hard to resist a childish impulse to open it just a whisker and peep. No! That would be ridiculous, she told herself, it wasn't as if she fancied him or anything. He wasn't exactly a hunk was he? No six pack and toned muscles about Simon Fenton, thirty four. No, but she liked the way the corners of his eyes wrinkled when he smiled; and the way he called her "Nat". Oh, and he had nice hands; dry and firm. With the memory of his hand holding onto hers as she had shared his pain and grief, Natalie drifted gently of to sleep.

CHAPTER EIGHTEEN

Detective Chief Superintendent Bell telephoned his powerful patron from his office as the evening rain began to fall on central London. He had put off the call as long as he dared in the hope of receiving good news from his Detective Inspectors, but there had still been no positive leads. The Governor remained angry and difficult. The only positive thing that Jimmy Bell had to report was that Stevens was most certainly dead. His body had been identified earlier. Of his girlfriend there was no trace, but both men agreed that she would probably know enough about what was afoot to pose a real danger to the operation. Her identity had been leaked to the senior Investigating officer of the Manchester force.

Since the publication of the CCTV images on the internet and via the television news stations in mid afternoon there had been numerous sightings of Simon Fenton and Natalie Robertson reported. The man had apparently been seen in Bradford, Newcastle, Blackpool, Harrow and Wigan while the girl had been reported in Morecambe, Palmers Green, Peterborough, Birmingham and Barrow-in-Furness. They had also been reported as a couple to be in Coventry, Leicester, Chesterfield and on the Isle of Wight. Each sighting was being painstakingly followed up by the local force concerned.

The Governor said that he suspected that the only worthwhile leads were likely to be the sighting of the man in Bradford and the girl in Morecambe or Barrow-in-Furness. He suggested that Bell enlist the help of local private investigators to keep watch on the man's house in Norfolk and the girl's flat in Manchester. As an afterthought he also suggested regular surveillance of the old bloke's house in Derby.

Bell's patron had an important dinner engagement later on and demanded an update at eight the following morning. Jimmy decided that he might risk a few hours at home and the luxury of sleeping in his own bed.

Back in his office well before eight the next morning, Bell still had little positive news. Stevens' girl had popped up on the passenger list of the Holyhead – Dublin ferry. The Detective Chief Superintendent had engaged a highly unofficial contact in Dublin to make sure she did not get a chance to tell her story. Of all the reported sightings, only the ones of the man in Wigan and the girl in Barrow-in-Furness had proved worth further investigation. A hairdresser in Barrow made a convincing case that she had dyed the girl's hair blonde early on Saturday morning and CCTV footage from Barrow town centre and railway station was being examined. The man seen in Wigan by an off duty policeman had been attempting to break into a lock-up garage but had run off and evaded pursuit. The Governor was planning to take his new trophy wife and several other minor celebrities sailing in the Channel aboard his motor yacht for the rest of the day. He demanded an update at ten in the evening.

CHAPTER NINETEEN

Monday morning dawned clear and bright. The heavy rain of Sunday had washed away the last traces of uncomfortable humidity and a pleasant late summer day was in prospect as Natalie took her early morning jog along the shoreline. Taking advantage of her absence, Simon showered and dressed quickly before beginning to prepare a breakfast of toast and tea. Upon Natalie's return he tactfully took station at the table in the awning while he listened to the "Today" programme on Radio Four. The lead story was still on the aircraft fire and the murder of Detective Inspector Gilroy had been pushed even further down the pecking order by floods in the Severn Valley caused by the torrential rain and an emerging scandal involving one of the potential candidates to succeed the Prime Minister. The drone of a hairdryer announced that Natalie had finished in the bathroom and Simon set about the now regular routine of taking care of the water and waste. Natalie had emerged by the time he returned wearing a light beige cotton dress and matching sandals. Simon took a sharp intake of breath as he saw her; suddenly relieved that he had not made any romantic overtures the previous evening. Way, way out of his league, he thought, a platonic friendship with this lovely creature was the only sensible game in town.

Natalie had slept soundly and had woken early, refreshed and alert. She had wriggled out of her night things and into her running shorts and top, intending to slip out into the morning sunshine and repeat her long run of the previous morning. Sitting up in bed, though, she had been unable to get the perplexing nature of her feelings for Simon Fenton out of her mind. Far from the relief she expected to feel at not having kissed him, she began to have pangs of regret at not having made the attempt. Retrieving her trainers from under the bed she had slipped them on and set off on her run. After fifteen minutes she had slowed to a walking pace. Not through fatigue, but because she could still not get her thoughts in order. She sat on a large rock overlooking the sea and watched the small waves breaking gently against the rocky coast. No matter how hard she tried to dismiss the idea she became more and more convinced that Simon was someone rather special, someone a girl could get to like very much; someone worth letting your defences down for. The only problem was she was not sure how he thought of her. He would never look at a tart like her would he? The disturbing paradox was that the more she thought about it the more she wanted him. No, that sounded too selfish; not wanted him, but wanted to be with him; well actually what she wanted was to give herself to him; completely. She wanted to lose herself in the safety of his arms and to do absolutely everything in her power to help him in his present dilemma and make him truly happy for ever. Devastating as the risk of rejection might be, she knew in an instant that if she didn't follow her instinct here the chance might never come again. He would never make the first move, she deduced, so it would be up to her to make the running. She levered herself to her feet and set off back the way she had come. As she jogged steadily along she began to plot the seduction of Simon Fenton; not for money this time and not simply for her own gratification, but because, for the first time in her life, she was beginning to understand what it really felt like to be in love.

By the time Natalie emerged into the awning after her shower both the tea and toast that Simon had prepared had gone cold. Despite her protestations he insisted on making more and breakfast was delayed. As they sat at opposite ends of the table drinking the last of their tea Natalie made her unorthodox opening gambit.

'Would you have done it?' she asked, leaning forward towards him, 'would you have gone to bed with me in the hotel if things had been different. I mean if I really was Samantha Evans and not Kelly the escort girl?'

Simon sat upright in his chair, his face rapidly turning crimson.

'That's not a fair question,' he blustered, 'do I really have to answer it?'

'Not if you don't want to,' she flashed him a wide smile, 'it's just a conversation starter,' she said.

'Er...er...I'd like to think...er... that I wouldn't, ' he finally replied, 'not that you're not drop dead gorgeous....oh shit, I'm digging myself deep here, aren't I?'

'It's just that we've told each other so much,' continued Natalie, mildly flustered by the consternation she had caused. Her intention had been to open a bout of flirting, but she was rapidly realising that she would have to be a lot more subtle, 'I just wondered what you thought of me the first time we met?'

Simon hesitated.

'Well,' he began, 'It's not just about looks, is it? I mean...er...when you came up to me I was pretty annoyed, I don't usually do social stuff very well, but when you started to talk about flying it was different. You were so obviously passionate about it; flying I mean and who you were started to become more important than how you looked, but...but...yes, if you'd led me on I might well have gone to bed with you Nat. I'm not proud of that, but it's the truth, but not just because of your looks.'

Regretting the line the dialogue was taking; Natalie made an attempt to redeem her disastrous start.

'I'm sorry, Simon,' she said, 'I shouldn't have asked you that. If it's any consolation I started to feel bad about what I was planning to do to you before I overheard Barry...oh shit, I'm lying...oh Simon I'm so sorry....so much has changed since then hasn't it. Can we start again...please, Simon, I'm sorry. I don't want to lie to you; not ever.'

With a total failure to comprehend anything that was going on Simon let out a sigh of relief.

'I think we better had, Nat, before things get any more complicated,' he replied. 'Now, do we need to make a shopping list?'

'No', she replied, 'let's live dangerously.' The irony of her statement reduced them both to giggles momentarily, 'When are we going?'

By the time the breakfast pots were dealt with the occupants of the other caravans had once again left the site and the sun was beating down from a clear blue sky. With the car windows wide open in response to the inadequacy of the air conditioning, and both of them wearing dark sunglasses Natalie and Simon drove off. Natalie donned the long blonde wig as they drove along the quiet country road and topped it with her floppy sun hat. They quickly located the railway station in Maryport and found a place to park the car a few hundred yards away. There was twenty minutes to wait for the Carlisle train and they joined the small group of waiting passengers. The crowded train arrived and they were forced to sit separately for the forty five minute journey. The train was an elderly one with no air conditioning and few opening windows and, by the time it discharged its human cargo at Carlisle the atmosphere inside was becoming unbearable. Simon joined Natalie on the platform and they enjoyed the relative coolness of the shade beneath the canopy before crossing the footbridge and orientating themselves on the station forecourt. Having agreed that the shops were most probably somewhere to their left they set off. As they walked past the imposing sandstone walls of the Citadel Natalie's hand sought Simon's. She entwined her fingers with his and let their forearms come into contact with each other. He turned sideways with a quizzical glance and was rewarded by another of her earth-stopping smiles.

'Good cover; for the CCTV,' Natalie said.

Hand in hand they mingled with the bank holiday crowd along the main shopping street.

'Come on, Mr. Executive,' Natalie grinned, 'there's M & S. Let's get you a suit.'

In the menswear department Natalie took charge of proceedings, persuading Simon to try on several suits before settling on a light grey pinstripe. She then chose him two shirts and ties before completing the outfit with a pair of smart black shoes, a leather briefcase and a large umbrella. Content to follow Natalie's advice, Simon rather enjoyed being fussed over. Sophie had never really shown much interest in what he wore and it was a novelty to him to have a girl giving her opinion. With a suit carrier and two large plastic bags in tow, Simon sought out the Carphone Warehouse outlet where he bought a notebook PC and a pre-paid mobile broadband dongle. Natalie dragged him into Boots, where she bought a pair of mens' mild reading glasses before taking him into a busy Specsavers store and repeating her substitution trick to provide him with a pair of plain glass spectacles. Tired by their exertions and burdened with their shopping they decided upon lunch in a Little Frankie's restaurant. Sitting in an alcove at the rear Simon began to study a complimentary newspaper which he had picked up as they had entered.

'Look, Nat,' he said quietly, 'we're on page seven now....they still think we're not together.....oh shit, they've found out a lot more about both of us....and they've got our passport photos in. It's a good job I look nothing like my passport picture....oh no....Barry's been shot...a gangland killing they call it.....'

Natalie turned the paper to face her and scanned the photographs and text, a frown furrowing her brow.

'They don't really seem to have much idea where we are though, do they?' she whispered.

The waiter arrived to take their order and Natalie turned the page.

The newspaper had taken the edge from their enjoyment of their little expedition and of each other. They ate their food in silence and both declined a desert. Over coffee Natalie once again began to thumb through the newspaper.

"Heat wave predicted" stated the headline on page two, opposite a photograph of a woman clad in a skimpy bikini.

'I know,' said Natalie, attempting to lift the mood, 'let's go swimming in the sea this afternoon.'

'But it's all rocky,' replied Simon, smiling.

'Then we'll get some crocs. Come on Fenton, Let's get you a pair of trunks and then you can help me choose a swimsuit.'

Fifteen minutes later a carrier bag containing two pairs of the soft plastic shoes and another containing a pair of black men's swimming shorts had been added to their burdens and Natalie had led Simon rather reluctantly into the women's department of House of Frazer were she swept up an assortment of swimwear and disappeared into the changing room. To Simon's bemused embarrassment she reappeared from time to time in a swimsuit or bikini to ask his opinion which, on each occasion was one of public affirmation and private admiration. After her last appearance she sent him in search of some more towels, telling him that he would get to see her final choice later in the day. After a major repacking of bags they struggled back to the station with their burdens in good time for the three twelve train. Once again the train was busy, but they managed to find seats together. Natalie allowed Simon the window seat and then sat close beside him. They were both conscious of the proximity of each others bodies throughout the journey.

Upon arrival back at the caravan the sun was still beating down as it dipped slowly towards the western horizon. After a brief flurry of unpacking bags and hanging clothes in wardrobes Simon began to unpack the notebook PC, intending to establish an internet connection. Natalie disappeared into the bathroom, only to emerge shortly afterwards in a pale green bikini that left very little to the imagination and a pair of white plastic crocs. She paused in the doorway and threw Simon's new pair of swimming shorts at him.

'Come on slowcoach, the water's lovely,' she shouted and nipped smartly through the door. From his seat Simon watched her lithe form disappear through the gap in the wall towards the beach. Pleasurably resigned to his fate he obeyed her last instruction, changed into his swimming things and followed. As he tentatively entered the water Natalie appeared to be standing in waist deep water only yards from the beach, with only her head and shoulders visible; but as Simon stepped gingerly towards her she leapt up from what was suddenly apparent as a sitting position and splashed torrents of water towards him.

'Can't catch me!' she shouted gleefully, falling forward and swimming steadily into deeper water. Catch her he did though. Seconds later they were caught up in a bout of wrestling. Natalie made a lunge sideways and evaded his grip; surfacing behind him she threw her arms around his neck and wrapped her legs around his waist. She nestled her head against his neck and Simon felt the blood begin to rise in his cheeks; and in an altogether different part of his anatomy. The softness of Natalie's face against his neck, the press of her breasts against his back and the grip of her thighs above his hips precipitated a few moments of anguished indecision for him. Surely, he thought, the girl was giving him the very clearest of signals that she wanted to move their relationship well beyond the platonic. In fact he was now convinced that she had been moving in that direction all day. All he had to do was to make the slightest of physical responses to her and that would probably be it; the point of no return. Yet still he held back. To do otherwise would be taking advantage of her vulnerability and youth, he reasoned; he felt a very deep affection for Natalie Robertson, of that he was certain, but rooted in that affection was an imperative to treat her with utmost respect and absolute integrity. He gently prized her arms apart and catapulted her backwards into the sea. The horseplay continued for a while, but Natalie had picked up Simon's indecision and interpreted it as a rebuff. She kept physical contact between them to a minimum and quickly made the excuse that she was becoming cold and walked back up the beach. On his part Simon lay in the shallows giving her plenty of time to get dried and changed before following her thoughtfully back to the caravan.

For the remainder of the evening relations were mildly strained. Simon began to make plans for his trip to Glasgow using the internet connection. He explained to Natalie that he proposed to leave from Dalston station on the seven twenty four train to Carlisle, wishing to avoid the car being seen at Maryport again. He planned to take the slow stopping train between Carlisle and Glasgow in both directions and return on an early afternoon service; he anticipated being back at the caravan by around five. He also planned to leave the Glasgow train at Barrhead and enter the city centre by taxi in order to avoid any scrutiny that might be in place at major mainline terminals. Natalie prepared a light meal of cheese on toast as they talked. After the meal, although both of them felt the need to address the unanswered questions from earlier in the day neither felt bold enough to make the opening move. For Natalie the burning question was whether or not Simon's apparent rejection of her advances was because of her past. Her fragile self-image told her that someone like him would probably see her as somehow tainted by her prior sexual behaviour and she was deeply troubled that the fist man that she had ever trusted completely might not think her worthy of his affection. Simon, on the other hand, felt increasingly concerned by his inept handling of the incident in the water. He had thoroughly enjoyed the company of Natalie all day. The memory of the banter and flirting, yes he decided, it actually had been flirting, was exhilarating and exciting. If only, he thought, he could be sure that responding to her advances would not be a breach of the deep trust that she had so obviously placed in him. He still felt a sincere gratitude to her for helping him to unburden himself of the last remnants of his grief and hurt over Sophie. With the benefit of hindsight he wished he had not pushed her away, What he felt for Natalie Robertson was very close to love; a different sort of love from that which he had once shared with Sophie. A love rooted in a sober reality and shared adversity; a love worth taking a risk for. On several occasions during the banality of their dialogue that evening he was on the verge of asking her directly about what might have happened if he had not pitched her headfirst into the water, but each time his courage failed him. Eventually Natalie drew a halt to the proceedings by suggesting an early night because of his mission the following day. With a sense of relief, but his heart heavy with lingering regret Simon performed his evening ritual with the water and waste while Natalie got ready for bed.

Sleep, however, eluded them both until well after midnight. At ten to one Simon realised that he had made a second major error. The last Monday in August was not a bank holiday in Scotland. He could have already retrieved the papers left in Glasgow by Michael Duckworth if he'd realised that earlier. He pondered the probability that if he had remembered in time he might not have blown his chances with Natalie Robertson.

CHAPTER TWENTY

There were no new leads for Jimmy Bell to report to the Governor when he made the call that evening. The Manchester enquiry was beginning to focus on Wayne Stevens as having been the murderer of Detective Inspector Gilroy with the motive having been revenge for the rolling up of the Liverpool gang for which Stevens had formerly worked. Simon Fenton and Natalie Robertson were obviously important witnesses and may well have been involved in some way, but checks into their backgrounds had thrown up no hint of involvement in organised crime.

'Let the local plods and the papers know she was on the game,' instructed the Governor, 'give them her website address. We need the locals to keep looking for them and we need their photographs all over the media every day until we get a lead.'

'Right, Guv,' replied Bell, 'The Dublin thing is sorted, by the way. She's floating down the Liffey as we speak.'

'The Barrow-in-Furness connection turned into a dead end,' reported Bell, 'the hairdresser was pretty adamant, but there was no sign of the tart anywhere on CCTV; bloody waste of time. I've no idea where they are or what they're up to.'

'It's all to do with whatever Fenton got from the old bloke's solicitor,' The Governor explained. 'We don't just need to see off Fenton and the girl; we need to get rid of the entire paper trail, Jimmy. If we don't it could all be over for both of us. I'm busy with engagements for the rest of the day, text me if there are any developments. If not I'll meet you in your office at ten tomorrow.'

CHAPTER TWENTY ONE

Natalie dozed fitfully throughout the night and was sitting up in her narrow bed fully awake as the first light of dawn filtered through the thin curtains. What a fool she had been. She had come on to Simon Fenton like a bitch in heat; using the whiles and devices she had developed as a professional sex worker to turn men on and make them feel good about themselves. No wonder he had backed off. Whatever must he think of her? Why should someone like him want a relationship with a common tart like her anyway? He had probably totally dismissed her by now as a right slapper. There he was; on the brink of discovering who had killed his father, why Inspector Gilroy and Barry had colluded to do them harm and why they were in the fix they were in. She should go, she decided, walk away; while he was in Glasgow she could probably get a fair distance; London or somewhere. She would do her best to avoid getting caught for as long as she could. She owed him that; and more. If she really cared for Simon that's what she should do; get out of his hair and let him get on with it. Knowing him he probably would sort this mess out; get the police off their backs, but he wouldn't want anything to do with someone like her, would he?

She opened the curtain separating her sleeping area from the rest of the caravan slightly. In the pale early morning light she could see Simon sleeping peacefully on the left hand bed. In a millisecond all her resolve dissipated. She could never run out on this man. While she had totally mishandled her attempted seduction of him, she realised that at a much deeper emotional level, they had developed a mutual care and intimacy that transcended anything she had experienced before. She would do all she could to repair the damage she had done. A shaft of sunlight penetrated through a chink in the curtains illuminating his face in a golden glow and her heart stood still. It was as if it was a sign. She slipped out of bed, smoothing her long t-shirt chastely down to cover her upper thighs and lit the gas under the kettle before moving over to kneel beside the sleeping man. She shook him gently by the shoulder.

'Simon,' she said, 'it's nearly time to get up.'

He made a quiet moaning sound and blinked his eyes several times.

'Nat, what time is it?' he asked, 'am I late?'

'No, Simon,' she replied, 'it's just twenty past six. I just wanted to apologise for yesterday. I was....'

'What are you on about, he interrupted, 'apologise...what...'

'Shhh,' Natalie placed a finger over Simon's lips as he levered himself into a sitting position, 'just let me speak for a minute and don't interrupt.'

She removed her finger and took a deep breath.

'I'm sorry for coming on to you like that yesterday; I was really stupid. I don't know what you must think of me, Simon, I was all over you, leading you on, trying to get you to make love to me. I was a selfish and stupid little cow....'

'No, Nat, don't say that. I liked it. That's what......'

She put her finger back over his lips.

'Please, Simon, just let me speak. I've never felt about anyone the way I feel about you, but it all came out wrong yesterday. Right from when I asked you if you would have slept with me in the hotel; I wanted to put that idea into your mind. I wanted you to be thinking about it all day while we were out. Then, when we were holding hands and shopping and stuff the idea of us being together just got bigger and bigger in my head; not just making love here and now, but long term. I thought that getting you into bed was the best way to make you fall in love with me, but I was wrong wasn't I?'

Simon lifted her finger gently away from his lips.

'Natalie…'

'No, Simon, let me finish. I just want to ask you three questions now and you have to answer "yes" or "no". Actually it would be better if you just nodded or shook your head. Nod now if you agree.'

Simon nodded his head.

'Right, I know this is a big day for you. I don't want to get in the way of you finding out about your dad and why we're hiding from the police and that, but I just wanted to clear the air before you go.'

Natalie felt her heart beating rapidly and knew that she was blushing. Glancing briefly downwards she realised that he had not let go of her hand.

'First question; you know all about my past. You know exactly who I am and what I've done. I'm a grubby little slapper and I've probably had sex with nearly a thousand different men. Is that why you turned me down yesterday? When you look at me is that what you think of?'

Simon shook his head and Natalie felt a first flush of relief spread slowly through her body.

'Second question; I know that we've been sort of thrown together by what's happening to us. I mean the stuff about your dad and the police, but we've really clicked with each other haven't we? I mean I've never told anyone else what I told you the other day and I think it was the same for you. Are we just friends, Simon or could we ever be anything more? What I mean is that, in spite of the mess I made of it yesterday, do you think we could ever have a relationship. Not just sex, I mean, but could we ever be together?'

Simon nodded his head gently and Natalie Robertson's smile melted his heart.

'Last question; would you like to go out with me; on a date; tonight. Please let's start again, Simon, give me another chance. We need to talk about so much. I promise I won't try it on with you, but let's go out somewhere; a restaurant or something; just like normal people. So, will you come?'

Simon nodded and drew Natalie into a gentle embrace, his mind and heart turning alternate summersaults. The brief hiatus was interrupted by the whistling of the kettle and Natalie drew away.

An hour later, dressed in his suit and with umbrella and brief case stowed safely on the rack, Simon sat on the local train on his way to Carlisle deep in thought. Things, it seemed, were turning out to be very different from how he had first anticipated. The whole issue surrounding Michael Duckworth's strange legacy and the incident in the Midland hotel had suddenly paled into virtual insignificance compared with the potentially life-changing experience of getting to know Natalie Robertson. Even in the headiest days of his relationship with Sophie he had not experienced the tumult of feelings he had for this extraordinary girl. He changed trains at Carlisle still reeling from the intensity of their pre-breakfast conversation, or rather Natalie's monologue. For most of the previous night he had laid awake; completely unable to come to terms with the possibility that Natalie might actually think enough of him to want a relationship. He had felt himself a little awkward and uneasy in her presence since their return from Carlisle but, until he had spurned her advances in the lukewarm waters of the Irish Sea, the day had been one of the happiest in his life. Afraid that he had messed things up, he feared that there would be no second chance. Now, he had been offered one without any effort on his part. What a way to wake up, he thought, with Natalie's face only inches away from his. As the train swayed and rattled through the barren lowland hills he dared to imagine what it might be like to wake up with his face inches from hers every morning. The motivation to survive the present threat to their lives; to follow the trail left for him by Michael Duckworth and to do whatever might be necessary to preserve the chance of a life with Natalie filled him with resolve. With a spring in his step and a renewed sense of purpose he passed out into the blazing sunshine searing the station forecourt at Barrhead just after ten thirty that morning and went in search of a taxi.

A short walk brought him to the main street and he soon located a private hire taxi office. A car would be available in five minute and he booked a trip to Paisley, anxious not to leave a clear trail. From Paisley he took another private hire car to the centre of Glasgow. By ten to twelve, having been dropped off on Renfrew street he had walked briskly southwards onto the parallel Sauchihall Street and followed it eastwards until, right on the corner with Rose Street he had located the Royal Bank of Scotland. After a short wait at the enquiries desk he was escorted into the vault and left the bank shortly afterwards with a bulky brown envelope in his brief case. With time pressing he took the risk of taking a black cab directly to Barrhead station, resisting the impulse to open the envelope until he could do so in relative privacy. During his twenty minute wait for the train he ventured back onto the main street and bought a pre-packed sandwich and a soft drink and, spot on time at fifteen minutes after one o'clock, the Carlisle train pulled into the station. There were few passengers; Simon located a seat at an unoccupied table and took the envelope out of his briefcase.

CHAPTER TWENTY-TWO

As soon as Simon had driven off Natalie began to put a plan of her own into action. Donning her thin black leggings and a blue t-shirt together with her sun hat and dark glasses she set out on her familiar morning route, but at a brisk walk rather than a jog. She reached the small harbour at Maryport an hour or so later, perspiring in the heat of another scorching day. Having located her first goal she wandered through the narrow streets of the small town following the cast iron signs for the railway station and caught the nine twenty eight train to Carlisle. The busy city centre held pleasant memories for her of the previous day and she wandered leisurely in and out of the shops making a few carefully considered purchases. From La Senza she bought a luxurious, but not exotic, matching black lace bra and brief set. From a nearby shoe shop she bought a pair of black patent leather sling-back shoes and a matching handbag. In the House of Frazer department store she spent almost a hundred pounds of the dead policeman's money on a plain black designer shift dress. She agonised for several minutes over whether or not to complete the outfit with a pair of sheer black hold-ups, but the association with a life she wanted desperately to leave behind forever was too strong and she decided that bare legs would be the safest option. Natalie Robertson was going out on a date and was determined to make the right impression.

With over an hour to wait for the next train back she collected a few toiletries from Boots, bought a newspaper and had a light lunch in the Starbuck's coffee shop opposite the shopping precinct. To her relief the story about the investigation into the murder of Detective Inspector

Gilroy comprised only a few paragraphs on an inside page. It was now thought that the perpetrator had been Wayne Stevens who had himself been killed in a gangland feud, but police were still keen to talk to Natalie Robertson and Simon Fenton.

By the time Natalie had returned by train to Maryport, paid a visit to the building close to the harbour that she had located earlier and completed the four mile hike back to the caravan site the sun still warm in the western sky. She put her purchases carefully away, changed into her bikini and dragged one of the sun lounger chairs out of the awning. Covering her exposed skin liberally in sun tan lotion, she settled down to daydream and pass the time before Simon's expected return.

Following her inept attempt at seducing him the day before, she was relieved that she had almost certainly managed to limit the damage done. She had been given a second chance and was determined not to waste it. She found it hard to comprehend why and when she had started to find him so attractive. When they had first met she had certainly been unimpressed by his looks. Getting rid of the beard and cutting his hair had helped, but he was certainly no trim and toned hunk. He was tall enough, but not good looking in a classical sense. He had lovely eyes, though; and there was something in the way he moved – a sort of gentle strength. It wasn't actually the way he looked at all that attracted her, she realised, although the very thought of him gave her a warm feeling in the pit of her stomach; it was the way he was. The whole package... that was it, the total person; that was what she had fallen for. He had accepted her for who she was and not what she did or could do for him. Might that be what love really was she wondered? She had thought that she had been in love with Matt, but even though he had been fun to be with and had made her feel good this was different. Her relationship with Matt, she had recently come to understand had been a series of transactions rather than the total surrender of her very being that she yearned to make to Simon Fenton. It didn't matter, she suddenly realised, whether their date that evening led to them making love or not. Although her body longed for his touch, there was so much more to it than that. If all they did was to talk and hold hands that would be more than enough for tonight. She had found a truly good man, she thought; someone she longed to share the rest of her life with. Whatever else the near future might bring, she had no shred of regret for becoming involved in this man's life. If today was her last day on earth she asked no more than to be able to share it with him.

The sun setting sun dipped behind a bank of cloud and a gentle sea breeze brought goose-bumps to her exposed skin. Natalie re-entered the caravan to shower and prepare for her date's return.

CHAPTER TWENTY-THREE

Simon laid the brown envelope on the table in front of him. Eager anticipation of his date with Natalie crowded his mind and distracted him from the task in hand. He felt as if somehow time and space had been suspended since he had arrived in Manchester only a few days before. At first, being drawn into a web of mystery and intrigue concerning the death of his father had seemed to be straight from the pages of a thriller. Then, when the beautiful woman had made her appearance, a James Bond movie had seemed more appropriate, but that had rapidly turned into a scene from a horror film when the policeman had died. The first twelve hours of being on the run had been a strangely exhilarating experience; an opportunity to take on the world and live by his wits. But the Cumbrian idyll of the last two days had pushed the urgency of his predicament far from his mind. When Sophie had died, and the active part of his Christian faith with her, he had never expected to fall in love again yet, here he was, like an eager teenager, far more worried about his date with Natalie than about the contents of the envelope and their probable implications. Steeling himself to his task he eventually opened the envelope and extracted bundle of A4 lined paper covered in the now familiar handwriting. He began to read:

Simon,

I guess that if you're reading this you've taken the plunge. First of all I need to tell you the name of the man I saw kill your father. The murderer is Eddie Duggan; the Home Secretary.

Troubled Legacy

Now, how to tell the story and what you need to do to bring him to justice is another matter. I'm writing this in a cheap hotel room and I've got all night, so forgive me if I ramble on a bit, Simon, but I think the best was is to tell you all that has happened in the order that it did.

Another thing is that my name isn't Michael Duckworth. It's Terry Clegg. It's really strange writing that because I haven't written or spoken that name for nearly thirty years. The story will tell you how I came to change it and why.

We were on detachment to Northern Ireland; you probably know that - half the squadron – two flights. Flight Lieutenant Lewis was in charge overall – he had B Flight and Eddie Duggan (we always called him Duggie behind his back) was OC A Flight. Anyway we worked in half-flights - twelve hours on and twelve off – two days on and two off - making four shifts altogether if that makes sense. There were six of us in each patrol. Your dad was the Corporal in charge of ours. The others were Tim Ellwood, Joe South, Danny Osterley and Ian Barker. We had to protect a radar station - Bishops Court it was called. There was one radar on the old airfield, one out on Killard Point beside the entrance to Strangford Lough and a domestic site with the barracks, the mess and the like in the middle. There were snowdrops and an airmen on backup on each site and we were a bit like the cavalry if anything went off, with out Landrovers ready to go. We were half way through our four month stint when it happened.

It was a Sunday night, well a Monday morning actually – that would be March 3rd. 1975, but I guess you know that. We were in the duty room, ready to go. We'd been out and about three or four times earlier on, but everything was dead quiet. Duggie was with us. He did a stint on patrol now and again – to show he was one of the lads I suppose – but we all knew he was a posh git who'd fluffed his A levels and couldn't get into university. Apparently his dad had told him it was either off to teacher training college or serving queen and country. The Regiment it was and he'd just made Flying Officer. Story was that his dad's firm went bust and the debts wiped out the poor sod's inheritance. Well, we got a shout from the Snowdrop on dog patrol at Killard about four in the morning.

He told us he'd seen a ship moving slowly about half a mile offshore and then he'd heard a car engine over the hill to the north. We went for a look see and Duggie came along. We parked well short and crept up on them. There were five of them – four Provos and another bloke – Columbian they said he was afterwards. They were carrying stuff from a little rowing boat to their car. Just off the Killard Road south of where the Coastguard Cottages were – bloody cheek of it. We could see them all right – there was a good moon and the sky was clear. I remember thinking how bloody cold it was when we came around the side of the hill. They were only fifty yards away. One of the Provos had a Thompson sub-machine gun. I didn't see any other weapons, but we found out later that they were all armed.

Anyway we all had a yellow card that said we couldn't open fire unless they were about to shoot someone. We had to shout out to them and tell them to drop their guns, but Duggie took no notice of that. He just grabbed Tim Ellwood's rifle off him and opened up. The rest of us sort of joined in. The Provo with the tommy gun got a burst off. That's what put me down. - two nine mills through my left lung. I passed out. When I came round your dad was bandaging me up but I was dead groggy and I couldn't speak. They all thought I was unconscious but I saw and heard everything after that. The bad guys were all dead. Duggie was down amongst them making sure. First he brought up their guns; the tommy gun and a handful of revolvers. Then he went back and brought up a bag. One of those airline ones- Pan-Am it was. He showed it to the lads. It was stuffed full with money. Sterling and US Dollars. Next trip he came back with three big plastic bags. Heroin he said it was. He said that the noise of the shooting would soon bring us an audience. Said that we had a decision to make. We could either tell it like it was – we gave them a warning and they shot me so we did for them all - or we could make the money disappear; and a couple of the bags. He said we deserved a reward of some kind and that was all we would get. Anyway your dad stood up to him and said that we hadn't warned them and we had no business breaking the law ourselves. I remember it clear as day. Duggie just picked up the tommy gun and put half a dozen rounds into his chest. We all knew what the right answer was after that.

The back-up turned up after ten minutes or so, an ambulance, lots of Snowdrops and B Flight. I passed out in the ambulance and the next thing I remember was waking up in Queens Med in Belfast two days later.

I was pretty poorly. They told me I nearly did so, in one way, every day was a bonus after that. Duggie came to see me the day after. I think he wanted to know what I remembered but I knew what he had done to your dad and kept quiet. I pretended I didn't remember a thing after we left the Landrover. He told me there was an unofficial reward and gave me five hundred quid in used fivers – told me to keep quiet about it and not to flash it around. The Docs said I would need to stay in three or four weeks and then a month's leave so I felt pretty good about that. I planned to go home to my parents' house in Hawes for my leave and then put in for a transfer to another squadron.

About a week later Tim Ellwood came in to see me. He was white faced and jumpy. He told me that Joe and Ian had been killed. Apparently they had been out on an unofficial trip with one of out Landrovers – a fish and chip run – and the brakes and steering had failed. They'd hit a brick wall at the bottom of a hill doing over eighty. Tim said he was becoming paranoid. He told me what had happened after the fire-fight, but I let on that I'd been awake for most of it. He thought Duggie was behind it – said he'd be looking over his shoulder from then on. Poor lad, he was always a bit camp – he got the piss taken all the time. Joe had been a particular friend of his and he was pretty much cut up about it.

The week before Easter I was up and about a bit. They'd brought me my civvies and I could manage to get down to the cafe and the TV room OK. Then, on the Wednesday morning Tim came again in a right old state. He said that Danny was dead. Apparently he'd nicked one of the Provo pistols and had accidently shot himself in the toilets. Tim was certain that Duggie was behind it, but he had a cast iron alibi – he'd been at Aldergrove for a security briefing all day. Tim said he must have had an accomplice but he didn't know who it was. Anyway, Tim was going AWOL. He was due back on duty at teatime and was planning to be long gone by then. He was on his way to the airport and said he would pay whatever it cost to get back across the pond. He told me that if I had any sense I would do the same. He only stayed ten minutes and off he went – scared shitless.

I thought about it for a bit and decided to follow him. I wasn't feeling too bad so I just got dressed, stuffed the cash into my anorak pocket and walked out at tea time. I headed for Donegal Quay and got a ticket on the Heysham ferry. I wasn't quite as well as I thought though and as soon as I got on I upgraded to first and booked a single cabin. Next morning I was back in England. I had no idea what to do. I had all my ID and stuff with me so I hired a car from Hertz; a Ford Escort and headed off towards home. I thought I'd let my parents know I was OK and just disappear. It was just getting light when I set off. I got lost on the Lancaster one way system and ended up heading for Skipton. Just after I went under the M6 I spotted a bloke about my age hitching and I picked him up. Good cover, I thought. He told me that his name was Mike and that he was originally from Stockport. He'd done time in Strangeways for burglary and was having trouble getting work. He had a smell of drink about him, though and I suspected work wasn't his top priority. I wasn't feeling too good again and missed the turning for Ingleton. We stopped at a Little Chef near Clapham. I bought him breakfast and he offered to drive for a bit. I was feeling so grotty that I didn't care and we set off for Hawes. He said that would be fine for him and he'd go on elsewhere if there was no work there.

I dozed off a bit and when I woke up we were on the back road near Selside. I know those roads like the back of my hand. It's not a very good road, or at least it wasn't then and he was going far too fast. I told him to slow down, but he just laughed. We'd just turned onto the B2655 when he lost control. We went flying through a dry stone wall and ended up against a tree. My chest hurt like hell, but I was OK. A branch had come straight through the windscreen though and his head was all mashed in. He was dead as a dodo. There was a smell of petrol so I got out fast. The back door had been busted open so I grabbed my bag and started to get as far away as I could before the petrol caught fire. Then it came to me. I dropped my bag on the grass about twenty yards from the car and went back for his. I lit the petrol with my lighter and walked away as Michael Duckworth. He had his prison discharge papers and his birth certificate in his bag. Terry Clegg had died in a tragic car accident. I felt bad about not telling my parents. They're both dead now. I went back to Hawes once, a few years later and saw our graves; my parents and mine, in the cemetery – about half a mile out of town on the Leyburn road. Very nice they are too, granite headstones and lots of blue pebbles.

I cut across country, hoping like hell that no one would spot me. I was in pretty bad shape and I had to rest every few hundred yards. Eventually

I ended up next to the railway line near Horton. I started following it downhill until I came across a platelayers' hut. It was a bit tatty and there was no glass in the windows, but I was cold and tired. I slept a bit and when I woke up it was nearly dark. There was a little fireplace, some lumps of coal and quite a bit of firewood. I lit a fire and slept a bit more. Next morning I followed the road down to Settle and got something to eat and drink. There was a train going to London at ten to two so I bought a ticket. I started feeling ill again though so I got off at Nottingham and tried to find a hotel to put up in. I couldn't find one nearby with vacancies though so I went back to the station. The next train was going to Derby so I bought another ticket and got on. There was a posh hotel just outside the station and I paid over fifty quid for three nights. I don't know what they thought of me. I was pretty grubby by then.

After a few days rest and a good bath I was a lot better. It was Easter Monday. I saw an advert for a lodger in a paper shop window so I spent a tenner on some new clothes and rented a room from an old lady for five pounds a week. I still had four hundred quid of Duggie's money so I spun her a yarn about convalescing after an operation and did not very much for a few weeks. Then I got a job on a building site. Proper companies don't like ex-jailbirds. I did casual work all summer, opened an account at the TSB and took my driving test again to get a license. Then I got a driving job in the October – not very good pay, because they knew all about my murky past, but it kept me going for nearly two years. I had a run to Barrow every five or six weeks; an overnight stay. I did some research in the library – newspaper archives and the electoral roll – and I found out about you. I visited a couple of times saying I was a mate of your dad's, but I stopped after a bit because I didn't want your grandparents asking too many questions. Then I got a start with British Rail – in the carriage sidings on shifts – just cleaning and stuff at first, but I worked my was up to maintenance after a while. That was my life, then. I got married to Julie in 1979. She was my landlady's niece – three years younger than me. She worked in Woolworths. With the shifts I was earning quite good money and we bought our own place on Chester Green Lane.

If you're reading this, Simon, I guess the house belongs to you now.

Simon paused in his reading. His eyes were moist and the poignancy of the letter penetrated his defences and nudged his preoccupation with

Natalie back into context. For them to have the future together that he so desperately hoped for he would have to find a way of completing the work that this unknown, but brave man had set in motion. He read on:

> *Anyway we only stayed together for six years. She left me for a furniture salesman and I had to remortgage up to the hilt to buy her out. There were no children, thank God. I didn't think too much about Duggie and what happened very often, but when he went into politics I couldn't help seeing his picture all over the place. I stopped voting after that.*
>
> *That was my life for the next twenty years. I never forgot what Duggie had done, but I didn't dare do anything or tell anyone. No one knows my real name, I didn't even tell Julie I just made stuff up about moving around a lot as a kid. Then, in November 2008 I met Tim Ellwood again. It was at Woolley Edge Services on the M1. When British Rail was privatised I went over to Virgin Trains and they sent me to the new depot at Central Rivers – it's about a forty minute drive from Derby – they became Cross Country later on. I had to go on a course to the makers in Yorkshire and I was on my way back when the car started playing up. I pulled into the services and called the AA, but they had to go and get a part so I was stuck there for ages. It was after tea and not very busy. I was on my third coffee when he came up to me. I didn't recognise him. "Terry", he said, "is it really you"? At first it made no sense at all and I thought he'd mixed me up with someone else, but when he said his name I recognised him straight away. Tim told me he'd got a flight to London that afternoon – after he'd left me in the hospital - and then he'd gone on to Paris by bus and ferry. He always told a good story and managed to pick up a job as a mercenary in one of those African places where there was a local war going on. Then he ended up in Rhodesia, he gave a false name and got into their army all right – they were in UDI then and weren't very choosy. When that went belly up he went on to South Africa and got into their army as well. The funny thing was that he told me he was gay all along. He certainly wasn't a natural soldier, but he seemed to have the knack of talking his way into stuff. In the end he left South Africa and ended up in Australia and took out citizenship – still in his false name. He took up with another guy and came out. They ran an arts and crafts business until his partner got aids and died, Tim was HIV positive by then and the stuff that happened*

at Bishops Court was haunting him, he said. He's come back to see if anything could be done before Duggie got to rule the world as he put it.

He knew his days were numbered and he was determined to make sure the boys that got killed got justice before he went off to join them. He'd been following up the various possible accomplices that he thought Duggie could have had. There were three Snowdrops that Duggie had been as thick as thieves with. A Sergeant and two Corporals. The Sergeant had died in the Falklands. He'd been to see one of the Corporals who was living in Durham then, he ran a pub there. Tim didn't think it was him though. His money was on the other one; Corporal Bell, who'd left the mob and made Detective Chief Inspector in the Met.

We talked for ages and we ended up staying the night in the Travelodge there. He came to stay with me for a few days afterwards and said he'd keep me in touch. It was about three weeks before I heard from him and he rang me up in a bit of a panic – said he was being followed. He wouldn't come to my place because he didn't want them to get onto me. We agreed that I'd meet him in Blackpool the next weekend if he could manage to shake them off. I booked a B & B and we met up on top of the tower. He had lots to report so he led the way back to his hotel and I trailed behind to check if he was being followed. It was all clear.

He'd been looking in to Duggie's business empire. Duggie had left the RAF about three months after the shoot out. He popped up in Tottenham running a couple of used car lots. Over the next ten years he opened or bought out half a dozen more. One of them, on Phillip Lane, was quite a big enterprise. Tim said that he was using dodgy accounting to launder money, probably from drugs or prostitution. He tracked down the mother of a girl who used to knock around with him in those days – she worked in the office at the big place. Her mother told Tim that Duggie used to buy cheap and tatty cars and sell them for a smallish profit, but he kept two sets of books. One set told the true story, but the other one showed that he was supposed to have sold the cars for a few hundred more that he actually did – the extra money was being laundered into the legit business. There were false invoices and everything – he used to claim the punters had paid big deposits when they usually hadn't paid a deposit at all.

Anyway this girl was apparently sweet on Duggie and he led her right up the garden path – promised her the earth while he was two or three timing her. Eventually she got fed up of him and started to make copies of some of the invoices and stuff. Her mum said she was planning to blackmail him. Then he bought a pile of clapped out motors and the same number of good ones the same model and colour and swopped over their identities. All the ringers were at Phillip Lane. Mary Soutar, the girl cottoned on to what was going on and took copies of the paperwork. She put it all in a biscuit tin in her bedroom.

One night she went back to the office late to photocopy the accounts books. She had brought one lot of copies home and then went back to do some more but there was a fire there that night and she was killed. Tim said Duggie torched it himself for the insurance. He didn't know if Mary getting killed was deliberate or accidental. The police investigated it all but, believe it or not, the investigating officer was one Detective Inspector Jimmy Bell. A couple of heavies paid a visit to Mary's mum a couple of weeks later asking questions, but she said nothing about the biscuit tin. Duggie used the payout to buy into a Ford main dealership and now he has a chain of them across the South East.

Tim had found the old lady and she had given him the papers, but he clocked two blokes following him around. He shook them off by jumping on and off tube trains half a dozen times before he caught a train to Blackpool. He had made copies of the stuff in a print shop in Blackpool. He said he was going to hide the originals somewhere they would never think of looking – I'll tell you where they are later – then take the copies to the press in London. He set off on his mission on the Sunday morning. The memories had been truly stirred up in me. I drove back via Hawes and sat for hours in the town thinking about my childhood and my dead parents. Bloody cold it was, I can tell you. That's when I remembered about you. When I got home I found you on the internet then I paid a private detective to find out all about you. I hope you will forgive me for that.

On the Wednesday I had a call from Tim. He was frantic. He said they were on to him again - the police this time. He'd made a run for it and had locked himself in his hotel room – he said they'd been waiting outside the Guardian office for him. He'd phoned the paper and they hadn't believed him so he was taking the stuff in, but they'd tried to arrest him outside. There was a banging noise and he hung up. It was on the news that night that an Australian tourist had fallen to his death from the twelfth floor balcony of his London hotel. Only I know that he didn't fall – he was pushed.

That was just before Christmas. In January my house was broken into and ransacked but they only took my TV and a digital camera. Then I spotted a red Audi following me to and from work. They must have traced his last call or something because they were on to me all right. I had another break in in February and my car was broken into in March. Then I knew for sure and I made my plans. I'm sorry to have burdened you with all this, Simon – I hope it doesn't get you killed as well.

I put in for a week's leave at the beginning of April, but I went to work on my usual night shift on the first day. The Audi followed me to work. I parked in my usual place and went in, but instead of working I hid in the train that was due to go out for the 05:55 Derby – York. By the time my shift was due to end at eight I was on an express to Edinburgh and they had no idea. I went on to Glasgow and here I am, booked in under another false name. After I leave this safe for you I'm going on to Manchester to make my will and you'll know the rest.

So, Simon Fenton, over to you. If I'm right I'll probably meet with some sort of fatal accident soon. I guess I'm too much of a coward to follow in Tim's footsteps and go to the papers, because they'll probably stop me. I hope they know nothing at all about you. That's why I'm going to find a solicitor in Manchester and not Derby. You should get a clear run at them. - Now for the important bit.

Tim told me he was going to bury the papers at the old radar site on Killard Point in Northern Ireland. It's all been closed and demolished now, but he's found out on the internet that the concrete bases for the height-finders are still there. He said he would bury them at the side of the northernmost base on the north side of it. That's where they are – I'm certain he would have done what he said.

So that's that. Good luck, Simon – your mission, should you choose to accept it is to bring down Eddie Duggan and avenge the death of your *dad and all the others that he's killed. If you choose not to do it then that's OK by me. You must do what you think is right and consider your own safety. If it ends up that Terry Clegg has taken his last secret to his grave with him then so be it.*

With my very best wishes,

Michael (or Terry – take your pick)

Simon put the sheets of paper back into the envelope and began to think through how he might go about getting hold of the incriminating papers.

CHAPTER TWENTY-FOUR

The first big break in the search for Simon Fenton and Natalie Robertson began to emerge just after lunchtime. A sharp eyed VDU operator in the Peterborough office of the Fenland Insurance Company was cross-checking details of new customers with the company's direct mailing database when he noticed the anomaly. A new motor policy had been taken out on the previous Saturday by a Mr. William Beavis. The name was already on the database for the same address; however the motor policy of the original William Beavis had been terminated by his executor following his death. The original Mr. Beavis had been seventy eight and had a full no-claim bonus whereas the "new" Mr. Beavis had given his age of thirty four and had claimed not to have been previously insured. In accordance with a company policy aimed at combating identity theft he reported the matter to both the DVLA and the police anti-fraud unit.

The operator at the police anti-fraud unit logged the concern into the police national computer system at three twenty and the pre-programmed police computer network uploaded the information onto the HOLMES system which had been asked to be on the look out for both vehicle crime and identity theft issues arising in Huddersfield since Saturday morning. A message notifying the matter appeared in the inbox of one the investigating officer at the headquarters of the Greater Manchester police who had logged the original search request. The officer opened the e-mail at ten past four and immediately contacted the DVLA who still had the car registered to its previous owner. The officer then filed a request with the West Yorkshire police for a visit to be made to the person registered on the DVLA database.

In Huddersfield police station the request was printed out by a civilian clerk and placed in the in-tray of a Detective Constable who was expected back from giving evidence in Leeds Crown Court before the end of his shift at ten that evening. In the event, the Detective Constable was delayed in heavy traffic and did not arrive back in the police station until seven thirty. He spent the remainder of his shift doing routine paperwork and picked up the printout as he left; intending to make the call on his way in the following morning.

CHAPTER TWENTY-FIVE

By the time Simon's train was approaching Carlisle he had read the letter for a second time and the glimmering of a plan of action was running round and round in his mind. He would have to discuss it with Natalie of course. The thought of the girl brought memories of his peculiar and unexpected awakening flooding back. Acting upon the contents of the letter was something that could be postponed for a few hours; he had a date with a lovely girl that evening. He had not blown his chances after all. For a moment he contemplated telephoning her on the so far unused mobile phone in his jacket pocket. They had charged up and switched on the unregistered phones in case of emergencies, but Simon had cautioned against using them unless circumstances were dire because calls could all too easily be traced. Resisting the temptation, he found it difficult to return his thought process to the letter. As he stepped off the train into the pleasantly warm cathedral-like railway station at Carlisle the excitement and anticipation of an evening out with Natalie remained in the forefront of his mind.

With an hour to wait for his connection he found a seat on a metal bench on the far platform and settled down to watch the trains go by and daydream about the coming evening. From time to time his embryonic plan of action re-surfaced and, by the time his train arrived he had a pretty clear idea of how to proceed. An added bonus of his tentative plan was that he and Natalie would be alone together for several more days.

As he drove back across the farmyard and into the small caravan site Simon felt a momentary pang of anxiety. Had it all been too good to be true? Did Nat really want to go out on a date with him? Was it real or had he imagined it? As he stopped the car and opened the door Natalie emerged through the flap of the awning. She was wearing a plain black dress and matching shoes. She smiled and her beauty literally took his breath away for a moment. She walked over to him as he retrieved his briefcase and umbrella from the boot. As he straightened up she kissed him fleetingly on the cheek and took a step backwards.

'Did you get it?' she asked. Simon nodded.

'Come on in, I've got the kettle on low,' she said, taking him by the hand and leading him into the awning.

Simon sat down at the small rectangular table.

'I don't know where to start,' he said. 'Here, read it for yourself.'

He handed the envelope to Natalie and she took out the papers and began to read.

'Shit, Simon, Eddie Duggan; the Home Secretary, no wonder the police are against us, 'she muttered.

'So where are we going tonight?' asked Simon, distracting her from her task.

'Oh, Maryport Tandoori; it's the best I could do; it was either that or fish and chips out of paper.' she replied, looking up from the letter, 'I've booked a table for seven thirty.'

'Nat, you look absolutely stunning,' commented Simon, 'what do you think I should wear?'

'You look just great as you are,' she grinned, 'why don't you take a shower and change your shirt and stuff while I read this?'

He took her advice and, presently, the thin buzzing of the water pump signified that the shower was running as Natalie became more and more absorbed in Michael Duckworth's letter. She finished reading as Simon emerged from the caravan, his hair still damp from the shower.

'I'm sorry, Simon,' Natalie said softly,' with all this about your dad. It must be tough on you and here I am acting like a silly love-struck teenager.' The phrase was not lost on Simon.

'It's funny,' he answered as he sat down beside her and began to sip the almost cold tea in his mug, 'but I don't seem to mind so much about my dad. He's always been a sort of abstract figure in my life; a sort of hero from long ago. I don't think Granny and Grandad could have liked him all that much; they hardly ever talked about him. What Duggan did to him was terrible, but reading the letter didn't make me want revenge the way I thought it would; it's Michael's story, or should I call him Terry, that bothered me the most. I feel really sorry for him; it's as if he carried some sort of guilt around with him for nearly forty years. He didn't even tell his wife the truth. I don't think he was a coward at all; just careful and sensible. If I could just disappear somewhere with you and forget all about this I would, that's for sure. I don't blame him for anything. I think he had big expectations of me and I'm not sure I'm worthy of them, Nat.'

'What are you going to do?' asked Natalie.

'It's we, not me,' answered Simon, 'I won't do anything unless you want to. We're in this together; equal partners.'

She reached across the table and touched his hand with hers, 'do you really mean that?' she asked, her voice catching in her throat.

Simon smiled.

'Yes I do,' he replied, 'it doesn't matter how we got into this or just how scary it all is. Meeting you was the best thing that's happened to me for a long time.'

The chill sea breeze drove them into the caravan and Simon explained his plan. His friend Kynpham Johal had moved on from local journalism and was now a junior reporter for the Independent. Simon would telephone him and give the briefest possible explanation. He would ask Kynpham to travel to Carlisle and then they would call him on his mobile with instructions about where to meet them. Kynpham would then rent a holiday cottage somewhere remote and stock it up with food and other supplies. Natalie and Simon would hide away in the cottage while

Kynpham travelled to Northern Ireland and dug up the papers. Once he had them he would return to London and show them to his editor. Their fate would then be in the editor's hands. Natalie suggested that Kynpham make copies and leave the originals with them in the cottage as insurance. Simon agreed and, still wary of using their mobile phones, they agreed that Simon would make the call to Kynpham's home number from a call box in Maryport on their way to the restaurant.

When the time came for them to actually set out on their dinner date, both of them were surprisingly nervous. Natalie, under the impression that she had given out the wrong signals the day before was very much afraid of being over-physical and flirting too overtly while Simon retained a slightly uneasy doubt that someone as young and attractive as Natalie really did want to become romantically involved with him. After some hesitation it was agreed that Natalie would drive so that Simon could have a couple of beers; neither of them thinking it incongruous that two fugitives from the law should be concerned with the dangers of drink driving.

They parked the car and walked arm in arm into the small town to locate a public telephone box. Squashed in together Simon dialled the number. Kynpham replied almost immediately. As single man on a junior reporter's salary living in London, he could hardly afford much of a social life and Simon had anticipated correctly that he would be at home with a few beers and a DVD for company. Once the Indian reporter had recovered from the shock of hearing his friend's voice on the end of the telephone he began to ask a torrent of questions, but Simon interrupted the flow.

'Kynpham,' he said, 'we've got the scoop of the century for you. I've got access to evidence of fraud and probably murder involving a very senior politician,,,,'

'We? Who's we?' interjected Kynpham, 'are you with that girl; the one from the hotel?'

'Look, Kynpham, Simon continued, 'just shut up and listen, will you. I can't tell you over the phone, but there are some papers that will give you a huge story; and probably save our lives into the bargain. There's corruption at the highest levels here and some of the police can't be trusted.

You may well put your life at risk if you help us; you know we're wanted don't you?'

'Don't worry about that,' reassured the reporter, 'I'd help you anyway, Simon, but this story, if what you say is right, could be my big break. I'll have to persuade my editor, though. I'm supposed to be doing a piece on an alleged cover up of delays to the building of the Olympic Stadium tomorrow. I'll tell him I know you and you won't talk to anyone else; that should do it. Where shall we meet?'

'I'm sorry for all the mystery,' his friend replied, but I reckon that it might be dangerous to plan too far ahead. How soon do you think you'll be able to set off?'

'The editor's usually in by ten, so I could be away before eleven. Where to?'

'Sorry, mate, I'm still being mysterious. I'll call you on your mobile at half ten. You'd better pack stuff for a few days away. Have you got a car yet or are you still using that grotty old bicycle?'

'Bicycle,'

'All right Kynpham, I'll work something out. I'll call you tomorrow.

'But can't you tell me anything now?'

'No,' replied Simon, 'we'll talk tomorrow.'

'Ok, mate,' was the reply. 'God bless.'

Natalie, who had been listening in with her face pressed close to Simon's heard Kynpham's final phrase quite clearly. She found his reference to God rather puzzling and alien to her experience, but derived a crumb of comfort from the distant possibility of help from an unexpected quarter as they walked back over the narrow harbour bridge towards the restaurant.

The food was surprisingly good and, ensconced in a secluded booth, Simon and Natalie sat opposite each other in the dim light enjoying each other's company and banal conversation. Although they had already shared their deepest secrets there was still a huge amount that they did not know about each other and, by tactfully avoiding the sensitive parts of their experiences, they learned a great deal about their respective life stories. Natalie's fears that Simon had a tendency towards geekiness were confirmed when he talked of his collection of railway books and obscure poetry. She also learned that he was a reasonably competent bass guitar player and had once played in a vicars versus imams cricket match at Lords. None of these facts altered the depth of her feelings for him. On his part, Simon learned that Natalie was addicted to "Eastenders" and "Casualty" on TV and that, apart from flying airliners, she had always dreamed of spending a long holiday exploring the Australian outback. Her favourite film of all time had been "Titanic" until she had seen "Mama Mia". Now she couldn't choose between them. She was allergic to shellfish and when she had too much to drink she couldn't stop herself from giggling. He still thought she was perfectly lovely. Like teenagers uncertain of what came next they lingered over coffee and mints; putting off their return as long as possible. Eventually Simon took the plunge and suggested that they return. They spoke little as Natalie drove back through the darkness; comfortable in their intimate proximity but acutely aware of the potential awkwardness of that same proximity in the cramped caravan. Natalie was determined that after the previous day's debacle she would not make the first move, but was also rather afraid that Simon would also hold back. Simon was anxious not to give her the impression that he did not find her overwhelmingly attractive, yet feared that an overt move might indicate a lack of respect for her. He was also far, far away from his comfort zone in all respects. His few relationships before meeting Sophie had been little more that adolescent flights of fancy. With Sophie their shared sense of propriety had regulated the pace of their physical relationship, and the lingering remnants of his faith painted a vaguely discomforting backdrop to his present situation. By the time Simon followed Natalie back into the caravan nothing had been said and nothing had been resolved.

As he came through the doorway she turned to face him, their eyes met and time stood still. Slowly Natalie reached both hands out and linked them behind his neck, pulling his face gently towards her. Simon slid his arms around her waist and drew her lower body towards his. Their first kiss began slowly, each taking time to savour the moments of intimate exploration. Natalie's arms tightened their embrace and Simon's hands responded by moving slowly downwards from her lower back to cup her buttocks, pulling her more strongly against his growing hardness. The tempo of their mutual arousal gathered momentum. Natalie loosened Simon's tie and started to unbutton his shirt; impatient with the time it took to undo each button, she pulled it over his head in one swift move. Pulling her gently back towards him, Simon unzipped the back of Natalie's dress and she pulled away from him and wriggled it to the floor at her feet. Within seconds they had completed undressing each other and their naked bodies gave frenzied expression to their love for each other as they intertwined, then writhed on the caravan floor in the narrow gap between the bench seats until the ecstasy of orgasm cemented and unified their relationship in a way that far exceeded either of their wildest dreams. As they lay in a tangled embrace on the floor the heat of their passion cooled gradually, yet they were both reluctant to move. Eventually Simon pushed himself up, rocking backwards onto his knees. He held out his hands and pulled Natalie into a sitting position.

'I love you, Nat,' he said.

'Me, too', she replied softly as a solitary tear escaped and trickled down her cheek.

Mindful of his modesty, Simon pulled on his boxer shorts as Natalie picked up their discarded clothing. Pulling a raft of tape-joined slats from the bottom of the miniscule chest of drawers Simon rearranged the cushions to form a large double bed. Onto this he placed the two sleeping bags, zipping them together into one large one. Still naked, Natalie climbed into the bed and sat with her back against two pillows as she watched Simon open a bottle of chilled white wine and pour out two glasses. She wanted to tell him a million things but somehow it didn't seem the right time. He passed her a glass and made as if to get into bed beside her.

Natalie pointed at his shorts.

'Boxers,' she said, grinning, 'I haven't finished with you yet, Simon Fenton, thirty four.'

Simon grinned back, discarded his underwear and climbed into bed beside her. For as long as it took to drink their wine they sat close to each other holding hands. Then Simon slid down into the giant sleeping bag and began to smother her toned stomach with a carpet of soft kisses. Natalie wriggled herself onto her side and they began to make love again;

slowly this time with each of them taking time and care to give pleasure rather than to receive it. With hands and mouths they explored the intimacies and eroticism of each others' bodies, taking turns to increase and decrease the tempo of their arousal until, after experiencing a wave of shuddering orgasms, Natalie sensed her lover approaching the point of no return and drew him into her most intimate place as they shared another overwhelming and all-consuming climax.

Natalie lay maintaining bodily contact with him, from her feet, which were comfortably entwined with his legs, to her face; which was nestled close alongside his neck. Her right arm lay between their bodies and, she gently ran the fingers of her left hand through the hairs on his chest.

'Simon,' she whispered, 'Even after all I've done, you know, all the bad stuff, I want you to know that you've just taught me the real difference between having sex and making love. Honestly, it's never ever been like that for me before. Thank you.'

He rolled towards her and kissed her.

'Nat, this has been the most perfect day of my whole life,' he said, 'it's me that should be thanking you, you're just fantastic. I don't care about anything else or about anyone else. Even if we both end up in prison tomorrow, or even worse I'm so glad this has happened. I wouldn't swop tonight for anything in the world. I love you, Natalie Robertson, twenty four.'

They maintained their gentle embrace. After a while the sound of rhythmic breathing told Simon that she was asleep. He lay there in the darkness holding her gently, the softness of her skin; the warmth of her lithe form next to his, the lingering scent of her perfume teasing his nostrils. This wonderful girl had dissolved the hard shell of hurt and anguish that had enveloped his heart since Sophie had died. His love for Natalie inundated all his senses and consumed his very being and, in that inner place of intimate and selfless giving of himself, he was fleetingly aware of the ephemeral presence of the God he had kept at arm's length for months.

Then, with the girl's breath gently brushing his cheek, Simon Fenton fell asleep.

CHAPTER TWENTY-SIX

In the bedroom of his London home Jimmy Bell sighed with relief as he disconnected the call. Although it was still dark and he had been woken up from a deep sleep the news was undoubtedly good. Fenton had called the journalist at home. The phone tap had recorded the call as it happened, but the electronic gadgetry at GCHQ had not flagged it as a particular priority. The intercept was eventually screened by an operator at three forty five in the morning. His instructions were to forward it as both an e-mail transcript and a voice recording to the intelligence unit at ICIS. The civilian clerk on duty telephoned her boss at ten to four with the news and read out the transcript over the telephone.

Jimmy Bell rubbed his eyes. So they either had the papers or they knew where they were. The call had been made from a call box in Maryport. Where the hell was that? He waddled into his study and booted up the computer. Twenty minutes later he had woken Detective Inspector Cavendish in his Manchester hotel room. He and Gerry Jewel were to get themselves up to West Cumbria as quickly as possible, Jewel having made arrangements to be informed of any other developments in the Manchester investigation by mobile phone. Paul Cavendish assured his boss that they would be in Maryport by breakfast time. For the time being, Jimmy Bell decided, he would not share the latest information with his colleagues in the Manchester Force.

Detective Constable Jason Entwhistle was not in a good mood. He had been up half the night pacing the bedroom floor cradling his three month old daughter while his wife, Ellie, had retreated to the sanctum offered by the spare room. Little Megan was both the joy and the bane of his life. Both grandmothers had been forced to agree that she was not proving to be an easy baby. With a mix of guilt and relief he had returned Megan to a still drowsy Ellie and slipped out of the house to begin his shift forty minutes early. The early morning sun bathed the streets of Huddersfield in a pale yellow glow as he drew up outside the white rendered council house. Although the paintwork and windows appeared well cared for, he noticed that the garden was overgrown with weeds and a rusty metal trailer lay at an odd angle against the wall.

His knock on the door was answered by a well build man wearing only a vest and a pair of black trousers. The occupant of the house was initially reticent but, on being reassured that there was no suspicion that he had done anything wrong, he grudgingly admitted that he had sold his car to a man matching the description of Simon Fenton the previous Saturday morning. In fact he still had the change of ownership slip. He had not got round to posting it because of the bank holiday, he said. When shown a printout of a CCTV image of Simon he was able to confirm that it was the same man. He also added the information that the man had also taken the number plate from the old trailer.

Detective Constable Entwhistle reached his desk in time for the beginning of his shift at nine feeling rather pleased with himself. He immediately e-mailed the investigating officer in Manchester with the news and confirmed the description and registration number of the vehicle. The Manchester officer concerned, however, had a dental appointment that morning and did not open the e-mail until nine forty. Within minutes details of the car had been circulated to police forces across the UK and it had been flagged on both the Police National Computer and the DVLA database. On hearing about the trailer number plate a senior officer added two and two to make four and also ordered a trawl of camping and caravan sites to be made by telephone. Four officers and six civilians began the process of telephoning them one by one at eleven fifteen.

CHAPTER TWENTY-SEVEN

Natalie awoke early. A deep contentment washed over her as memories of the previous evening surfaced. The reassuring presence of Simon in the bed beside her sent a shiver of thankfulness throughout her body. If anyone had suggested a week ago that she would meet and fall in love with a pretty ordinary looking guy ten years older than her who was undeniably a bit eccentric she would have laughed at the idea, but that was exactly what had happened to her; an attraction that transcended the mere physical. She had been so afraid that she had blown her chances through her inept and overplayed flirting, yet in the end it appeared that she hadn't. Pushing herself slowly into a sitting position she carefully unzipped the side of the sleeping bag and slid gently out of bed to avoid disturbing the sleeping man. She dressed in her running gear and crept out of the caravan into the sunrise. For almost an hour she jogged relentlessly; as far as the Golf Club and back, allowing the endorphins to boost her deep sense of well being as she exorcised the mild aches caused by the late night activities in the caravan. When she returned Simon was still asleep. She paused for a long moment just looking at his sleeping form silently thankful for the new and totally unfamiliar dimension he had added to her life. For the first time that she could remember Natalie Robertson did not feel in the least bit lonely. She had experienced and received real love. She cast off her clothes and went into the tiny bathroom.

The buzzing of the water pump roused Simon from his stupor. As consciousness dawned so did the realisation of what had passed between him and Natalie the night before. He smiled, sitting up in bed and stretching. Presently the bathroom door opened and a naked and dripping Natalie emerged, grabbing a towel which was draped over the gas hob. Winding the towel round her wet hair, she filled the kettle from the gas and put in on to boil.

'Morning, sleepy head,' she smiled.

Simon sat staring at her open mouthed.

'Wow, he croaked, 'tell me I'm not dreaming, Nat. Did we? I mean are we? Oh shit, Nat, did we really make love to each other last night?' Oh, bugger, I'm staring, sorry.'

Natalie stooped across the bed and kissed him, droplets of water falling from her skin as he reached up and drew her closer. Natalie pulled gently away.

'Slow down, lover boy,' she grinned, 'there'll be plenty of time for that later. Nnow are you going to get out of bed today or aren't you?'

'Well, 'responded Simon, 'the idea of a day in bed…..'

'I told you... later,' replied Natalie, 'right now I want my boyfriend up and dressed. Then he can take me out somewhere in this lovely sunshine while we wait for Kynpham.'

Simon sheepishly complied and took his turn in the bathroom. By the time he was dried and dressed Natalie was dressed in her leggings and a crop top and had prepared coffee and toast for breakfast. As they ate they agreed that they ought to make the most of the day until Kynpham was able to join them and help move the quest for Eddie Duggan's papers forward. With hints of innuendo and occasional bouts of giggling they began to plan how they might spend three or four days hidden away in a remote holiday cottage in the Scottish Borders. Using the road atlas from the car they decided to risk a day playing at being tourists in Keswick. With Natalie wearing her long blonde wig and both of them their plain glass spectacles they were now sufficiently confident that they looked very different from the images of themselves that so far had appeared in the media. There had been no mention of the murder of the Detective Inspector on the radio for over twenty four hours and their growing fascination with each other also served to inhibit their previous caution. Simon suggested that they pack a few essentials as he thought it probable that they would not return to the caravan so, with his holdall and Natalie's rucksack, they were on the road by ten; Natalie once again doing the driving. They paused outside a telephone box in Cockermouth so that Simon could make the call to Kynpham. This time she waited in the car for him.

Upon his return he announced that Kynpham had thought better of involving his editor on the basis that his boss might either not agree to a junior reporter tackling such a big story or could say or do something to endanger Simon's life. Instead he had proposed to take a week's leave beginning that evening. He would be free to travel as soon as he had filed his story on the delays to the Olympic Stadium. Simon retrieved the notebook PC from the car boot and switched it on. With an internet connection established he looked up trains from London to Carlisle and returned to the telephone box to pass on the information to his friend. When he returned again he told Natalie that Kynpham proposed to catch a train which arrived in Carlisle at twenty one seventeen. He would book a hire car before he set off and await another call on his mobile; both men having agreed that making too many arrangements too far in advance would pose too great a security risk. Natalie started the car and they drove off towards Keswick.

Neither of them noticed the small white van that was conducting a DVLA photographic check on vehicles travelling eastbound on the A66.

Keswick was packed with visitors. The late summer heat-wave was continuing unabated, blessing the holidaymakers with weather they had barely dared hope for and supplementing their numbers with a horde of day trippers. The central car parks were all full. They eventually located a space near the old railway station, paid and displayed and set off hand in hand towards the town centre.

After a light lunch in an old fashioned tea shop Simon and Natalie ambled towards the lake shore, enjoying the apparent anonymity of being in a crowded tourist destination on a warm and pleasant day. They had to queue for over half an hour, but they eventually managed to hire a rowing boat. Natalie dissolved in giggles at Simon's inability to row in a straight line. Changing places almost resulted in the boat capsizing and Simon had his revenge as Natalie proved no better at manoeuvring the boat than he had been. At a safe distance from the shore they gave up any attempt at rowing and let the boat drift in the light breeze as they talked. Both fascinated by each others lives, but careful to avoid their shared secrets of difficult days gone by, they chatted animatedly. Simon admitted to having neglected his little house since moving in. Although he had needed to have the rotting doors and windows replaced he had not done any decorating and, apart from a new flat screen TV, his furniture was an eclectic mix of cheap IKEA chic and hand me downs. Natalie took him to task and suggested various colour schemes and options. She told him that he had better put his house in order if she was going to spend any time there. Simon shivered with anticipation and delight at the prospect. She told him about her little flat and about her work at the bank. It was funny, she said, how the attraction of high pressure sales seemed to have faded over the last few days; she was not sure at all that she wanted to carry on there, although she had no idea now how she was ever going to achieve her dream of becoming an airline pilot. She certainly wouldn't be carrying on her life as Kelly, anyway; that was absolutely certain. Simon came close to telling her that he had already decided to help her out financially, but held back, fearing that it might not be the right time. As their hour on the water drew to an end Simon rowed the boat erratically back to the landing stage as Natalie trailed her fingers in the water. Back on the shore they strolled hand in hand into the quaint town centre where they bought immense ice-cream sundaes and lingered over wide mugs of cappuccino before making their way slowly and contentedly back to the car.

It was still late afternoon; far too early to position themselves for the meeting with Kynpham. Natalie drove slowly along the Braithwaite road and continued up a series of steep and sinuous hills, deliberately taking the side roads to pass the time until nine seventeen. Following a brown road sign she pulled into a small picnic area amongst the dense woodland of Whinlatter Country Park.

'Why are we stopping here?' asked Simon.

Natalie unbuckled her seatbelt and leant across to kiss him. Pulling away she gave her reply,

'Because we're going for a walk in the woods,' she said, ' and we're going to find somewhere quiet and make love.'

CHAPTER TWENTY-EIGHT

The Home Secretary was fifteen minutes late for his meeting with Detective Chief Superintended Bell. He had been delayed by dealing with urgent papers returning a number of important calls from his office in Marsham Street. He had made the short journey on foot, dismissing his protection officer at the ground floor entrance to the building on Broadway. Still relatively fit at fifty eight, he took the stairs rather than the lift and was only very slightly short of breath when he entered the ICIS Office Suite.

To Jimmy Bell's relief there was good news to report. Fenton had been in contact with the journalist and was due to telephone him again within the next half hour. An alert had been issued and a call to either the reporter's office or mobile would be traced immediately. Jewel and Cavendish had recently arrived in Maryport and were awaiting instructions and, within the last few minutes, there had been a positive lead on a car that Fenton was almost certainly driving. When Eddie Duggan arrived Bell briefed him quickly and was rewarded by a grudging acknowledgement. The two men decided to await the call to the reporter before deciding whether to collaborate with the local force or play their own hand. The Home Secretary favoured dealing with the matter "in house" if at all possible. They were still not absolutely certain whether or not Simon Fenton was on his own or in the company of the girl. He had used the word "we" in his conversation with the journalist and that implied that he probably was, but the girl was a loose end that was in urgent need of tidying up.

Their speculation was interrupted by a telephone call. Fenton had called the reporter again; from a call box in Cockermouth. The journalist was planning an unofficial trip to Carlisle to help Fenton and would arrive on the evening train and would be hiring a car. Bell relayed the information to Cavendish and Jewel; ordering them to pick up the journalist on Carlisle station and use him to lure Fenton and the girl, if she was with him into a trap.

A report from the DVLA reached the police in both Manchester and Cumbria in early afternoon. The dark blue Mondeo that they were looking for had been spotted by an Automatic Number-plate Recognition Camera heading east along the A66 between Cockermouth and Keswick. All traffic patrols in the area were alerted and the beat bobbies and traffic wardens in Keswick were asked to keep an eye out for the car. The information was relayed by the Manchester force to Gerry Jewel at two fifteen and he immediately passed the report on to his boss.

A Keswick beat bobby finally spotted the car in late afternoon leaving the car park on the site of the old railway station. There were two occupants he later reported, but the distance was too great for him to see them clearly. The car left the car park heading westwards along Brundholm Road. The battery in his radio was low and he was unable to raise his control office. It was not until the end of his shift at five thirty that the information reached Keswick police station and was immediately passed on to Cumbria Police Headquarters and onwards to their colleagues in Manchester. Jimmy Bell knew all about it by six twenty; as did Jewel and Cavendish.

With the growing trail of evidence the officer in charge of searching Cumbrian caravan and camping sites began to home in on the Maryport area. Although there had been no success from contacting licensed sites one of the civilian staff was a keen caravanner and suggested that they try the smaller Caravan Club members' only sites, which did not require a license because they could only accommodate five or fewer caravans. They struck gold at six fifteen. The owner of a tiny costal site between Allonby and Maryport confirmed that a couple broadly matching the descriptions of Natalie Robertson and Simon Fenton were staying there. The car was not present at the moment. A call was made to the Cumbria force requesting that a visit be made. Once again the information reached Jimmy Bell and his two assistants within minutes. Bell decided to keep to his original plan of using the journalist as bait. He would much rather that Fenton and the girl fell into the safe hands of Jewel and Cavendish than into the custody of the local force.

Kympham Johal's train pulled into Carlisle railway station spot on time at seventeen minutes past nine. As he carried his small suitcase through the small booking hall he found his path blocked by two burly men.

'Kynpham Johal?' asked the taller man.

'Er, yes,' answered Kynpham hesitantly.

'Police,' the man flashed an identity card under Kynpham's nose, 'I wonder if you would mind coming with us.'

The reporter's heart sank. It was pretty apparent that things were every bit as serious as Simon had suggested they might be. With a policeman on either side he was escorted across the station forecourt into a dark coloured Vauxhall Vectra. One man got into the back seat behind him while the other opened the driver's door. Suddenly the man beside him pushed him violently sideways, grabbed his arms and quickly handcuffed them behind his back. It was strange, he thought, that neither officer had informed him of his rights or told him he was under arrest. Perplexed and increasingly anxious, Kynpham stared out of the window at the unfamiliar streets as the car moved off. Five minutes later they were parked up in a deserted industrial estate. The man beside him pulled a flick knife from his pocket and pressed the button which released the blade with a terrifying thud. He held it to Kynpham's throat.

'Listen to me,' the policeman hissed, 'Your pal is going to call you in a couple of minutes. This is what you're going to tell him.'

CHAPTER TWENTY-NINE

The sun was dipping towards the horizon and there was a chill in the air when Simon and Natalie returned to the car, once again hand in hand. The few other vehicles that had been parked in the picnic area had left. With Natalie again doing the driving they set off on the next leg of their mission. At eight forty they drew into the small town of Dalston, which Simon had decided was sufficiently close to Carlisle for them to await Kynpham's arrival in his hire car, yet far enough from the public gaze of the ubiquitous CCTV. They found a small car park, close to the town centre and parked in the furthest corner from the street lights. Claiming to be worn out from Natalie's energetic demands, Simon went in search of refreshments and returned a few minutes with an assortment of chocolate bars and a couple of newspapers. Their hunger satisfied, Simon switched on the courtesy light on the car roof and began to leaf through a broadsheet. Natalie followed his lead and picked up the other paper, a red-topped tabloid. The photographs on the fifth page caused her to take a sharp intake of breath. "Has anyone seen the vicar and the tart?" the headline read. Underneath was a fuzzy photograph of Simon with longish hair and a beard dressed in clerical robes. Next to it was the one from the homepage of "Kelly's" website. In full colour there she was with long auburn hair; wearing black bra, thong and hold-up stockings, leaning against the brass headboard of a bed with the tip of her right index finger seductively between her lips and two fingers of her left hand slipped down the front of her thong.

Her first instinct was to close the paper so that Simon wouldn't see the photograph. Reacting to her sudden movement he turned towards her, noticing her anguished expression.

'Nat, what's up?' he asked.

Natalie shook her head slowly from side to side. In an instant the bubble of her romantic dream had burst. While they had been cocooned together in the intimacy of the caravan the past seemed almost not to matter. Telling Simon all about it had been cathartic and he had not condemned her; far from it, he had told her that he loved her. Now, faced with the harsh truth that not only Simon, but the whole country knew about her double life, the prospect of any sort of future with him seemed to be receding rapidly. It was not what he thought that mattered, she reasoned, but what all his friends and everyone they met would think. In her misery she had all but put out of her mind the fact that they were on the run and probably in danger of their lives. All she could think about was the shame of being known as the vicar's tart. She put her head down and began to cry.

'What is it, Nat?' Simon asked again, reaching out to put an arm around her shoulder. She dissolved into him, the tears dampening his shirt as he held her close.

'Its....it's the paper, Simon,' she sobbed.

Reaching across her he picked up the newspaper and awkwardly turned the pages with one hand while holding Natalie with the other. He found the page in question and smoothed it out on the dashboard.

'Oh, Simon,' she sighed, 'don't look. I don't want you to see....'

'Don't be daft, Nat,' replied Simon, squeezing her shoulder, 'You told me all about that. It doesn't make any difference, to us I mean. I love you; that's all there is to it.'

'Maybe now,' she answered, reaching into her bag for a tissue, 'but what about everybody else. They'll all know at work and at the flying school and all your friends. How can we be together after this?'

'Nat, it makes absolutely no difference. Sod everyone else. I still think you're the best thing that ever happened to me,' he said crumpling the newspaper into a ball.

Natalie wiped her eyes, but the sparkle had gone out of them. She leant against Simon's shoulder taking comfort from his presence, but the incident had served as some kind of unwelcome jolt back to reality for her. With the melancholy glimpse of future challenges came a deep foreboding about their present predicament.

'What if Kynpham can't find the documents?' she asked, 'and what if his editor won't print the story? We're still wanted; it said so in the paper. They think Barry, or Wayne, or whatever his name is killed the cop, but I did didn't I? They'll find out and I'll go to prison.'

'Look, don't worry about that now,' reassured Simon, 'Kynpham will be here soon. I think we'll get him to book a couple of rooms in a Travelodge somewhere tonight; at a motorway services might be best. Then he can track down a cottage tomorrow; I'll use the notebook to find one.'

'But it won't be the same now,' muttered Natalie, 'oh shit, Simon, why did they have to publish that picture?'

He held her close until a fresh episode of sobbing subsided, desperate to find a way to let her know that it really didn't matter to him what anyone else might think. He loved her and wanted to spend the rest of his life with her. Words failed him though, it was not the right time, he realised, to try and paint a rose coloured picture of their future together. First they had to deal with their present situation. Simon powered up the notebook and checked the train arrivals for Carlisle. Kynpham's train was shown as running on time. The clock on the computer screen read nine fifteen. Only two minutes to go. He would give his friend ten minutes or so to pick up the car before telephoning, so fifteen minutes; that was all. Then things would start to move more quickly. He switched of the courtesy light and Natalie nestled her head into his neck as they waited.

If Simon had not been distracted by the article in the newspaper and Natalie's distress he would have sought out a public call box. In the circumstances, however, he decided to risk using one of their emergency pre-paid mobiles. He carefully dialled Kynpham's number. The call was answered on the fifth ring.

'Kynpham Johal, is that you Simon?' said a familiar voice.

'Yes, sure is,' replied Simon, 'did you arrive all right?'

'Yes, fine.'

'Listen Kynpham,' continued Simon,' have you got the car yet?'

'Er..yes,' replied the reporter, 'where shall we meet? It's been a while hasn't it; do you remember our day out in Clacton?'

'Er, yes,' answered Simon hesitantly, his mind working overtime.

'We'll let's hope we have as much fun this time, mate,' continued the reporter.

'Hope so,' said Simon, thinking rapidly, 'we're at Southwaite Services on the M6, southbound. I think it will take you about twenty minutes from where you are.'

Natalie looked up in surprise. Simon gestured for her to stay quiet.

'Southwaite Services, southbound,' echoed Kynpham, 'see you there in twenty. Are you parked up or in the cafe?'

'Cafe,' replied Simon,' I'll get you a cappuccino, two sugars isn't it?'

'Sure is,' replied Kynpham, 'bye Simon.'

Simon pressed the end call button.

'Oh shit!' he exclaimed, 'something's very wrong, Nat.'

'What's going on, Simon?' she asked, sitting upright in her seat.

'He mentioned Clacton,' replied Simon,' we were there last year and we both got mugged at knifepoint. I thought he was trying to warn me so I said that stuff about sugar in his coffee. He doesn't take sugar. When he agreed I was certain something was up. We've got to get moving, Nat. Let's go back and pack up the caravan and hit the road. I don't have a plan.

We just need to get away. I hope Kynpham's OK. I just don't know what's going on.'

'You drive,' said Natalie, opening the door, 'give me the map and I'll navigate.'

They changed places and Simon drove off, retracing the half-familiar route to the little caravan site. As he drove Simon was desperately trying to come up with some sort of plan. You could get a ferry to Ireland from Liverpool. Perhaps if they picked up the caravan and found another site in that area one or both of them could slip across and dig up the papers? Now that they were back in the newspapers hiding would be more difficult. They both probably needed another change of appearance.

The urgency of the situation calmed Natalie's raw emotions. By the time they approached Allonby she had half persuaded herself that there would be plenty of time to worry about the future if only they could survive the present.

Simon slowed down and turned the car into the short driveway and, out of habit, Natalie reached for the door handle, intending to get out and open the gate. As the car straightened up there, in the beam of the dipped headlights they could both see the florescent yellow squares of a police car which was parked in the farmyard. Simon threw the car into reverse and back onto the road. Natalie saw a flash of yellow as a burly policeman ran from the door of the farmhouse towards the closed gate as his companion, who must have been sitting in the car, activated the blue flashing lights. Simon put the car into first gear and accelerated rapidly, taking the narrow road northwards. Within a minute they passed across a small bridge in the centre of the village. With a squeal of tyres, Simon turned right onto a narrow road that was barely wider than the car. In the rear view mirror he could see the flashing blue lights of the police car as it turned out of the farmyard and set off in pursuit. Natalie gripped tightly onto the armrest and looked over her shoulder as the car raced along the narrow road. In the distance the lights of the police car turned onto the road behind them. Grazing the verges, Simon pushed the car as hard as he dared.

'Shit, Nat, I'm out of ideas,' he shouted several minutes later.

'Keep going!' replied Nat, 'I don't think they're gaining at the moment.'

A "give way" sign loomed ahead and Simon braked slightly. The moon was high in the sky, bathing the hedges and fields on either side in a pale wash of silver. Simon switched off the car's lights and released the brakes. Immediately ahead was a cross roads. Without slowing further Simon drive straight across a deserted main road and onwards along another narrow road. The lack of illumination slowed their progress but, to Natalie's delight the blue lights of their pursuer halted at the junction behind them then moved off at right angles to their route.

'Lost them!' exclaimed Natalie.

Simon slowed further; his eyes having adjusted to the moonlight.

'We've got to dump the car,' he said, 'they'll be out in force soon; any ideas?'

Natalie remained silent. Without Kynpham's help, she realised, their chances of unearthing the papers which were the key to resolving their predicament were very slim indeed.

'Simon, let me take the car and lead them on a wild goose chase,' she said, 'you bale out and hide up somewhere while I get as far away as possible then you might have a chance.'

Simon could see the logic of her idea, but was loathe to agree; he worried that she might get hurt in the chase; that she might take the consequences of the policeman's death and even more that the long tentacles of Eddie Duggan might do her even more serious harm.

'I think we should stick together,' he said gruffly, a catch in his voice.

They crossed another main road; Simon choosing to stay on narrow country lanes, still driving without lights. At a fork in the road he chose to veer left and the lane became even narrower.

'Oh no!' exclaimed Natalie, pointing to their right, 'I think that's a bloody helicopter.'

A tiny cluster of flashing lights in the sky seemed to be hanging stationary in space. Simon lowered the car window and a distant whumping sound confirmed Natalie's suspicion. Up ahead on their left was a semi-derelict industrial unit with a collection of sheds and more substantial buildings. Simon pulled into the yard, and then edged the car slowly through a gap into an old barn where a broken door hung precariously upon one hinge and the other lay broken on the ground.

'This will keep the car off their Infra-red sensors,' said Simon, 'and us; if we stay inside.'

They got out of the car into the stygian darkness of the barn. As their eyes adjusted they could make out an assortment of rusting machinery and piles of wooden palettes strewn around. The noise of the helicopter got closer; then began to recede. Simon reached out for Natalie and drew her close to his side.

'I'm sorry, Nat,' he said, taking hold of her hand, 'I think this might be as far as we get. I think it would be safer if we gave ourselves up.'

'No, Simon,' she answered, turning towards him and slipping her free hand around his waist, 'not yet. Let's make one more effort, shall we?'

They repacked their belongings, cutting down on clothing and packing the remainder of the money with the notebook and mobile phones into Natalie's rucksack and discarding Simon's holdall. After a tentative peep outside the barn door confirmed that the helicopter was no longer in the vicinity they set off on foot. An area of dense woodland beckoned and they crossed the small yard and sought a degree of refuge amongst the trees. The moon was sliding towards the horizon and little light penetrated the foliage, seriously hindering their progress. Simon tripped over a root, falling awkwardly and cutting his arm. Natalie roughly bandaged the cut with a strip torn from a shirt in the rucksack. They sat down with their backs against a tree.

'It's no good,' said Simon, 'we'll have to lie up and wait for daylight.'

'Just let me have a look up there,' Natalie gestured to the top of a gentle slope, 'it looks a bit brighter up there, do you think we could risk open country; the helicopter seems to have gone.'

She carefully picked her way up the slope, leaving a despondent Simon propped against his tree. That was that, he thought, he had done his best and there was no way he would have traded the past few days for a lifetime of his previous humdrum existence. Natalie was the best thing that had ever happened to him, but now it was just about all over. They would just have to take their chances with the police. Surely Eddie Duggan couldn't harm them in a big police station? Perhaps they should try and reach Carlisle at first light, maybe even in the car?'

'Simon!' Natalie's excited voice penetrated his growing depression, 'there's an airfield just over the hill and perhaps we could get away in an aeroplane?'

She dragged him to his feet. He picked up the rucksack and followed her up the slope. From the edge of the tree-line they could see a large airfield laid out at the foot of a shallow escarpment; the moonlight illuminating a dark ribbon of the runway in front of a collection of hangars and buildings. Several light aircraft were parked in front of the control tower.

'Look,' said Natalie, I can't see any houses or anything. If we could get one started up we could be away at first light and there's a chance no one would know we were gone for hours. We could go all the way to Ireland and land in a field or something.'

'Are you sure you could fly one?' asked Simon, cautiously.

'I think so,' answered Natalie, 'anything with a fixed undercarriage and a single engine, anyway. I won't say it would be elegant, but I could probably get it up and down safely enough. Come on, let's have a closer look.'

Her earlier anguish at the publication of "Kelly's" photograph momentarily forgotten, she led the way down the slope and across the moonlit expanse of the airfield.

'Won't they all be locked up?' asked Simon, 'and do we need a key to start them up like a car?'

'Yes and yes,' replied Natalie, 'but lots of light aircraft are owned by a group or consortium. It's not likely that they all have their own keys. My bet is that if we can break into the clubroom or hangar we can probably find a set of keys hidden away somewhere. The aeroplanes in the hangar probably won't be locked, anyway and I reckon the keys will be inside them. After all people don't steal aeroplanes...' She began to giggle and Simon smiled at the incongruity of it all. Compared to murder, the offence of taking an aeroplane without the owner's consent seemed to pale into insignificance. So be it, he thought. He began to giggle along with her as they crossed the grey tarmac of the runway and closed in on their target. Five aircraft were lined up outside the control tower, four of them with their cockpits obscured by canvas covers. Natalie worked her way along the line, delving where necessary below the canvas to try the doors. All of them were locked. From there they approached the club-house cum control tower and peered through a window.

'No go,' said Simon, 'there's a burglar alarm. With no one around to hear it probably dials the local police if there's a break in.'

'Oh shit!' exclaimed Natalie, 'there's bound to be sets of keys for some of them; let's try the hangar.'

The distant sound of a car engine disturbed the silence. Instinctively both crouched down at the side of the building. The sound faded and, sobered by the reminder that a search for them was underway, they walked slowly towards the hangar. The main door was fastened shut with a formidable-looking padlock.

'I can't see us getting in there without a hacksaw,' said Simon, the earlier mirth rapidly receding into the dark corners of his memory.

'Try the side,' said Natalie, 'the big door is for aeroplanes, there's usually a little door for people somewhere else.'

They found a small wooden door at the rear corner of the hangar. Once again this was fastened shut by a padlock, but a rather less substantial one. Simon ferreted around on the ground nearby and returned with a large stone. After a quick circuit of the hangar to make sure they were as alone as they hoped, Simon began to hammer at the lock with the stone. After a dozen blows the padlock flew off and a firm push resulted in the door creaking open. Natalie led the way inside and Simon followed, divesting himself of the rucksack beside the doorway. After the moonlit landscape outside the cavernous interior seemed to be pitch dark. It took several minutes before either of them could see anything at all and, even then, vision was extremely limited. Natalie, her arms held out in front of her, edged slowly towards the centre, locating the dim outlines of a number of aircraft while Simon slowly explored the wall next to the still open door.

'It's no good,' he said, 'we can't see a thing in here. We'll have to wait for daylight.'

'This one's open,' replied Natalie, her voice echoing from the metal walls and roof.

'Where are you?' inquired Simon, 'I can hear you but I can't see you.'

'Wait a minute,' exclaimed Natalie, 'watch this?'

A dull glow emanated from the cockpit of an aeroplane parked in the centre of the hangar. Immediately afterwards a number of different coloured lights spilled out in a variety of directions; a bright beam shone from the aircraft towards the front of the hangar while a flashing red light illuminated the roof and a red and green lights shone from the wingtips.

'Shut that outside door, Simon,' called Natalie.

Simon complied and then, drawn towards the source of light, he found her in the cockpit of a high wing monoplane.

'No keys here,' she reported, 'but at least we can see what we are doing.'

Moving swiftly from aircraft to aircraft, Natalie carried out a search of each cockpit. After climbing on the wing of a low-winged aircraft right in front of the door and sliding into the right hand seat she squealed in glee.

'Keys! We've got a set of bloody keys, Simon.' She manoeuvred herself into the far seat, allowing Simon to join her. Deftly she began to press a series of rocker switches in the centre of the instrument panel. Then she turned a small wheel beside them and a dim glow illuminated the cockpit instruments.

'Not much fuel,' she commented, 'about a quarter each side; probably good for an hour and a bit.' She turned the wheel back and the instrument lights went out as she rocked the switches back into their original positions.

'Can you fly this one?' asked Simon.

'No problem,' replied Natalie, 'it's an older version of the Warrior I fly from Leeds. Probably twenty horsepower less and its got old fashioned control yokes. It's called a Cherokee and is about forty years old, but it should be a piece of cake.'

She grinned broadly in the diffused light. Simon was reminded of the evening they had met. Her eyes had sparkled when she spoke of flying and he could sense that overwhelming enthusiasm again.

'Nat, when we get out of this mess,' he began, intending to make his offer of financial support for her advanced training.

'Shh,' she interrupted, 'let's not think too much about the future right now. Go and see if you can find any tools to get rid of the big lock on the main door while I do the pre-flight checks.'

Simon left her alone in the cockpit and retraced his steps towards the door. In the multicoloured confusion of light he could see a long work bench running along the wall. In minutes he had located a large hacksaw. He picked it up and waved it at Natalie who was now outside the cockpit running her hands over the wings and control surfaces.

'Hold on a minute,' she said, 'let me finish this first. Then we'll put the lights out and go back outside.'

Good to her word, Natalie finished checking over the little monoplane and then climbed back into the cockpit of the first aircraft. One by one the lights went out leaving the interior of the hangar in pitch darkness. Simon opened the door to admit a glimmer of half-light and waited patiently by the door listening to Natalie's footsteps as she gingerly made her way towards him. She flung her arms round him and kissed him.

'Simon Fenton, thirty four,' she said, 'I really think we're going to make it; now let's see to the front door.'

A bank of high cloud had all but obscured the moon when they left the hangar. Only a lingering luminescence gave shape and form to the hangar as they returned to the front door. The rasp of the hacksaw seemed inordinately loud in the still cool air and Natalie looked anxiously around as Simon attacked the lock. He was sweating freely and breathing heavily by the time it finally fell to the ground with a resounding clang. With no sign that they had been detected, they began to heave on the sliding door which, with an alarming squeal, began to slide on its rusty runners. Slowing their pace, Simon and Natalie eased the door into a fully open position and, following Natalie's instructions, they pushed the Cherokee out onto the tarmac. With another startling cacophony of squealing and creaking they closed the doors behind it and stood leaning against the aircraft's rear fuselage regaining their breath.

'Helicopter,' exclaimed Simon in a hoarse whisper.

In the eastern sky the tiny Christmas tree of flashing lights and the familiar sound of rotors signalled approaching danger and spurred them into action. Darting back to the side of the hangar they re-entered the dark cavern and closed the door firmly behind them. For several minutes they listened to the sound of the helicopter as it seemed to criss-cross the area before the sound gradually faded in the west. Sitting with their backs against the hangar wall, they began to make their plans.

'We'll get off as soon as we can see the runway,' announced Natalie, 'I had a quick look at the map in the cockpit. We'll head straight for the coast, them turn left onto about two three zero until we pick up the northern tip of the Isle of Man. From there it's about zero nine zero and we should make landfall in the vicinity of Ardglass; that's where we need to be isn't it. There's an airfield at Newtownards but that's about thirty miles north of there. At that time in the morning we could probably slip in without anyone being there, but they'd find the aeroplane. I don't know how we'd get to the old radar place from there, though.'

Simon recognised and admired her undoubted competence. For the first time since they had been spotted by the police car he began to feel truly optimistic. If they could get across the Irish Sea undetected that might well give them a serious advantage. Even if the aircraft was found after an hour or two no-one would know where they were heading. You could cover a lot of ground in a couple of hours.

'We need to try and avoid taxis or buses close to where we land,' he said, 'and if we stole a car it wouldn't take long for them to catch on. Perhaps we could walk or something. Dress up like hikers and buy a tent?'

'Or what about bikes?' asked Natalie, 'if we bought bikes we could move faster. Even if they recognised us at the bike shop afterwards, I mean the photos and stuff might not be so public over there....' The memory of the photograph and her perception of its implications surfaced again and halted her in mid flow.

'Not a bad idea,' replied Simon, 'have we still got the road atlas?'

'Er..I think I put it in the rucksack, you could have a look once we get airborne.'

She snuggled into Simon's side and, almost immediately, she felt her confidence ebbing. As they sat in silence, Natalie felt the unaccustomed pang of truly caring about someone else more than herself. It just wouldn't do to expect this man - this lovely wonderful man that she had unexpectedly fallen head over heels for - to be lumbered with an ex-prostitute; especially one who had set out quite ruthlessly to abuse his trust. In the cool night air the truth gradually dawned on her; she loved Simon Fenton more than she had ever thought it would be possible to love anyone. While the old Natalie – whoever she really had been – would have been busy calculating how to manipulate the situation for her own benefit the New Natalie just couldn't bring herself to do it. If, and that was a big if, they got out of this mess intact, she perceived that Simon would feel a debt of gratitude towards her that, the honourable man that he was, might lead him into offering her the relationship that she so desperately desired. But she just didn't deserve that and he certainly didn't deserve to be known as the vicar who'd fallen for the tart and her cheap tricks. No; she would have to put aside all her hopes and dreams and devote herself entirely to doing everything in her power to help him in his quest for justice for his father and for Michael Duckworth or whoever. With a sudden flash of realisation Natalie Robertson knew that she would gladly give her very life for the man who was leaning against the wall next to her snoring gently into the darkness, but could and would expect nothing whatsoever in return.

CHAPTER THIRTY

At Southwaite Services Jerry Jewel had remained in the car with Kynpham Johal while Paul Cavendish went in search of his quarry. Twenty minutes later he returned. There was no sign of either Simon Fenton or Natalie Robertson anywhere on either the north or south side of the M6. Muttering under his breath he set out again to search the car parks for the Mondeo. While he was searching Jewel's mobile phone rang. The suspects' car had been seen at Allonby on the coast. A police car had set off in pursuit, but had lost the fugitives amongst the narrow Cumbrian lanes. Jewel swore as he punched the buttons of his phone to inform Paul Cavendish who returned immediately. Without a word being exchanged Cavendish started up the car and they returned to the deserted industrial estate where Kynpham had been coerced into taking the call from Simon. The car pulled up in the centre of a large car park and Jewel freed the Indian journalist from the handcuffs. Cavendish opened the car door and Jewel roughly pushed Kynpham through the door onto the hard tarmac.

'Piss off,' ordered Cavendish as he walked back round to the driver's door. Kynpham picked himself up from the ground and began to walk unsteadily across the car park. Cavendish gunned the car's engine and accelerated away rapidly. When the car was fifty yards away from Kynpham the driver swung it round in a tight circle and drove it straight at the reporter accelerating rapidly. Realising what was intended Kynpham dodged to his right and began to run, but Cavendish had anticipated the move and the car unerringly altered course towards the running man. At the last moment the beam of the headlights illuminated a discarded wooden palate directly in front of the speeding car. Cavendish hauled on the steering wheel, drawing a scream of protest from the tyres, but it was too late. The offside front wheel clipped the corner of the palate and the steering wheel was momentarily wrenched from the driver's grip. The car was almost parallel with the running man as Cavendish threw the steering wheel in the opposite direction. With a dull thud the nearside wing caught Kynpham a glancing blow just below his hip and catapulted him into the air. Milliseconds later he landed head first on the dark tarmac and was still. Cavendish braked to a halt, stepped out of the car and walked slowly towards the recumbent figure. As he approached the fallen man the squeal of tyres announced the imminent arrival of another vehicle. Paul Cavendish turned on his heel and sprinted back to the car, slammed the door behind him and drove off into the night.

Jimmy Bell's late night telephone call to the Home Secretary was not a pleasant experience. The admission that his plan to use the journalist as bait to reel in the fugitives from under the noses of the local constabulary had failed was bad enough; but the fact that the locals had also lost contact with them added injury to insult and the Home Secretary made his feelings known in no uncertain terms. Eddie Duggan's worries were compounded by the fact that, for the third time in three weeks the thirty year old former pop singer that he had married the previous spring had not returned home for the night. It was not so much that he particularly minded if she was being unfaithful to him; it was the fear of what the discovery of any illicit liaison might do to his chances of becoming Prime Minister that brought him out into a cold sweat.

In Carlisle the Assistant Chief Constable of the Cumbria police had been summoned to headquarters from the comfort of his home. Simon Fenton and Natalie Robertson had evaded arrest earlier in the evening, despite the presence of the police helicopter which had been diverted from another job. Although neither of them was deemed a prime suspect in the murder of Detective Inspector Gilroy the Manchester force was very keen to speak with them and, apparently, the Home Secretary was taking a particular interest in the case. Road blocks were in the process of being set up on major routes and the police helicopter had been authorised to conduct a further infra-red search of the area in which they were thought to have gone to ground. After less than an hour in the air, though, the helicopter had developed a fault in its fuel system and had been forced to return to its base at Carlisle airport. A new fuel pump was required, but no spares were held there and a new one would not be available until mid morning. The Assistant Chief Constable began to make arrangements for a large scale manhunt to begin soon after first light.

Eighteen year old Danny Mantle's pride and joy was his six year old Vauxhall Astra SRI. The second most important thing in Danny's world was the possibility of having sex with his new girlfriend; seventeen year old Vicky Litton, a busty blonde with an outrageous taste in brightly coloured boob tubes and an infectious laugh. The laugh was ringing in his ears as she sat beside him in the car. He was driving fast, but with all the confidence of youth, he considered the speed to be well within his capabilities. Every squeal of tyres on tarmac unleashed another laugh and, determined to make the best possible impression on the girl he headed into the deserted industrial estate on the western side of the Carlisle railway station in which he intended to demonstrate his skill in handbrake turns. As he skidded into the approach road he noticed another car, a newish Vectra, coming the other way. Dodging neatly around the other vehicle, Danny began to accelerate hard as he approached the large car park in front of a vacant unit. In the glare of his full beam he saw what looked like a bundle of rags in the centre of the car park. Curiosity curbed his performance and, with a screech of brakes, the Astra drew up beside it. Both he and Vicky got out of the car. Lying on the ground was a man dressed in smart casual clothing. He was bleeding heavily from an ugly head wound. Vicky, who had recently completed first aid training as part of her college course, established that he was still breathing while her boyfriend dialled nine, nine, nine on his mobile phone; the adrenalin fading rapidly from his bloodstream as the hand holding the handset began to shake.

CHAPTER THIRTY-ONE

Simon wriggled his numb bottom gently on the hard cold floor of the hangar, taking care not to move too abruptly for fear of waking the girl who was fast asleep with her head resting against his shoulder. In the almost total darkness of the hangar he could not see her, but the feel of her hair against his cheek and the faint trace of her perfume in his nostrils filled him with an unreasonable sense of well-being. Since Sophie's death there had never seemed to be the remotest possibility of him falling in love again. Yet here he was, intimately entangled with Natalie Robertson; the most beautiful, intelligent and truly wonderful woman in the world. Early birdsong signalled that dawn was not too far away. He gently withdrew his arm from around her shoulder to look at his watch, but the movement roused her from her sleep before he could interpret the dull pinpricks of its luminous dial.

'What time is it?' asked Natalie anxiously as she arched her back and stretched out her arms in front of her.

'I think it's about ten to six,' he replied slanting his watch from side to side as he struggled to read the time.

'Come on, let's have a look outside,' said Natalie as she stood up.

There was no more than a glimmer of lighter indigo in the eastern sky as they exited the hangar through the side door. The grass outside was wet with dew as they trudged slowly along the building's side in the half light and located their escape vehicle. Natalie busied herself taking the filler caps off the aeroplane's wing tanks, feeling inside with her fingers to ascertain the fuel level.

'Should be OK for an hour or so,' she said. 'Listen Simon, this could be a bit dangerous so you'd better know the facts before we go any further. First of all I'm going to take off without doing all the proper checks. Once the engine starts we don't want to be hanging around on the ground running up the engine. We want to attract as little attention as possible, so I'm just going to start up and go. That'll mean taking off with no certainty that the engine will keep going; the oil will be cold and the pressure will be low so the engine might cut out after take off. It will still be dark so there's no chance of a proper forced landing. We will both probably die if that happens. Then I'm going to keep low; five hundred feet. That way we won't appear on anybody's radar so they won't be able to track us. Again, one blip of the engine and that could be that. If it's dark or we're over the sea we'll probably not survive. Then there's the fuel. There's not much wind so it should take us about forty five minutes to reach the Irish coast. If we run out of petrol before then we've got very little chance. By the time we get to Ireland It'll be just about light, so we might manage to put down in a field or on a beach. We won't be using radio or showing navigation lights to avoid being spotted, but if anything goes wrong that also means there'll be no one to help us. Do you still want to do this?'

Simon reached out for her hand.

'Yes, absolutely,' he replied, 'we don't have a choice really, or at least I don't Nat. If you think it's too dangerous it's fine with me if we just run for it, but I'm not scared, not if you're not...I mean I'd rather like to see this through now.'

'Right, then, follow me,' she said, letting go of his hand and pulling herself onto the top of the metal wing and opening the cabin door. Natalie slid across into the left hand seat and Simon followed her, taking the seat nearest the door. Natalie reached across him and pulled the door closed with one hand while operating the catch with the other. Under Natalie's instruction Simon located the lap belt and strapped himself in. She passed him a bulky headset and gestured for him to put it on. Her voice sounded metallic and echoed in his ears, 'OK, it's getting lighter all the time, here we go.'

She operated a series of levers and knobs and the engine burst into life with a roar that was muted by the headphones. Almost immediately Natalie started to taxi the aircraft towards the barely visible runway. Without a pause she turned the aircraft onto the dark ribbon, heading towards the lightening sky and opened the throttle. The little aeroplane accelerated slowly at first, but rapidly gained momentum until, with a lurch, they were airborne and the darkness of the earth began to fall away as the pre-dawn glimmer from the east seemed to rise with them above the horizon. The engine note changed and a frisson of fear flushed through Simon's veins, but Natalie turned to him and grinned; her face illuminated by the glow from the instrument panel.

'Five hundred feet; that's high enough, let's get out of here.'

She levelled off and banked the aircraft to the left. The glow in the eastern sky moved slowly from straight ahead to their right. As they progressed northwards Natalie kept up a running commentary on the flight, pausing from time to time to adjust various controls. The lightening sky began to illuminate the ground below and Simon noticed that they were passing over the coastline and out into the Solway Firth. Natalie studied the map and announced that they would need to turn left again onto a heading for the northern tip of the Isle of Man. From the right hand seat Simon was filled with awe and admiration for the competence and self-assurance of the pilot beside him. There was no trace of the low self-esteem or vulnerability in the way she went about her business in the cramped cockpit and Simon realised that flying had been and would always be the most significant vehicle in Natalie's journey from her troubled past into an indeterminate future. He wondered what part he might play as a companion in that journey, hoping against hope that their current intimacy and deep affection would continue.

The eastern sky began to turn orange and the dark smudge of the Isle of Man became visible ahead of them. Natalie turned to him and grinned.

'Right on the button,' she exclaimed as she once again picked up the map and orientated it on her lap. 'About twenty one minutes,' she continued, 'I've plotted the course to overhead the old airfield at Bishops Court. The radar station was on Killard point so we should get a good look as we pass. I don't know what the airfield's like, but we might be able to get down there. It depends on what's around; we don't want to be seen or heard do we?'

With a gentle turn the aeroplane settled onto its new course as the rising sun painted a scattering of sparkling orange ripples on the sea below. As they closed with the coast though, thin tendrils of water vapour began to swirl past the windscreen, merging together ahead of them into a thin layer of misty cloud. Natalie slowed the aircraft and lowered the flaps to their first setting as she gently descended to stay in sight of the sea. Levelling off at three hundred feet the waves below were clearly visible.

'It's getting pretty ropey,' she announced, 'keep your eyes peeled for the coast, we won't have much chance to work out where we are in this, never mind land.'

Simon strained his eyes against the mist. Then suddenly, almost directly below the nose he made out the dark shape of a headland.

'There!' he shouted, pointing, 'land, just below.'

Natalie put the aircraft into a steep left hand orbit and glanced in turn at the shape of the land below and her map. On closer examination there were two headlands with a wide gap between them.

'That's the entrance to Strangford Lough,' said Natalie, 'I'm going to follow the Lough shoreline northwards, that should lead us directly to Newtownards airfield. It's right on the side of the Lough. We'll need to risk no-one seeing us arrive and then get away as quickly as we can.'

She rolled out of the orbit with the rocky coastline on their right and throttled back slightly as she held the aircraft about a hundred yards offshore. Ten minutes later a black asphalt runway loomed out of the mist and Natalie jinked the aircraft hard to line up the nose with the runway threshold. At that moment the engine spluttered and she deftly reached down to her left to change fuel tanks. The engine picked up again as she pulled on the lever between the seats to fully lower the flaps before pulling the throttle right back as the dark expanse of the runway appeared below the nose. The touchdown was smooth and Simon felt himself pushed forward in his seat as the pilot braked rapidly before turning right at the runway intersection and gently opening the throttle to taxi the aircraft towards the apron. Natalie parked the aeroplane neatly alongside several others before closing the throttle and weakening the mixture to stop the engine just as the sun broke through the mist above the eastern horizon. In the peculiar silence that followed they both removed their headsets. Natalie reached into the rucksack on the rear seat and fumbled about for a few moments before producing a notebook and a wad of banknotes. She scribbled a brief note.

Sorry about the unannounced early arrival, Please take the landing fee & top her up with 100ll.

She signed the note with the aircraft's registration number which she copied from a plate on the instrument panel before peeling off three fifty pound notes.

'We'll put this under the club house door,' she said, 'it might just buy us some time.'

Ten minutes later they were walking briskly along the Portaferry Road towards the town centre. Their arrival had appeared to have been unobserved. They were passed by on or two early morning commuters in their cars as they walked, but few people seemed to be up and about at that hour. A part demolished factory building offered them a temporary refuge and they slid through a narrow gap in the fence and sat down in the corner of a roofless building. Simon powered up the notebook and began to plan their next move.

Ten o'clock found them cycling back along the lake shore in the opposite direction to their airborne arrival; the sun having dispersed the last remnants of low cloud. Their first call after the shops had opened had been to an outdoor activity specialist where they had bought two smaller day-sacks to replace Natalie's rucksack; which they had dumped in a skip next to a partly-built house, waterproof jackets, woolly hats, a map and a pair of folding spades. From there they had sought out a bike shop and bough a pair of mid-range mountain bikes. Their final call was at a newsagent's where they stocked up on pre-packed sandwiches, chocolate bars and bottled water.

Despite the unfamiliarity of riding bicycles, they made good speed along the flat costal road and covered the nineteen miles to Portaferry in less than two hours including a ten minute stop for refreshments. They wheeled their cycles onto the ferry to make the short crossing of the mouth of Strangford Lough and settled onto a hard wooden bench.

'I'll tell you something,' Simon said quietly, 'my arse hurts.'

'Mine too,' replied Natalie.

'Well I'll just have to rub it better hadn't I?' replied Simon with a grin as he slid his arm around her narrow waist and then lower until his hand cupped her buttock.

Natalie felt all her resolve and reservations melt away as she nuzzled her face into his neck and kissed him gently. Perhaps there would be a way for them to stay together after all. Maybe they could go and live abroad; start a completely new life where no one would know about her past? At the back of her mind though was a persistent niggle that wouldn't completely go away. Why should he turn his back on his work and friends just to be with her? And what about all the God stuff that he had told her about? Did he still believe deep down, she wondered; and if he did what did that imply? Still, they were together for the time being; and very much in love. She had heard it said that love could conquer all. She wondered if she could dare to hope that it just might be true as the ferry pulled out into the Lough.

'Later,' she replied, nibbling his ear lobe, 'let's find ourselves a great big bed tonight.'

Re-mounting their bicycles on the concrete ramp leading from the Lough shore towards the small town of Strangford was a painful experience for both of them. The short enforced rest had allowed their muscles to relax and the discomfort of their saddles did little to help as they wobbled up the short hill. Once back on the open road Simon allowed Natalie to draw ahead and closed in behind her. From the back, he thought, she was unbelievably beautiful. In fact she was absolutely stunning from any angle. How could it be possible that someone like her could actually like someone like him, he wondered; someone as boring and ordinary; someone who had hidden himself away in a safe little world; someone who had thought himself content with his lot? Although he had no clear plan for what he would do if and when they retrieved Tim Ellwood's papers, he spent several long minutes daydreaming about a future with Natalie Robertson. Where would they live, he wondered? Should he travel to the USA with her while she gained her airline pilot's license? What then? Would they live somewhere close to an airport, or perhaps in her flat in Leeds or his house in Wroxham? Still musing on a rose-coloured future he was brought to an abrupt halt when Natalie braked hard and let her bicycle fall onto the grass at the side of the road. She had the map in her hand and was comparing it to the surrounding landscape. Simon lay down his cycle and went to stand beside her.

'I think this is the place, Simon,' she said softly, 'the place where Duggan killed your dad.'

They had stopped close to a small beach in a curved bay with high ground rising to the south. A short row of cottages lined the narrow road on the landward side. Simon looked over Natalie's shoulder at the map.

'Yes,' he said slowly, 'I think you're right.'

'Do you really hate him?' asked Natalie, 'Duggan I mean. I think I would if he had killed my dad....not that I know who my dad is anyway...'

Simon put his arm around her shoulder and drew her close.

'I don't know, Nat,' he replied, 'I didn't ever know my dad. I suppose I should hate him, but I just don't know. It's Michael or Terry or whoever he was...and Tim Ellwood. Now I can't help thinking something bad might have happened to Kynpham too and I feel responsible for that. I'm not sure that hate is the right word. I'm angry about it, but hate is different. Hate just eats you up. I want to try and do something about it, though. People often say that they want justice when what they mean is that they want revenge. I don't think I'm wired like that; to hate I mean. We all make mistakes; for goodness sake I've made enough, but I do think that Duggan needs to be stopped. Stopped before he does any more harm to anyone and stopped before he becomes Prime Minister. Only God knows what sort of stuff he'd get up to then.'

'Do you really mean that,' ventured Natalie hesitantly, 'er about God knowing. I don't think I believe in God, Simon. Could that be a problem between us..er..do you still believe and that?'

'I don't know what I believe about God any more, Nat. But I'll tell you what I do believe; I believe in you. You're the best thing that ever happened to me. Nothing is going to be a problem between us; nothing. I used to think that God had brought me and Sophie together; like us being married was what He had planned; that he was pleased about it. Look what happened. I don't blame Him or anything, what went wrong was our fault; Sophie's and mine, but I don't think it was really God's doing that Sophie cheated on me or got killed. Bad stuff happens and we can't just blame God. To answer your question the answer is probably "yes". I do believe in God, but I'm not sure what I really believe about Him any more. He's good, I know that, but I'm not sure people, especially people in the church have ever really got a handle on Him. Look, let's stop this conversation where it is. I love you, Nat. That's all that matters.'

'Shall we stay here a bit?' asked Natalie, 'do you want some space or something; because of your dad?'

'No, not now, Nat,' he replied, 'perhaps one day; after all this is over we'll come back. It would be nice to have a picnic here on a nice summer day and think about him, but I guess if he was here now he'd probably want us to get on with the job. It's not far to the old radar site now, just up the hill. Come on.'

They wheeled their bicycles up the hill and, just as the letter had described, there were two grey concrete plinths still standing on the cliff top. A layer of high cloud diffused the heat of the early afternoon sun and a stiff offshore breeze ruffled Natalie's hair as they stood next to the plinth. Simon took the folding spades from his bag and they began to dig. In less than five minutes they had found it; a medium sized Tupperware container housing around a hundred sheets of A4 paper. Simon wiped off as much soil as he could before peeling back the lid. The top sheets appeared to be almost undecipherable very poor quality photocopies of some sort of ledger. Below them were equally pale copies of what might be sales invoices and one or two almost illegible handwritten letters. The top three sheets were lifted from the box by the breeze and Natalie chased after them, managing to collect all three before they disappeared over the cliff top.

'Better put them back and have a proper look later,' suggested Simon as he replaced the lid.

'So what now?' asked Natalie, 'how do we use this lot to stop Duggan?'

'I'm not sure, Nat,' he replied, 'we're not too far from the Irish border. We could probably get across by tonight. That might keep the police off our scent, but I think Duggan must have some kind of private army as well. What we really need to do is to get the media interested without Duggan or the police cottoning on. I'm not sure that the Southern Irish press would be very interested, though.'

Natalie sat down on the plinth and pulled her waterproof coat around her shoulders in deference to the cool wind.

'Couldn't we just let him know what we've got; make copies or something and send him some samples?' she asked, 'we could threaten to publish them if he didn't withdraw from politics.'

'I don't think that would put us out of danger, Nat,' replied Simon, 'so long as we were alive he would be threatened, but if he got rid of us he could just carry on. I don't mind admitting that I'm scared. I don't know what to do for the best. I think we need to try and get back across to England. If we could get to London or somewhere we might find the BBC or someone who would have a look at the evidence.'

He sat down beside her and they stared out across the grey-blue Irish Sea towards the purple hills of the Isle of Man, which were clearly visible along the horizon. A fishing boat was chugging slowly out to sea from the mouth of Strangford Lough.

'I've got it!' exclaimed Simon, 'a boat. If we could just get hold of a small boat we could get over to the Isle of Man tonight. That might throw them off our trail.

'As long as we don't have to go by bike I'm up for anything,' said Natalie, rising to her feet. Simon studied the map. '

'There's a small town just to the south of us; Ardglass. The map shows a marina so we might find something or other. Come on, Nat, 'it's downhill all the way.

In the event they did not have to travel as far as the marina. They pulled up outside the village shop in Ballynahornan; a wayside hamlet on the Ardglass road to replenish their supply of chocolate and Natalie spotted a handwritten advertisement in the window. By three thirty they were the proud owners of a twelve foot inflatable boat with a ten horsepower outboard motor. The vendor had even driven Simon to the marina and back to enable him to buy and fill a large jerry can of petrol. The boat was on a trailer, which the vendor did not want to include in the sale but, again obliging, he had agreed to deliver the boat and outboard onto the beach opposite the former coastguard houses to the north of Killard Point where Simon had told him he and Natalie were renting a holiday cottage.

With no little trepidation on the part of her crew, the little craft had set sail with Simon and Natalie's meagre luggage stowed safely on board at three forty five in the afternoon. There was a slight swell running and, at full speed, waves broke over the bow of the boat. Simon reduced power and their abandoned bicycles on the shoreline slowly disappeared from view behind them as they huddled together in the stern, their few possessions contained in large plastic bin-liners that Simon had obtained from the marina along with the fuel can. Grey cloud obscured the sun and both of them, in turn, struggled into warmer clothing before zipping their waterproofs up to their necks.

CHAPTER THIRTY-TWO

The Chief Constable of Cumbria felt a perceptible sense of disquiet. He had arrived in his office at the usual time of seven thirty that morning to discover that a major manhunt was underway on his patch. Apparently the material witnesses to the murder of Detective Inspector Gilroy had been traced to a caravan site near Maryport the previous evening. Less than twelve months from his retirement, Ian Saunders was not afraid to speak his mind. He had immediately cancelled the manhunt, leaving just a few roadblocks in place on major routes. For the past few days he had become increasingly concerned about the hue and cry surrounding Simon Fenton and Natalie Robertson. Especially as the strongest suspect for the policeman's murder had already been found; albeit murdered himself.

The Chief Constable had been paid a visit by a Detective Inspector from ICIS shortly after his decision to scale down the search had become known. This, however, had left him less than impressed. He had paid little attention to the sharp suited cockney and little more to the subsequent telephone call from Detective Chief Superintendent Bell, the head of ICIS, who had informed him that there was considerable evidence to suggest that the pair were key links in a chain of drug traffickers. Ian Saunders had irritably requested that ICIS e-mail him some of the evidence and hung up. An hour and a half later; at ten fifteen, no e-mail had arrived bur there had been a telephone call from the Home Secretary. Mr. Duggan, it appeared, was keen that the fugitives were found and reiterated the ICIS suggestion that a major drugs ring was involved. The Chief Constable telephoned his counterpart in Manchester who apparently had also been pressurised by the Home Secretary to keep the case open. He had, he said, scaled back the investigation and only three detectives were active in following up leads and collating information. He also informed his colleague that there seemed to be a peculiar loose end with regard to the murder of Detective Inspector Gilroy. Apparently a hoax call alleging a sexual assault had been made by an un-named woman from the room in which Gilroy's body had been found the previous evening, but the officers following it up had been warned off by Gilroy himself. The Chief Constable of Greater Manchester police went on to speculate that the Home Secretary might be concerned with appeasing the popular press, which had taken some delight in the "Vicar and Tart" angle, to add kudos to his quest for higher office. Ian Saunders decided to follow his colleague's example. He allocated a Detective Inspector and three Constables to the inquiry and agreed to double the number of cars on patrol in North West Cumbria for the next twenty four hours.

The duty operations officer at Kirkbride airfield arrived at eight thirty. He filled the kettle in the clubhouse and then settled down with a mug of tea and the morning paper to await the arrival of any flying club members or aircraft owners who had decided to fly that day. After the recent run of goods weather most pilots had satiated themselves with flying hours and, with the forecast for a strengthening westerly wind and rain by late afternoon, he did not expect to be very busy. In fact it was almost lunchtime when the owner of an ex-RAF Chipmunk trainer arrived to fly; collecting the hangar keys from the clubhouse. Within minutes he had returned and reported that the locks on both doors were missing. The duty officer went out and verified the facts and was on his way back to the clubhouse when he realised that the elderly Piper Cherokee that usually inhabited the front space in the hangar was not there. A telephone call to the member of the owning syndicate responsible for collating bookings confirmed that no-one had booked the aircraft out. Utterly perplexed the duty officer made a telephone call to the local police station to report a stolen aircraft.

At Newtownards Aero Club the Duty Instructor had opened up the clubhouse at five past nine to find a three English fifty pound notes and a brief letter had been pushed under the door. Irritated that a flight seemed to have arrived without the requisite prior permission, she went out to inspect the line of parked aircraft. Sure enough the Cherokee was there; neatly parked alongside the other visiting aircraft. Grumbling to herself, she made out a docket for the landing fees and sought out the club mechanic; instructing him to put fifty litres of avgas in each wing tank. She then calculated the charges and fumbled about in the cash box for the correct change, which she put in an envelope. She would give the errant pilot a piece of her mind when he or she returned, she decided; after all rules were rules. It was not just the unauthorised arrival that bothered her. If the flight had originated on the mainland permission would also need to have been obtained for the flight from the Police Service of Northern Ireland. Having no way of knowing from where the aircraft had come, however, she decided against calling the police for the time being, fearing that she might look foolish if the aircraft had taken off from somewhere else in Northern Ireland.

Detective Chief Superintendent Jimmy Bell was still reeling from the dressing down he had received from the Home Secretary. Not only had the plan to lure the fugitives into a trap by using the journalist as bait failed miserably, the journalist was still alive; albeit in a coma with a fractured skull and potentially serious brain injuries. The hospital in Carlisle described him as "very poorly"; Eddie Duggan had described the situation in much less polite terms. To add to his woes, the Home Secretary had fielded concerns from the Chief Constables of both Greater Manchester and Cumbria complaining that the use of their resources in pursuing suspects who may or may not be involved as drug couriers was disproportionate to the seriousness of the alleged crimes. Although he had leant heavily upon them both, he suspected that both forces had scaled back their inquiries to a minimal level. Jimmy Bell had been given twenty four hours to bring matters to a satisfactory conclusion. His two acolytes had now been briefed quite specifically; the reporter, who was apparently under police guard in a the Cumberland Infirmary in Carlisle was not to be permitted to wake up and Simon Fenton, Natalie Robertson and any papers that were in their possession were to be taken out of circulation; permanently.

The Cumbria police made the breakthrough at two thirty in the afternoon. A quick witted detective constable on the Fenton and Robertson inquiry team was scrolling through crime reports for the last twenty four hours, hoping to discover the theft of a car in North West Cumbria when he stumbled across the report of a stolen aeroplane. He remembered that Natalie Robertson was a qualified pilot and put two and two together. He began telephoning airports and airfields throughout the country to check if the aircraft in question had arrived early in the morning. Unfortunately for the progress of the inquiry, however, he started with the large commercial airports whose names he was familiar with. It was ten to five when he struck gold in Northern Ireland.

The Police Service of Northern Ireland responded quickly to their Cumbrian colleagues' request for help and a patrol car reached the clubhouse at Newtownards just as the duty Instructor was about to lock up. An appeal for information, accompanied by photographs of Simon Fenton and Natalie Robertson, was carried by the TV stations in their late evening bulletins. By midnight information had been received indicating that the two fugitives may have bought bicycles from a shop in the town centre and another report suggested that they might have been on the Portaferry – Strangford ferry at lunchtime. Sean O'Mally, the man who had sold them the inflatable boat, also saw the report on the BBC ten o'clock news. Although he was no republican activist, O'Mally was Catholic by birth and tradition. His brother had suffered a beating at the hands of the Royal Ulster Constabulary for no more than whistling a revolutionary folk song in the late 1970s. He was no friend of the police. Despite recognising the photographs he chose not to call the number on the screen. He raised a glass of whiskey to his lips and silently toasted the man and girl; really pretty she had been, he thought; that bloke was a lucky bugger all right.

CHAPTER THIRTY-THREE

The fugitives' sea voyage had proved tiring, uncomfortable and, at times, alarming. The noise of the engine and the rhythmic slapping of the hull against the waves had made conversation all but impossible apart from during the two occasions that Simon and Natalie had needed to stop to refill the small tank on top of the outboard motor. On the second occasion the dark bulk of the Isle of Man seemed to fill the entire horizon and Simon briefly consulted their road atlas before re-starting the engine. They decided to head for a small bay on the southwest coast as it appeared to be remote and unpopulated. As they drew closer to the shore in the gathering gloom of twilight it began to rain and pools of water sloshed about under their low seat in the stern. It was almost fully dark when; wet and bedraggled, Simon and Natalie beached the boat in Fleshwick bay. They dragged the boat across the narrow beach into a small copse and upturned it between two bushes to provide a modicum of shelter from the now persistent rain. Simon dragged the faithful outboard motor into the copse behind them and they huddled together on a pair of black bin-liners, spread out on the ground to protect them from the damp eatrh below, utterly exhausted. Simon again powered up the notebook and immediately encountered a 'low battery" warning. In the few minutes remaining he managed to download am Isle of Man bus timetable and details of the ferry service between Douglas, the island's capital, and Heysham in Lancashire. If they walked the two and a half miles into Port Erin they could catch an early morning bus to Douglas that would get them there in time for the eight forty-five ferry.

The scrawny trees and a tangle of brambles sheltered them from the worst of the wind and the upturned hull of the boat did a fair job of keeping them dry. Simon and Natalie were both worn out, but their overnight accommodation was far from comfortable. A further change of clothing exhausted their supply of dry garments and they sat close together with their backs against a large tree stump in the darkness listening to the howl of the blustery wind and the intermittent patter of rain squalls on the foliage above them and the hull of the boat.

'So where do we go from Heysham?' asked Natalie.

'I'm not sure,' replied Simon, 'I think we need to find somewhere to hide up for a day or two. We could do with having a good look at Tim Ellwood's papers; not to mention a decent sleep. I still think the best bet is to get the papers to the press, but it all takes a bit of figuring out. I wish I knew what had happened to Kynpham. Perhaps the Independent would be the best bet if the BBC won't help. I hope he's OK. In any case I don't think we can do much until Monday, we really do need somewhere to stay until then.'

'Surely they won't have harmed him,' ventured Natalie, 'not if they're the proper police, anyway.'

'I don't think they were, the proper police I mean,' answered Simon, 'I think it was Duggan's thugs. I'm scared that I've led him into trouble. He could be dead for all we know.'

They shared out the last of their chocolate and sat glumly in the darkness. Simon rummaged in his bag and produced the roll of unused bin-liners, which he spread out under the upturned boat to permit them to lie down on the lumpy earth. Using their small bags as rough and ready pillows they both attempted to find a comfortable position. In spite of their fatigue neither of them was able to sleep and they lay close together in an uneasy silence. Replaying the day's events in his mind, Simon pondered Natalie's words spoken next to the beach where his father had been killed. He had surprised himself when he had put into words thoughts of which he had barely been conscious. It was true, he reflected, that he found hatred difficult. He had been deeply hurt by Sophie's betrayal. He had been badly bruised by the fact that the God he had given his life to had seemed strangely absent in his hour of need, but there was a deeper truth behind it. He had not actually stopped believing he realised, he had simply opted out of the implications of living out that belief. There had been no way in which he could maintain a public front, though. In his pain and grief he had found no comfort in his faith, but that same faith had not completely left him. It was true that he did not blame God for what had happened. He had tried to shoulder a large portion of any blame that might be going himself. That was probably one of the reasons that he had walked away from the church; not that many church people had offered him any more than vague platitudes. To discover that he still retained a spark of the life that he had pushed from his mind for so long was mildly disquieting. Natalie had been perceptive in asking him if his faith might cause a problem between then, he thought. For the first time since he had met her, a tiny niggle of reservation crept into his mind. He loved her. He loved her with everything that he was and everything that he had. There was no problem with that. Making love with her had been a beautiful and utterly all consuming experience. He had no regrets. Yet, a still small voice somewhere deep within his being reminded him of the obedient chastity of his pre-marital relationship with Sophie and a tiny spark of dissonance burnt a hole through the fragile membrane of his contentment.

Lying beside him, Natalie tossed and turned in an increasingly irritable discomfort. Her body hurt in too many places to count and she could not get even the least bit comfortable on the hard ground. She knew that she was utterly exhausted and willed her mind to close down, but thoughts continued to tumble round and round in her head. Not twenty four hours ago she had vowed to herself that it would not be fair on Simon to expect him to carry on a relationship with her if and when the Eddie Duggan issue was resolved. Where once there had been an aura of amorality, there now seemed to be a deep desire to do right by the man she had fallen for. How could she, a woman who had sold herself for sex, not because she needed the money to survive, but because she wanted to follow a selfish dream, dare to hope for true acceptance from someone like Simon? Even the way she had met him had been tainted by her sordid intent to have sex with him in return for a large amount of money. Yet the hope within her just would not die. With a degree of pride she recalled the early morning flight across the Irish Sea. It had been her; Natalie Robertson, who had flown a strange aircraft in dreadful weather into an unfamiliar airfield, helping the man she loved to escape the dragnet closing around them. In their present predicament she was not entirely useless, then; she had a part to play. She had never wanted anything in her life as much as she wanted a future with Simon, but she was dreadfully afraid that one day he would wake up and wish he had never set eyes on her. She had deliberately provoked him by suggesting that his faith could come between them, but she had a vague idea that his god had little time for prostitutes. In all honesty he would probably just want to get back to his old life when all this was over and she wouldn't blame him a bit if he did. He might even take up being a vicar again. Still there might just be a chance, if only a tiny chance, that he really meant all the wonderful things he had said to her. Perhaps, she thought as she rolled over onto her other side once again, she ought to back off a bit from the physical side of things for a while and spend the time really letting him get to know her; whoever she really was or whoever she might one day become.

The luminous hands of Simon's watch told him that it was not yet midnight. Sleep had remained elusive amid the damp discomfort of the tiny patch of woodland. Natalie seemed to have stopped moving around for the past few minutes, suggesting that she might have finally dropped off. Too tired to think straight, yet becoming increasingly anxious about both what to do with the plastic box of papers and about what his future with Natalie might hold he considered slipping away from the makeshift refuge and walking on the rain-swept beach, but fearing that moving would disturb her, he rolled over and tried to adjust the lumpy bag under his head into a more comfortable position. It was then that he found a temporary solution to one of his problems. The small bunch of keys that the solicitor had given him in Manchester the previous Friday poked him in the ear as he settled his head back down onto the bag. He had a house in Derby! A place in which it was unlikely anyone would be looking for them. He sat up and eased the keys out of the bag. Natalie stirred beside him.

'Nat,' he whispered, 'are you awake? I think I know where we can hide out when we get across the water.'

Five o'clock on Friday morning found them trudging slowly through the rain. A steep, narrow lane led inland from the beach and, having slept little if at all, Simon and Natalie had packed up their bags and dragged the discarded evidence of their presence on the island into the dense undergrowth on the landward side of the copse. In the pre-dawn darkness their aching limbs responded slowly and their progress was sluggish. Simon had calculated that the walk to Port Erin would take under an hour, but restlessness and anxiety had prompted an early start. Wearing their waterproof coats and woolly hats against the cool rain it took them almost half an hour to reach the summit of the lane. Before them lay a scattering of orange street lights, delineating the thoroughfares of the small town which lay at the foot of the hill. The streets were deserted as they passed dark houses and closed up shops in the first half-light of a grey dawn. The rain continued unabated and they finally arrived at the bus stand on the promenade with half an hour to wait for the Douglas bus. As the departure time approached a smattering of early-morning commuters joined them and a short queue had formed by the time the red and cream double-decker pulled in. They found seats near the back and the dry soporific warmth of the bus lulled them both into a doze as the bus meandered its way across the island.

It was still raining heavily when the bus disgorged its passengers onto the damp streets of Douglas an hour later. The cold morning air caused Natalie to shiver as she walked silently beside Simon the short distance to the ferry terminal. Anonymous in their baggy coats and woollen hats Simon booked their tickets and took advantage of the offer of the use of a four berth cabin for the three hour crossing. There was a short wait before boarding, but less than half an hour after stepping off the bus they were ensconced in the luxury of their cabin.

'A shower!' exclaimed Natalie as she threw off her damp clothing and turned on the tap. Simon looked on in admiration at her lithe naked form as he gathered up her clothes and, together with the soggy contents of their bags, laid them out on the top bunks. As she gyrated distractingly under the jet of hot water he plugged in the charger for the notebook and set it to charge before undressing himself. Natalie emerged wrapped in a large white towel and Simon took her place under the comforting stream of warm water. By the time he re-emerged she was fast asleep under the covers of one of the narrow bottom bunks. Within minutes Simon was also asleep in the opposite bunk.

CHAPTER THIRTY-FOUR

The trail in Northern Ireland had gone cold. No further sightings of Natalie Robertson or Simon Fenton had been reported. With a suggestion that they were most probably now in the South, the Senior Officer co-ordinating the search informed his colleagues in Cumbria and Greater Manchester and closed down his small team. The Chief Constables of the two mainland forces conferred once again and decided that they would pay only lip service to the demands of ICIS and the Home Secretary. To all intents and purposes the active search for the two fugitives was over.

Moreover the Chief Constable of Cumbria was becoming slightly uneasy about the activities of Inspectors Jewel and Cavendish. Upon learning that the victim of an apparent hit and run in a deserted Carlisle industrial estate was an up and coming journalist on a prestigious daily and that there was absolutely no trace of alcohol or proscribed substances in his bloodstream the Detective Inspector leading the investigation had posted a police guard on the side ward where he was fighting for his life. Apparently Paul Cavendish had appeared late the previous night showing an unexpected interest in the journalist's prognosis. The constable on duty had informed the Inspector in charge who, in turn, had mentioned the fact to the Chief Constable. Frustrated at what he saw as unwarranted interference in a local matter, he had bent the ear of the beleaguered Detective Chief Superintendent Bell in his London office demanding that his ICIS officers either shared their evidence with their colleagues in Cumbria or, as he put it, 'pissed of back to London.'

Eddie Duggan was like a bear with a sore head. Aware that his frantic quest for Natalie Robertson and Simon Fenton was beginning to draw unwelcome attention from his subordinates he instructed Jimmy Bell to recall Jewel and Cavendish and to make use of his contacts on the other side of the law to track them down. There had been another story in the tabloid gossip columns concerning his wife's late night revelries and he could sense that his one chance of higher office might be about to slip gently away.

Although Jimmy Bell had no shortage of contacts in low places, he was experienced and intelligent enough to know that, even if he called in every favour that he was owed, they had little chance of locating two people who could be anywhere between Dublin and Dungeness. He made one or two desultory telephone calls to a few old pals before checking his office safe for the passport he kept in a name that was not his and a bundle of bearer bonds and financial documents which were also held in the name in the passport. He slipped the documents into a thick brown envelope and stowed it in his brief case. If things went totally pear shaped he did not want to have to return to his office.

In Carlisle, a neurosurgeon was just completing a delicate operation to patch up the damage to Kynpham Johal's skull. There was still a worrying amount of brain swelling, but a scan had shown that the clot-busting drugs were doing their stuff. Although he was still officially described as "poorly", the prognosis for the journalist had significantly improved over the last twelve hours. After some complicated detective work his family in India had been traced and the man's sister was booked on a flight leaving Delhi the next morning; his parents apparently being too old and frail to contemplate such a long journey.

CHAPTER THIRTY-FIVE

A voice over the ship's public address system announcing their imminent arrival in Heysham roused Natalie from her sleep. Rubbing her eyes, she swung her legs over the side of the bunk and stretched. The pain from her exertions on the bicycle had dulled slightly and she dressed quickly and began to pack the two bags while Simon slept on. The bump of the ferry's hull against the pier signalled their arrival and Natalie shook Simon gently to wake him. By the time Simon was dressed disembarkation had begun and they were able to walk ashore through a light drizzle and into the austere greyness of the adjoining railway station. A notice informed them that the one and only train of the day was due to depart at one thirty for Lancaster and Leeds. Around half a dozen other passengers were scattered on benches along the solitary functioning platform. While Simon powered up the ubiquitous notebook once again to plan their onward journey Natalie ventured out into the small town in search of food and drink. When she returned with fish and chips twenty minutes later Simon informed her that the BBC News website was carrying the story that Kynpham had been seriously injured in a hit and run in Carlisle. He was in hospital and said to be "very poorly". Simon had little appetite for his meal and Natalie sat silently beside him; holding his hand as the fat congealed on the cooling fish and chips.

'It's all my fault, Nat,' he whispered, 'I knew it might be dangerous. Oh shit! What if he dies or ends up a vegetable or something. What on earth have I done?'

'Shh,' Natalie placed her finger gently on his lips, 'he wanted to help. You're his friend. It might not be as bad as that.'

'Shit, Nat, it is bad, though. If they tried to kill him once they'll probably try again,' he muttered.

Natalie squeezed his hand.

'I don't know what to say, Simon,' she said softly, 'except that it was me that got you into this and I'm sorry.'

'No it wasn't,' replied Simon, looking directly at her, 'your fault I mean. If it wasn't you they would have just found another way to get me. What you did was save my life. Anyway, whatever happens I don't regret being here with you. I just wish we could do something to help Kynpham.'

'We've got the papers,' replied Natalie, 'perhaps we can end all this in a day or two?'

'Let's hope so,' replied Simon, 'the good news is that there's nothing about us on the web. Perhaps they're losing interest. We still need to be careful, though. Duggan will still be after us I'm sure.'

Holding hands on the hard metal seat, they waited patiently for the train to arrive. Simon explained that he thought they should just book a ticket to Lancaster on the train in case the conductor recognised or remembered them later. At Lancaster they would book to Manchester, but get off at Bolton and from Bolton they would book tickets to Buxton but get off at the wayside station of Furness Vale. There was a bus service from Manchester to Derby which passed Furness Vale and they could travel onwards on that. Simon suggested that they alight at either Belper or Duffield then take a taxi to Chester Green, but not quite all the way to the house. He said that he hoped the convoluted journey would cover their tracks. Eventually the short train trundled slowly into the platform and disgorged its complement of passengers for the afternoon ferry. Still hand in hand Natalie and Simon got on and their odyssey continued.

The journey towards Derby continued along the lines that Simon had planned. They left the little train at Lancaster and booked their new tickets before boarding the Trans-Pennine Express to Manchester. The train was busy with Friday afternoon travellers and they were not able to sit together. Perched on a tip-up seat next to the door, Simon's thoughts returned to his friend fighting for his life less than a hundred miles north of their present location. A huge burden of guilt descended upon him like a dark cloud. In all his previous troubles, Kynpham was one of only two friends who had always been there for him. Kynpham had never tried to pontificate or preach to him and, despite the Indian's strong personal faith he had never given the slightest hint that Simon's own spiritual crisis was in any way a failure or a matter of religious culpability. Now Kynpham was badly injured and he was unable to help in any way, well, any way except maybe to pray for his friend. In the silence of his heart Simon called out to the God he had all but ignored since Sophie's death, asking him to be with his friend and to heal him. Feeling slightly foolish and quite acutely hypocritical he looked up from the floor and watched the passing countryside under its thick overcoat of scudding grey cloud.

The damp windswept platform of Bolton railway station provided an inhospitable welcome to the weary travellers. A short expedition to the ticket office provided them with tickets for the next leg of their journey before the warm sanctuary of the station buffet drew them into its garish interior. Seated at a small table with insipid coffee and unappetising sandwiches, Natalie and Simon began the forty minute wait for the Buxton train.

'My arse still hurts,' whispered Natalie.

'Mine too,' replied Simon.

'Do you want me to massage it?' asked Natalie innocently, a sparkle in her eyes.

Simon was instantly jerked from his period of introspection.

'Only if I can do yours first,' he replied, stifling a giggle. Natalie reached across the table and took his hand.

'Just you wait, Simon Fenton,' she said quietly, 'when we get to that house of yours I'm going to show you just how much I love you.' All her fears melted away as he smiled back at her. She would do whatever it took to stay with this man, she decided, pushing away her resolve not to burden him with her past. A love like theirs would surely find a way through any difficulties. In any case they had a whole weekend alone together to look forward to.

'Simon', she said, 'I know that you feel bad about what happened to Kynpham; and I know that we've probably got a few more problems ahead of us, but do you think we could just try and get to know each other a bit better this weekend?'

Simon smiled.

'I know, Nat, nothing that's happening at the moment is your fault. There's nothing we can do for Kynpham; or about Duggan at the moment, so yes. Let's just spend time together. I can't wait to stop travelling for a bit. I've no idea what the house will be like, but let's make the most of our time together...' He had been about to say *because we don't know what will happen on Monday,* but he held back. Monday could take care of itself, he thought. Saturday and Sunday belonged to them.

Their next train was also busy, but they managed to squeeze together on a seat, drawing comfort and hope from their enforced proximity. An hour later they were walking wearily up the short slope from the railway station onto the main A6 in search of their bus stop. It was raining again and they were once again damp and cold by the time the gaudy green "Trans-Peak" bus pulled up a quarter of an hour later.

Condensation masked the view from the window. At Natalie's suggestion Simon began to tell her anecdotes about his childhood; he told her about his earliest memories of his grandparents; of his first day at school; of his early friendships and falling outs. By the time he began to tell her about his secondary school he found that she was no longer listening. Natalie was fast asleep on the seat beside him. The bus wove its way through the rain-drenched towns and villages of the Peaks and Dales; passengers joining and leaving at almost every stop. The journey gave him time once again to think. The anticipation of a weekend of domestic simplicity with the girl that he loved filled his mind but, once again a faint but persistent sense of unease and foreboding took the edge from his happiness. Even if it proved possible to circumvent Eddie Duggan and escape from their present predicament he had a feeling that there might still prove to be troubled waters ahead. While the prospect of returning alone to his former humdrum existence now seemed unthinkable he was quite unable to articulate any coherent alternative in his mind. Yes, he wanted to be with Natalie; there was no doubt about that, but he could not visualise the what, where and how of that might come about. He wiped the condensation from the window beside him and watched the wets pavements pass by in the orange glow of the early street lights which were fending off the gathering darkness.

Natalie was awakened from her sleep by Simon shaking her by the shoulder.

'We've just passed a Supermarket, Nat,' he said, 'it's a good place to get off.' Rising unsteadily to her feet, Natalie picked up her bag and tottered down the aisle while Simon pressed to bell. They emerged into the rain opposite a small cottage hospital.

'It's back the way we've come,' announced Simon,' about a quarter of a mile. We're in Belper; about six or seven miles from Derby. We can pick up a taxi at the supermarket.'

'We could do a bit of shopping as well,' suggested Natalie, 'we'll need bread and milk and stuff won't we?'

A five minute walk brought them to a Morrison's which was set back from the main road behind a large car park. They collected a small trolley and perambulated up and down the aisles choosing a variety of everyday essentials. Simon added a new pair of mobile phones, explaining that one of their old ones may have been traced via Kynpham's. Burdened with baggage, they called a minicab from the public telephone in the lobby and waited under the shelter of the canopy. It was dark when the cab arrived and the rain was getting even heavier. The journey into Derby took less than a quarter of an hour. Simon paid the elderly driver as he dropped them off outside the church in Chester Green. Ominously, the city's police headquarters was opposite and they set off rather furtively on the short walk to the junction with Chester Green Lane. The lane proved to be a cul-de-sac, running at right angles to the main road. The small terraced houses were huddled on each side of the deserted street, their front doors opening directly onto the pavement. They located number twenty two, about half way along. Simon took the small bunch of keys from his coat pocket and managed to open the door with the second key he tried. Natalie led the way into a small lobby, fumbling on the wall for a light switch.

'Hold on Nat,' cautioned Simon, 'we don't want to draw attention to ourselves. Leave the lights for now; let's try and have a look round first.' He pulled the external door closed behind them.

As their eyes became accustomed to the gloom it became apparent that the lobby led into a square living room containing a fabric-covered armchair and a matching sofa. There was a wide-screen television in the corner and a large coffee table in the centre of the room. They gingerly crossed the room and passed through another door on the far side. On their left a staircase led upwards, while the rest of the space contained a small kitchen area, a dining table and four chairs accompanied by two battered armchairs next to a gas fire. At the rear another door led into what was obviously the bathroom. Simon crossed the floor and peered out through the window. Behind the house was a small yard bounded by a high wall. On the other side of the wall was a series of pre-fabricated buildings which appeared to be some sort of industrial area. Simon retraced his steps and closed the door behind them as Natalie found the light switch. The room was a little musty, but had obviously been cleaned and tidied since its former inhabitant's death. The fridge was empty and smelled faintly of disinfectant. Simon plugged it in and was rewarded with a reassuring hum as Natalie began to unload their shopping onto the table. Leaving Simon to prepare a simple meal, she ventured upstairs.

'There's a double bed in both rooms,' she called down, 'I've shut the front room door to keep us secret.... Oh here's the airing cupboard.... there's clean bedding and a quilt... I'll make the bed up.'

By the time she returned Simon had produced a simple meal of omelettes and toasted teacakes and they sat comfortably at the table to eat.

'I think I'll have a go at getting the television set up in here,' said Simon as they sipped mugs of tea. 'We don't want to go into the front rooms if we can help it. I'm pretty sure we're safe here for a few days, but we'd better not take too many chances.'

'I'm knackered,' replied Natalie, 'I'll go and warm the bed up. Don't be long, Simon.'

In the event it took him longer than he had anticipated. There was an aerial point in the kitchen, but the TV went into some kind of auto-setup mode when he connected it and, following the on screen prompts, it took him a while to get the channels tuned in. When he eventually climbed the stairs and found the bedroom Natalie was fast asleep. She was lying face up in the semi darkness and had thrown the quilt cover aside, exposing the naked form of her body. Smiling inwardly, Simon stripped down to his boxer shorts and crawled in beside her. Whatever happened next, he thought, he would do absolutely everything in his power to love, protect and cherish this wonderful girl. The trace of a smile was still visible on his face when he too dropped off to sleep moments later.

CHAPTER THIRTY-SIX

As the urban sprawl of Delhi faded into the mist below Rebecca Johal settled her petite frame back into her window seat aboard the British Airways Boeing 777 as it began its eight and a half hour journey to London Heathrow. The previous twelve hours had passed in a blur. The telephone call from the hospital in England had been made at lunchtime. Upon her return from her work as a teacher in the Bishop's Lower Primary School in the former Hill Station of Shillong in North East India Rebecca had stumbled into the midst of a family in chaos. Her mother, confined to a wheelchair because of severe arthritis, was sobbing uncontrollably while her father was pacing up and down wringing his hands risking, in Rebecca's opinion, another heart attack. Kynpham, it appeared had suffered a serious injury somewhere in the north of England and was dangerously ill. Her father intended to fly out immediately, but her mother was afraid for his health and had suggested that Paul, their eldest child should go instead.

The Johals were very wealthy by Indian Standards. Rebecca's father had made his money in property development; buying small plots of land carved out of the steep hillsides in the bustling city and building residential and commercial developments which he then sold at a healthy profit as property prices had rocketed upwards. Their three eldest children, Paul, Peter and Lumlang, all worked in the business. Paul, in his early forties, was now to all intents and purposes the driving force behind the firm and was ably assisted by the other two who were in their late thirties. The twins, Kynpham and Rebecca, had come along later. Now twenty five years old, Rebecca had lived as a pampered and rather spoiled girl for most of her life. After graduating from University in Delhi four years previously she had been given a junior position in the family firm but had taken advantage of her status as the boss' daughter to do as little actual work as possible while enjoying a salary which far outstripped her contribution. After a couple of years she had finally thrown in the towel and abandoned the pretence, choosing instead to travel in Europe. It had been while she was staying with her brother in Norfolk that she had rediscovered her dormant Christian faith. Her father was a Lay Reader at Shillong Cathedral. The three eldest children had attended worship regularly all their life; giving great pride and joy to their father. Kynpham too had not wavered in his faith, but she had kicked her heels as a teenager and had not been seen at Sunday worship since she left for university. With the benefit of hindsight she realised that her restlessness and indolent lifestyle were symptoms of a deeper spiritual hunger. Within the gentle fellowship of believers that she had been readily welcomed into while staying with her brother; she found the peace and contentment she had craved. Upon her return to Shillong she had immediately volunteered to teach; for a nominal salary, at the Bishop's School. The school served families at the extreme of poverty and those facing social taboos. The children of beggars, prostitutes and vagrants were educated free of charge and provided with a hot meal every day through the generosity of local Christians. In her work Rebecca found true fulfilment and a purpose for her life.

When the other two brothers arrived a full family meeting was convened. All the children present agreed with their mother. Father was far too ill to embark upon such a journey. Paul was in the midst of heavy negotiations regarding the prospective sale of a new office block, so the early consensus favoured Peter. Apart from attending Kynpham's graduation ceremony in Norwich, however, he had never been out of the country and was obviously a little anxious at the prospect. When Rebecca had volunteered there had been a stunned silence, followed by a dawning realisation that she was probably the right choice after all. Her English was fluent and she had spent several weeks in England two years previously. Moreover she had already obtained a six month tourist visa for the UK in anticipation of a trip planned for the long school holidays which started at the end of November. Within minutes she was packing her bag while her father telephoned the school principal to obtain permission for her to have leave of absence. Meanwhile Paul had booked her air tickets over the internet: a helicopter trip from Shillong to the nearest regional airport at Guwahati leaving in just over an hour followed by a late evening Kingfisher Airlines flight to Delhi from where she could catch the early morning British Airways service to London. Without her having time to catch her breath Paul had driven her to the heliport in his jeep and pressed a large bundle of thousand rupee notes into her hand to cover expenses. After an uncomfortable night at the airport she had virtually cleaned out the foreign exchange desk by swapping her rupees for one thousand five hundred and eighty four pounds sterling before boarding her international flight.

As the aircraft climbed out of the hazy cloud the white peaks of the Himalayas became visible to the north. Rebecca Johal slowly drank a cup of tea while she collected her thoughts. She ran a hand through her straight black hair, which framed an attractive, small-featured brown face, and closed her eyes. Although deeply anxious and upset by the news of her twin's condition, she was forced to concede that compassion had not been her only motive in volunteering for the trip. She was very much hoping that she would get the chance to meet up with Simon Fenton again.

CHAPTER THIRTY-SEVEN

Eddie Duggan was caught up in a whirl of political manoeuvring which left him little time to plan his next move. He was fairly certain that the potentially damning evidence was in the hands of Simon Fenton. Unusually for a Saturday, though, he was scheduled to host a seminar for aspiring Chief Constables in a central London hotel. Following that he had a conference call scheduled with the BBC to agree in principle the nature of the questions that would be put to him the following morning on the Andrew Marr programme. While there was a the clear potential for the interview to provide the sound-bites he needed to help boost his campaign for the highest office he would have little chance to confer with his acolyte in ICIS. The Home Secretary decided that it would be best to visit his acolyte and the two remaining henchmen in the ICIS office after his return from the BBC the next morning. He consoled himself with the thought that at least his wife had not disappeared again for a day or two as he sat glumly in his car being driven into the city in the dampness of early morning.

Jimmy Bell had spent the previous evening and most of the hours of darkness making a contingency plan. Things had reached the point where he could no longer attempt to bring pressure to bear on senior officers in regional police forces. The Chief Constables of Greater Manchester, Cumbria and now the Police Service of Northern Ireland had let it be known in no uncertain terms that they did not feel that a major search operation for Simon Fenton and Natalie Robertson was justified by the almost total lack of any substantive evidence of wrongdoing. Indeed, the senior officer from Cumbria had as good as told him that he suspected that there was some kind of inappropriate interest in the couple emanating from ICIS. Bell had little doubt that Eddie Duggan would fall from grace without dragging his long time partner with him. The options were stark; either to get hold of the incriminating papers and make Simon Fenton and the girl disappear or to make a run for it leaving his salary, pension and good name behind. Over the years he had accumulated more than two million pounds in ill gotten gains. A quarter of a million was tied up in bearer bonds, stored in his safe. A further hundred and fifty thousand he had in cash, stowed away safely in the loft of his house. The remainder he had injudiciously invested in the development of a holiday villa complex on the Costa Brava three years previously. Spanish property prices had bombed ahead of the so-called credit crunch and there still seemed little prospect of recovery. The one and a half million he had invested was now apparently worth less than a third of that – even if it was possible to find a buyer. Realistically he could only rely on around four hundred thousand plus whatever he could raise on his house before he left. While he could flee the country easily enough, he was far from certain that, even in a part of the world where the cost of living was low, there would be enough money to keep him in comfort for the rest of his life. He logged on to the internet and clicked on the Halifax Online website. The balance of his mortgage was a little more than sixty two thousand pounds. More significantly there was a drawdown facility for a further eighty five thousand. He clicked on the various boxes and requested that the full amount be transferred to his current account. On the Nat West website he applied for a personal loan of twenty five thousand pounds on the pretext that he was buying a new BMW.

With more hope than expectation he had made a series of early morning telephone calls to a variety of underworld contacts and private detective agencies to remind them of the need to keep a good look out for Natalie Robertson and Simon Fenton. He then called Paul Cavendish and Gerry Jewel, recalling them to London for a conference the following morning. He also, pretending to be a close friend and colleague, checked on Kynpham Johal's progress at the Cumberland Infirmary. After some wrangling about him not being a relative he managed to persuade the ward sister to tell him that the operation had gone well, but the young man had not yet regained consciousness; nor was he likely to for a two or three days as he was still under heavy sedation.

In the cold grey dawn that Saturday morning, Bell concluded that unless Fenton, Robertson and the journalist were taken out of circulation by Wednesday at the latest he would have no alternative but to make his escape. Using a credit card belonging to the alter-ego of his false identity he booked a seat on a flight to Rio de Janeiro leaving at half past eight on Thursday morning.

CHAPTER THIRTY-EIGHT

Natalie awoke to the sound of birds singing. As the dull morning light penetrated the thin curtains she gradually recalled where she was and how she had come to be there. She was lying on her side with her right hand resting on the pillow just behind Simon's head. The warmth of his body next to hers and the now familiar smell of him in the bed beside her brought her a surge of reassurance. He was snoring gently, still fast asleep. Natalie slid her hand around his broad back and gently ran her fingers through the hair on his chest. He made a small groaning sound, but remained defiantly asleep. Natalie's hand began to make its mischievous way downwards, across his lower abdomen and then beneath the elastic in the waistband of his shorts. He would be wide awake soon enough, she thought.

Exhausted by their love-making Simon and Natalie lay naked on the bed. With all their anxieties and reservations temporarily forgotten, they maintained a light-hearted banter, arguing about which one of them most deserved to be treated to breakfast in bed by the other. After a while Natalie graciously gave in and pulled on a long t-shirt and a pair of briefs. When she returned with tea and toast Simon was asleep again. She put the tray down on the bedside table and retreated to the kitchen where she opened the Tupperware box and began to leaf through the upper layers of its contents.

Simon finally arrived in the kitchen; fresh from the shower, to find that Natalie had began to sort the papers into a number of piles.

'Look,' she said, 'once you decipher this lot it's easy to see what was going on.' She held up a sheet of paper and tilted it against the light from the window and the pale grey typescript became easier to read. 'This is a list of cars bought at an auction in March 1983. The prices and mileages are listed beside the registration numbers.' She picked up a separate bundle of papers. 'There are sales invoices; the registration numbers and mileages check out. The deposit shown is either ninety nine pounds or a part exchange allowance.' Natalie put the papers down and picked up a third pile. 'These are sales invoices for the same cars, but on all but three they show cash deposits of between five hundred and a thousand pounds; even on top of the part exchange. That must be how he was putting illegal money into the business. These,' she gestured to yet another sheet of paper, 'are entries from some kind of accounts book that show the higher prices. I've done March and April so far and the same pattern is there.'

'So there's proof of money laundering,' commented Simon as he filled and switched on the kettle. 'Is there evidence of any more scams there?'

'I don't know,' replied Natalie, 'I've only looked at the top few sheets so far.'

Simon made tea and they began to make plans for the weekend. Natalie pointed out the lack of washing powder and the bedraggled state of much of their clothing. She suggested either a trip to the supermarket or a further shopping expedition. Taking the cue Simon encouraged her to join him in a trip to the city centre; they could also pick up some washing powder while they were out, he ventured. Fortified with tea and cakes they donned their all enveloping waterproofs and ventured out through the back door and along a short alley way into the rain once again.

A short walk brought them into the centre of Derby. The rain drove them into a large shopping centre where they replenished their stock of clothing from a selection of department stores but, somehow the light-hearted spontaneity of their earlier bout of retail therapy in Carlisle was absent. Increasingly preoccupied with the challenge of persuading either the BBC or the Independent to run the corruption story on Eddie Duggan, Simon allowed Natalie to choose a couple of casual outfits for him as well as several for herself. An air of deep-rooted anxiety permeated the experience for him. It was as if the weekend was marking some sort of transition between a lovely, but haunting, idyll with a wonderful girl and the grim reality of holding on to her when some kind of normality returned. He had experienced a faint pang of pre-conditioned guilt, but no real regret, after they had made love that morning. Concerned that he might be taking advantage of the girl in the difficult situation they were in had taken the edge from his joy. Although his love for Natalie was undiminished he feared for their future together and began to seriously doubt that a girl as attractive, intelligent and wonderful as her would find him so attractive if and when the time came when they were not held together by circumstances.

Natalie too felt a shift in the dynamic of their relationship that afternoon. It was as if things were drawing inexorably towards some sort of climax. Not just in terms of their success or failure in exposing Eddie Duggan, but also in the transition of her relationship with Simon from the overwhelming intensity of first love into something more tangible; something that she half dreaded. A place in which the cliché of vicar and tart might just spell the end of a dream that she held so closely to her heart. As she stood waiting patiently for Simon to emerge from the gents' toilet she mouthed a silent prayer to someone or something she was almost certain did not actually exist;

God, if you are ther, and as it says on the busses you probably aren't, just give me a sign, will you. Just tell me somehow that it's all going to be all right.....oh shit, no sorry, you don't approve of language like that do you? .... oh bugger, just tell me...if you're there that is....and if you're not, well...well if you're not I'm turning into a bit of a loony aren't I?

They soon tired of shopping amongst the Saturday afternoon crowds and sought out a pizza restaurant where they had a late lunch before, burdened with their purchases, they took a taxi back to the main road close to their little temporary sanctuary.

CHAPTER THIRTY-NINE

Making up for the uncomfortable night she had spent at the airport, Rebecca Johal had slept for most of the flight to London. The moving map display on the seat back in front of her showed that the aeroplane was flying over Germany when she woke up. An attentive steward brought her tea and sandwiches as she peered out of the window at the dark green patchwork of fields visible through gaps in the grey clouds. Simon Fenton; she had been thinking about him when she dropped off to sleep. She had first met him at Kynpham's graduation ceremony on her first visit to England. He had been a curate at the Church her brother had attended. Rebecca remembered him as he had been then; tall and broad shouldered with longish hair and a neat beard. Kynpham had introduced them and she had immediately checked out his left hand, finding to her disappointment a wedding ring on his finger. Later on she had asked her brother about him. Apparently he was married to a workaholic corporate lawyer. Kynpham had grinned at her and told her to keep her hands off. She had grinned back and announced that she would do exactly as she liked. In truth there had been several romantic liaisons during her time at university and she had lost her virginity to a tall postgraduate student from Agra during the first term of her second year, but she had tired of the Indian attitude to women which, even in the twenty first century, frequently consigned them to the role of mother and homemaker as soon as they married. Her secret hope on this first trip to England was to meet a man who would treat her as an equal. Rebecca had been ready for romance and, marriage apart, Simon Fenton had fitted right into her fantasy.

Back home again she had played the role of the wealthy single woman with gusto and although there had been one or two sexual encounters, her outspokenness and feisty attitude to the cultural norms surrounding her had dissuaded any serious potential suitors. She had also strongly resisted the efforts of her parents and older brothers to arrange a suitable match. It had been on her second visit to England that things had changed. Her ready acceptance into the warmth of the Christian community had surprised her. In England, it appeared, women were seen as important in the life of the church as men. In addition, the big skies and green countryside of Norfolk had given Rebecca time to take stock of her life and for her dimly remembered God to whisper his words of love and acceptance into her heart. With the rekindling of her faith came a wholesale shift in her attitudes and priorities and, in the background to this life-changing experience had been Simon Fenton. Only a few months after the death of his wife he had been living in the vicarage but taking no part in the life of the church. He and Kynpham, however, seemed to have become close friends and she had joined in wholeheartedly with her brother's mission to draw the grieving man out of both his vicarage and his despair. They had dragged Simon along on several day trips that autumn. She had cooked the three of them a couple of Indian meals at Kynpham's flat and, on one occasion, she had persuaded Simon to accompany her to the cinema to see a film that her brother had seen already. Throughout her gentle courting of him though, she had remained sensitive to the rawness of his grief and had made no overt moves. Realising that any reciprocation of her interest would not be either appropriate or likely for many months in the future, she had returned to her homeland with a new sense of purpose and the hope that one day she and Simon Fenton might become more than friends. Before she had left she had confided her hopes in Kynpham, who had wisely replied that either her preoccupation with Simon would soon fade away once she got home and was therefore no more than infatuation or would remain until an appropriate time in the future when she might visit again. Since then Simon Fenton had figured significantly in their exchanges of e-mails. She learned from her brother that he had left his work in the church and moved out into the countryside, finding employment in an office. Later, when Kynpham had moved to a new job in London, she was relieved to learn that the two men had remained close friends. Throughout the months since her visit that time Rebecca had sought and received Kynpham's reassurance that he had not even hinted to Simon of her feelings for him. Although slightly disturbed that Simon's faith seemed to have, as Kynpham put it, "gone into hibernation" she still dared to hope that she might soon become part of God's plan for waking it up. Gazing at the clouds below, she pulled the crumpled print out of her brother's last e-mail sent two weeks previously out of her pocket and re-read the last paragraph for the umpteenth time;

And now to the matter of Simon Fenton, dear sister. He does not seem quite so sad these days, although he is not yet fully back into the fold of the church. I think that he would never admit it, but there is now perhaps some small space in his life for a new romance. I have, as you know, a photograph of you on top of the fireplace in my flat and when he visited at the beginning of July he picked it up and asked for news of you, so he had not forgotten your last visit completely. If you were to arrange to come and stay with me after your school ends for the long holiday in November perhaps it would be possible for the two of you to spend some time together, but go gently, sister, for he may yet be a little fragile. What I can say is that it would be a great joy for me if my twin sister and my closest friend here in England could bring happiness into one another's' hearts.

May God bless you,

Kynpham

Rebecca folded the paper and pushed it back into the pocket of her jeans. The visit had come a little earlier than she had anticipated. Her brother was seriously hurt and he would, of course, be her first priority. Surely, though, his closest friend would have learned of his accident and have travelled to be with him. There was a very real possibility, she thought, that that very day she would come face to face with Simon Fenton again. As the note of the engines changed and the aircraft began its descent towards Heathrow Rebecca took a deep breath and began to pray silently to her God for the safety and well-being of both of the men who meant so much to her.

CHAPTER FORTY

Paul Cavendish was exhausted. With Gerry Jewel by his side he had driven the three hundred miles from Carlisle to North London in just under six hours. It had been a tiring journey. Since running over the wooden palette while attempting to run down Kynpham Johal, the Vectra had developed a bad habit of veering to the left and he had needed to make constant small corrections to the steering wheel. In addition there had been an accident on the M6 south of Preston that had slowed them to a crawl for nearly an hour. Jimmy Bell did not want to see them until ten the next morning so, after dropping Jewel off outside his home in Palmers Green, Cavendish was making slow progress through the Saturday tea-time traffic on the North Circular on his way to his studio flat in Tottenham Hale. He knew that he ought to try and have the car's steering looked at by a garage rather than the police mechanics in case there were any traces of the collision with the Indian reporter, but the garages would soon be closing. Perhaps he would be able to call in a Kwik-Fit or somewhere after the meeting with the boss the next morning. In any case he was knackered. A hot curry, a few beers and a night with his feet up in front of the telly was what he needed.

For some reason that he found hard to understand, Eddie Duggan's young wife seemed to be in a particularly affectionate mood when he returned from his engagement with the budding Chief Constables. It was as if, without using words, she was trying to put things back onto an even keel after her late-night revelries. She had dismissed the staff and greeted him as he came through the door wearing only a lacy black bra with a matching thong, suspenders, stockings and a pair of patent leather shoes with ridiculously high heels. For over an hour they had performed a series of sexual gymnastics in various rooms and positions before, utterly drained, he had finally collapsed in a heap on their queen-sized bed. In the indolent afterglow even his worries about Simon Fenton receded into the background of his mind. The call from the BBC half an hour later confirmed that there were no potentially damaging questions planned for him the following morning. He knew from the anti-terrorist unit that they had a major operation underway in more than a dozen towns and cities across the country and, although they were still several days away from making several co-ordinated dawn raids on a number of addresses, he felt that the time was probably right to give an obscure hint about the importance of homeland security and the high priority he had given it during his time as Home Secretary. If he played his cards skilfully there would be a stock sound-bite from the recording of the Andrew Marr programme ready for when the operation took place; just before the Party Conference. Things might not be looking too bad after all.

Jimmy Bell was at home. The strain of the past week had taken its toll and he found it increasingly difficult to come up with any coherent plan of action. It was most likely, he thought, that Fenton and the girl had crossed the border into the Irish Republic; possibly posing as a couple on a cycling holiday. It was also probable that they had whatever paperwork the Governor was afraid of. What would he do if it he was in their shoes? He knew full well that Eddie Duggan had killed Fenton's father in cold blood. From behind the barbed wire fence enclosing the radar station he had witnessed it himself that night in the early spring of 1975. If only... he thought...if only he had reported it as he should have done instead of confronting Duggan and demanding a share of the spoils. Duggan had readily agreed to his request, but only on the condition that he reduced the number of others with a claim on the booty. Since then he had killed them all; every one of the surviving members of the patrol.

With his share he had purchased his discharge from the RAF, put a deposit down on a small house in Colindale and applied to join the Met. His application proved successful and, after his training and probationary period, he had opted for the CID. That was when he had run up against Eddie Duggan again. When he had taken up his first plain clothes job in Wood Green, Duggan had sought him out. Using the threat of exposing him as the murderer of the two RAF men who had died when the brakes on their Landrover had been sabotaged and the "accidental" shooting of the other one, Duggan had called in a number of favours; each of which was rewarded with a cash handout. The irony was, thought Jimmy, that he had actually been a pretty good cop until then; he still was for that matter. Once crooked, always crooked was the old adage though. Complicit with his paymaster in one matter it was a short and very slippery slope into the tangled web of corruption. He had proved himself as a successful legitimate detective many times over; well enough to thoroughly deserve every promotion upon merit until Duggan had become Home Secretary and manipulated him into his present post. There had, however, been a long trail of "unofficial" work performed to order; including the enlistment of his three juniors into the dark side of policing. Still, what was done could not be undone. The three threats were Fenton attempting to exact a personal revenge on his father's killer, Fenton going public with what he knew and the journalist identifying Jewel and Cavendish as the men who abducted him and ran him down. The first he thought unlikely. Simon Fenton did not seem to be a man of action and Eddie Duggan had a police protection officer when he was out and about. Even when he was at home an armed dog handler and his dog were on patrol in the grounds. The second scenario was more frightening. When the old guy had attempted to go to the press ICIS had intercepted the telephone call. Unknown to anyone but ICIS and the Home Secretary the switchboards of all the major newspapers, radio and TV channels were still illicitly tapped. If Fenton called ahead they stood a good chance of intercepting him. That was why he had recalled his Detective Inspectors to London; he sensed that the next move would ultimately be made in the capital. As for the journalist, it seemed that they had a couple of days grace before he regained consciousness. The presence of a police guard outside his room was a serious problem. While Jewel and Cavendish could probably hatch some sort of plan whereby one of them lured the guard away while the other gave Kynpham Johal a lethal injection there would inevitably be a murder inquiry afterwards. Still it might prove to be their only option. In the meantime the threat of Fenton going to the press over the weekend was the highest priority, but the likelihood of emerging from the situation unscathed still seemed to be more of a hope than an expectation. He checked the travel documents in his briefcase again before taking two sleeping pills and retiring early to his bed.

CHAPTER FORTY-ONE

Natalie switched on the television and curled up in an armchair, flicking through the channels as Simon settled down at the table to sift through the remaining papers from the Tupperware box. He removed several sheets which, upon careful examination, appeared to be copies of pages of a cash book of some sort. Under the income column amounts of between two hundred and a thousand pounds were listed next to various names: *The Pelican, Calico Joe's, Sweetbox* and *Hot Mary's* seemed to appear on a daily basis. Someone had written annotations next to the names. *The Pelican* and *Calico Joe's*, it appeared, were strip clubs while *Sweetbox* and *Hot Mary's* were identified as brothels. There were also a large number of initials shown as sources of income, but no indication of what they represented. In the expenditure columns various amounts were listed against car registration number. Simon backtracked through the pile of papers. The amounts shown proved to be the difference between the deposits shown on the two invoices for the vehicle in question. Again there were several sets of initials listed against expenditure. He noticed that someone or something listed as *JC* seemed to be receiving three hundred pounds each week. He shared his suspicions with Natalie, but she was absorbed in the TV and did no more than look up and smile as he explained what the papers appeared to be showing.

The next bundle of papers showed that two separate sets of identical makes and models of cars had been purchased at a series of half a dozen auctions across Greater London over a period of three weeks in June 1985. For each car the registration number and mileage was listed. For each make and model one example had a low mileage while the other had an exceptionally high mileage; the difference being reflected in the prices paid. A set of sales invoices showed that the high mileage examples had subsequently been sold from several outlets for prices two or three times as much as had been paid for them.

Paper clipped to the bottom sheet was a photocopy of the newspaper cutting about a fire at the Phillip Lane site in which Mary Soutar had been killed. With a chill he realised that the cutting had almost certainly been attached by the dead girl's mother. The clear implication was that the cars' identities had been swapped and that the insurance claim for the more expensive cars had been fraudulent. The next step, he realised, would be to obtain police and insurance records of the fire. It seemed pretty likely that they would confirm his suspicions. That, however, would be a matter for the press.

Natalie had found a re-run of "Titanic" on one of the TV channels and, with her feet tucked up underneath her, appeared absorbed in the film as Simon took out the last few sheets of paper. They were rather patchy photocopies of letters written in a girlish hand. At first he struggled to decipher the faded form of rounded script but, after standing up to switch on the overhead light and angling the paper away from it, he began to read;

12th September 1984

Dear Eddie

I know you are busy, but I have really tried to get to see you last for the last week. I have some good news for you. You are going to be a dad. I came to the flat three times – on Monday, Wednesday and Thursday last week but you wasn't in. It looked all shut up so I think you might have moved. I know you don't like me to bother you at work, but I'm sending this to the garage 'cos I thought you'd want to know right away.

I know you love me Eddie and I think we can be really happy together – all three of us. Please can you come and see me at the bedsit or at the club if you can't 'cos we need to make plans and stuff – for us and for the baby. Do you want it to be a boy or a girl Eddie. I expect you want a boy but I don't mind.

I do love you so much, Eddie. It's such good news isn't it? We can be together properly now can't we?

Do come and see me soon because we've got so much to talk about.

Love and kisses,

Sue xxxxxxx

Simon frowned. This was something different. Scandalous, perhaps, but they were not in the same league as the financial records. Then he remembered; Mary Soutar who had made the copies in the first place had been in a relationship with Eddie Duggan. Here was the evidence of his infidelity. He took the next sheet and the sorry tale continued;

21st. September 1984

Dear Eddie

I was wondering if you got my last letter- the one about me being pregnant I mean. In case you was worrying I can promise you the baby is yours. I might take my clothes off for men – that's what Johnny pays me for and you know that, but I swear there's not been anyone else – not since that first time with you last May.

I'm getting a bit worried about not hearing from you Eddie. I know you've gone from the flat 'cos some bloke I've never seen before opened the door to me yesterday. He said he didn't know you – he just got if from the agency he said. Is it that you don't want me to have the baby? If you truly don't then you know I'd do whatever you wanted, but I just need to see you Eddie. I haven't seen you in the club for weeks and I came to the garage, but that snooty secretary told me you wasn't there and she wouldn't tell me when you'd be around.

I really do love you, Eddie and I know you love me too 'cos you've told me often enough. You even bought me that gold necklace. Please get in touch soon.

Love

Sue xxxxxx

Simon felt a surge of anger rising within him as the sorry tale unfolded before his eyes. The next letter continued the saga.

2*nd*. October 1984

Dear Eddie

I don't know why you haven't been in touch. I haven't done this on my own, you know – got pregnant. I'm sorry if it's not the news you wanted, but like I said just say the word and if it's what you want I'll get rid of it. I miss you something rotten Eddie and I just can't find you anywhere, even though I keep looking.

I've been to the doctor and the baby's due next April. It will be nice to have a baby in the spring. It would be nicer if there was two of us together 'cos children need their mums and dads don't they?

I do hope you will be in touch. I still love you even if you're not so keen on me anymore.

Love

Sue xx

There was a gap of several weeks before the date of the next letter.

25*th*. November 1984

Dear Eddie,

I am writing because really need your help. Even if you have gone off me it's still your baby that's growing inside me. The trouble is that it's starting to show now. Johnny says I can't keep on working. He says the punters don't want to see a stripper with a dirty great bump in their belly and he's probably right.

I've got a little bit saved up, but I can only afford one more month's rent. If you don't help me out I'll have to go back home to my mum and dad only you know we don't get on – that's how I ended up in London. Do you remember my dad threw me out when I was eighteen? I know I was a bit of a cow and got drunk and stayed out all night and that, but he really had it in for me. Please don't make me go crawling back to them. I don't want a lot Eddie, just enough to get by on until the baby's born and I get my figure back. I haven't passed any exams or anything and I can't get another job while I'm knocked up anyway so please, please will you help me out - or should I say us — me and our little one?

Looking forward to hearing from you soon.

Sue

Simon glanced up at Natalie. She was still absorbed in the film. He got up from his seat and made coffee for them both. Natalie smiled as she accepted the mug, but did not speak. He sat down on the other armchair. The doomed ship had just struck the iceberg and its passengers were going about their business seemingly unconcerned. Content to sit in a companionable silence with her Simon sipped his coffee slowly, somehow reluctant to return to the anguish and pathos of the series of letters written almost twenty five years ago.

For Natalie the film on the television provided her with the opportunity to engage in some deep thinking without alerting Simon. What had she been like? Attempting to pray to a God she had paid scant attention to since primary school and who almost certainly was a figment of peoples' imagination. Still, this God seemed to figure in Simon's life in some important way, so perhaps a quick prayer now and again might be a sensible sort of insurance after all. When the opening titles to "Titanic" had began to scroll across the TV screen it had initially seemed that it might be some sort of divine sign that things would be fine. It was her joint favourite film. Did that mean something? Then, as she reflected on the plot and the inevitable sad ending with the death of the boy, sacrificing himself to save his girl, she realised that it might also be a sort of portent that things would end disastrously for her and Simon. Unsettled and listless, she continued to stare through the screen, lost in her worries.

Simon rinsed his mug under the tap and resumed his seat at the table.

13th December 1984

Dear Eddie,

Well, here I am – back home with my mum and dad. In case you want to get in touch we live at 47 Curzon Avenue, Oldham. My dad says that I've brought so much shame on him that he daren't show his face at the club again, but he still seems to go somewhere or other for a few beers every night. Mum's been quite nice really, but I can tell she'd rather I'd stayed away. I've got nowhere else to go, though.

I went to see the midwife last week and she says everything is going OK – with the baby and that. I so wish you was here with me Eddie, or I was there with you. I'm getting a bit scared now, about giving birth. I'm frightened that it will hurt and I'll be on my own. I asked mum if she'd be with me when the time came, but she just said that I'd got myself into the mess and I'd just have to get on with it. I haven't told a soul who the father is and I won't unless you want me too Eddie.

I can't help wondering what happened to us. We seemed to be so happy together and you just couldn't get enough of me.

Anyway, I won't write to you again – not until the baby's born. It would be really good to hear from you, Eddie and I'm really short of money so any help you could give would be really welcome.

Bye for now

Sue.

Simon put down the letter and sighed. Eddie Duggan, it seemed, was a first class shit; murderer, money launderer, fraudster and possibly pimp and drug dealer. Now it was also clear that he was an insensitive and uncaring bastard. He had obviously taken advantage of a youngster who had fallen for his charms hook line and sinker then cut her off without a word or a penny when he found out that she was carrying his child. He picked the last piece of paper out of the box.

15th. April 1985

Dear Eddie,

Hello. It's me – Susan Robertson – remember? The girl who you knocked up and abandoned. I suppose you've a right to know – your daughter was born two days ago on April 13th at two in the afternoon. I haven't chosen a name yet, but I quite like Rachel, or Natalie or Carrie.

With a sickening lurch of his stomach Simon looked up at Natalie with a deeply disturbing suspicion growing in his mind. She was still staring at the television screen He tore his eyes away and, with a deep foreboding, forced himself to read the rest of the letter.

Anyway it's crunch time for you and me. I still love you, Eddie and if you want us to be together just say the word. Even if you don't want me, the least you could so is to provide for your daughter. If you write to me before next week I'll put your name on the birth certificate, but if you don't I won't.

The truth is Eddie that I've met someone else. I don't love him – not really – not the way I love you, but he's nice enough. His name is Paul. He's got a good job and a house with a garden on the edge of town – and his own car. He's soft on me and he says he'll make a home for me and the little one and things are so bad at home that I'm probably going to say yes and try and make a go of it. Unless you write that is. So there you are, Eddie.

Deep down I still hope you will write or just come and knock on the door or something, but now I don't think you will but if you ever want to get to know your daughter you can always write here and my mum will pass it on.

Take care of yourself. What we had together was special and I'll never forget you.

Yours,

Sue.

Stupefied, Simon was frozen in his seat. The awful truth was there to see. This was no simple tale of lust and parental irresponsibility. It was a profound and deeply significant truth that the girl sitting across the room had absolutely no inkling of, but most certainly had the right to know. For several minutes he stared unseeingly at the sheet of paper, not daring to raise his eyes to look at Natalie. He considered hiding the incriminating sheets and destroying them later, but to do that would be to deny Natalie her birthright; and if hid did take that course of action his motivation would be partly his own self-interest. He owed her more than that.

'Natalie,' he asked, his voice breaking, 'when's your birthday?'

Natalie looked up from the television, but Simon would not meet her gaze.

'April 13th,' she replied, 'why do you want to know?'

'And is your mum called Susan?' he continued.

'Yes, she is,' replied Natalie in a puzzled voice.

'Then I think you probably ought to come over here and read this.' He said softly.

Simon replaced the letters in order and stood up, guiding Natalie to sit in the chair he had vacated. He rested his hand on her shoulder as she began to read. At first she could make little sense of the concern indicated by Simon's tone of voice, but as she finished reading the first letter the awful realisation began to tear at her heart. She read on in silence with a deep sense of dread; hoping against hope that the ending would not be the one she half suspected. It was every bit as bad as she had begun to fear, though, and, as she read the last letter, the tears began to flow, dripping from her cheeks to stain the surface of the faded photocopy. Simon reached for her chin and tried to gently turn her face towards him, but she shrugged him of and recoiled from his touch.

Natalie had been given her sign; in fact not one sign, but three. She thought that she remembered having heard somewhere that God often did things in threes. First of all there was the fact that her mother had seriously been prepared to have an abortion; to end her prospect of life before birth. Secondly there was the sign that her father had simply not, ever, wanted to know her or care for her. Her sense of rejection was palpable and her fragile self-esteem deflated like a balloon with a slow puncture. Finally, and most uncomfortably and unequivocally of all, her father was Eddie Duggan. It was her own father whose underhand dealing had caused his own daughter to be prostituted in an attempt to preserve his own reputation; it was her own father who was behind the police pursuit that had hounded her and Simon for the last week and, most painful of all, it was her own father who had cold-bloodedly murdered the father of the man she had dared to fall in love with. It was clear to her now; she could not ever be with Simon Fenton. How could she ever expect him to return the love of someone whose father had murdered his father? How could he ever contemplate spending his life with anyone as unworthy and tarnished as she was?

Seeing her distress, Simon made another attempt to hold her, but she pushed him roughly away, ran out of the door, slamming it behind her and disappeared from his sight. He could hear the sound of her footsteps on the stairs and then the slam of the bedroom door. He had absolutely no idea what to do. For several minutes he stood rooted to the spot before had sat down despondently in the armchair Natalie had recently vacated. He would give her time, he decided; he could think of no alternative.

CHAPTER FORTY-TWO

With the formalities of immigration and customs behind her Rebecca Johal made her way into the Heathrow Tube Station and located the platform for the train into the city centre. It was late afternoon and the cool air chilled her bare arms. She struggled to find a coat from her bag and put it on just as the train rattled into the platform. Her brother Paul had texted her mobile phone to let her know that she could get a train to Carlisle from Euston station; she had studied the complicated underground map and deduced that she would need to change at Green Park. The journey to Euston took her almost two hours. She had got hopelessly lost during the transfer at Green Park and had ended up travelling in the opposite direction; away from Euston rather than towards it. A kindly old lady had helped her out and given her directions. Flustered and tired, Rebecca eventually joined the short queue at the Euston ticket office and succeeded in booking a single ticket to Carlisle which cost her almost a hundred pounds. The three and a half hour journey passed slowly and, as the train drew closer to her destination, the level of anxiety she felt for her twin brother increased. By the time she reached Carlisle it was almost ten o'clock and she immediately took a taxi to the hospital. Although visiting time had ended much earlier, the woman on the reception desk had taken pity on the diminutive brown girl who had travelled half way across the world and called the ward. The sister in charge immediately offered to come down and meet her.

Rebecca's first shock was to see that a policeman was sitting on an armchair outside the door to Kynpham's room. Her second came moments later when she saw her brother lying prone on a hospital bed, his head swathed in bandages and with a tangle of wires and tubes connecting him to various drips and pieces of machinery. The sister explained that an operation had gone well, but a scan showed that there was still considerable swelling of the brain. While the prognosis had improved considerably, Kynpham was still under heavy sedation and was unlikely to regain consciousness for a few days. Rebecca's first duty was to phone home with the news; the kindly ward sister reassuring her that it would be quite all right if she used her mobile phone. Rebecca then pulled up a chair and sat holding her brother's warm hand. A while later the ward sister returned; she told the Indian girl that she had made up a bed in a side room. Rebecca was welcome to make use of it and stay in the hospital until she could make other arrangements. An hour later, as she was just about to succumb to sleep between the crispy white sheets, Rebecca realised that she had not thought about Simon Fenton once since she had got off the aeroplane at Heathrow. She wondered where he was.

CHAPTER FORTY-THREE

Simon sat in the kitchen armchair for almost two hours, oblivious to the television which was still on. The virtual certainty that Eddie Duggan was Natalie's father had come completely out of the blue and had shaken him to the core. Not that it had changed in any way his feelings for her. He still loved her with all his heart, but he just had no idea what to do or say. A hostage to his gender, he felt intuitively that whatever he said would probably be the wrong thing, anyway. So he had remained rooted to the chair. He had heard no sounds from the bedroom and felt an odd reluctance to intrude on Natalie's privacy. Eventually hunger drove him into action and he began to prepare a light meal for them both; taking Natalie's upstairs, he reasoned, would give him the excuse he felt he needed to check on her condition.

When he took the tray upstairs, however, he found her fast asleep on the bed. With a half smile he recognised the ironic symmetry with the situation that morning when he had fallen asleep after their lovemaking. He pulled the quilt over her shoulders, switched off the light and returned downstairs, deep in thought. He felt helpless and alone. If only he had not read the last few papers this might not have happened. If only he had hidden them and destroyed them later...but he also knew that a relationship based on falsehood; on withholding the truth was not the sort of relationship he wanted. Total honesty, total faithfulness and total commitment; that summed up his inmost desire where Natalie was concerned. For the first time his thoughts strayed to the contemplation of asking her to marry him. He found that idea rather attractive.

With no more than a half-formed plan of action in his head he rooted out a blanket from the airing cupboard at the top of the stairs, tiptoed into the front lounge and settled down on the sofa, bathed in the orange glow from the street light outside. After an hour or two he slept.

Natalie awoke to find herself covered by the quilt. She felt around in the bed for Simon, but soon realised that he must have covered her up and left. She groped for the switch on the bedside light and screwed her eyes up against the resulting brightness. Her watch showed her that it was ten past three. Driven downstairs by the need to use the toilet, she was surprised not to find Simon sitting in the kitchen. Panic seized her for a moment. She was terrified that her rebuff might have driven him away. Finding him asleep in the front room brought an overwhelming flood of relief. She sat down in the armchair next to him and watched him sleep for several minutes. Her love for him was undiminished, but her mother's letters had shot a hole in her fragile sense of self-worth and the fear had returned. How could he possibly want a relationship with the daughter of his father's murderer? Not to mention the fact that she was damaged goods; nothing more than a cheap tart. And then there was all this confusing God stuff. She wondered if Simon finding the letters actually had been something to do with that; the sign she had asked for. No, that was just being irrational, she convinced herself. It was pure coincidence and there was no God! But she knew that Simon wouldn't agree with that. He still had a faith – probably quite a bit more of it than he was willing to admit to, in her opinion. She knelt down on the floor beside him and gently stroked the hairs on his arm with her fingertips. How she loved this man. Yet she sensed that her love for him might well be destined to become more of a burden than a joy. What they both needed, she decided, was a bit of time and space; time and space not to talk, but just to be and to think. She would tell him in the morning. He was far too good and kind to step back from her so it would be her responsibility to cool things off between them. While her heart would not permit her to give up hope completely on a future with Simon Fenton, her head was screaming at her that she must give him the chance to walk away. She would tell him that she wanted time to think. That would make him take time to think as well. With a quiet sigh she stood up, climbed the stairs, undressed and crawled back into bed.

Breakfast was a quiet and rather sombre event. Natalie had been up and dressed first. She was cooking bacon when Simon walked into the kitchen on his way to the bathroom at seven thirty.

'I'm sorry about last night,' she said, 'I know it's not your fault, Simon. You were just there. It's all too much to think about...Eddie Duggan and my mum...'

'It doesn't matter, Nat,' he began, but Natalie held up a hand in front of him, palm outwards.

'I really don't want to talk about it; not at the moment, just leave me to get on with things...'

'But don't push me out,' retorted Simon, 'I love you, Nat. Who your father is makes no difference to that.'

'It might not to you, but it does to me!' she exclaimed. 'Just leave it. Here's your bacon, I'm going out for a run.' She stamped angrily up the stairs.

Ablutions complete, Simon sat at the table, but had no appetite for breakfast. Natalie returned wearing shorts and a t-shirt. She passed through the room without a word and disappeared through the back door.

She was gone for more than an hour. Simon idly powered up the notebook and looked up trains to London for the following day. With a gathering sense of foreboding he recognised that he was still planning to bring down Eddie Duggan, Natalie's natural father; not out of any sense of revenge for the death of his own father, but because he was absolutely certain that it was the right thing to do. He wondered what Natalie thought now that she knew the truth about her paternity.

Pounding the empty Sunday morning streets gradually began to sooth the rawness from Natalie's anger and frustration, but the pain deep within her would not go away however hard she pushed herself. Exhausted and covered in perspiration, she slumped down on a bench seat set into the side of a modernistic metal footbridge above the dark swirling waters of the river on the fringe of the city centre. The rain had passed, leaving a blue sky punctuated by fluffy white clouds which were chasing each other across the sky in the cool breeze. It had all gone so completely and absolutely bloody pear shaped, she thought. It wasn't just the fact that she still felt unworthy of Simon's love, although she did. In addition to her desperate fear that he would regret getting close to someone like her once he got back to his old life and his friends, she was now acutely aware of the huge rift between them caused by an accident of genetics. She felt only contempt for Eddie Duggan; she couldn't bring herself to think of him as her father. Yet he had put the final nail into the coffin in which the last shreds of her hopes for any sort of future with Simon Fenton had just been buried. With sudden clarity of thought she realised that on every occasion that they had made love it had been she who had instigated it. The cheap tart making the first move every time to entice him into fulfilling her carnal needs; that was probably how he had seen it; some self-seeking temptress luring him away from his beliefs and his integrity. The tears once again began to flow freely as she sat in the cool air with goose bumps forming on her exposed arms and legs. Yet, into her despair she also sensed another voice telling her that her love for the man had brought out the very best in her. Even if this was the end of it all, she decided, she would have no regrets. Even at the bottom of the pit of misery she discovered that there was still a selfless dimension to her love for Simon. She did not deserve him; she would not impose herself upon him in any way, but she would do whatever might be necessary to preserve his well-being and help him in his mission. She hoped fervently that, together, they would succeed in bringing Eddie Duggan to justice; not just as the fraudster and murdered that he was, but also because of his treatment of her estranged mother. She stood up and began to jog slowly back towards the house.

When she returned Simon was watching highlights from the previous day's football on the TV. He looked up as she walked in and was rewarded with a shy smile.

'I'm a total prat, aren't I?' she said.

'No you're not...' he began, but Natalie would not let him finish.

'Yes I am and I'm sorry. I just think we both need a bit of time and space to come to terms with everything. '

'What are you saying, Nat,' he replied anxiously, 'are you telling me it's all over between us?'

'No, I'm not telling you anything,' she answered, 'Let's just get on with what we were planning before you found the letter. I will say one thing, though; I think Eddie Duggan is a complete shit. He might be my dad in a biological sense, but I hate the bastard. Let's do for him, Simon, any way we can. I'll use these letters. The press would love the story wouldn't they; "Home secretary has love child by Stripper" can you just imagine the headlines?'

'I don't think we should, use the letters,' said Simon, 'I mean... we've more than enough without it. You don't need that sort of exposure...I mean your reputation and that.'

Natalie smiled wryly.

'Reputation, what reputation,' she muttered, 'my reputation's not worth a bean, Simon Fenton, I'm the tart that seduces vicars, remember.'

Simon coloured up in embarrassment.

'I'm sorry, Nat, but that's not how I think of you, you know, not a bit. I'm in love with you; all of you past, present and future. Just let me love you, Nat. Please.'

'I meant what I said, Simon, I don't want to think about the future until we've done what we have to do. Now put the kettle on while I have a shower.'

While Natalie was in the bathroom the football came to an end and the Andrew Marr programme began. There, large as life was Eddie Duggan on the TV screen not three yards from where he was sitting. Transfixed he turned up the sound and began to listen in earnest as his adversary began expound his views, skilfully deflecting the direct questions and making a fairly overt bid for the leadership of his party. Oblivious to the fact that Natalie had returned wrapped in a large towel he sat forward in his chair hanging on every word as he contemplated the possible news stories which would inevitably follow if they succeeded in reaching a sympathetic journalist.

'Shit!' hissed Natalie venomously. Simon half turned and noticed her standing beside him. 'He's nothing but a shit, Simon. I don't care what it takes, he's not going to get away with it; any of it.' She slipped up the staircase as Simon resumed his gaze at the screen.

CHAPTER FORTY-FOUR

The after effects of long distance travel and anxiety held Rebecca Johal in her hospital bed until much later than she had intended to be up and about. The ward sister who had looked after her the previous evening had gone off duty but had obviously briefed her replacement well. After a quick shower and a cup of tea, Rebecca was once again at her brother's bedside. The policeman on guard duty had been replaced by a young policewoman with short blonde hair who also seemed to know exactly who she was. Kynpham was still unconscious, but appeared to be sleeping peacefully. No sooner had she sat down beside the bed than a doctor appeared. He was very reassuring. He told her that there was no good reason why he should not, in time, make a full recovery, but there was always the possibility that he wouldn't. Kynpham would be having a further brain-scan that afternoon and, if the swelling was still reducing, the doctors planned to gradually reduce the strength of the intravenous sedative over the following twenty for hours. The earliest he might be expected to regain consciousness was on Tuesday.

The new ward sister enquired about Rebecca's accommodation arrangements and helped her to book an inexpensive room in the County Hotel, a short bus ride away in the town centre. Promising to return for evening visiting after Kynpham's scan, she collected her belongings and went in search of her hotel. Once installed in her room she bought lunch in a nearby fast food outlet and set out to explore the compact shopping centre. Although the big stores were open there were few shoppers about and, calculating the time in India she made a very short call on her mobile, promising to follow it up with an e-mail. After asking several passers by she located an internet cafe in a side street, paid for the minimum of thirty minutes and quickly dashed off her message. Unwilling to waste the remainder of her time she typed Simon Fenton's name into the search engine. Rebecca was still surprised that Simon had not arrived in Carlisle to be with his friend. Thirty seconds later she discovered the reason. He was, apparently, a wanted man and was on the run with a prostitute. Rebecca was both disappointed and confused. The man she had thought about almost every day for almost two years was not the sort to be involved with either crime or prostitutes. Her romantic dreams slowly dissipated as she trawled though news report after news report about the shooting of a policeman, drugs and a nationwide hunt. On one site a grainy photograph of Simon was shown next to a much clearer one of am auburn-haired girl wearing sexy underwear posing provocatively. If Simon had chosen to be with someone like that, Rebecca thought, how could she possibly stand a chance with him?

For the first time since Andrew Gilroy had been dispatched to Manchester to deal with Simon Fenton all the members of ICIS and their political master were gathered together in one place. They were the only people present in the ICIS office that Sunday lunchtime and, seated around a small table in the conference room they began to review their options.

They had absolutely no idea where Simon Fenton and Natalie Robertson were. Jimmy Bell had heard nothing from his illicit contacts or from the handful of private investigators he had employed to keep watch on their homes and other likely hideouts. Phone taps on the mobile phones which had been used and the fugitives' most likely contacts had revealed nothing and the remainder of the police service had lost interest. The tabloid press, while certain to make much of any new developments involving an ex vicar and a high class call girl, had also let the story drop. All four of them agreed that Fenton was likely to approach the media if he had the incriminating papers in his possession and a number of contacts placed in TV and newspaper offices had been slipped a fifty pound note with the promise of making ten times that if they tipped Bell off before Fenton arrived and made contact with the journalists. These unofficial informants remained their best hope. Even if the papers fell into the hands of a reporter there was always the possibility of an "official" visit by Jewel and Cavendish to attempt to recover them before any harm resulted. As for Kynpham Johal, the prognosis remained uncertain. An old friend of Gerry Jewel on the Cumbria force had agreed to tip him the wink if and when the injured man regained consciousness, believing Jewel's tale that the reporter was operating on the fringe of an Islamist terror cell as part of an investigative journalism assignment and might have fallen foul of the militant leadership. They did not know the extent of Kynpham's knowledge of the situation, but all for agreed that there was a strong possibility that, if the reporter recovered, he would probably be able to identify Jewel and Cavendish. Should he regain consciousness, it was decided that Cavendish would be tasked with taking care of the reporter while Bell and Jewel would remain in London and attempt to thwart any attempt that Simon Fenton might make to approach the press.

Eddie Duggan left the meeting in mid afternoon to return to his Kent constituency. He hoped that his wife might repeat her welcome of the previous afternoon.

The three corrupt police officers retired to a nearby bar and consoled themselves with beer and sandwiches. Paul Bell remembered the problem with the Vectra's steering, but the attraction of a second pint won out. He could always pop into a garage first thing in the morning, he thought.

CHAPTER FORTY-FIVE

Sunday passed slowly for Simon and Natalie. Although friendly on the surface, there was a strain on their relationship that had not been present before. Unresolved issues bubbled just beneath the surface as they made their plans. Determined not to use the letters from Natalie's mother, Simon had opened the back of the TV set, unscrewing it with a knife from the kitchen, and had hidden them, folded into a small square, amidst the wiring. They would form, he said, their last line of defence. He alone would go to London; taking the first train of the day at five to five in the morning. That would give him time to disappear into the morning rush hour and turn up at the BBC with the day shift. If he did not succeed there he would try the Independent. Natalie would stay in Derby. Simon agreed to telephone her at nine twelve and three. If he had not succeeded in interesting anyone in the story by three he would return. If he was not back by six, or if he missed a call, Natalie was to assume the worst. Simon suggested that she would probably be safest if she walked the few hundred yards to Derby police station. He tried to persuade her that she should turn herself in and refuse to say anything at all to the police for a period of forty-eight hours, just in case he had got caught up in something dangerous and had to lie low for a while. Natalie refused to agree to his suggestion. She would, she said, follow in his footsteps the next day and give the copies of the letters written by her mother to the tabloid press, hoping that whoever had intercepted Simon was assuming that they had all the papers, and break the story of Eddie Duggan and her mother before going on to the nearest police station to give herself up and keeping her right of silence.

As day turned into evening, hunger drove their thoughts to food. Natalie suggested a Chinese take away from a local outlet whose leaflet had popped through the door earlier on. For a few minutes they debated whether or not to go and collect it or to telephone their order and have it delivered. Lulled into a sense of security by the domesticity of the quiet street they opted for the telephone. When the doorbell rang half an hour later Natalie answered it, giving the delivery man a twenty pound note and telling him to keep the change in order to keep her time in the doorway to a minimum.

After the meal there was a degree of unspoken unease about the sleeping arrangements. Reluctant to bring the issue into the open, Simon suggested that he prepare everything that he would need for his early start and sleep on the sofa again to avoid disturbing Natalie. With a degree of relief Natalie agreed, although part of her still longed deeply to hold his naked body close to hers and bury her anxieties in a warm cocoon of physical affection. They parted with a brief embrace and gentle kiss before bedtime.

Although neither of them slept well, Natalie remembered later that she must have dropped off eventually because she had no recollection of Simon leaving to catch the early morning train.

CHAPTER FORTY-SIX

David Wallace was the shadow of the man he had been twelve months before; both mentally and physically. He had lost his job as a quantity surveyor when the firm he worked for had made almost half of its staff redundant in the summer of 2008; an early portent of the recession. The worry of it had also led him to lose almost two stones in weight. Although his wife earned reasonable money at the Royal Derby Hospital where she worked as a medical secretary, the heavy mortgage on their detached house in prosperous Allestree, and the myriad needs of their two primary school aged children, ensured that expenditure was in constant danger of running ahead of income. His relatively generous redundancy package had kept things ticking over for the first couple of months but, after over thirty job applications had brought no result he sank the last of their money into taking a training course as a driving instructor and buying into a national franchise. The promised thirty thousand pounds a year, however, was still to materialise. He counted it a good week if his earnings amounted to half what they would need to be to make that salary. To supplement his income he had made the most of his brief and not particularly successful stint as a Special Constable several years ago and set up as a part time private investigator. A trickle of matrimonial surveillance cases and a successful search for a missing teenager made a small but welcome contribution to family finances; and he had been delighted to receive a commission by telephone; backed up by the arrival of two hundred and fifty pounds in cash, to keep an eye on an empty property in Chester Green Lane for a couple of weeks. He was to telephone a mobile number if he noticed any sign of occupation.

For the first week he had contrived to take all his pupils onto the narrow cul-de-sac to practice their three point turns. There had been no trace of occupation. On Thursday morning however, a careless pupil had backed the car into a wall while attempting a reverse parking manoeuvre in a quiet residential street. He had taken the vehicle straight to a local body-shop for repair and expected to be back on the road by Tuesday. In the meantime he had needed to cancel over a dozen lessons and Chester Green Lane had remained unobserved all day. The telephone call on Friday afternoon had jolted him back into action. He had paid a visit immediately, checking both the back and front doors on foot but had detected no sign of habitation. On Saturday afternoon he had braved the rain once again with the same result. Sunday had been a precious family day. They had made the most of the better weather by spending the morning at the swimming pool and the afternoon in Markeaton Park. David had almost decided not to bother with another surveillance visit; after all, no one would ever know would they? An honest man at heart, however, his conscious would not permit him to willingly fail to do what he had already accepted payment for and he set out once again into the twilight on the forty minute walk to Chester Green Lane.

The Sunday evening streets were quiet and he had the strong suspicion that his trip would prove fruitless, but David Wallace found the solitude of his walk comforting. Time from the unending busyness of family life was a welcome respite and he whistled softly as he approached the cul-de-sac. To his surprise there was an elderly Nissan Micra parked outside number twenty-two. The dark figure of a small man emerged from the car carrying a white plastic bag and knocked on the door. David increased his pace and was almost directly opposite when the door was opened by a pretty blonde girl who handed something to the man, took the bag and quickly closed the door. David continued to the end of the cul-de-sac as the car executed a neat three-point turn and drove off. He then slipped along a narrow alleyway to access the rear of number twenty two. Although the downstairs curtains were closed their thin material could not obscure the fact that a light was on behind them. Realising that he had forgotten to bring the piece of paper with the contact number written on it with him,

David Wallace rapidly retraced his steps. He wondered if there would be a bonus for his successful surveillance.

Jimmy Bell was not available to answer his mobile phone when David Wallace called. The Detective Chief Superintendent was fast asleep in an armchair beside the gas fire in his house after consuming a little too much lager with his two colleagues during the course of the afternoon. He had left his telephone in the pocket of his coat which hung in the hallway and the faint sound of the ringtone before the call was diverted to voice-mail failed to rouse him. It was only when the urgent need to urinate penetrated his stupor that he heard the bleep signifying a missed call as he made his way upstairs to the bathroom. It was well after midnight but, elated at the news from Derby, he immediately dialled the private number of Eddie Duggan, waking him up to share the good news. His next calls were to Detective Inspectors Cavendish and Jewel. His instructed them to proceed northwards immediately. They were to force an entry into the house, do away with Simon Fenton and the girl, retrieve any papers that they could find and then set fire to the property to eliminate as much of the evidence of their visit as possible. Both officers were asleep in bed when the calls came. By the time Paul Cavendish had dressed, thrown a few things into a small suitcase, driven across North London, picked up his colleague and joined the M1 at Staples Corner it was almost two thirty in the morning. The ailing Vectra weaved its way along the motorway at a steady seventy five and they paused at Castle Donnington Services for a couple of cups of strong coffee and to pick up a street map to supplement the meagre detail provided by their satellite navigation system at just after four. A careful scrutiny of the map showed that Chester Green Lane was too close for comfort to the main police station in the city and that a cautious approach would be needed. The car drew up outside the darkened house at twenty past five. Jewel stood guard at the front door while Cavendish scuttled along the alley to the back door, a heavy battering ram concealed in the folds of his coat.

A repeated crashing noise from below woke Natalie up with a start. She sat up in bed, switched on the light and screwed up her eyes against the brightness as she groped for her watch. Five twenty two. Simon would be on his way to London. With growing fear she began to comprehend what was happening. A cry of 'Armed Police!' from below signalled that the kitchen door had been battered open and she grabbed the mobile phone from the bedside cabinet and pressed the speed-dial button for Simon. The sound of the front door opening downstairs signalled the arrival of at least one other intruder. The call was answered on its second ring.

'Nat?' said the familiar voice.

'Simon, they're here,' she hissed as feet pounded on the stairs. Just as the bedroom door began to open she slid the still active handset under the bed as she pulled the quilt up to cover her nakedness.

The two men burst in, Cavendish brandishing an automatic pistol.

'Fuck!' he exclaimed, scanning the room, 'where's Fenton?'

Jewel followed him in before rapidly turning on his heel and smashing open the door of the front bedroom.

'Not bloody here,' he shouted, re-entering Natalie's room, his face dark with anger. He ripped the quilt from her grip and punched her in the face before she had time to make any attempt at defending herself. He grabbed her arm and jerked her roughly onto her feet before punching her again, this time in the stomach. Natalie doubled over in agony.

'Where is he?' the burly policeman demanded, again jerking her upright by the arm. Through her pain and shame Natalie drew on all the resolve she could muster.

'I'm not telling you,' she gasped. She felt her feelings for Simon welling up within her and giving her strength as she prepared herself to endure whatever might be coming next. She would buy him as much time as she could. The next blow caught her on her left breast, bringing a new flash of nauseating agony. She fell backwards onto the bed, sobbing. As Jewel raised his arm for yet another blow a thin distended cry of anguish rose from the telephone handset beneath the bed.

'Nat, tell them where I am.' Jewel stopped in his tracks.

'Shit, she's got a mobile with an open line under the bed!' he exclaimed. While Cavendish kept her covered with the gun Jewel groped beneath the bed and lifted the phone to his ear.

'Fenton,' he said, 'if you ever want to see this tart alive again, you'd better do exactly what I tell you.'

'No, Simon,' shrieked Natalie, 'don't. Just get the bastard behind all this.'

'You'd better listen, Fenton', Jewel continued, but the line had gone dead. The corrupt policeman pressed the redial button but, there was no reply. Instead he was redirected to voicemail.

'Fenton, you'd better call this number. Now! If I don't hear from you in the next ten minute's the tart's toast!'

Natalie curled up on the bed and attempted to draw the quilt again up, but Jewel snatched it away from her again.

'Get these on,' he said, 'tossing a t-shirt and a pair of leggings at her. One wrong move and my friend here will shoot.' Sobbing gently in despair, Natalie complied. As soon as she was dressed Jewel pulled a pair of handcuffs from his pocket and secured her hands behind her back, throwing her face down on the bed. She felt a pinprick in her upper arm; then nothing.

Paul Cavendish returned the gun to his coat pocket and called Jimmy Bell to explain the situation while his partner ransacked the house in search of the incriminating papers. In response to Bell's questions he read off Simon Fenton's mobile phone number from Natalie's handset and grunted a few times before disconnecting the call.

'Boss says we're to get out quickly in case Fenton calls in the local plods and take her to the Warrington place,' he announced to Jewel who had returned unsuccessful from his search. 'Keep trying Fenton and offer a trade, the papers for the girl, then reel him in, get the stuff and get rid of the pair of them. Taking hold under her arms, the two men dragged Natalie's inert form off the bed and down the stairs. Jewel bolted the back door, which was swinging in the wind, then opened the front door slowly. The street was deserted and he detected no twitching of curtains in the pre-dawn gloom. The two of them frogmarched the drugged girl the few feet to the car, pushed her into the back seat, covered her with a coarse blanket and closed the house door before driving off into the darkness.

CHAPTER FORTY-SEVEN

Simon had left the house in good time to catch the five to five train. The walk through the dark streets to the station had taken him half an hour and there had still been twenty minutes to wait. The train was standing in the platform and, as he settled into his seat, he was glad of the distraction the day would inevitably bring to the unresolved and perplexing enigma that was his relationship with Natalie Robertson. There was no doubt that things had quite significantly cooled between them. He thought that Natalie was probably right; they both needed some time to come to terms with what the future might hold once the Eddie Duggan stuff was resolved. While he was unwavering in his commitment to her, he was also aware of the very real practical issues that would need to be dealt with if they were both to want any form of long-term relationship. For him, he suddenly realised, that still meant marriage. Although he loved her with all his heart and had participated fully and completely in their lovemaking he knew that he would only feel absolutely content if they were to be married. The problem was that she might well not see things that way and he knew that he was likely to be helpless to resist her physical charms now that Pandora's Box had been well and truly opened.

There was also what she had called "the God stuff". With the experience of human love had come a gentle nudge in the direction of his past faith. It was as if being loved by the girl had opened up to him the possibility that the God who he had kept at bay for so long might still be watching over him after all. It was all too much to think about. He turned to look out of the window, but could see only the reflection of the interior of the carriage in the darkness beyond as the train pulled out of the station and began to gather speed.

Simon's mobile phone rang just as the train was pulling into Leicester. As he reached into his pocket for the handset he was mildly irritated. Natalie knew that using their mobiles ran the risk of detection. He pressed the answer key. 'Nat?' he gasped and then abject fear coursed through his veins as the drama began to unfold over the airwaves. He could hear the sound of shouting, then a voice demanding that she tell them where he was. Her brave refusal melted his heart, but the obvious sound of someone hurting her brought him out into a cold sweat. He leaped from his seat, dragged his bag from the rack and made for the door as he shouted for her to tell them. As he stepped down onto the platform a voice threatened that if he wanted to see her again he'd better do what they wanted. In the background he could clearly make out Natalie shouting at him not to comply. In a moment of pure anguish he pressed the power off button and the line went dead. Pushing his way through a small crowd of waiting passengers he slumped onto a bench seat. Utterly despondent, Simon tried to force his mind into action. He knew that he had to think. All his instincts were drawing him back to the little house in Derby where the woman he loved was in mortal danger. He glanced at the departure screen. A train for Derby was shown leaving at six thirty three; perhaps it would be quicker if he took a taxi. In any event, he would probably arrive far too late to help her. He contemplated dialling nine, nine, nine and reporting the assault, but his instincts told him that the Derby police would arrive too late to make a difference. Calling the police would also draw unwelcome attention to him and he still had the papers to offer as a trade; that might be Natalie's best hope. As the beginnings of rational thought began to filter through his mental torment he realised that going back was almost certainly what they wanted him to do. They wanted the papers. He contemplated hiding them somewhere before returning and then trying to bargain with them to release Natalie, but he was certain that these people had killed before. They would undoubtedly kill him and Natalie given half the chance. No, he reasoned, the best way of keeping Natalie alive was probably to bargain from a distance. He would offer them the papers in exchange for proof that Natalie was alive, well and free. In despair he sat on his lonely seat and plumbed the recesses of his mind for some sort of coherent plan of action.

The only option, he realised, was to try and keep the initiative. Whatever it took he must attempt to call the shots. While he was free and had the papers, Natalie was reduced to being no more than a bit player in the drama. Of course if they ever did get hold of the papers her life would be worth nothing to Eddie Duggan, except that if he knew that she was his own flesh and blood it might make some difference. That would be his ace in the hole. He must do all he could to make sure that Eddie Duggan knew that he was about to kill his own daughter. If only he could get Natalie released and safe somewhere he could then try and somehow carry on with the mission entrusted to him. Natalie came first, though; that much was obvious to him. He would ultimately trade his own life for hers willingly, but if he could take down Eddie Duggan and his evil empire at the same time so much the better. Simon removed the phone from his pocket and was about to switch it on when the thought struck him. They, whoever they were, might well have already traced the previous call to Leicester. He had to keep moving and also, if at all possible, never call more than once from the same handset. He glanced again at the departure screen. A train to Peterborough was due to leave at eleven minutes past six. He would move on; and keep them waiting. Natalie would probably be reasonably safe while he was at large, he reasoned. He would travel to Peterborough; then on somewhere else and buy a bundle of mobile phones before he called Natalie's number again. He would play a game of bluff and double bluff. The only problem was that the stakes were as high as they could be. The most important thing in his life was his love for Natalie and it was her life that would be forfeit if he made the wrong decision.

CHAPTER FORTY-EIGHT

Natalie's limbs felt unreasonably heavy. She had a blinding headache and dull angry pains in various parts of her anatomy. As the realisation of her predicament forced its way through her drug induced lethargy, Natalie's mental anguish pushed the physical pain into the background and she attempted to push herself up into a sitting position. Her right arm however would not do what she wanted it to. As her eyes regained their focus she realised that her wrist was securely manacled to the heavy iron frame of a grubby bed. Thin light penetrated the room through faded curtains and, as she wriggled her legs over the side of the bed and finally managed to sit up, she saw that she was imprisoned in a small bedroom. Beside the bed was a large plastic bucket, which she viewed with distaste, but the very sight of it prompted an urgent need to urinate. Crossing her legs did little to help and she self consciously struggled to push her leggings down to her ankles using her free hand in order to make use of the primitive facility before attempting the equally difficult task of readjusting her clothing and sitting back on the soiled bed. She could hear no sound of habitation in the house, but dared not make any unnecessary noise, fearing a repeat of the physical violence she had experienced earlier.

Time passed slowly and Natalie was both frightened and despondent. She had no idea how long she had been unconscious. Her thoughts turned to Simon. She fervently hoped that he had not been deflected from his mission. She strongly suspected, however, that he might have been. She had no doubt that he loved her very much and that gave her some comfort, but her new fear was that he would put himself into more danger in an attempt to come to her aid. She was under no illusions; in all probability she would not be allowed to live once Eddie Duggan and his thugs got hold of the papers. If Simon tried to trade them for her life then they would probably both die anyway. Still, the last week had been the best time of her life. Whatever the consequences, and they would undoubtedly be dire, she was glad that she had met and fallen in love with Simon Fenton, thirty four. She tried to convince herself that giving her life that he might live was the only way she had left to express her very deep love for him. She would tell them nothing, she promised herself. Yet, even as she made the vow fear welled up within her. She did not want to die. Her imagination played on her fear. She wondered how they would kill her. Would they shoot her? Or would they continue to hurt her if she refused to tell them Simon's plan. It was all good and well to say that love would keep her strong, but she was not at all sure that she could hold out if they tortured her. She pulled her knees up to her chin with her free hand and began to cry. Natalie cried for the man she loved; she cried for all her wasted years and she cried for herself. She wondered what Simon would do if he was in her predicament. Being the man he was he would probably pray, wouldn't he? But she didn't believe in all that. The tears rolled freely down her cheeks as her aching body heaved with sobs. So this was it, she thought, this is where it all ends. With nothing left to lose she finally cried out to the God she did not believe in.

'Oh, God, please get me out of this and please make Simon live,' she sobbed, 'and if you do that for me I promise I won't drag him down to my level. I promise I'll walk away from him and give him back to you.'

The sobs gradually subsided and Natalie Robertson slipped gently back into an exhausted and fitful sleep.

CHAPTER FORTY-NINE

At Peterborough Simon bought a ticket to York after carefully consulting the timetable. The next train would get him there just before the shops opened at nine o'clock. He walked to the far end of the platform to wait; seeking solitude amidst his despair. With a pen and paper ready he switched his mobile phone on and transcribed Natalie's number onto a scrap of paper before switching it off again immediately. If the local network had picked up enough signal to trace he hoped that he would be long gone before anyone had the time to take any action. In spite of having the glimmering of a plan in his mind, he still felt helpless. Natalie was in the hands of the enemy. He had no idea where they might have taken her, but he was fairly certain that she would no longer be in Derby. One thing was clear to him, though, he would have to do whatever was necessary to save her. As he paced slowly up and down the windswept platform, though, he was deeply troubled. At that very moment they might be hurting her again; torturing her to get her to reveal where he was going and what he was planning to do. The mental picture of the woman that he loved being deliberately hurt filled him with anguish and his pain drove him to the deepest place in his being.

'Oh God,' he prayed, please help......' But a wave of even deeper despair overcame him. How could he possibly call upon the God whom he had turned his back on? With an inner cry of anguish too deep for words he wrung his hands in desperation.

A sudden gust of wind stirred up a collection of discarded chocolate wrappers and paper cups into a noisy spiral on the platform in front of him and Simon dared to hope that his God might just have been listening after all.

Pale morning sunlight illuminated the ancient walls of York through a gap in the rainclouds as Simon strode briskly from the railway station into the city centre. Mindful of the difficulties of charging batteries while on the move he bought four handsets which were identical to the one in his pocket, planning to move the almost fully charged battery between them before each call. His next stop was a high street copy shop where he enquired about making photocopies of the documents. After some experimentation, however, the shop assistant apologetically explained that the contrast and clarity of the originals was so poor that it was quite impossible to obtain legible photocopies. The results were either too pale for the text to be distinguished or so dark that the sheets turned out almost completely black. Disappointed, Simon was left with no fall-back plan. On impulse he asked for and obtained good copies of all the letters from Michael Duckworth, with only a sketchy idea of what use they might be put to. From then on it would be all or nothing; there would be only one chance of success and that would entail drastic measures. He retraced his steps towards the railway station and paused by the city wall. Taking a deep breath he inserted the live battery into one of the new handsets, powered it up and, with trembling fingers, began to dial the number.

'Fenton, what the fuck do you think you're doing?' snapped a voice as the call was answered. 'You'd better do exactly what you're told if you want to see your girlfriend again. Now, where are you?'

Simon felt the anger rise within him. With a silent prayer that Natalie would not hear what he was about to say, he began to put his embryonic plan into action.

'What girlfriend?' he retorted angrily, 'she's no more than a cheap slapper. You're welcome to her, but just watch out you don't catch something nasty. I don't give a damn about the girl, but I think your boss should; after all, she is his daughter.'

'Now just you listen to me....' replied the voice.

Troubled Legacy

'No, you listen,' hissed Simon, 'Natalie Robertson is Eddie Duggan's daughter and I've got letters to prove it. You just ask him if he remembers Sue Robertson, a stripper that he knocked up in 1984. The tart was born on 13th April 1985. Just think what the papers would make of that – the Home Secretary and the Stripper – sure beats the vicar and tart stuff doesn't it. Anyway I'm not dealing with the monkey; it's the organ grinder I want to talk to. Tell Duggan that if he wants a deal he'll need to be the one answering that telephone when I call again and it's hard cash I want, not some shagged out tart. I'll give you five hours. When I call at half past two it had better be Duggan on the other end or this lot will end up all over the Daily Mail.'

Simon powered off the phone and slumped against the wall. His legs were weak and he could feel his heart beating rapidly in his chest. He had, he hoped, bought himself some time and taken the fight to the enemy. He did not think that whoever was holding Natalie would dare to harm her any further if there was a suspicion that she could actually be Eddie Duggan's daughter. Even if Duggan denied paternity there would be the seeds of doubt in his mind. With the possibility of DNA matching, his denials might not stand up indefinitely. A real red herring had been introduced. Simon allowed himself a brief smile of satisfaction and prepared to move on to the next step in his plan. He had also realised how the photocopies of Michael Duckworth's letters could be used to his advantage.

He took a train to Leeds, where he checked into a large hotel adjacent to the station under an assumed name. As he did not have a credit card, the hotel demanded a two hundred pound deposit, but cash was a commodity of which he still had no shortage. In his room he plugged in the chargers for the notebook PC and the unused mobile phones before making a foray into the city centre shops. Upon his return he laid out his purchases on the bed; a large rucksack, an Ordnance Survey map of part of North Yorkshire, a bundle of long cable ties, a dark green jacket and a matching pair of trousers, a small tent and a lightweight sleeping bag, a wind-up torch, a slab of blu-tak, a packet of plain postcards, some writing paper, envelopes and stamps and a wooden rounders bat. Alongside these he unpacked the contents of his day-sack. Apart from the plastic box containing the pale photocopies, a couple of shirts and some spare underwear and the day-sack he discarded the remainder of his few possessions into the bin. Upon reflection, however, he reclaimed the folding spade. It might just come in useful, he thought.

After sitting at the small table and writing two letters he stuffed the small day sack into the large rucksack along with the rest of his remaining equipment and set out on the next leg of his journey. Although he had no intention of returning to the hotel Simon did not check out.

CHAPTER FIFTY

In the Warrington council house Simon Fenton's call had caused a great deal of consternation. Far from being prepared to trade the papers for the girl as they had expected him to, Simon Fenton seemed to have grasped the initiative. Paul Cavendish put down the telephone handset.

'Shit!' he exclaimed, 'I wonder if she is; Duggan's daughter, I mean.'

Jewel, who had been able to hear the whole conversation via the speaker option on the telephone, shrugged his shoulders.

'I've no bloody, idea,' he replied, 'but we'd better kick this upstairs and no messing about.' He took a second handset from his pocket and dialled Jimmy Bell's private number.

After making Jewel repeat the story and subjecting him to a rigorous cross-examination, Jimmy Bell called Eddie Duggan. At first Duggan's reaction was a mixture of apoplexy and rage. After a few minutes, though, his tirade lost some of its impetus. He ordered Bell to make sure the girl's telephone reached the ICIS office by two at the latest. He would deal with Fenton himself, he said, and would be there by two thirty.

Jimmy Bell ordered Jewel to take the first possible train to Euston, leaving Cavendish to keep an eye on the girl. The Detective Chief Superintendent told his Detective Inspector that he would meet the train at Euston and collect the handset, freeing Jewel to get back to Warrington without further delay.

Eddie Duggan took stock of his options. The view from his conservatory, over the gentle rolling hills of south-east Kent, held little fascination for him as he tried frantically to find a way to put his troubled past behind him without risking his bid for the highest office. The past had come back to haunt him in more ways than he had ever imagined would be possible. For many years he had almost succeeded in erasing the memory of Susan Robertson and her unplanned pregnancy from his mind. Now, out of the blue, it seemed that the prostitute Andrew Gilroy has suborned to seduce Simon Fenton might very well prove to be his illegitimate daughter. While he had been most afraid of the documents pertaining to his shady business dealings and the shooting of John Fenton, he now had to come to terms with the fact that, because of their respective paternity, both Simon Fenton and Natalie Robertson posed an even more significant threat to his plans. Ruthless logic told him that killing them both remained the best guarantee of his success and, ultimately, his freedom. The prospect of killing Simon Fenton caused him no concern whatsoever. Natalie Robertson, however, posed him a dilemma. Neither of his marriages had produced children. At the age of fifty eight he had no pressing desire for his current wife to conceive; nor did she appear to have any ambitions in that area. He had long resigned himself to remaining childless although, once or twice he had wondered about Susan Robertson's baby; for some inexplicable reason he had kept her letters at the back of his desk drawer at the Phillip Lane car dealership. He had always assumed that they had been lost in the fire. At the time he had doubted that he was the father; suspecting Susan of having singled him out from a list of potential fathers on the grounds of his wealth. But he had always wondered. Now it seemed that she might well have been telling the truth. It was possible that he actually could have a daughter. DNA analysis could either confirm or deny the fact; a daughter who had been working as a prostitute; a daughter who had taken up with Simon Fenton against him; a daughter over whom he now held the power of life and death. Bell had informed him that Fenton was not prepared to trade the papers for the girl and logic told him that the safest course of action would be to have her killed and her body disposed of where it would never be found. A remnant of conscience, however, tormented his mind. If Natalie Robertson was his own flesh and blood she was the only means by which his genes could survive into another generation. He felt a strange reluctance to order her execution. Torn with indecision he dismissed his driver and protection officer, telling them that he was planning to remain at home for the next few days. Only the armed dog-handler in the grounds would remain on duty and Eddie Duggan knew that if he timed his departure for when the officer was at the far end of his large garden no one would ever know that he had left the house.

For Jimmy Bell the news of Natalie Robertson's probable paternity came as a body blow. He was already up to his neck in the highly irregular, totally illegal and potentially career-destroying mess that The Governor had blackmailed him into. He was sickened by what he had done. The ghosts of both the men he had either killed and those he had ordered others to kill troubled him in increasingly regular nightmares. Each time he had followed Eddie Duggan's illicit orders he had sworn to himself that it would be the last, but there had always been something more; not that he had grumbled about the payoffs, he reflected wryly. Now, though, the prospects of success in the present operation seemed to be fading hour by hour. The idea of starting over in Rio was becoming more and more attractive. Only a few more days, he thought; then he would be on his way. For a moment he was sorely tempted to just walk out from his office with his bonds, money and false identity and hide up somewhere until Thursday morning. Financial reality however reined him in. He would try and extract some more money from Eddie Duggan before then, he thought. If he could help to obtain the incriminating papers from Simon Fenton he was likely to be rewarded appropriately. He would hang on in there until the last minute, he determined. Another quarter of a million might make all the difference. He called his contact at GCHQ in Cheltenham. Fenton's call had been made from York. He alerted the listener to be prepared to track another call to the same number that was expected at around half past two.

CHAPTER FIFTY-ONE

Simon Fenton's next rail journey involved crossing the Pennines to Manchester. As the train pulled out of Leeds he watched from his window seat as the train accelerated past the modern tower blocks, the windows behind the tiny balconies reflecting the blue-grey sky; one of them, he mused, belonged to Natalie. He thought of her, his eyes moist with tears. He was carrying the responsibility now for her well-being and her future. Although he still had serious doubts about his ability to carry off his audacious scheme, he was utterly determined that he would do everything in his power; she was more important to him that life itself.

    The stark familiarity of Piccadilly station would not allow Simon's mind any respite from his awesome responsibility. Having sought out a post box and posting one of his letters he mentally ticked off the days since he had last passed through Manchester; since he had first been in the company of Natalie Robertson; ten days, eleven if the fateful Friday evening when he had eaten dinner with her in the restaurant at the Midland Hotel was included. Eleven days that had changed his life forever. With almost an hour before he was due to make the call, he took the escalator onto the mezzanine and ordered a latté and a sandwich from Costa Coffee, but he had no appetite and ate very little. The hands on his watch moved interminably slowly. Eventually, just two minutes before the half hour, he powered up the phone and waited for the signal that it was within the coverage of the network. There bars signified success and he slowly and carefully dialled the number.

The call was answered immediately.

'Is that you Fenton?'

Simon rocked backwards on his seat, intimidated by the ferocity of his protagonist's voice which he recognised immediately.

'Er.. I want a million, 'he said, 'in used notes. A million and you can have the stuff.'

'No way, Fenton,' came the reply, 'if you give me what you've got you can walk away. That will be the end of it. You can go back to your sad little life and forget all this. Take it or leave it.'

'A million in cash,' Simon repeated, 'you can take it or leave it. You've got two hours.' He powered off the 'phone and sat upright in his chair. Duggan's response had been more or less what he expected. By turning the power off the handset he felt that he had maintained the advantage. They might very well trace the call, but he would have moved on again before they could act. The danger would come the following morning when his freedom of movement would be curtailed. Still, he would still be calling the shots, even then. If all went according to plan he would, anyway. He stood up and walked the short distance across the concourse to platform three where he boarded the fourteen forty two service to Middlesbrough. When the train reached Leeds he got off and found a vacant table in the McDonald's fast food outlet in the station concourse where he sipped a cold drink and nibbled on a hamburger until the time reached four thirty. Determined to keep up the pressure on Eddie Duggan he did not call right away. He waited a further fifteen minutes.

'Six hundred thousand, Fenton, 'Duggan's voice was less confident this time, 'that's the best I can do at short notice. Now where shall we meet?'

'Oh no, you don't,' replied Simon, 'You'll do as I say. Make sure you're at Kings Cross station by ten to six tomorrow morning with the money in a suitcase; and make sure you're on your own, Duggan. No hangers on or hired help. Have this telephone with you and I'll tell you where then. Oh, and as proof of your goodwill I want the tart released tonight. Unless I read on the BBC News website tomorrow morning that she's given herself in at a police station the deal's off.'

He powered off the handset once again. The dye was cast. There was no more he could do. Either Natalie would be relatively safe in the custody of the proper police and he would have his confrontation with the man who had killed his father or it would all come grinding to an end. He dared not contemplate the latter. With a shiver running up and down his spine Simon joined a train for Skipton at platform one. After a short wait at Skipton, where he purchased an assortment of pre-packed sandwiches, chocolate bars and bottled water, he joined the last train of the day to Carlisle and alighted into the darkness at the highest mainline station in England fifty minutes later.

CHAPTER FIFTY-TWO

When Natalie awoke again it was dark outside. A faint orange glow from a streetlight on the other side of the curtains gave some measure of illumination to her prison. Her mouth was dry and her headache was considerably worse although the pain from her bruises had dulled slightly. She could hear voices from somewhere nearby and considered calling out to ask for a drink, but fear kept her lips sealed. Although she could not be certain, she assumed it was the same day that she had been abducted. She wondered if Simon had managed to reach the media with the incriminating documents. The thought of him still free and determined to bring Eddie Duggan to justice gave her a degree of comfort, but little hope. If she was to survive this, she reflected sombrely, it would be a miracle; she simply knew too much for Duggan to risk her staying alive. Even if he was to discover that she was his daughter his track record of ruthless self-interest would be more than likely to overcome any glimmer of paternal instinct. After all, he hadn't wanted anything to do with her when she was born – why should anything be different now. A daughter who was on the game would be no asset to an aspiring Prime Minister. Tears of despair filled her eyes and she curled up into a foetal position on her side with her manacled wrist splayed out towards the corner of the bed.

Suddenly the door crashed open and the overhead light was switched on. Screwing her eyes up against the sudden glare, she recognised the figures of her two captors in the room. The taller one was standing in the doorway with an automatic pistol levelled at her while the other man stood menacingly at the side of the bed. The closer man unlocked the handcuff from the bedstead and roughly flipped her over onto her front, twisting her free arm behind her and cuffing her wrists together. Natalie was petrified, fearing that the final act in her short life was about to be played out. The man beside her jerked her to her feet and, with the gunman covering their every move. Tthe smaller man pushed her roughly through the door and down a steep flight of stairs. In a small hallway he pushed her face-first against the wall and wrapped a blindfold tightly over her eyes. No words were spoken and Natalie heard the sound of a door being unlocked and opened before she was frogmarched for a short distance, with a captor on either side of her. She could feel the cold damp air on her exposed skin and a chill wind penetrated her thin clothing as she heard a car door being unlocked and opened before she was pushed through in and left lying on a bench seat. She heard the door being closed behind her and then sensed her captors opening and closing the front doors. The engine started and Natalie Robertson steeled herself for what she believed would be her final journey before oblivion.

The drive was shorter than she had anticipated. The car drew to a halt and the engine was turned off. She was dragged backwards out of the car and forced upright by a strong pair of hands. The blindfold was torn from her face. Rather than the lonely countryside she had been expecting to see, she was in an urban street. The car was parked in the shadows beneath a broken street light. Ahead of her she could see an illuminated blue sign proclaiming the building almost opposite to be a police station.

'Listen to me!' a voice hissed in her ear. 'In a minute I'm going to take the cuffs off. You're going to walk straight ahead – don't you dare look back – and go and give yourself up to the police. Only you don't say a word about anything about us or Eddie; not if you value your life. We can get to you in there and we know where you live, Natalie Roberson. So keep quiet like a good little girl and maybe, just maybe you'll stay alive.'

Natalie felt the handcuffs being released from her wrists and then a push in the small of her back. With the rough asphalt pricking her bare feet she tottered unsteadily across the road, up the ramp and through the glass doors. A bored-looking woman was seated behind a glass partition at the reception desk. Natalie stumbled up to the speaking grille.

'I'm Natalie Roberson,' she croaked, 'I think you've been looking for me, only please could you tell me where I am and please could I have a drink of water.'

CHAPTER FIFTY-THREE

Dent, apart from being the highest mainline station in England, suited Simon's purposes for two other reasons. Apart from the ex-stationmaster's house and the station building itself, both of which were now converted into holiday lets, there were no occupied buildings in the vicinity. Although another former railway building was in the process of being converted into holiday accommodation the work was not yet complete. The village itself was almost four miles away in the bottom of the valley. Secondly, because of the surrounding hills there was no mobile phone reception. Simon knew all of these facts because he had spent a week in the former stationmaster's house a few weeks previously. The brochure had made clear that none of the mobile networks could be accessed. Seeking solitude, scenery and a view of the passing trains on the Settle to Carlisle railway he had spent a week of his annual leave there in July. Although he had not been the slightest bit concerned about not being able to use his mobile phone, he had a mobile internet connection on his laptop that needed network coverage. He had discovered that a walk of half a mile or so up the old Coal Road and then a short sharp climb over rough ground to the summit of a rounded hill enabled his modem to make the connection.

He paused on the platform as the train rattled its way into the darkness, then he took out his torch and made a careful inspection of a number of fittings and features on both platforms, crossing under the railway by means of following a tumbling stream under a small bridge. Satisfied with his reconnaissance, he set off up the Coal Road, glancing back at the general layout of the station from above. The electric lights in their reproduction lamp stands cast a soft light over the platforms and a yellow glow from behind the curtains signified that holidaymakers were present in both buildings. He trudged upward for ten minutes, then, recognising the location from his earlier visit, climbed over a low wall and struck off across country. In the pale moonlight that filtered through the thin clouds he found the going difficult, frequently stumbling as he climbed the barren hillside. Eventually he reached the summit and checked the signal on both his last unused mobile phone and the notebook. All was well and he slithered his way down into a shallow depression on the far side of the summit where he pitched the small tent on a reasonably level piece of ground and dragged his rucksack inside after him. After a rudimentary meal he re-emerged into the damp night air. The cloud had thickened and the feeble moonlight was all but obscured. Apart from one or two isolated lights in the far distance he could see nothing at all. The deep rumble of a goods train climbing from Blea Moor Tunnel distracted him momentarily from his solitude. He wondered if Natalie had been released. The temptation to switch on the notebook and trawl the web for news of her was very strong, but the need to conserve the limited battery life won out and he reluctantly conceded that it would not be sensible to look until the following morning. He crawled back into the tent, took off his shoes and pulled the sleeping bag up around him. The next day would be both the most dangerous and important in his life.

CHAPTER FIFTY-FOUR

Eddie Duggan had managed to return to his house undetected. His wife was not at home. From Jimmy Bell the Home Secretary had learned that Simon Fenton was making his calls, never on the same handset twice, from various locations in Northern England. He had instructed Bell to arrange for Jewel and Cavendish to release the girl in Warrington, along with a dire threat to keep her silent, then to stay on call in the Manchester area. Bell was tasked with collecting him from his home at four fifteen and driving him to Kings Cross. If Fenton appeared at Kings Cross Bell was to ride shotgun and use his warrant card to stage his abduction. If the rendezvous was in the north, the two Detective Inspectors would fulfil a similar role.

In the lonely solitude of his grand house Eddie Duggan began to make preparations for a final showdown with Simon Fenton. Accepting that he may well have to produce the money in order to entice his adversary into close proximity, he went to the safe in his bedroom and took out the six hundred thousand pounds agreed on. He placed the bundles of notes in a sturdy suitcase and then took out a large brown envelope. Like Jimmy Bell he too had an emergency escape plan, but he had fake identities in not one, but two other personas. The first was as London businessman Eric Blackheath. In addition to the passport though, Eric Blackheath had several bank accounts, a villa in the Vendee and the sole directorship of a shell company registered in Bermuda which owned a number of businesses in the UK, France and Spain. His other alter-ego was Peter Lord, a Canadian who also owned property in both France and Austria and had a balance of almost two million in a Swiss bank account. He tipped the various documents onto the bed and fingered through them. If worst came to worst he would be prepared.

Jimmy Bell was also reviewing his contingency plan. The problem was simple; he did not have enough money to be certain that he would be comfortable for the rest of his life if he disappeared. With over thirty years of police service he was already eligible for retirement on a handsome pension. This Simon Fenton business, he decided, was the last straw. If Fenton, the girl and the journalist could be taken out of the picture and the documents recovered it would be his last job. He would give in his notice and call it a day. If only he had not invested in the Spanish property, he reflected, he would have had a real choice; but now it seemed that success in his present illicit venture was the only option.

Gerry Jewel and Paul Cavendish had obtained rooms at the Travelodge at Birch Services, between Manchester and Leeds on the M62. Their orders were to remain available at short notice in case Simon Fenton attempted a meet with Eddie Duggan anywhere in the north of England. The two men were sitting in the self-service restaurant eating a late meal. They were discussing the excessive play in the Vectra's steering. Jewel, who had driven the car from Warrington that evening was concerned that, unless they got the problem rectified soon, they might need to hire an alternative car. In the end they decided that they would await Jimmy Bell's instructions in the morning. If Fenton travelled south to meet with Eddie Duggan they would find a local garage and have the car repaired.

In the Cumberland Infirmary Rebecca Johal was sitting quietly beside her brother's bed. The sedative drip had been removed before lunch and Kynpham had become progressively more restless during the afternoon. The medical prognosis was good and Rebecca was determined to be beside him when regained consciousness. Sally Chamley, the staff nurse on night duty in the ward, had kept Rebecca fed and watered as evening became night. Sally and Rebecca were of a similar age and the visitor from India had been delighted to learn that Sally was also a Christian. As the demands of duty had slackened off in the early hours of the morning Sally had pulled up a second chair in the ward and the two girls were talking quietly when Kynpham's eyes opened for the first time in almost a week. Sally was the first to notice.

'Look, Rebecca, 'she whispered excitedly, 'I think he's back with us.'

Rebecca stood up and looked down upon her brother. He half smiled in recognition and emitted a low croak.

'Hello Kynpham,' Rebecca said, 'You've had a bit of an accident.'

Ten minutes later Kynpham was sitting up in bed propped up by several pillows. The junior doctor had been summoned and affirmed the reporter's recovery and Kynpham had managed to drink a little water. He was surprised and delighted to see Rebecca, but said that he had no memory whatsoever of the accident or what had led up to it. He was somewhat incredulous to discover that he was in Carlisle; a place he had never before visited. His last recollection was interviewing an engineer on the site of the new Olympic Stadium in East London about the reasons why, despite official statements to the contrary, the project was running almost four weeks behind schedule. The policewoman on guard outside was informed of Kynpham's progress and the reporter was once again incredulous upon discovering that he had a police guard. The policewoman radioed the information to the control centre, but she was told that no detectives were available to interview Kynpham and that she should stay where she was until her relief arrived in the morning.

Natalie's reception at the police station had not been what she had expected. The woman behind the desk had noticed her bruised face, bare feet and general state of distress and had immediately unlocked the access door and led her onto the other side of the desk. She had then made Natalie a cup of tea and offered her chocolate biscuits. A Sergeant was summoned. He took details of Natalie's name, address and date of birth before disappearing once again. Twenty minutes later he returned and took Natalie to an interview room where she was given a second cup of tea and a plate of sandwiches. As she ate, the Sergeant told her that a doctor had been summoned to have a look at her injuries.

The doctor duly arrived and, after a cursory examination, pronounced her unfit to be questioned. He prescribed paracetomol for her multiple pains and a good night's rest. The Sergeant replied that he was relieved about that because he didn't know what questions he should be asking her anyway. It was, he said, the Greater Manchester police who would like a word with her. He had informed them, but did not expect them to send a car to collect her until the following morning anyway. Eventually she was offered a bed for the night in a cell, which she was more than happy to accept. The bed was hard and the blanket coarse, but Natalie Robertson didn't mind. Although logic told her that the arms of Eddie Duggan had a long reach she felt somehow safe in her austere surroundings. If he had been going to have her killed, she reasoned, his henchmen would not have released her. In spite of the raucous singing of a drunk in the next cell, Natalie quickly slipped into a sound and dreamless sleep.

CHAPTER FIFTY-FIVE

The shrill sound Jimmy Bell's alarm clock jerked him from an uneasy slumber at ten to three. In the pitch darkness he fumbled for the button to silence the incessant warble before locating the switch for the bedside light. He was due to pick up Eddie Duggan at four fifteen.

At a few minutes after four Eddie Duggan, unshaven, dressed in the clothes he usually wore for gardening and sporting a woolly hat and tinted sunglasses, slipped unnoticed from his house. His young wife had still not made it home which gave him one less problem to solve in the short term, but the possibility of a much larger one to address at a later date. He was carrying a shoulder bag containing an assortment of items which included his false identity papers and dragging a substantial wheeled suitcase very slowly along the unlit lane in an attempt to avoid making so much noise that someone noticed him. Shunning the illumination of the few street lights in the centre of the village, he remained in the shadows. Detective Chief Superintendent Bell pulled up at the agreed rendezvous less than five minutes late.

Despite the early hour there was considerable traffic on the M20; mainly heavy goods vehicles processing to and from the Channel Ports. Bell maintained a steady eighty miles per hour in the outside lane. Neither man was in the mood for conversation, but the Home Secretary took pains to remind his subordinate of the back up he wanted in place for his meeting with Simon Fenton. As they pulled up outside Kings Cross, Bell gestured to a constable of the British Transport Police. The junior officer approached the car and Bell got out, flashing his warrant card.

'Keep an eye on the car, son,' he ordered as Eddie Duggan slipped furtively out of the passenger door, 'and get on your radio for armed support, I may need to make an arrest in a couple of minutes.'

There was no sign of Simon Fenton amongst the early morning travellers. Jimmy Bell made contact with an armed officer carrying a sub-machine pistol and the two of them loitered outside the W H Smith bookshop while Eddie Duggan stood listlessly beneath the huge electronic departure board. At exactly five fifty the mobile phone in his hand began to ring. After a matter of seconds the Home Secretary dropped the handset back into his coat pocket and scurried towards the ticket office where he joined a short queue. In possession of a ticked, Duggan then sprinted across the concourse and through the barrier of platform three. The departure board indicated that the train in platform three was the six o'clock for Leeds. Jimmy Bell kept the armed officer talking for a few moments, anxious that the man made no connection between his encounter with a senior officer and the unkempt-looking man who had needed to run to catch his train. He then dismissed the constable and returned to his car, within seconds his own mobile phone rang.

'Leeds, Jimmy, it's Leeds. Get Jewel and Cavendish there before the train.' Slightly bemused, Jimmy Bell disconnected the call and pressed the speed-dial connection for Gerry Jewel.

CHAPTER FIFTY-SIX

Simon had slept reasonably well on the hard ground. The alarm on his watch galvanised him into action at four forty five. After pulling on his trainers he took the notebook and picked his way through the rough scrubland to the summit of the hill where he switched the computer on and waited for it to make an internet connection. He could feel his heart beating rapidly and his breathing was erratic as he watched the screen. He was about to find out if the first part of his double bluff had paid off. In a state of deep anxiety he awaited confirmation that Natalie Robertson was alive and relatively safe. The glow of the screen was the only light in the pitch darkness of the North Yorkshire wilderness; a tiny ray of hope in a world of near despair.

Then there it was. A one line link on the BBC News website: "Fugitive call girl gives herself up." Relief flooded through him like a rising tide on a tropical beach. Natalie was alive! He clicked on the link and began to read the story.

"Cheshire Police announced this morning that call girl Natalie Robertson (24), who is wanted for questioning with regard to the murder of Detective Inspector Andrew Gilroy of the Independent Criminal Investigation Service in Manchester a week ago last Saturday walked into Warrington police station late yesterday. She is expected to be collected by detectives from Manchester later today and taken there for further questioning. Miss Robertson is thought to be a key witness in the investigation. Police sources indicate that the suspected murderer of Inspector Gilroy was gangland

enforcer Wayne Stevens, who was himself shot dead by persons unknown shortly afterwards. A spokesman said that Miss Robertson was not under arrest, but is simply helping the police with their inquiries. Ex- vicar Simon Fenton, who is also thought to have witnessed Inspector Gilroy's murder, is still at large. Miss Robertson and Mr Fenton were last reported to be travelling in Northern Ireland ont Friday."

It was all that he had hoped for; Natalie in a police station and the world aware of the fact. Although he had no illusions as the ruthlessness of Eddie Duggan and his associates, Simon felt fairly confident that, along with the newly planted suspicion of her paternity, events in Warrington and Manchester might keep Natalie out of harm's way while he put the second and most crucial part of his plan into action.

His next move was to re-trace his steps to the narrow road and return to the deserted station, where he opened in turn the grey housings of the Network rail telephones on each platform and secured small pieces of paper to the upper inside surfaces of the doors with blu-tak before closing them again. The telephones were provided so that passengers could check the progress of trains with the signalman; there being no public address or information screens on the remote rural station. He hoped that no passengers would make use of them and notice the papers before they had served their purpose. It was still dark and the journey back to his camp took him longer than he expected. There was just enough time for him to re-pack the items that he needed into the small day sack before he trudged the last few yards back to the summit of the hill. Dawn was beginning to illuminate the eastern sky as he once again powered up the notebook.

After checking the electronic departures board for London Kings Cross, he waited impatiently for the luminous hands on his watch as they moved painfully slowly, but inexorably towards five forty nine. He switched on the mobile phone handset and quickly dialled the number.

'Duggan, you're going to Leeds on the six o'clock. They won't let you through the barrier without a ticket, so get a move on. I'll be waiting.'

Simon did not bother to disconnect the call; he simply switched off the handset and checked his watch again. Nine and a half minutes to six. Then the train of events would be well and truly underway. He smiled at the mental pun and whistled soundlessly as he scrambled back down the hillside to his makeshift camp. It was time for some breakfast.

CHAPTER FIFTY-SEVEN

As the Leeds train snaked its way through the tunnels outside Kings Cross and began to gather speed Eddie Duggan hid his face behind a copy of the Train Operator's in-house magazine in his corner seat. Unusually, but quite appropriately for someone dressed as he was and who was trying to avoid drawing attention to himself, he was travelling standard class. The carriage was less than half full and the airline-style seat beside him was unoccupied. He hoped it would stay that way. The high seat back in front helped maintain his privacy and the Home Secretary remained mercifully anonymous as the first pale traces of the dawn painted the eastern horizon above the unmistakable minaret of the Finsbury Park Mosque.

Jimmy Bell parked his car in the basement beneath New Scotland Yard and completed the short journey to Broadway on foot. He let himself in to his office and sat in on the worn leather sofa while he waited for the kettle to boil. He was half way through his second cup of strong black coffee when a call on his mobile from his contact in GCHQ informed him that it had not been possible to obtain an accurate fix on the call made to Natalie Robertson's mobile. Only one phone mast, it appeared, had registered the handset and that was located between Skipton and Settle in North Yorkshire. The signal had been of low strength, suggesting that the call had been made from between eight and twelve miles away, but it was not possible to determine in which direction. Jimmy Bell thanked his informant and passed on the information to Eddie Duggan who circumspectly concurred with Bell's view that Leeds probably was the appointed meeting place and thanked him for the information that

Jewel and Cavendish would be on hand when the train arrived. He also texted the Home Secretary the mobile numbers for both Gerry Jewel and Paul Cavendish so that they could be contacted directly should the need arise. Bell's next task was to inform Jewel and Cavendish. A sleepy Jerry Jewel agreed that they would be in position on the platform at Leeds ten minutes before the train was due. The strong coffee seemed to be playing havoc with Jimmy Bell's digestive system: he felt physically and mentally worse than he could ever remember.

In the Cumberland Infirmary Kynpham Johal was making excellent progress. Rebecca had eventually left by taxi a little after one in the morning and was back at her brother's bedside by six with the complicit assistance of Sally Chamley. Kynpham was clearly on the mend. When Rebecca arrived he was sitting up in bed drinking tea and nibbling toast. Still completely oblivious to how he had arrived in Carlisle, never mind the Cumberland Infirmary, he announced that it had all probably been worth it to bring his twin sister to visit him in England two months earlier than he had expected. After breakfast a detective sergeant arrived to ask Kynpham a number of questions, to which the reporter was able to give few coherent answers. Having established that there was no question of Kynpham being involved in any form of undercover investigation he made a brief phone call to his Detective Superintendent, who ordered the police guard outside the ward away. Another police officer overheard the conversation and passed the information on to Paul Cavendish who, in turn, informed Jimmy Bell. Relieved that Kynpham was unable to remember anything at all about his abduction and attempted murder, Jimmy Bell mentally filed the information away. Eliminating Kynpham Johal could wait until the more pressing matter of Simon Fenton had been resolved.

CHAPTER FIFTY-EIGHT

As daylight chased the last shadows from the bleak fell-side above Dent railway station Simon left his camp for the last time. The heat of the early morning sun promised a fine day, but he donned his dark green coat; a degree of camouflage would be important later on, he thought. A quick check of the station area revealed two cars parked; one next to the station itself and one outside the former station master's house.

Satisfied with his reconnaissance, he regained the summit of the hill and checked the progress of Eddie Duggan's train via the National Rail website. It was running on time. After searching the web for the telephone numbers of several national and local newspapers and writing them down he settled himself relatively comfortably, sitting on a flat stone between two large boulders, and laid out the notebook his mobile phone and his watch beside him. In the brief morning idyll his thoughts turned to Natalie. By this time tomorrow he hoped that she would be free and that Eddie Duggan would have been exposed as the liar cheat and murderer that he was. It would all depend on what was about to happen on a hillside in Dent in less than three hours time.

The six o'clock from London was due to arrive in Leeds at eight thirty-two. At eight twenty five Simon made his next call. It was answered on the first ring.

'Wait on the big footbridge; outside Starbuck's. I'll come and find you,' he snapped and powered off the 'phone.

On the notebook the live departures and arrivals for Leeds updated themselves as the London train drew ever closer. It was shown as arriving at eight thirty-four; two minutes late. Simon checked the screen and smiled in satisfaction. Everything was going according to plan. At eight forty six he switched on the phone and made the next call, which was also answered immediately.

'Change of plan Duggan. If you look at the departure screen you'll see a train for Carlisle leaving at eight forty-nine. Get on it and get off at Skipton.'

Once again he switched the phone off straight away. A band of high cloud partially obscured the sun and sent a shiver down Simon's spine. Perhaps it was all going too well, he thought. He was aware that Eddie Duggan would almost certainly have one or more of his hired thugs in tow, but he was relying on them shadowing him by road and not being on the train with him. If they were driving then he was confident that he would have the advantage. He had not chosen Dent only because of the lack of mobile phone coverage in the area. He knew that no car on earth could possibly keep pace with a train because of the narrow and tortuous roads from the south. By the time the hired help arrived he planned to be holding all the aces.

The hands on his watch crawled past nine o'clock and the National Rail website told the story of the train's journey through the Aire Valley. The timing of the next call would be crucial. Simon took the risk of switching on the phone more than a minute before the train was due to call at Skipton. and a few seconds after nine twenty-four he made the call.

'Duggan, are you at Skipton?' he said.

'Yes,' was the reply, 'where the fuck are you?'

'Not there!' snapped Simon, 'get back on the train. Get off at the sixth stop. Now, listen carefully, you'll be looking for a grey box with a passenger telephone in it. There's a piece of paper stuck to the inside; at the top. Do what it tells you.' Again he powered off the phone. That was it; the die was cast. Simon slipped the Tupperware box into a bright yellow plastic bag that he had obtained in Leeds the previous day and put it on one side while he packed up his day sack and made his way gingerly down the steep hillside which was still wet with the morning dew. After about three hundred yards he placed the yellow bag where it was clearly visible from below on a large stone. He then sat down on a rocky outcrop in the concealment of a small indentation in the hillside. Below him; through a dense tangle of gorse bushes he could see the full panorama of the railway station. Above him the yellow bag was clearly visible. From the day sack he took six long cable ties, the rounders bat and a cotton shirt, which he tore into long strips. He contemplated laying the folding spade along side the bat, but thought better of it and put it back in the bag. After a few minutes he also returned all but two of the cotton strips to the bag. He could always retrieve them later if he needed to.

CHAPTER FIFTY-NINE

The journey from London to Leeds had seemed interminable to Eddie Duggan. In his anxiety not to be recognised he did not dare to venture out of his seat except for a brief excursion to the toilet in the vestibule behind his seat. Having read and re-read the magazine, he contemplated his predicament. Although he was still confident that, with the support of his corrupt acolytes, he would be successful in detaining Simon Fenton as soon as he arrived in Leeds and in destroying the papers, there was an uncomfortable feeling at the back of his mind. For one thing, involvement in cleaning up the present messy situation kept him out of the public and media eye. That was not an advantage in his bid for leadership of his party and the country. Secondly, Simon Fenton had proved to be rather more resilient and resourceful than he had expected; there might well be some more twists and turns to come. Then there was the matter of Natalie Robertson and her paternity. It was possible that she was his daughter. He felt no familial affinity for her, but there seemed to be some sort of deep reluctance to do her further harm somewhere within him. Logic told him that it would be safer if she simply disappeared. He wondered if the six hundred thousand pounds in his suitcase would serve to buy her off and send her away to start a new life somewhere once Simon Fenton had been dealt with. Finally, there was the matter of his wife. He was now certain that she was being unfaithful to him and the media might well already be on her tail. He would have to do something to either enforce her loyalty or put her out of the picture altogether. By the time the train was approaching Leeds he was morose and unsettled. The strident ring of Natalie's mobile phone in his pocket came as an almost welcome relief.

After listening to Simon Fenton he replaced the phone in his pocket and took out another, upon which he dialled Gerry Jewel's number.

'On the footbridge outside Starbuck's,' he hissed, 'keep your eyes peeled.'

The train drew into the platform and the heavily disguised Home Secretary took his time in alighting; waiting for all the other passengers in the carriage to leave before him. It took him a few moments to orientate himself on the platform, but he eventually located the wide mezzanine that spanned the platforms and rode the escalator upwards. Gerry Jewel was sat on a bench seat facing the Starbuck's coffee stall. Duggan caught his eye and the policemen acknowledged him with an almost imperceptible nod of his head. Duggan could not locate Paul Cavendish, who was actually sitting in the car which was parked beside double yellow lines on the street outside.

Simon's second call took him by surprise. Again he made no reply, but swore audibly as Simon disconnected the call, scanning frantically for the departure board.

'Carlisle train,' he yelled at Gerry Jewel as he started to stride briskly towards the down escalator, dragging the suitcase behind him, 'he's at Skipton!'

With less than a minute to spare Eddie Duggan slipped through the rearmost door of the train and slumped into one of the few empty seats. He had no ticket, he realised. That meant that he would have to buy one on the train and that carried yet another risk of recognition. A staccato bleeping sound announced the closing of the doors and the train moved off. Red-faced and flustered, he bought a return ticket to Skipton from the guard and then half-turned to face the window as the train rattled its way through the suburbs of the northern city.

By the time Gerry Jewel got back to the parked Vectra the Carlisle train was well on its way. The combination of heavy traffic and unfamiliar roads conspired to hinder their progress and it was only by Cavendish exceeding the speed limits and adopting a very aggressive driving style that the two policemen were able to overtake the train before it arrived in Skipton. A call from Jimmy Bell confirmed that Simon had made the call from somewhere north of the small market town. They parked hastily in a supermarket car park which was adjacent to the railway station and Jewel crossed under the line by the subway to await the train while Cavendish remained close to the entrance. No sooner were they in position than the train ran into the platform. As Eddie Duggan stepped down the sound of his mobile phone stopped him in his tracks. With his eyes scanning form side to side in search of his quarry he answered the call. Almost immediately he stepped back onto the train heaving the suitcase through the narrow doorway, leaving Jewel and Cavendish in a state of bemusement. The train departed and Gerry Jewel rejoined his colleague. After a brief conversation they walked the short distance to the car where they waited for further instructions.

Eddie Duggan fought back a rising tide of panic. Simon Fenton had stolen the initiative; he had no idea where the sixth stop would be. He frantically sought out the conductor, having weighed up the risk of recognition against the imperative to make sure his back-up was in place. By the time he had ascertained that the sixth stop was Dent and purchased yet another ticket the train was already slowing down for its next stop. A frantic telephone call, made from the sanctuary of the toilet cubicle, galvanised Jewel and Cavendish into action and the Vectra left the car park with a squeal of tyres. Paul Cavendish was frantically programming the satellite navigation system while Gerry Jewel concentrated on finding the quickest route back on to the by pass. The satellite navigation system calculated the route and predicted a journey time of an hour and fifteen minutes. Cavendish very much doubted that the train would take that long and urged his partner to keep his foot down.

The Vectra was overtaking a slow-moving tractor on one of the series of sweeping bends on the A65 between Hellifield and the Settle by-pass when it happened. At a speed of over seventy miles per hour Paul Cavendish had just swerved back onto the left hand side of the road when the front offside wheel struck a pot hole. The coil spring forming part of the offside front suspension snapped, causing the weight of the front part of the car to fall upon the already weakened steering joint which also fractured. The tyre came into contact with the lower part of the suspension mounting and burst. The resultant deceleration swung the rear offside of the car across the carriageway right into the path of an articulated lorry which was climbing the hill at a steady forty five. The impact hurled the Vectra onto its side before the lorry driver lost control and veered sharply to the left. The remains of the car were splayed against a dry stone wall. Both occupants were dead before the car stopped moving.

Eddie Duggan tried four times to check the progress of Jewel and Cavendish in the Vectra. Mobile phone coverage was becoming patchy as the train began its ascent into the high Pennines, but on the two occasions he did manage to find network coverage the call was redirected to voicemail.

CHAPTER SIXTY

Simon Fenton checked his watch. The train was not due for another ten minutes, but he knew that a southbound service should be arriving in a couple of minute's time. He switched on the notebook once again and there was just sufficient signal for him to make a connection to the internet. The southbound train was shown as running just under an hour late; things would be resolved one way or another before it arrived. He stood up to ease the numbness of his limbs and carefully scanned the scene below him. The car which had been parked alongside the station building had disappeared and, as he watched, a two adults and a child emerged from the former stationmaster's house and made the short journey onto the platform where they stood in the lee of the waiting shelter. Simon smiled. If they got onto the train from which Eddie Duggan was about to alight the locality would be completely deserted. There would be no one to interfere with his plans.

Within the next half an hour his future would be decided; and in all probability Natalie's too. The messages in the telephone housings were intended to lure his adversary up the hillside towards the yellow bag. To get there Duggan would need to pass close to his place of concealment. His intention was to leap out behind the Home Secretary and knock him out with the rounders bat; then he would use the cable ties to secure Duggan's arms and legs, gag him with the cotton strips and drag him the few yards into a shallow depression concealed from both the railway and road by a crumbling dry stone wall. Simon would then climb back up the hillside to inform the news desks of the BBC, several national newspapers and the local radio station that he was holding the Home Secretary hostage along with papers that implicated Eddie Duggan in fraud, money laundering and murder. On impulse he took the letters written by Michael Duckworth from the flap of his bag and checked that they were all present. Reassured, he replaced them and made a few experimental swings with the bat. Violence of any sort was alien to him and he was concerned that if he did not hit Duggan on the back of the head hard enough the man might be able to fight back and overpower him. On the other hand if he hit him too hard he might do him severe damage or possibly kill him. The thought of Kynpham Johal lying gravely injured in his hospital bed flashed into his mind and Simon resolved that he would not hold back.

He was under no illusions as to the likely course of events that he would unleash. Undoubtedly the local police would rapidly appear on the scene, but hopefully some media representatives would also arrive with them and whatever happened would take place in the sight and hearing of the press. He would, of course, give himself up immediately, but Eddie Duggan would have to give an account of what he was doing in the Pennine wilderness and the incriminating evidence would be there for all to see. His hope and prayer was that the subsequent publicity would prove to be the catalyst for Eddie Duggan's downfall. The matter of six hundred thousand pounds in cash would also be powerful evidence of Duggan's complicity in wrongdoing. He would, Simon thought, be hard pressed to explain why he had brought such a large sum of money to trade with a known fugitive.

The sound of the train as it emerged from the northern portal of Blea Moor tunnel brought Simon's musings to an end and he slowly lowered himself into his hiding place. Through the gaps in the gorse bushes he watched transfixed as the drama began to unfold below him.

CHAPTER SIXTY-ONE

As the train began to slow Eddie Duggan could not dispel a deep sense of disquiet which had become considerably more acute since he had failed to make contact with Cavendish and Jewel. He checked his phone once again, but there was still no network coverage. Things were going very badly. He had lost the initiative and was clearly dancing to Simon Fenton's tune. Although he was still fairly certain that Simon's motivation centred around the six hundred thousand pounds there was now a seed of doubt in his mind. After all he had killed the man's father. With no alternative plan in the offing he steeled himself for the confrontation.

Only one other person alighted at Dent; a fit-looking young man toting a large rucksack. The young man strode purposefully out through the gate and disappeared from view as Eddie Duggan pretended to scrutinise a timetable encased in a Perspex frame. There was a brisk wind blowing along the valley and a bank of grey cloud was rolling in from the south. Eddie Duggan shivered as he began to scan the platform for the telephone. He quickly located the grey box and opened it. As promised a folded sheet of paper was stuck inside. He removed it, unfolded the message and began to read.

Turn to your right. At the end of the platform there is a stream running under a bridge under the railway. Leave the money on the rock shelf under the bridge on this side of the stream then carry on under the bridge and up onto the other platform. There is also a telephone on that platform. In the box is your next instruction. Do exactly as you are told – you are being watched.

The Home Secretary felt the hairs on the back of his neck stand on end. For the first time in many years he was experiencing real fear. Somewhere out there Simon Fenton was almost certainly watching him. A man whose father he had killed over thirty years ago in what had become the defining moment in his life; the moment at which he had irrevocably set himself on the wrong track. When he had chosen self interest above duty and had drawn others into his web of deception, power and greed. Fighting the instinct to turn round and search the hillside above for any trace of his enemy Eddie Duggan turned to his right and began to walk slowly along the platform. The platform end was fenced off to prevent trespass on the railway and he levered himself down from the platform edge onto the track, dragging the suitcase behind him, before walking the few steps to the parapet of the bridge. Again he had to lever himself over the low rail and back onto the side of the embankment, his progress severely hindered by the not insubstantial weight if his suitcase. The banking was slippery and he slithered his way down to the rocky outcrops at the side of the stream. Under the bridge he quickly located the ledge. It was well clear of the water and was formed by a deep cleft in the rock. He slid the suitcase in until it was barely visible and sat on a large stone for a few minutes while he regained his breath.

To regain the opposite platform Eddie Duggan had to perform the same pattern of gyrations, but in the reverse order. Unencumbered by the suitcase, however, he found progress easier and located the grey telephone housing at the far end of the platform. Again he found his instructions inside:

Now carry on along the along the railway line and follow it until you come to a tall aerial. You will see a dry–stone wall running up the hillside on your left. Follow it up the hill. After about a hundred and fifty yards you will see a yellow plastic bag on top of a big stone. The papers are in the bag. Take the bag and get back to the station. Wait there and get on the next train.

He took a deep breath and continued on his quest. It was still just possible, he thought, that Simon Fenton had set all this up in advance and was not actually in the vicinity. In that case he would have been able to get away with both the documents and the money, though, so it was unlikely. After a brief walk beside the railway line he spotted the aerial, climbed through a wire fence and began to follow the wall uphill. The hill was extremely steep and the damp ground was slippery underfoot. Despite his relative fitness, he was only able to make slow progress, pausing frequently to regain his breath. As he climbed higher the brow of the hill appeared over a ridge ahead of him. Below it, as promised, was a bright yellow plastic bag on top of a large rock. He continued a straight course towards the bag, stumbling frequently on the rough ground. Just ahead and to his left was a clump of gorse bushes. Beyond that there was only a matter of yards left to climb. As he drew level with the gorse bushes he determined that he would not stop again; he would make one last effort and continue all the way to the his goal.

CHAPTER SIXTY-TWO

Squadron Leader Greg Rennie was literally in his element. After nearly two and a half years marking time as a Range Safety Officer at the RAF bombing range at Wainfleet he was once again alone in the cockpit of a fast jet aircraft, snaking through Pennine valleys two hundred and fifty feet above the ground. After his initial training he had flown Jaguar ground attack aircraft for more than six years, but when the last Jaguars had been retired in May 2007 Greg Rennie had been consigned to watching his erstwhile colleagues refining their skills using live munitions on the flat costal plain of Lincolnshire. Now, newly promoted to Squadron Leader, he was en-route to an appointment as Flight Commander on a Tornado squadron. As a precursor to learning to fly the complex bomber he had been posted to RAF Valley in North Wales for a fast jet refresher course. Having completed the dual instruction part of his training the previous afternoon he had lost no time in booking himself a solo flight in the sleek black Hawk advanced trainer.

Rennie's initial plan had been to fly a low level sortie amongst the hills and valleys of Snowdonia, but the approach of a warm front from the south west signalled the probability of a low cloud-base and intermittent rain. Instead he had climbed out of RAF Valley and headed northwards, dropping to two hundred and fifty feet over the exposed mudflats of Morecambe Bay before accelerating to four hundred and twenty knots and storming along the course of Lake Windermere. From there he had hopped from valley to valley across the ridges then turned eastwards over the fertile floodplain of the River Eden. Overhead Appleby he had turned southwards and followed the sinuous route of the Carlisle to Settle railway, relishing the challenge of keeping his aircraft within the confines of each valley. As the Hawk skimmed over the railway cottages at Garsdale its pilot noticed that a bank of grey cloud lay across his route some ten miles to the south. A quick check of his fuel state confirmed that it was time to climb back into the upper air, where his engine would be much more efficient, if he was to get back to his base with adequate reserves. Squadron Leader Rennie advanced the throttle against its stop and allowed the speed of his aircraft to reach five hundred knots. As he flashed along the hillside on the eastern side of the railway station at Dent he pulled gently back on the control column; the nose of the aircraft pitched up and the black shape of the Hawk disappeared from view as the tendrils of grey stratus closed around it.

CHAPTER SIXTY-THREE

From behind the tangle of yellow gorse Simon Fenton watched the train pull out of Dent railway station. There, standing in front of a notice board with a suitcase on the ground beside him, he saw in the flesh the man who had killed his father for the first time. Strangely, he felt little emotion; just a nagging anxiety about whether he could succeed in subduing and restraining his adversary and whether the media would take the news of the Home Secretary's predicament seriously. The figure he knew to be Eddie Duggan moved off slowly once the only other passenger had disappeared from view. Duggan appeared to be following instructions; he dropped down onto the rails and slithered down the steep embankment next to the bridge. After a minute or two he emerged from the other side of the little bridge and climbed awkwardly back up on the opposite side of the railway. A high retaining wall then hid him from view and Simon spent several worried minutes watching and waiting before Eddie Duggan became visible once more, climbing the steep hillside parallel with the dry stone wall. He was making heavy weather of the steep climb, frequently stumbling and slipping and was taking a route slightly further away from the wall than Simon would have liked. If he maintained that track, Simon calculated, the Home Secretary would pass his hiding place five or six yards further away then he had planned. As Eddie Duggan drew closer Simon slipped off his coat, folded it into his bag and made one or two tentative swings with the rounders bat. He would probably have to sprint the five yards or so to his quarry just after Duggan had passed the clump of gorse bushes, hit him hard on the back of the head and take it from there.

Red-faced with exertion Eddie Duggan drew ever closer. Twenty yards, fifteen, ten, five. Simon crouched with his knees bent; bat in hand, ready for action as Eddie Duggan drew abreast of his hiding place.

The sudden roar from behind his position startled Simon, causing him to take an involuntary glance over his shoulder as a black swept wing aircraft tore over the hillside. When he turned back Duggan stood facing him. For a millisecond Simon stood transfixed as he watched his father's murderer begin to draw a small pistol from his coat pocket. In a flash of lucidity he hurled the bat at Duggan, spun on his heel, scooped up his bag and began to run. As he accelerated rapidly along the hillside his left foot slipped on the damp ground and he lunged desperately in the opposite direction in an attempt to regain his balance as the crack of the pistol signalled imminent and very real danger. Simon kept on running, not daring to look over his shoulder as two more shots rang out. Then he felt a searing pain in his side, just above the waistline of his trousers and lost his footing completely. His considerable impetus sent him tumbling diagonally downhill until he reached the rim of a steep gully, at the bottom of which the stream that crossed beneath the railway line at the north end of the station plummeted down the hillside. Simon felt himself falling over the edge; then he struck his head violently on something hard. Everything went dark and he knew no more.

CHAPTER SIXTY-FOUR

Eddie Duggan had been nearing exhaustion as he closed in on the bright yellow bag on top of the large flat stone. The direct route up the steep hillside had taken its toll; his breathing was ragged and his face flushed. The sudden roar of the jet aircraft drew his eyes away from the summit of the hill and there, only a few yards to his left, he recognised Simon Fenton who was holding a substantial wooden bat in his hand. Duggan's hand flew to his pocket and he began to tug free the .32 calibre automatic pistol that he was carrying as a weapon of last resort. Before he could aim the pistol, however, Simon Fenton flung the wooden bat directly at him. The bat headed straight towards his face. With his free arm he pushed out his hand to protect himself while dodging fiercely to his right. His right foot slid from under him and all his weight fell upon his left foot as he staggered sideways. He felt something tear in his left ankle and fell awkwardly face down upon the damp hillside. When he looked up Simon Fenton was running away. Grasping the pistol with both hands, and struggling to control his breathing, he loosed off four shots at his fleeing adversary. The fourth shot sent Simon staggering sideways for a few paces before he lost his footing completely and began to roll over and over down the slope. After a few seconds Simon's body disappeared from view.

After taking a minute or so to get his breath back Eddie Duggan rolled over onto his back and eased himself into a sitting position. His first attempt to stand returned him rapidly to the mud-streaked ground. The pain in his ankle was excruciating. He could put no weight on it whatsoever. A second more tentative try resulted in him regaining an upright posture with only his right foot in contact with the ground. He hopped awkwardly the few feet towards a stunted tree and gripped a flimsy branch while he weighed up his options. The yellow plastic bag was less than ten yards away. A short crawl brought him to it and he gratefully slithered back down the hill on his bottom with his left leg held carefully clear of the ground, towing the yellow bag behind him. Once he reached the dry-stone wall he manoeuvred himself through a narrow gap and continued his descent holding on to the wall for support. A little lower down the hillside were a series of palisades made of rotting railway sleepers running parallel to the slope. He put the bag down on the ground and gingerly he hopped the short distance from the wall to the highest palisade and picked his way carefully along it. From the far end he could see down into the gully where Simon Fenton had fallen. His adversary's body was lying close beside the stream about thirty five yards from where he was standing. He could see that Simon's shirt was red with blood and a small trail of the red liquid led from under his head to a small pool on the rock below. Eddie Duggan took the pistol from his pocket and attempted to aim at the recumbent form, but his hands were shaking badly. Logic told him that Simon's body lay beyond the effective range of the weapon and he returned it to his pocket. The body would not be visible, he realised, from either the road or the railway station. Even if Simon Fenton was not dead already the chances were that he would not survive long in the inhospitable and inaccessible gulley. He painfully began to retrace his route on the opposite side of the palisade before hopping once again to the wall, collecting the bag and continuing his difficult descent. Close to the bottom of the slope he was able to break a reasonably sturdy branch from a wizened tree and use it as a makeshift walking stick. Wet, muddy and bedraggled he eventually negotiated the wire fence and regained the relative sanctuary of the railway station. A small group of passengers on the opposite platform eyed him suspiciously and he recoiled from both the physical exertion and the risk of unwelcome attention from the bystanders in any attempt to retrieve the suitcase full of money. It was pretty unlikely to be discovered, he thought, and he could send someone to get in, and to confirm the demise of Simon Fenton, after nightfall. To his relief a southbound train rattled into the platform within minutes. Eddie Duggan painfully dragged himself through an open door and slumped in a corner seat. As the train drew closer to Leeds it became quite busy, but no one chose to sit alongside the dishevelled and mud-stained tramp sitting in the seat nearest to the door.

CHAPTER SIXTY-FIVE

The police car did not come to collect Natalie until late morning. To her surprise she had slept soundly in the cell. After being given an unappetising breakfast of soggy corn flakes with lukewarm milk and weak tea in a cardboard cup she had been left alone. Worry about the whereabouts and fate of Simon had preoccupied her thoughts during the wait and she was relieved to be on the move again when the two police officers from Manchester had arrived. She was not handcuffed, but a female officer sat beside her in the rear seat while a male officer drove. The policewoman made several attempts at polite conversation, but Natalie remained silent; determined to buy time for Simon to do whatever he had to in order to deal with Eddie Duggan. However hard she tried she just could not think of Eddie Duggan as her father. He was the enemy. He had killed Simon's father and rejected his own daughter even before she had been born. If he was her biological father, she thought, it would make no difference whatsoever to how she thought of him. She pushed the unwelcome thought from her mind as the car sped along the motorway on its short journey.

Although Natalie had no inkling of the fact, the Chief Constable of Greater Manchester was aware of her impending arrival. The fact had been made known to him at his regular morning briefing and mention of her name had sparked his interest. He had no particular interest in re-opening the case of the murder of Andrew Gilroy. The chief suspect, who was almost certainly guilty, was now also dead. Like his Cumbrian colleague he was more than a little disconcerted at the interest shown in

Natalie Robertson by both ICIS and the Home Secretary. He instructed a female Detective Inspector to take charge of questioning Natalie and suggested that a softly, softly approach might be best. He ordered that she should not be charged with an offence if she was willing to stay on police premises, but suggested that a charge of obstructing the police might be used if she showed any inclination to leave. In no circumstances were any officers from ICIS to be allowed access to her. He also asked to be kept informed of developments.

When the car arrived at its destination Natalie was greeted by a smiling woman in civilian clothing who looked to be in her early thirties. She introduced herself as Alison Frith and took Natalie into what seemed to be some sort of staffroom. When offered the chance of a shower and clean clothes Natalie was glad to accept and within the hour she found herself sitting down to a ham salad sandwich and a mug of tea with her still damp hair dripping onto a borrowed sweatshirt. Alison Frith was friendly and attentive, but made no attempt to engage Natalie in anything other than banal conversation. Increasingly at ease, Natalie began to chat quite happily with the policewoman about films, television, books and shopping. On several occasions Detective Inspector Frith attempted to move the conversation on to boyfriends and other more personal areas but, refreshed by her good night's sleep, Natalie was astute enough to recognise the overtures as a prelude to interrogation and neatly side-stepped each time by changing the subject. By tea time the cards were on the table. After ducking out of leading questions for a fourth time Natalie took a deep breath and said her piece. She would not talk about either Simon Fenton or anything either of them knew about or had seen or done until the day after tomorrow, she told her tactful interrogator. Then she would tell the whole truth to anyone who cared to listen.

Alison Frith pressed Natalie to give explain why she had chosen to remain silent for another thirty-six hours, but Natalie just shook her head and smiled. Nothing on earth, she told the policewoman, would change her decision. She would be content to spend two more nights in a cell and would tell them everything on Thursday morning. After giving her a meal of sausages and mash, Alison Frith took Natalie at her word, escorted her to a cell and left to inform the Chief Constable of developments.

CHAPTER SIXTY-SIX

Detective Superintendent Jimmy Bell received two telephone calls in as many minutes. The first was from the North Yorkshire Police informing him that two of his officers had been killed in a road accident near Settle. The second was on his mobile phone; the display indicated that it was Eddie Duggan calling. Jimmy Bell pressed the reject button and switched off his phone. He needed time to think.

Eddie Duggan had somehow managed to negotiate his way across the platforms at Leeds railway station using his makeshift walking stick. From a kiosk he bought a packet of over the counter painkillers and took three of the tablets, washed down by a soft drink. Once again he was aware that people actively avoided getting too close to him; for that at least he was grateful. He had tried to contact Jerry Jewel, Paul Cavendish and Jimmy Bell on his mobile phone once the train had dropped down into the Aire valley, but his calls to Jewel and Cavendish were directed straight to voicemail and his attempts to call Jimmy Bell were no more successful. A London train was waiting in the platform and he staggered onto it and laid claim to a double seat by placing the yellow bag prominently alongside him. He would be back in London by four, he thought; now all he had to do was to arrange for someone to meet him.

By early afternoon Kynpham and Rebecca Johal had migrated from the tiny side ward to the coffee bar on the ground floor of the Cumberland Infirmary. The reporter's head was still swathed in bandages, but all the tubes and wires had been disconnected. He felt much better and was listening with increasing incredulity to his sister's account of Simon Fenton's apparent involvement with a lady of ill repute following the murder of a policeman in a Manchester hotel. Behaviour of the sort was so alien to the Simon Fenton that he knew that he was inclined to disbelieve Rebecca until she produced printouts of some of the news stories to back up her tale. Kynpham expressed deep concern for his friend and Rebecca became more than a little embarrassed at the turn the conversation then took. Her feelings for Simon were well known to her brother and he quickly deduced the question of Simon's involvement with a prostitute was troubling her. Changing the subject he gave her the task of buying him some clothes from the shops before they closed and they made their way back to the ward. Sally Chamley was just about to go off duty and offered to give Rebecca a lift into the city centre. By the time Rebecca returned with her purchases she had agreed to meet up with Sally after visiting ended the following evening for a pizza.

In his London office Jimmy Bell had reached a decision. He would leave his old life behind and try and start over in a new country. Before that, however, he would exact a fair price from Eddie Duggan for his continued silence. He was sickened by the death of his three colleagues. All of them had died either directly or indirectly because of Eddie Duggan. In recent weeks, the murders he had carried out himself at the bidding of the man he had once tried to blackmail had begun to haunt him. Every time another innocent person had needed to die in order to preserve their shameful web of conspiracy he had vowed to himself that it would be the last act in the tragedy, but there always seemed to be someone else to take their place. Now Simon Fenton, Natalie Robertson and Kynpham Johal were living on borrowed time; unless Duggan had already disposed of Simon Fenton that was. No, for Jimmy Bell enough was enough. He would play along with Duggan only in order to extort one last payment. He would be on the flight to Rio in just over thirty six hours, hopefully with enough money to live comfortably into old age. He switched on his mobile phone and called Eddie Duggan's number.

The pain in Eddie Duggan's ankle had eased slightly since he had taken the painkillers. As the train sped through the Home Counties he was relieved when his mobile phone indicated an incoming call from Jimmy Bell. With some difficulty he extricated himself from his seat and hopped into the vestibule to take the call in a greater degree of privacy. Jimmy Bell agreed to pick him up where he had dropped him off that morning at Kings Cross and to chauffer him for the rest of the day. The cogs in Eddie Duggan's brain began to whirr as he began to make damage limitation plans.

CHAPTER SIXTY-SEVEN

It was late in the afternoon when Simon regained consciousness. In the encroaching twilight his eyes were slow to focus as he lay on the rocky side of the steep gulley. Memory began to seep slowly back into his befuddled mind. He had failed. Eddie Duggan had got away, probably with the papers. With full consciousness came the pain. He had been shot. There was a sharp pain in his side and the blood pounding through his head sent stabs of excruciating agony through his brain. Slowly and painfully he rolled over onto his back and forced himself to sit up. For a few minutes the pain threatened to return him to a state of semi-consciousness, but the world around him gradually stopped spinning and he began to examine his injuries. Beneath his blood-soaked shirt he discovered a six inch long furrow in his side. The blood had clotted into raw scabs, but the slightest pressure from his fingers reopened the wound and it began to bleed again in several places. He also located a deep cut in his scalp above his right ear and a number of grazes on various other parts of his anatomy. His bag was only feet away and he manoeuvred himself cautiously towards it, causing fresh waves of pain and nausea. After a few minutes rest he took out the torn cotton strips and manufactured a makeshift pad, which he placed on the wound in his side and fixed in place with several of the other strips. Sweating from the effort, he hauled himself slowly upright and took a few tentative steps towards the stream. Although the pain from his head and side slowed him considerably, everything seemed to be more or less in working order and he crouched down beside the fast running water and drank copiously from cupped hands. Having washed his hands and face to the best of his ability he paused to examine the contents of his bag. The notebook and mobile phone were damaged beyond repair but his coat, spare shirt, the folding spade and the remains of the money were all present. In the flap on the lid he was relieved to find Michael Duckworth's letters. At least Eddie Duggan had not got the lot; he still had something to fight with. Simon sat down on a flat rock and tried to get his mind into focus. Natalie! He wondered what had happened to her. He hoped that she had told her story to the Manchester police. He hoped that she had caused such a fuss that the whole world knew about what had been happening, but nagging doubts caused his real distress. He had no way of knowing whether or not Natalie had been able to do anything to harm Eddie Duggan; or to protect her own life for that matter. It was still up to him, then; to do what he could to keep both of them alive. As the last glimmers of daylight began to fade from the sky Simon Fenton picked his way carefully and painfully down hill towards the little bridge that allowed the stream to pass beneath the railway. After a few minutes he found his way blocked by a wooden fence across the surface of the stream intended, he surmised, to keep grazing sheep away from the railway. With some difficulty and a great deal of pain he slowly edged himself over it. By the time he reached the bridge it was dark. The faint glow of the lamps on the station failed to penetrate beneath the bridge, but he located the narrow shelf by touch and was surprised to discover that Duggan had left the suitcase there. The money, if the case actually contained any, however, was of little consequence to him and he made a final effort to climb up the banking onto the platform. The printed timetable confirmed his suspicion that the last train had long gone and the warm yellow glow of light from behind the thin curtains in the station building almost tempted him to knock on the door and seek assistance. That, though, would almost certainly involve the necessity of a call to the local police and bring to an end his freedom to act. Standing still after the exertion of movement had made him feel cold. He slipped into the small waiting shelter and put on his coat. Suddenly exhausted he eased himself down onto the long bench seat and tried to work out what to do next.

Fatigue gradually overcame him and he dozed fitfully for a while. When he awoke again the station lights had gone off but thin moonlight was filtering through the scattered clouds and illuminating the four silver threads of the rails as they traced their way along the hillside. The pain in his head had subsided to a dull ache but the wound in his side was throbbing. Shivering with cold he levered himself to his feet and began to pace slowly up and down trying to force his brain to engage. Still at a loss as to how to use the little ammunition he had left to curtail Eddie Duggan's nefarious activities, he decided that the best way to get warm again would be to keep moving. The bench in the shelter was tempting, but there was also a risk of either hypothermia or discovery. Leaving his temporary sanctuary, Simon lowered himself gently over the platform edge and began to walk northwards on the slippery ballast beside the railway. On two occasions the approach of goods trains drove him away from the track but, step by step, he made progress and the exertion brought pain and warmth to his body in equal measures. The stygian gloom of a tunnel loomed ahead of him but he was not deterred. For almost half an hour he stumbled his way through the darkness, keeping his left hand on the brick lined tunnel wall to orientate himself. Just as a pale arch of moonlight signified that he had almost reached the other end another goods train coming in the opposite direction forced him to crouch beside the wall in the hope that the driver would not be able to see him in the beam of the train's headlight. Simon emerged from the tunnel utterly exhausted. Ahead was the shape on a precast concrete platelayers' hut. On closer inspection it proved to have been long abandoned, but the roof and walls were intact. Simon staggered in through the gap where a door had once been and gently lowered himself to the floor in the far corner. He remembered that Michael Duckworth, or Terry, or whoever he was, had also spent a night in a platelayers' hut many years before. He wondered if it had been the same one for a while, but realised that Michael Duckworth's escape had been made a good ten miles further south. He still had no coherent plan of action and his anxiety about Natalie Robinson's welfare penetrated his pain and discomfort to the level that she was soon all that he was aware of. Natalie; he loved her so much, yet he could do nothing to help her. He had let her down and there was no one else who could help her. Semi-delirious with fatigue and blood loss he could not get the image of her out of his mind. He would do anything for the girl he loved, but he could devise no coherent plan at all. In the darkness of his despair he began to utter the half-forgotten words of the Lord's Prayer. In a twilight state between sleep and wakefulness he began to pour out his heart to his God. Somewhere in the conversation there seemed to be times when he was angry with God and others when he wept with shame at having let God down. Then there was Natalie; he mumbled out the story of his love for her and called out to God to protect her. He tried to articulate his uncertainty about what to do next, but the words just jumbled in his mind. One moment he felt the sweat pouring from him and the next he found himself shivering with cold. Nothing made sense any more and, with his mind still reeling with increasingly inarticulate intercession, his head drooped onto his chest and Simon Fenton slipped gently into a deep sleep.

CHAPTER SIXTY-EIGHT

Eddie Duggan managed to slip into the car beside Jimmy Bell without drawing undue attention to himself. A second dose of painkillers had helped him navigate his way across the crowded station concourse with his stick and yellow plastic bag with the agony from his ankle only just bearable.

Bell pushed a copy of the free London evening paper onto his mentor's lap.

'Sorry, Guv, but take a look at page five. You won't like it,' he said.

Duggan turned the pages. Under the Headline "Who were you with last night?" there was a grainy photograph of his wife and a well known premiership footballer hand in hand emerging through an unfamiliar front door. The story underneath reported that the couple had left a night club together the previous evening and had been followed to the footballer's London flat, from which they had been photographed emerging at ten thirty that morning. Although the news was not completely unexpected Eddie Duggan experienced a fresh churning in his stomach. He wondered if he could make some sort of play for public sympathy by making a statement that he still loved her and was willing to completely forgive her. Whatever happened next, his wife's public infidelity would probably damage his political aspirations beyond repair, but perhaps his affluent and indulgent lifestyle might still be salvaged. In any case he would make sure that the cheating bitch didn't get a penny more of his money than the two million contracted in their pre-nuptial agreement.

The evening rush hour was beginning and the car crawled across London at a snail's pace. Duggan directed his driver to a small and very discreet clinic in Kensington. With Jimmy Bell's elderly Saab parked in a nearby meter bay the policeman had helped the Home Secretary into the salubrious waiting area and, almost immediately Eddie Duggan had been whisked away by an Asian nurse, leaving Bell with instructions to go and buy him some smart casual clothing.

An x-ray examination indicated that no bones were broken. After luxuriating briefly under a hot shower Eddie Duggan was laid out on a treatment table while his badly sprained ankle was strapped up by an attentive young doctor who also administered a pain killing injection. The Home Secretary requested and obtained three more doses of the pain killer and three syringes. Wearing a thick white dressing gown he sat on a comfortable chair in a small cubicle and began to examine the contents of the yellow plastic bag. The papers were contained in a plastic box. He peeled off the lid and recognised faded photocopies of papers from his past. Right on top though was a brown envelope with his name written on it. He tore it open, extracted a single sheet of paper and began to read.

Hello Eddie, or perhaps I should call you Duggie?

If you are reading this it probably means that I am dead – that makes two generations of us that you've killed. I won't say murdered, Eddie, because I hope I gave you a run for your money. My dad wasn't expecting what you did to him, but I know exactly what you're capable of.

I expect you think you've won, but think again. Eddie. You may have all the papers about your past life as a fraudster and money launderer, but you forgot about Michael Duckworth' letters. You will also find the letters to you from Susan Robertson are missing.

Now we get to the good bit. If anything bad happens to either Natalie Robertson or Kynpham Johal you can be sure that these letters will get to the press. I've made all the arrangements. If either of these people dies – of anything at all – while you are still alive it all hits the fan Eddie, so you'd better do all you can to make sure they stay fit and healthy.

Goodbye, Eddie

Simon Fenton

Eddie Duggan's hands began to tremble. He had been planning to dispatch Jimmy Bell on a final tidying up mission; to travel north and make sure that Simon Fenton's body would not be found easily and to remove anything that would help in its identification; to silence Kynpham Johal permanently and to wrest Natalie Robertson from the Manchester police. He had still not been able to decide what to do about the girl. He would never publicly acknowledge her as his daughter; of that he was certain, but the prospect of ordering her death disturbed him. Simon Fenton's testament had at least solved that problem for him. His hopes and dreams were in tatters. He would never realise any of his ambitions. Simon Fenton had defeated him after all. The shadowy figures from his past had finally conspired to take their revenge. A wave of exhaustion washed over him as the Home Secretary realised that the way of life he loved so much was drawing to an end. There was no doubt at all; he must put his escape plan into action. First of all though there were still some loose ends that needed tidying up.

Dressed smartly once again, and with his mobility improved considerably as a result of his medical treatment, Eddie Duggan hobbled back to Jimmy Bell's car with the aid of a proper walking stick. He had transferred the pistol to the pocket of his new jacket and replaced the papers in the plastic bag. With the car doors closed, Jimmy Bell made his pitch.

'I want out, Guv,' he began, 'I've done all you've asked, but things are getting too hot and I want out.'

Eddie Duggan smiled inwardly. Bell's statement was pretty much what he had been expecting.

'OK Jimmy,' replied the Home Secretary, 'but first I need you to make sure there's no trail to follow. Get yourself up to Dent. Find Fenton's body and get hold of any ID and paperwork. Don't worry about the body; just leave it where it is. Oh and make sure there's no tell-tale traces of anything at the office. Get rid of all the mobiles and take the hard drives out of the PCs.'

Troubled Legacy

'What about the reporter and the girl?' asked the policeman.

'Just leave them, Jimmy, just leave them.' replied Duggan.

'But Guv, it's a bit risky and...'

'I know Jimmy, you've been a good mate. I've no cash left; it's all in a suitcase under a bridge in Dent. You can have it if you go and get it. I've got a packet of uncut diamonds at home; worth about a million. They're yours as well if you do this one last job for me.'

Jimmy Bell grimaced; he had no intention of spending all day on some wild goose chase in the high Pennines. Even the lure of six hundred thousand pounds was not enough to deflect him from his long list of things to do before boarding his flight to Rio. The prospect of another million pounds however, was attractive; it might just enable him to spend the rest of his life in relative comfort. In any case Duggan need never know.

'OK, Guv, he replied, just one last job.'

'Good man,' replied Eddie Duggan, 'meet me on the cliff top where the old road branches off at Capel-le-Ferne tomorrow night at midnight. I'll have the diamonds by then.'

Jimmy Bell knew the place. There had been several clandestine meetings there between them in the past few years. Since Eddie Duggan had bought his motor yacht and berthed it at Folkestone Marina the Kent coast had very much become the Home Secretary's back yard.

'OK Guv, tomorrow at midnight,' he replied.

CHAPTER SIXTY-NINE

Simon Fenton spent the night slumped in the corner of the derelict railway building in a blissful oblivion brought on by absolute exhaustion. When the morning light penetrated his consciousness he was immediately aware of numerous aches and pains, but his mind was clear. He knew exactly what he had to do. It took him almost five minutes to push himself into a standing position. He had a throbbing headache and a sharp pain shot through his wounded flank each time he tried to move. In addition, his peculiar sleeping position had induced stiffness and discomfort in both legs and his neck. Spurred on by his renewed motivation, Simon quickly removed his coat and examined his wound. It had bled some more during the night. He discarded the makeshift dressing and made a new one from the remnants of his torn shirt. He then re-read several paragraphs of Michael Duckworth's letters. Yes, he had remembered them correctly. All might not yet be lost, but he had to move quickly. Hawes, then; he must reach the small Wensleydale town and make sure. He knew that there had once been a branch line connecting Hawes with the Settle to Carlisle line at Garsdale and Garsdale was probably no more than a mile or two from his present location. He could not recall the distance between Garsdale and Hawes, but thought it was probably somewhere in the region of six or seven miles. Even in his present state surely he could follow the relatively level route of the abandoned railway and arrive in Hawes in three or four hours time. By staying clear of roads and civilisation, he reasoned, he would minimise the risk of being spotted by Eddie Duggan's henchmen who he had little doubt would be searching for him by then.

Emboldened by a renewed sense of purpose he donned his coat, swung the day-sack onto his back and stepped outside. A thick blanket of hill fog obscured his view. He could see the railway lines stretching ahead of him for perhaps thirty or forty yards. Well, the fog would help him to stay out of sight. He was aware that he probably looked quite a mess with a barely scabbed over cut on his head and dirty blood-stained clothing. He began to walk beside the track. After a few minutes he spotted a fast-flowing stream burbling under the railway in a culvert and painfully scrambled down the embankment where he splashed his face with cold water and quenched his raging thirst. His watch had been broken in his headlong tumble into the gulley and he had no idea of the time as he trudged slowly along the ballast. After what felt like an hour or so the dark gritstone buildings of Garsdale station loomed out of the mist and he crossed quickly to the other side of the twin tracks. There was a signal box on the platform at Garsdale and he did not want his arrival to be spotted by the signalman. In the event, both the signal box and the station were deserted. Simon rested for a while in the waiting shelter and watched the passing of two goods trains before he forced himself to his feet once again and searched for the old junction. In the poor visibility traces were hard to find, but he eventually detected what could only be a raised railway embankment curving off to the right from the rusty sidings to the north of the lonely platforms. He soon found his way blocked by a wooden fence. Despite having taken the greatest of care when climbing over it Simon detected a fresh trickle of warm blood from his side as he trudged away from the fence towards his goal. He felt lightheaded and very hungry; it was more than twenty four hours since he had last eaten. A quarter of a mile further on he encountered his next obstacle; a low dry stone wall. In the years since the railway had been abandoned and the track lifted farmers had reclaimed and enclosed the land. In the first mile Simon encountered no fewer than five walls or fences across the track bed. In some cases there were convenient gates, but all too often the painful climb had resulted in fresh bleeding. Utterly exhausted he was compelled to rest for longer periods after surmounting each obstacle and his progress was painful and very slow.

Simon had lost all track of time. Putting one foot in front of the other like an automaton he made wraith-like progress through the fine grey vapour, only an image of Natalie in his mind and a relentless determination to do right by her keeping him from slumping to the ground and giving in. Yet somehow, the very thought of Natalie also brought a disturbing sense of foreboding. Something seemed to have changed deep within him. He still loved her with all his heart, but there was something else; a sense that true selfless love must never constrain her. If they both emerged intact from their present predicament he concluded that it must be all or nothing between them. He would not try to persuade her to be with him against her will. Things had not been quite right between them when they had last been together. While he was absolutely certain that what he wanted more than anything else in the world was to be married to Natalie Robertson he was not at all sure that she felt the same way. He would ask her to marry him, he decided. If she accepted he would be the happiest man alive. If she turned him down then he must let her go. There would never be anyone else, though. It would be Natalie or no one.

The cool damp air seemed to have permeated Simon's very being. Wearily he climbed one more fence and, after taking ten minutes or so to recover from the exertion, trudged on. To his right the muted glow of lights through the mist and the sound of traffic indicated that he was closing in on his destination. He cut across a field, through a gate and found himself standing in a narrow street outside a rope-maker's factory in what could only be Hawes. Reaching the town gave him renewed strength and twenty minutes later he was standing quite alone in the cemetery before a light grey headstone as the light of day began to fade. He took Michael Duckworth's letters from his bag and re-read the paragraph;

> *I felt bad about not telling my parents. They're both dead now. I went back to Hawes once, a few years later and saw our graves; my parents and mine, in the cemetery – about half a mile out of town on the Leyburn road. Very nice they are too, granite headstones and lots of blue pebbles.*

One down one to go, he mused. Resting the bag on the headstone he took out the folding spade and began to sweep aside the blue pebbles. Presently he began to dig a series of small holes in the earth where the pebbles had been. He found it at the fifth attempt. With a wry smile he re-read another page of the letter in the last glimmer of dusk.

You must do what you think is right and consider your own safety. If it ends up that Terry Clegg has taken his last secret to his grave with him then so be it.

Spurred on by his success he quickly excavated a dark and rusty biscuit tin. Inside, wrapped in a black bin liner, were duplicates of the papers that had been in the Tupperware box inside the yellow plastic bag that Eddie Duggan had taken. The light was almost completely gone. Simon quickly rifled through the papers and took out the letters from Natalie's mother. Unlike the pale photocopies concealed in the case of the TV set in the house in Derby, these were the originals; handwritten on cheap lined writing paper. He tore a broad strip of the bin liner away and carefully wrapped them in it before replacing them in their hiding place. Once the blue pebbles were back in place there was no trace that the grave had been disturbed. Only the weight of the papers in the day sack on Simon's back served as evidence that Eddie Duggan was no longer in the driving seat.

As darkness fell he slowly and painfully made his way into the almost deserted town centre; the poor weather having confined the few late-season holidaymakers to the pubs and restaurants. A SPAR shop beckoned him with a yellow glow from its windows. He was by then very weak and very hungry. Just as he was about to enter however, he caught sight of his reflection in the window. His hair was caked in what he surmised to be dried blood and his filthy coat was torn in several places. With his mission far from over, Simon reluctantly walked on by; not daring to draw any unnecessary attention to himself. A few yards further on he found a telephone box that accepted coins opposite a fast food outlet proclaiming itself to be "Paul's Pizzas". Pasted up inside the red call box was a card displaying the number of a local minicab firm. He fed in a fifty pence piece, dialled the number and requested a pick up from opposite Paul's Pizzas, giving his intended destination as Carlisle.

CHAPTER SEVENTY

Natalie Robertson woke up cold and hungry. Her second night in a police cell had passed a lot less comfortably than the first. She had been left alone since early evening the previous day and sleep had proved elusive. For one thing she had no inkling of what Simon was doing. For all she knew he might even be dead. The agony of ignorance had played on her mind as she concocted mental scenarios of what might have happened to him which became more and more bizarre as thee night went on. Her second area of deep uncertainty was bound up in the first. She had done a deal with God, whoever he might or might not be, that if he got her out of being held captive by the renegade police officers she would let Simon Fenton go. In the lonely reality of her relatively safe police cell she felt foolish at the memory. She did not really believe in God, did she? Yet something seemed to have changed. If, and it was still quite a big if, she and Simon emerged free and unscathed from their current ordeal what would the future look like? No matter how hard she tried Natalie could just not imagine then being together for the long term, no matter how much she wanted it to happen. Simon Fenton, she thought, would not easily fit into the mould of the stay at home partner of a busy airline pilot. She could not really expect him to give up his job, home and friends to travel to the USA while she completed her training, nor could she envisage him living in a flat close to Heathrow or Gatwick, left alone for days on end while she lived her dream. The alternative was even more difficult to comprehend, though. How could a girl like her, especially one that everyone knew all about from the newspapers, go and live with him in his small Norfolk town? All his friends and neighbours would be talking behind his back; telling each other that he could and should have done better and speculating about the ways and whiles of an ex- call girl. Natalie's third worry arose as a direct result of her second. It would almost certainly be up to her to break off their relationship. She knew that she had to spurn any further advances that Simon might make. She loved him far too much to ask him to give up all he knew in order to be with her or to impose herself and her reputation upon his laid back and comfortable lifestyle. The crux of the problem was that she feared that she would not have the strength of character to do what she knew was right. The very thought of him sent her weak at the knees and caused the hairs on the back of her neck stand up. More than anything else she longed to see him again, to hold him close to her; to abandon herself completely to his touch. Deep anguish and an endless cycle of worry robbed her of sleep. She had no watch, and hence no way of measuring the passage of time but when the arrival of a rudimentary breakfast in the cold grey light of dawn dragged her into full wakefulness it felt as if she had hardly slept at all.

Alison Frith's arrival a little later on lifted Natalie's spirits a little. Once again she was taken to the relative comfort of the staff room, but this time there was less banal conversation. Within minutes Natalie realised that she was actually being subjected to extremely skilful, if subtle, interrogation. Simon Fenton's name was repeatedly injected into the proceedings, causing a pang of emotion that Natalie was finding it increasingly difficult to conceal. The Detective Inspector also dropped in a number of facts or suspicions that way-marked the last week and a half of Natalie's life. Comments about dinner in the Midland Hotel, a night spent at Manchester Airport, a makeover in Barrow in Furness and a caravan holiday by the sea gave Natalie frequent opportunities to comment, but she managed to remain silent at all the pertinent points. After the caravan the police seemed to be less certain, although Alison did bring up the unauthorised flight of a light aircraft across the Irish Sea and alluded to cycling in Northern Ireland. Natalie was sorely tempted to pour out the whole story, but she had promised Simon that she would keep silent for two days after giving herself up. She would save it all for the next day; and the bit about who her father was and what he had done. At lunchtime Alison Frith left Natalie alone for a while. On the staffroom table were several daily newspapers. Natalie searched them avidly for any mention of Simon or the fall from grace of Eddie Duggan, but there was no mention of either. When the policewoman returned she brought a pre-packed ham salad and a selection of magazines with her.

'Look, Natalie,' she said, 'I know you've told me that you'll answer all our questions tomorrow. I probably shouldn't tell you, but the Chief Constable himself is interested in what you've got to say. If I leave you in peace for now do you promise to give me the full story tomorrow?'

Natalie nodded.

'Right, then, eight thirty on the dot; you, me, one of my team and a tape recorder, then. No excuses. If you're not forthcoming I'll have to arrest you on suspicion of obstructing the police. No more softly, softly, we'll have you up before the magistrates and you'll be in prison on remand by lunchtime. Understand?'

'I'll tell you, then,' replied Natalie, 'I really will; and I think you'll be pretty interested. Will you just tell me one thing now, though?'

Alison inclined her head inquisitively,

'What?' she asked.

'Simon Fenton, do you know where he is? Has anything happened to him?'

Alison Frith remained silent for a few seconds.

'Honestly, Natalie, if you told me what was going on I might be able to help.'

Natalie felt her eyes becoming moist and screwed up her eyes to hold back the tears. There was a long silence.

'No, I don't know anything. We don't know where he is. Actually that's one of the things we wanted you to tell us. Honestly, Natalie, I'm not playing games with you. We don't know where he is or what he's up to. That's the truth.'

Natalie nodded her head gratefully.

'Thanks, for telling me that,' she said softly, 'I really will tell you everything in the morning, but it might already be too late.'

After lunch Natalie was returned to her cell. The magazines made the waiting a little easier, but the day passed excruciatingly slowly and faded once again into the dark solitude of night.

CHAPTER SEVENTY-ONE

Jimmy Bell dropped Eddie Duggan off in Parliament Square where the Home Secretary hailed a black cab and made the driver's day be hiring him to take him to his home in Kent. The journey took the best part of two hours due to road works on the M20. Duggan phoned ahead to alert the police dog handler on patrol in the grounds and the gates were opened just before his arrival. Turning away from the intrusive flashguns of a small posse of paparazzi as he passed through, he paid off the cabbie and limped up the short flight of steps. Inside he was greeted by an irritated armed protection officer, but no wife. The protection officer politely admonished his charge for leaving the premises alone, but the Home Secretary countered with the argument that if he was not allowed to be about his business on his own during the summer recesses it was a poor do. A frosty impasse was quickly reached. Eddie Duggan would only be leaving his house once more and had no intention of announcing his departure to anyone. He dismissed the policeman, promising that he would be at home waiting for his wife for at least the next forty-eight hours. In the ensuing privacy he took the incriminating bundle of papers from their Tupperware container for the last time and fed them sheet by sheet into the heavy duty shredder in his study. Exhausted by travel, disappointment and the still nagging pain from his ankle, the Home Secretary took another dose of painkillers and went to bed.

He slept late the next morning. Despite the strapping and painkillers he was still unable to put much weight on his left foot and washing and dressing took him considerably longer than usual. He was tempted to use one of his syringes, but logic persuaded him that he would have more need of them later. After a makeshift breakfast Eddie Duggan sat down before his computer, logged on to the internet and began to move money electronically into accounts from which they could be discretely moved around the world time after time until the trail of transactions became so complex as to be virtually untraceable. Once his electronic preparations were complete he turned his attention to more material matters. He packed a few items of clothing into a small suitcase and limped through the internal connecting door into his garage. Of his two cars he chose the Audi A8 because it had an automatic transmission and could be driven using only his right leg. The suitcase went into the cavernous boot together with a long woollen overcoat. In the pocket of the overcoat nestled his automatic pistol, which he had just wiped clean with a damp cloth, and two pairs of latex gloves.

Upon returning to the main part of the house he opened the safe and removed two packets of documents comprising the fake identities and an assortment of other papers proving ownership of various properties and investments by his two alter egos. Next he extracted not one, but three, black cloth bags each containing uncut diamonds to the value of around a million pounds. Lastly he took out several bundles of banknotes consisting of almost three hundred thousand Euros and just over a hundred and fifty thousand US Dollars. He swung the safe door shut and spun the combination lock before stowing the booty in a large leather holdall and limping back to the garage to complete the loading of his car.

A light lunch from the freezer via the microwave followed and he settled down before his enormous plasma screen TV to wait out the time before his planned departure by watching some of his favourite films.

At eight thirty he injected a dose of the powerful local anaesthetic into his ankle, slipped into the garage, locking the connecting door behind him, opened the electric garage door by means of a button on the car's key fob and drove slowly out; the door closing automatically behind him. The gates at the end of the drive were also opened in a similar manner and the sleek silver Audi sped off into the night past the now diminished gaggle of photographers. Before any of them had either the opportunity or the gumption to reach their various modes of transport and give chase he was well over a mile away travelling at a speed well above the legal limit.

Eddie Duggan's first destination was his motor yacht, which he kept moored in the marina at Folkestone. He parked his car in his usual space and made two slow trips out to the vessel taking both the suitcase and leather bag and stowing them in the spacious cabin. He then unpacked a few items from the suitcase before hobbling back to the car park and driving off.

CHAPTER SEVENTY-TWO

After the Home Secretary had levered himself out of Jimmy Bell's car in Parliament Square on Tuesday evening there were some similarities between the actions of Eddie Duggan and those of the corrupt policeman, but there were also a number of significant differences.

Bell's first port of call was his office, where he checked the latest updates on the Police National Computer for any news of Simon Fenton or, for that matter Natalie Robertson. The lure of six hundred thousand pounds in cash hidden under a bridge somewhere in North Yorkshire was a powerful incentive to carry out Duggan's instructions, but first of all Jimmy Bell wanted to make sure that he would not be heading into danger. No new information had been logged. Natalie Robertson still appeared to a guest of the Greater Manchester police and there was no mention whatsoever of Simon Fenton. Weighing up the possibilities, he reaffirmed his original view that the potential gain did not justify the risk. A very large amount of cash would not be easy to get through check-in at Heathrow and the last thing he wanted was to draw unnecessary attention to himself. His thoughts strayed to his estranged wife and his two boys, now aged seventeen and thirteen. There was no love lost between Jimmy Bell and his ex-wife. The decree absolute may only have been six months old, but the love between them had died many years previously. He felt guilty about the boys, though. He had been tardy in his visits, often leaving five or six weeks between brief excursions to the cinema or bowling alley. Although he had already put in place a rudimentary plan to furnish both boys with some sort of nest egg, the possibility of increasing that many times over by using a degree of subtle subterfuge seemed infinitely more attractive than taking undue risks to immediately secure the suitcase full of money. He pulled a wad of paper from the tray in his computer printer and began to compose a letter to his ex-wife. An hour later, with more than half a dozen sheets having been consigned to the shredder he was reasonably pleased with his efforts and he sealed the letter, together with a rudimentary sketch map of the railway station at Dent, as described by Eddie Duggan, into an envelope. He would post it second class from the airport just before he checked in. He did not want his departure to be noticed too soon. He put the thin envelope into his brief case beside his fake ID and airline tickets.

After a restless last night in his lonely double bed Jimmy Bell used his laptop to check on the balance of his current account. Both his personal loan and the money he had drawn down from his mortgage were shown as cleared funds. He drove around the North Circular and cut down the A10 to Wood Green where he parked in a supermarket car park. From there he made the short journey onto the High Street where bought two matching shoulder bags before locating a branch of his bank. The request for a cash withdrawal of a hundred and twenty thousand pounds brought the unwelcome attention of a supervisor but Bell's police warrant card and driving license seemed to reassure her and the cash was paid over in bundles of twenty and fifty pound notes. Bell stowed the cash in one of the shoulder bags and left quickly, returning to his car where he locked the cash in the boot. On his way home he called in at a branch of Staples and purchased two large postal cartons and a roll of parcel tape.

Over a makeshift lunch, in the privacy of his dining area he counted out the money into three piles; two of fifty thousand and one of twenty thousand. Each of the larger bundles he placed carefully inside a shoulder bag which, in turn, he packed and sealed in the cartons. He wrote the name and address of each of his sons on the cartons and picked up the remaining money from the table. He then retired to his bedroom where be packed a suitcase with a few items of clothing and some toiletries. He also packed framed photographs of the two boys. Finally he added the twenty thousand pounds to the rest of his cash, put it into the suitcase and closed the zip.

Troubled Legacy

A short walk took him to his local sub post office where he posted the two cartons by the slowest service on offer; again mindful of the need to be as far away as possible when his absence became apparent. Upon returning home he rang his office administrator, saying that he had a bout of flu and would not be at work for at least the rest of the week. With a heavy heart Jimmy Bell locked up his home for the last time and drove northwards to join the M25 as the evening rush hour traffic began to build. He crossed the Thames at the Dartford Crossing and took the M20 towards the Kent coast. With time on his hands at his destination he treated himself to a fillet steak with all the trimmings at the Beefeater restaurant just outside Dover. Lingering over coffee, he took the opportunity to review his plans. After collecting the diamonds from Eddie Carlton he would drive slowly through the night to Turnpike Lane tube station, where there was ample street parking. He would abandon his car with the doors unlocked and the keys in the ignition in the near certain expectation that it would be stolen within the hour. By then, however, he would be well on his way to Heathrow; the Piccadilly line ran straight from Turnpike Lane to Terminal Five and he intended to be aboard the first train of the day.

The restaurant closed at eleven and Jimmy Carter drove slowly along the A20 towards Capel-le-Ferne. A few hundred yards after passing West Hougham he turned left onto the old coastal road and immediately pulled off into the cliff-top lay-by. He was surprised to find Eddie Duggan's Audi already parked there. A cursory examination showed the car to be empty but the familiar silhouette of the Home Secretary was clearly visible against the moonlit sky. He was sitting on a wooden seat and looking out over the English Channel where tendrils of silver mist were rolling from the west and dimming the lights of the steady procession of ferries making their short voyages across the Straits into faint pinpricks.

CHAPTER SEVENTY-THREE

Alec Leonard had been sitting comfortably in the minicab office watching TV when the call came in. His son and daughter in law had arrived back from New Zealand only that morning for a month's holiday. Accompanying them was Alec's first grandson, a handsome toddler who was just a few weeks short of his second birthday, who had come to meet his proud grandparents for the first time. Alec had only been able to spend half an hour with them before he had needed to leave for work after lunch and he was very much looking forward to the end of his shift at ten o'clock. Little Jack would probably be in bed, but at least he would be able to catch up on all the news from Daniel and Katie. A three hour return trip to Carlisle on a foggy night was the last thing he wanted. Alec checked his watch; eight fifteen. If he pushed it a bit there was still a chance that he might be home not long after eleven. Perhaps they would wait up for him. He pulled on his coat and walked the few paces to his car.

Pulling up outside the post office, he took one look at his customer in the orange glare of the streetlights and almost decided to return to the office. The man was unkempt and gaunt. Something which looked suspiciously like blood was matted in his hair and he was slumped against the door of the telephone box. Alec lowered the driver's window.

'Are you for Carlisle, mate?' he asked warily. Simon straightened up and took a step towards the car. 'Only you know it'll be eighty quid; I'll not get a fare back like.'

Simon reached into his pocket and took out a roll of money. He peeled off six twenty pound notes.

'Here,' he said, his voice faltering, 'I'll give you a hundred and twenty up front.'

The driver eyed him suspiciously. A tip of forty pounds would go a long way towards treating the family to a meal out the following afternoon.

'You'd better get in, then; the back seat mate if you don't mind,' answered Alec as he held out his hand to take the notes.

Simon eased the back door open and slid carefully into the plastic-covered seat, closing the door behind him. By the time the street lights of Hawes faded behind them Simon was fast asleep.

For the first few miles the fog kept Alec Leonard's speed to no more than twenty miles per hour, but as the road dropped towards Sedburgh the fog began to thin and by the time he joined the M6 at junction 37 he was able to accelerate safely to a comfortable cruising speed of seventy-five. Alec was glad that his passenger seemed to be asleep. He was still half afraid of the man in the back seat. As the car sped northwards the driver allowed thoughts of his grandson to run through his mind and a faint smile turned the corners of his mouth upwards. Little Jack had been a bit wary of him at lunchtime, but they would soon get to know one another better. A whole month of kicking balls in the park, walks through woodland where the leaves would soon be beginning to turning brown and falling from the trees and trips to playgrounds and other places of fascination for the little lad lay ahead. Alec Leonard was so engrossed in his daydream that he completely missed junction 42. As he sailed past the turnoff he realised his mistake but it was too late. He swore gently to himself; it was another three miles to the next junction and time was passing.

After leaving the motorway Alec's progress was slowed by a succession of red traffic lights. Increasingly anxious to be on his way home he pulled over and stopped just short of the city centre and turned in his seat. He shook his passenger gently by the shoulder.

'Carlisle, mate, we're here,' he announced.

Simon came round slowly, rubbing his eyes and stretching in his seat. A fresh pang of agony from his side caused him to grimace as he realised where he was.

'Do you know where the Bishop lives?' he asked groggily.

'No mate, I've got to go back now, you'll have to get one of the locals to take you. There's a rank at the station; straight on then left. You'll see it on your right. You can't miss it.'

Simon slowly opened the door and levered himself out to the accompaniment of yet more agony from his wound. He pulled himself fully upright and closed the car door. The minicab moved off smartly, leaving him dizzy and lightheaded. A few people were about, but no one paid him any particular attention. A few tentative steps brought him to a shop window and he rested his shoulder against it while he hefted the day sack onto his back and waited for his head to stop spinning. He vaguely recognised his surroundings from the shopping trip with Natalie. He estimated that the station was about half a mile distant. Agonisingly slowly he began to put one foot in front of the other, keeping his left hand on the walls and windows of the shops for support. In front of him the challenge of crossing a busy road loomed. After halting the traffic at a pelican crossing he ambled his way hesitantly across the intersection, but stumbled as he stepped back onto the pavement on the opposite side. For two or three steps the momentum of his body outstripped the capacity of his legs to keep up and he fell to the ground. His side hurt badly. He tried to check the security of the makeshift bandage, but his hand came away sticky with fresh blood. No matter how hard he tried, he just did not have either the strength or mental coordination to get back up onto to his feet. He tried to call out for help, but all that emerged from his mouth was a feeble moan. He noticed a young couple cross the street in order to avoid him. Simon let his head rest on the cold pavement and began to sob gently. Even in his befuddled state he knew that he was at the end of his strength and he had failed. He had failed Natalie, failed himself and failed to right the many wrongs that Eddie Duggan had done.

CHAPTER SEVENTY-FOUR

When Sally Chamley picked up Rebecca Johal in her car outside the Cumberland Infirmary the Indian girl was in high spirits. A scan had shown that Kynpham's fractured skull was healing well and his brain had returned to its normal size. The prognosis was excellent and the reporter was likely to be discharged before the next weekend.

Sally drove into the city centre and found an on-street parking space in a side road close to the Citadel. From there they walked to a small Pizzeria on Cecil Street. Over the meal the two girls told each other about their families and work. Sally lived with her parents in the nearby village of Wreay, attended a large Church on the southern side of the city and had recently broken up with her boyfriend. Over coffee Rebecca began to confide in her new friend about her affection for her brother's friend Simon Fenton. Sally remembered having read something about him in the papers and tactfully avoided any mention of his alleged travelling companion.

As Rebecca began to tell Sally about how, since meeting Simon shortly after the death of his wife, she had not been able to get him out of her mind, the nurse ordered more coffee and listened attentively as the brown skinned girl poured out her heart. Rebecca admitted that she had actually spent very little time in Simon's company, but that she had been unable to completely absorb herself into her life in Shillong with the prospect, however remote, of a relationship with Simon somewhere in the background. She explained how she had planned to visit the UK during the school holidays in December and make her move on him. She just had to know whether or not she had a chance, she said. Until then her life would have remained partially on hold; as it had for the previous two years. Now everything seemed to have changed. Kynpham had been injured in mysterious circumstances; the object of her affections seemed to have become involved in some shady business and had been on the run with a girl of ill repute and it was now almost certain that her planned trip in December would be not take place. In any case if Simon Fenton really was involved in something illegal and had taken up with prostitutes, she wasn't sure that he would be the least bit interested in a good Christian girl from North-East India anyway. A tear trickled down her cheek as she rounded off her tale and Sally passed her a tissue. Rebecca blew her nose, Sally paid the bill and they set left the restaurant. Rebecca's hotel was not far from where Sally had parked the car and the nurse had insisted on walking Rebecca back to the door. Arm in arm they turned onto Warwick Road.

On the pavement right in front of them was a scruffy and unkempt man lying right across their path. He was emitting a low moaning sound. Rebecca wrinkled up her nose.

'Is he drunk?' she asked her companion.

Sally crouched down beside the prone figure. 'I don't think so, I can't smell drink,' she replied, 'I suppose it could be drugs or something.' She lifted the man's head from the kerbstone and the orange light from the streetlamp fell across his face as Rebecca crouched beside her friend.

'Blimey!' Rebecca exclaimed, 'it's Simon; the one I was telling you about, it's Simon Fenton and he looks as if he's hurt.'

The two girls half lifted and half dragged Simon back from the kerb and managed to prop him in a sitting position with his back against a shop doorway. Sally made a cursory examination of his injuries.

'He's got a deep gouge out of his side and a bad cut on his head,' she announced, 'and he's lost quite a bit of blood. I'll call an ambulance.'

'No,' gasped Simon, 'please, please don't call an ambulance.'

'Simon,' Rebecca cupped his face in her hands and gently turned it to look towards her, 'it's me, Rebecca Johal, you know, Kynpham's sister.'

'But you're in India,' replied Simon in a shaky voice, 'I must be dreaming or something.'

'No it really is me. You've been hurt and we need to get you to hospital.' Sally had her mobile phone in her hand and was beginning to dial.

'Please, no,' implored Simon, 'I'm in a bit of trouble and I don't want to go to hospital. Where's Kynpham? Is he all right?"

Sally looked at Rebecca who shrugged her shoulders, her finger poised above the keypad.

'Rebecca,' pleaded Simon, please help me. I need to get to the Bishop's house, but I don't know where he lives. It's really important.'

'Is this to do with what happened to Kynpham?' asked Rebecca, 'he's doing fine by the way.'

'Sort of,' muttered Simon, 'can you just get me a taxi to take me to Bishop Tim.'

Sally looked down at the couple. Rebecca had sat down on the floor beside Simon and had her arm around his shoulders. The Indian girl looked up at her imploringly and, moved by compassion, Sally put her common sense aside and slipped the handset back into her bag. .

'I know where the Bishop lives,' she said, 'I went to a picnic at his place at Rose Castle with my youth group a few years ago, when the old Bishop was there. You wait here with him Rebecca. I'll go and get the car.'

The journey took them less than a quarter of an hour. Rebecca sat in the back seat with Simon Fenton's head laid across her thighs. She gently stroked his matted hair and her eyes filled with tears. The object of her affection had literally fallen into her lap.

Sally drove boldly up the drive and stopped the car a few feet from the door of Rose Castle. Although the house was grand Bishop Tim and his wife Carrie lived there alone Their elder daughter was married and living in London, while their younger one was just beginning a gap year between school and university by backpacking in Thailand. It was the Bishop himself who answered Sally frantic knocking. He had been about to watch the BBC ten o'clock news on the TV while his wife finished washing the pots after their evening meal.

'Bishop,' exclaimed Sally breathlessly, 'sorry to disturb you, but we've got Simon Fenton in the car. He says he knows you and he wants to talk to you but he's been badly hurt and he won't go to hospital…'

Tim Baxter had dealt with more than his share of crises during his twenty five years in ministry and he quickly calmed Sally down and took stock of the situation. With his help Simon Fenton was quickly brought into the warmth of the kitchen and seated in a comfortable old armchair next to the Aga. Carrie had been dispatched to get the first aid kit from the garage while the Bishop organised a mug of hot sweet tea and began to heat a carton of chicken and leek soup in the microwave. In the light Simon looked considerably worse than he had seemed when the girls had found him. Under his torn coat his shirt was brown with dried blood; as was the left leg of his trousers. There was an ugly cut in his scalp which had scabbed over, but a trickle of fresh blood trickled from his side. Carrie returned with the first aid kit and Sally carefully eased the soiled shirt over Simon's head, exposing the deep weal in his side. With a pad of cotton and a pan of warm water she bathed the area gently and covered it with a large dressing before transferring her attention to his head wound. As Simon sipped at his tea, Tim Baxter went and got a sweatshirt and a pair of jogging bottoms. With Sally's help they eased Simon up from the chair and slipped off his soiled trousers and replaced then with the joggers, then helped him into the sweatshirt.

Rebecca looked on in silence, mildly embarrassed by the sight of Simon wearing only his boxer shorts. Her mind was reeling. Even in her most vivid daydreams about him she had never envisaged anything like this. With absolutely no idea of what it might be that Simon was mixed up in, and not an inkling of what would happen next, she sat at the kitchen table lost in her thoughts as Sally and the Bishop tended to his needs.

The warmth of the kitchen and the sweet tea helped revive Simon. His spirits rose as he realised that in the bag beside his seat lay all he needed to triumph over those who had so ruthlessly abused their positions and ended the lives of so many innocent people. As the Bishop's wife placed a bowl of hot soup and a plate of crusty bread on the table he slowly levered himself up and tottered a few places across the room to take the seat opposite Rebecca.

'Tell me what happened to Kynpham,' he said.

Rebecca explained how her brother had been badly hurt in a hit and run accident and how she had travelled from India to be with him. Kynpham, she said, had no recollection of the two days before his accident and could give no explanation whatsoever about what he was doing in Carlisle. Simon nodded, evaluating the information. It seemed that Kynpham was well on his way to making a full recovery and was safely out of the firing line for the timer being.

'Thanks, Rebecca,' he said, 'and thank you for what you have done for me tonight. You too,' he gestured at Sally. 'Between you, you have probably saved my life – in more ways than one.' Rebecca smiled shyly as Simon continued. 'Now, I'd really like to talk to Tim on his own if that's all right,' he glanced at the Bishop who nodded his head.

Sally announced that she had better be on her way and offered to drop Rebecca back at her hotel. While the last thing Rebecca wanted was to leave, she dared not put all of her cards on the table. With Simon badly hurt and obviously in some sort of trouble, affirmations of love from a virtual stranger would certainly not be appropriate and she reluctantly accepted Sally's offer. Rebecca stood up and walked over to where Simon was sitting. She took both his hands in hers.

'Take good care of yourself, Simon Fenton,' she said, 'and I hope we will be able to meet up again soon, you, me and Kynpham I mean.' She bent over and kissed him briefly on the forehead and was rewarded with a smile that made her heart skip a beat.

Carrie Baxter saw the girls out and went to busy herself elsewhere leaving the two men alone. Simon took a deep breath and began to tell his story, omitting only the fact that it had been Natalie who had been struggling with Andrew Gilroy when the gun went off, any reference to his intimacy with Natalie or the fact that Natalie was almost certainly Eddie Duggan's illegitimate daughter. He produced the brittle papers from his bag, along with the letters from Michael Duckworth also known as Terry Clegg. Tim Baxter had not risen to the position of Bishop of Carlisle without developing superb skills in both listening and seeing beneath the surface of what was being said and, in less than half an hour, he had grasped not only the complexities and implications of the situation, but was pretty sure that Natalie Robertson had become an extremely important factor in Simon's life. He was not displeased with the idea. He had known Sophie well and had often thought that Simon Fenton had been very much the junior partner in their marriage. When Sophie had been killed he had shared Simon's pain but he had also prayed that one day the rather intense and serious young man might discover the kind of sustaining and enduring love that he and Carrie had shared for almost thirty years.

'So what part do you want me to play in this?' asked the Bishop as Simon drew to the end of the tale.

'Help me get to the media with this lot,' answered Simon, 'they'd take notice of you and we could get to them before the police or any of Duggan's mob can stop us.'

'I'm not sure about that,' replied Tim Baxter, 'I mean about not involving the police. They would soon get onto it anyway.'

'I know,' replied Simon, 'but they can't all be trusted. Duggan has some sort of hold on some of them and if it was his lot we went too things would get very bad very quickly.'

Tim Baxter remained silent for a while, mulling things over. A few minutes later he began to unfold an alternative plan.

'First of all you need proper medical treatment,' he began. 'Now I know you can't just turn up at A and E, but will you let me call a doctor? Not a GP; a member of the congregation at the Cathedral. She's an A and E consultant and a good friend.'

'But wouldn't she be obliged to report a gunshot wound to the police?' asked Simon, 'I'm pretty sure all doctors have to do that.'

'Just hear me out,' said the Bishop, 'I also want you to agree to speak to a policeman. He's another good friend. Carrie and I play badminton with him and his wife every couple of weeks. His name is Ian Saunders and he's the Chief Constable of Cumbria. I'd trust my life on him being straight, Simon. There are issues here that the media would have a field day with. At the end of the day they're more interested in making money than the truth and it seems to me that with people as influential as Eddie Duggan involved we need to tread carefully.'

Simon thought for a moment or two before he replied.

'All right, Tim,' he answered, 'let's try it your way. I suppose that one of the reasons I came to you is that you always seem to know the right thing to do.'

CHAPTER SEVENTY-FIVE

The consultant was the first to arrive. Hefting a large bag she bustled into the kitchen and eyed Simon up and down.

'Now then, laddie,' she said in a soft Scots burr, 'what seems to be the trouble?'

Tim Baxter introduced her as Elspeth Duncan and she gently removed the recently applied dressings to Simon's wounds before filling a syringe with local anaesthetic and beginning her work. By the time the Chief Constable arrived twenty minutes later both wounds had been thoroughly disinfected and stitched. She was just applying new dressings as the burly policeman made his entrance.

'You'll do for the time being,' the doctor said to Simon. 'You've likely had a bit of concussion from that bang on the head. The wounds themselves are clean enough, but there'll be a bit more pain when the local wears off. You've also had a narrow squeak with hypothermia, but you're warm enough now. Make sure you get properly checked out in a hospital tomorrow, though and if you feel ill before then get Tim to give me a call.'

The Chief Constable and doctor appeared to know each other and held a brief conversation just out of earshot as Tim Baxter helped Simon to put his sweatshirt back on.

The policeman sat down at the table opposite Simon. Tim Baxter escorted the doctor to the door and the policeman introduced himself as Ian Saunders. He was tall and broad with a reddish complexion and short grey hair. Tim Baxter returned and brewed more tea while Simon placed the papers on the table and began to tell his story all over again. He told only one lie and again omitted the details of his relationship with Natalie and any reference to her likely paternity. The clock in the hallway chimed midnight as Simon completed his account and Ian Saunders excused himself saying that he had to make a number of calls. Simon was utterly spent and retired to the armchair where he was fast asleep when the Chief Constable returned.

'I'm sorry,' he said, having shaken the sleeping man gently to wake him up, 'I know it's late and you've had a hell of a time, but I'm going to need to keep you up for another hour or so. Let me tell you what's going to happen.'

Simon ribbed his eyes and nodded.

'First of all, this is far too important to deal with in Carlisle. Secondly I want you to know that I believe you. I suspected that something peculiar was afoot when certain senior officers from a semi-detached unit at Scotland Yard and the Home Secretary were taking an undue interest in finding you and Miss Robertson last week. I never thought for a moment, that it was a serious as this, though. I've got the Metropolitan Police Commissioner out of his bed and he seems to think I've done the right thing. I've also spoken to my colleague in Manchester and we should be hearing back from him soon. We'll all be meeting up at Scotland Yard tomorrow; at twelve noon. I don't know how far the rot has spread through high places so we're keen not to involve anyone else for the time being. I have to say at the outset, Simon, that you are most definitely not under arrest. As far as I can see you've not only done absolutely nothing wrong, but if what you say can be proved you and Miss Robertson have done this country a considerable service. I do have to ask you, though, are you willing to come with me to London in the morning?'

Simon nodded his assent.

'I think I'd like to come along too,' interjected Tim Baxter, 'I know all about it anyway and I think it's in Simon's best interests if there is someone independent with him if that's all right Ian.'

'No problem,' replied the Chief Constable, 'but I'll be driving you myself. I'm going to leave a message that I'm needed for a special briefing in connection with a big secret operation; that's not far from the truth, actually. We don't want anyone at all to know anything at all for the time being; not until we're in a position to reel in Duggan and his crew.'

The mobile phone in the policeman's pocket began to ring and he ducked back into the hallway to take the call. He was smiling when he returned. He passed the handset to Simon.

'Here,' he said, 'there's someone on the other end of this that I think you wouldn't mind a word with. It would be really helpful if you could let her know that it's all right by you if she tells my colleague in Manchester what you've just told me.'

CHAPTER SEVENTY-SIX

Eddie Duggan arrived early for his rendezvous with Jimmy Bell; he had a particular reason for wanting to get there first. No sooner had he parked up and hobbled awkwardly over to the seat overlooking the Channel when the lights of a second car signalled the arrival of the policeman. As the car drew to a halt the Home Secretary snapped on a pair of latex gloves and thrust his hands deep into the pockets of his overcoat.

Jimmy Bell ambled over to the bench and sat to the right of Eddie Duggan.

'Have you got them?' Bell was forced to raise his voice over the incessant noise of heavy goods vehicles climbing the hill from the ferry terminal at Dover. Duggan flapped his right hand in his pocket.

'In here, Jimmy, just be patient,' he replied, 'now did you find Fenton's body and the money?'

'Yes,' lied Bell, 'I've burnt all of his ID; and the letters from the fat bugger, oh and those about you being er...related to the tom.'

'What about the money?' asked the Home Secretary.

'The suitcase is at the bottom of a lake in Yorkshire and the cash is and safe and sound at my place,' continued Jimmy Bell, 'don't worry Guv, no loose ends.'

'If that's the case, then, Jimmy, this is the end of it,' exclaimed Eddie Duggan. He pulled the gun from his pocket, swivelled to face his erstwhile junior partner and shot him in the head before the policeman had time to realise what was about to happen. Bell's body slid off the end of the bench and Eddie Duggan scanned rapidly in all directions in an attempt to ascertain whether or not the shot had been heard. Apart from the noise of traffic from the road behind him, all seemed quiet. He had deliberately chosen the spot because of the virtually constant traffic noise. Duggan slid across the seat and checked for a pulse in Bell's neck with his left hand. He did not find one. He then, again using his left hand, felt in the dead policeman's pockets and took out his car keys. He then pressed the pistol into Jimmy Bell's left hand and closed his dead fingers around it before squeezing the corpse's finger on the trigger to send a second bullet out over the cliff top in order to ensure that any forensic investigation would find Bell's fingerprints on the gun and firearms residue on his hand. He had known for many years that Jimmy Bell was left handed. The fact that forensics would almost certainly identify the unlicensed gun as the one that had also killed Simon Fenton, together with the copious amount of money in Bell's house, would muddy the waters still further, he thought.

Eddie Duggan snapped off his gloves and immediately replaced them with the second pair. After another scan for any unwelcome attention, he unlocked Bell's Saab, removed his suitcase and brief case and locked them in the boot of his Audi before returning the keys to the dead man's pocket. After a final look around to reassure himself that there had been no witnesses, Eddie Duggan slipped gingerly into the driving seat of his car, started the engine and drove off.

The Home Secretary was back aboard his yacht by midnight with Jimmy Bell's suitcase and briefcase open on the table in the salon. With a degree of satisfaction he extracted the bearer bonds and cash before placing the brief case, still containing its identity documents, an airline ticket and an envelope addressed to Jimmy Bell's ex-wife into the top of the suitcase. He then made his tortuous way down the narrow companionway into the engine space with his ankle protesting at the abuse with a series of sharp stabbing pains. From the machinery space he collected half a dozen heavy spanners and wrenches and a sharp knife. After a pause for the pain in his ankle to ease he hobbled back into the salon. The spanners and wrenches he placed into the suitcase. With the knife he punctured the fabric of the case in around twenty places before placing the implement next to the other tools and zipping the suitcase closed. It would be at the bottom of the channel as soon as he was clear of Folkestone Harbour.

His mission complete, Eddie Duggan undressed and lay down in the queen-size bed in the master cabin. As soon as it was daylight he would be leaving the United Kingdom for the last time.

CHAPTER SEVENTY-SEVEN

Natalie was sitting up on her hard bed with her knees under her chin and her arms wrapped round her lower legs when they came for her. She had slept a little during the early evening but her anxieties had returned in full force after nightfall and robbed her of sleep. The rattle of the cell door lock was a precursor for the bright overhead light coming on and, for a few moments, Natalie could not focus her eyes on whoever had just stepped into her cell.

'Natalie, I'm sorry to disturb you, but something's come up.' Alison Frith's voice drew her attention and the trim figure of the detective gradually resolved in her still blinking eyes. Beside her stood a tall thin man of about forty with dark wavy hair and deep-set grey eyes. 'This is my boss,' continued Alison, 'Adam Morgan, the Chief Constable of Greater Manchester.'

Natalie's heart lurched. Had something terrible happened to Simon, she wondered, or had Eddie Duggan's tentacles penetrated right to the top of the police service in north-west England?

'We'd like you to come and have a chat,' the Chief Constable's voice was deep with just a trace of a Welsh accent, 'It's nothing to worry about, Miss Robertson, but we really do need your assistance.

Helpless to resist, Natalie meekly allowed Alison Frith to guide her along a series of corridors and up several flights of stairs with the tall policeman following behind. Eventually they reached a large well-furnished office with panoramic windows on two adjacent walls which afforded an eye-catching view of a galaxy of streetlights stretching into the distance and reflecting their orange glow from a canopy of clouds. Alison gestured for Natalie to sit on one of a group of chairs clustered around a low table next to one of the windows.

'Welcome to my office,' said the Chief Constable, 'I've just been speaking to my counterpart in Carlisle and there's someone with him that I think you might want to talk to.' The only person that Natalie knew to be anywhere near Carlisle was Simon's friend Kynpham. She looked at the senior officer with a puzzled expression as he dialled a number on the telephone.

'Hello, Ian,' he said into the mouthpiece, 'yes she's with me now. I'll just pass you over.' He walked over and gave the handset to Natalie. She put it to her ear with an uneasy sense of trepidation.

'Hello, 'she said tentatively.

'Nat, oh Nat, it's so good to hear your voice,' exclaimed Simon.

'Simon.......' Natalie was momentarily lost for words. 'Simon...' she spluttered. She was overwhelmed with relief and joy; the tears began to flow freely down her face. Alison Frith passed her a tissue and Natalie gradually regained her composure.

'Simon,' she sniffled, 'is it really you, are you all right?'

'Yes Nat, I'm fine really, well actually I had a bit of a dust up with Eddie Duggan and I think he probably came out of it a bit better than me, but I'm fine. I really am.'

'I'm in the police station, Simon,' she continued hesitantly, 'they had me locked up somewhere, but they told me to turn myself in so I did. I wouldn't tell them anything even when they knocked me about. I'm OK though; just bruises. Simon, I won't tell the police either, I said I wouldn't talk to them until tomorrow like we agreed, or is it today. What time is it?'

'It's nearly one in the morning Nat,' he replied, 'and you can tell them everything now. Don't worry I'm not being forced to say this; I've not been to Clacton or anywhere.'

Natalie smiled weakly, recalling the cryptic warning that Kynpham had given them the previous week.

'Tell them it all, Nat,' he continued, tell them everything from when we met and when the gun went off when I was fighting with Inspector Gilroy. They don't want to know all the trivial stuff like what we watched on telly, Nat, but tell then what we've done and about Duggan and that.'

Despite her heightened emotional state Natalie recognised both of Simon's other cryptic comments for what they were. He was obviously trying to shoulder any blame that might accrue for the death of Andrew Gilroy and he was not going to say anything about the copies of the letters her mother had written to Eddie Duggan that were concealed in the television set at the house in Derby.

'I understand,' she replied, hoping he would know exactly what she understood and what she was going to say, I'll tell them the whole truth.'

It was Simon's turn to read meaning into her words. He suspected that she would not allow him to take responsibility for the shooting of Inspector Gilroy. He thought, however that she had probably understood what he meant about the letters.

Acutely aware of the audiences at both ends, Natalie and Simon exchanged a few brief pleasantries. In response to a gesture from Adam Morgan Natalie brought the conversation to an end; promising Simon that he would see her soon and passed over the handset. The Chief Constable gestured for Inspector Frith and Natalie to leave the office and they found seats in a small reception area. Ten minutes later they were summoned back into the office. With all three of them seated around the low table, Natalie began to tell her story while Alison Frith made handwritten notes in a large hard-backed notebook.

CHAPTER SEVENTY-EIGHT

Although Simon only managed four hours sleep before a knock at the bishop's guest bedroom door woke him he could not remember when he had last slept in such blissful comfort. His head was clear and the pain in his side had subsided to a dull ache. Dressed in borrowed clothes that were a size too large for him, clean shaven and feeling better than he had for several days, Simon joined his host for breakfast in the kitchen as they waited for Ian Saunders to arrive.

The unmarked Volvo drew up outside at the agreed time of six fifteen and the two passengers embarked. Alone on the back seat, Simon was asleep again before they reached the motorway. His next recollection was of the car drawing to a halt. Rubbing his eyes saw a sign welcoming them to Keele Services. The clock on the dashboard showed it to be ten past nine. Refreshed by coffee and pastries, the three travellers resumed their journey making light conversation and studiously avoiding any mention of the business upon which they were engaged. Ian Saunders drew in to the underground car park at New Scotland Yard a few minutes after eleven thirty.

By the time Natalie's interrogation had ended the clock on the Chief Constable's office wall showed it to be two thirty in the morning. Alison Frith offered Natalie the choice of returning to her cell or a makeshift bed made up from a couple of easy chairs in an empty office. As she was utterly exhausted Natalie chose the cell and was asleep within minutes. The next morning Alison Frith arrived with a change of clothes for the erstwhile prisoner and, after a much better breakfast than had been served the previous morning Natalie, Inspector Frith and the Chief Constable were on their way to London. From the basement car park they were ushered into an austere office where Natalie and Alison were asked to wait while the senior officer went to confer with his colleagues. A member of the civilian support staff made drinks while they waited. Presently the Chief Constable returned and led them up several flights of stairs into a large conference room. On the table was a brand new laptop, still in its box. The Chief Constable asked Inspector Frith to get the computer up and running while he went to inform someone he referred to as "The Commissioner" that they were ready. Alison Frith followed her orders, unpacking the machine, connecting up the power and loading an enclosed copy of Microsoft Office while Natalie stared out of the window. She was not particularly familiar with London, but the view encompassed Big Ben and Westminster Abbey. She felt small, insignificant and more than a little frightened as she started across at the well known landmarks and awaited her fate.

With the computer up and running Alison Frith joined Natalie at the window and gave her forearm a reassuring squeeze.

'Don't worry so much, 'she said, 'I think they're really pleased with you. You're not in trouble you know.'

Natalie shivered. Now that the dangerous contest with Eddie Duggan and his henchmen seemed as if it might be drawing to an end a whole new set of challenges were emerging for her.

A young man wheeled in a trolley loaded with sandwiches, fruit and insulated flasks. He began to set them out on a side table, together with crockery and cutlery which had been stowed on a lower shelf. The man left and Natalie risked asking the question she had been longing to ask all day.

'Is Simon Fenton here?'

Alison Frith shook her head.

'I don't know, Natalie. I think the Commissioner wants to speak to you both, but I don't know if that will be at the same time. It's all a bit hush, hush. They haven't told me any more than I found out from you last night.'

At that very moment the door swung open and Adam Morgan returned along with a broad shouldered black man wearing a police uniform that was obviously a cut above that worn by the rank and file.

'Miss Robertson?' he asked, walking up to Natalie and shaking her by the hand, 'My name is Denzel Goodman, pleased to meet you.'

Natalie half smiled, but made no reply.

'Come on everyone, get something to eat and drink. The others won't be long.' He ushered Natalie towards the table where the food had been set out and she awkwardly selected a couple of small sandwiches and poured herself a cup of coffee. Behind her she heard The Chief Constable of Manchester talking to the man who had introduced himself as Denzel Goodman. Adam Morgan, she noted, was calling him "Sir Denzel". She felt completely out of her depth. Natalie walked slowly back to the window and stared absently over the rooftops at the pods on the London eye making their almost imperceptible progress across the skyline. Lost in her thoughts and oblivious to the buzz of conversation behind her she was unaware of the presence of anyone immediately behind her until she felt a hand on her shoulder.

'Nat,' whispered a familiar voice, 'I've missed you so much.'

CHAPTER SEVENTY-NINE

Eddie Duggan had been lying awake in the comfort of the sumptuous surroundings of his yacht since well before dawn. He had named her "Cabinet Minister II" in honour of the ship that had been wrecked off a Scottish Island in the 1940's; shedding its load of whisky for the lucky islanders to salvage in an Ealing comedy inspired by an actual event. The thirty two foot motor yacht was his pride and joy. Her twin engines were capable of propelling her at a speed of twenty three knots for hours on end and she had sleeping accommodation for eight guests in addition to the crew of four that were required when he was entertaining. She had been his favourite plaything for more than three years. As he lay in the darkness the Home Secretary gave his mind free reign to recall how he had bought her at a knock down cash price from an investment banker who had been caught insider trading.

At first he had employed a professional skipper to run her, but his confidence in handling the boat had grown and within a year he was taking her out into the Channel for day trips on his own. His first overnight trip away had been a jolly to Cherbourg with the fading starlet who was later to become his wife. After the break up of her girl band she had only managed to reach the top forty with one of her five singles and sales of her solo album had been disappointing. He had met her at a party where she had told him that she intended to re-launch her celebrity status in a jungle survival TV show. He had invited her to sail to France with him and an alternative and much more lucrative opportunity had presented itself. With grim satisfaction he recalled that if he managed to successfully disappear she would have to wait seven years to inherit his house, legitimate business interests and the assortment of remaining assets that he had not been able to move offshore. She would probably be ten times better off than she would have been if they divorced. He hoped vindictively that she would start losing her looks before she was able to start spending his money.

Dawn broke over the marina and Duggan showered and dressed as he made his final preparations for departure. A glance outside, however, revealed that the mist of the previous evening had coalesced into a thick sea fog. The maritime forecast on the radio confirmed that the fog bank extended right across the channel and was not expected to disperse before noon. Eddie Duggan swore copiously. The Cabinet Minister boasted both a state of the art radar and a sophisticated GPS system, but he was not at all confident in his ability to sail safely across the busy Channel to Boulogne in such poor weather conditions. His plan had been to arrive in the French port using his own passport then take a slow train to Paris and disappear into the evening rush hour. His Canadian identity would then come into play as he booked into a mid-range hotel for the night and hired a car the next morning. Eddie Duggan would never be seen again. With growing frustration he retired to the salon, switched on the radio and cooked himself a breakfast of bacon and eggs.

Surprisingly, now that the die was cast, he was not sorry to be leaving his old life behind. Politics, he thought, had been like an addictive drug. Once he had tasted the first fruits of political power he had sought more and more of it; ultimately to the extent that his ambition had overridden every other aspect of his life. Divorced ten years ago after seven years of marriage to the daughter of a wealthy businessman, he had only married his second wife as a prop to enrich the backdrop of his quest for power. There had never been real love between them, but she had stayed in line for almost two years enjoying the expensive accessories and lifestyle that he was able to provide her with. Ultimately they had not been enough for her and she had sought her thrills elsewhere. On sober reflection he realised that, even if the whole Simon Fenton business had not reared its ugly head, his wife's affair would probably have been enough to have doomed his bid for leadership of the country to failure. At lease with a new life, in a new place and with a different name he might have the time and space to enjoy the small things in life; to perhaps discover love and be loved in return; to be free to make choices without having to worry about the way in which others would see them.

Eddie Duggan's train of thought was interrupted by an announcement on the ten o'clock news on the Radio Two. The body of a man had been discovered on the cliff top between Dover and Folkestone and the man appeared to have been shot. A tremor of anxiety ran through him. The fact that Jimmy Bell's body had been discovered made him uneasy. His plan had been to leave harbour at first light; before there was any realistic chance of the body being discovered. Instead he was stuck at his mooring in the marina not three miles from where the body had been found. After a few moments of hesitation he hobbled decisively up the short flight of steps into the cockpit, powered up the radar and GPS and prepared to put to sea. It should be safe enough if he kept a careful eye on the twin screens and took it steady. The rumble of the twin diesel engines from below sent a surge of adrenaline though Eddie Duggan's body. He checked that his wallet and passport were securely zipped into his weatherproof coat and pulled on a lifejacket before he manoeuvred himself awkwardly out onto the deck, cast off the mooring lines and moved off slowly out of the marina. He estimated the visibility to be in the region of eighty meters, but the crystal clear multicoloured moving map on the GPS display gave him an accurate indication of his position and course. Duggan advanced the throttles slightly until the display showed a speed of five knots and slipped past the breakwater and out into the channel. Five minutes later Jimmy Bell's suitcase was on its way to the sea bed.

The places of greatest danger were the twin shipping lanes which were followed by ships of all sizes transiting the narrow straits. They were well known to be the busiest shipping lanes in the world. Calculating that the safest way to proceed was to cross each lane at a right angle he set his course to due south and cranked out the range on his radar display to ten miles. A line of ships was clearly visible and, calculating angles and relative speeds he increased speed to ten knots; aiming at a blip on the screen three miles distant in the intention of crossing between the ship and the one following around four miles behind it, He watched the screen with fascination as things went exactly according to plan. With growing confidence, and no ships indicated on the radar in the sea ahead of his course he accelerated to fifteen knots. The GPS screen told him exactly where he was while the radar showed him that all was clear ahead. He wondered what he had been worried about. This was proving to be much easier than he had expected. Twenty minutes later the second stream of ships following the invisible navigation lanes resolved itself onto the radar screen ahead of him. Once again he performed a series of mental calculations. With growing bravado he aimed for a much narrower gap of just two and a half miles. With a mile left to run he noticed that he would come rather too close to the bow of the rearmost ship. He increased speed to twenty knots. Hurtling through the fogbank at twenty knots filled him with a growing sense of invincibility as he slipped neatly through the exact centre of the gap between the two ships. The GPS showed that he had only eleven miles to run to his destination; less than half an hour at twenty knots. With no warning whatsoever the radar screen went blank. Duggan recycled the switch several times and checked the circuit breaker. The screen remained blank. The GPS, however continued to give him a detailed map of his position and the coast of France was clearly visible. What the hell, he thought; he'd passed neatly through the danger areas, hadn't he? Surely there would be no other ships or boats between him and Boulogne in such appalling weather conditions. He left the twin throttles where they were and watched the miles count steadily down on the GPS display.

As oil tankers went the Panamanian registered Jurassic Voyager was little more than a tiddler. Weighing in at only eighty five thousand tons she had been plying between the Gulf States and the spot market in Rotterdam for almost thirty years. Her present owners were not renowned for either their compliance with maritime safety regulations or the quality of accommodation and conditions of service offered to their crews. Inbound to Rotterdam from Kuwait with a full load of crude, the voyage had already taken three days longer than planned because of persistent engine problems. Her Venezuelan Chief Engineer had informed the South African Captain that he suspected fuel contamination. Both engines had proved troublesome, but with one stopped for the fuel filters to be cleaned the other one had managed to maintain a speed through the water of just over five knots. The port engine had failed for the fifth time when the Jurassic Voyager was abeam Hastings and the engineers had not even completed stripping down the fuel system when the other engine gave up the ghost two hours later. There was no wind to speak of, but the ship had begun to drift slowly south-eastwards in the Channel swell. Five miles outside Boulogne the captain had dropped the anchor and retired to his cabin with a bottle of Whisky to await notification from the engineers that power had been restored. In the absence of their superior, the officer of the watch and the three seamen on duty sought out the comfort of a nearby mess deck and settled down for a game of cards.

To Eddie Duggan the flank of the tanker which loomed out of the fog less than a hundred yards ahead of him looked like a giant black cliff. In the two seconds that it took him to recognise it for what it was the Cabinet Minister II had already covered half the distance. Duggan threw both engines into reverse and spun the wheel hard a starboard, but the motor yacht was still travelling at sixteen knots when she struck the plates of the tanker an angle of forty five degrees two seconds later. No one aboard the tanker knew what had caused the explosion two thirds of the way between her bow and stern for several minutes. It was only when the flames died down that the wreckage of the yacht could be made out bobbing gently on the swell. The Captain ordered a boat to be lowered. The entry in his log stated that the charred body of a man was recovered on board at one zero five eight Greenwich Mean Time.

CHAPTER EIGHTY

The unexpected sound of Simon's voice, together with the warmth of his hand on her shoulder, caused Natalie to drop her plate on the floor. She spun around and there he was, smiling down at her. Instantly she folded herself into his embrace as the hubbub of conversation from the others side of the room came to a halt. Oblivious to the stares of the onlookers Natalie lifted her face to his and their lips met. Natalie ran her tongue teasingly across his semi-open mouth and held on to him as if there was no tomorrow. The mildly embarrassed onlookers averted their gaze and dialogue was resumed as Simon took her gently by the shoulders.

'Let me look at you,' he said, pushing her gently away, but keeping hold of her shoulders. 'You've got a whopping bruise on your face, Nat. Did they do that to you?'

Natalie touched her cheek. 'Yes, and some more, but all they did was hit me; look at you,' she touched his head just below the adhesive dressing. How did the happen?'

Simon grinned.

'I've got worse than that to show you. There's a blooming great bullet hole under my shirt. Eddie Duggan shot me; then I fell over a cliff and got this,' he gestured to his head, 'knocked me out for hours.'

'What happened to Duggan?' asked Natalie.

Simon pulled two chairs over from the table to the space in front of the window and, in hushed tones, they brought each other up to date with their respective stories. As Natalie sat opposite Simon the enormity of the task she had pledged herself to seemed overwhelming. The very sight of him caused a peculiar longing in the pit of her stomach. The memory of the taste of his lips on her tongue sent her heart turning summersaults. Giving up this man; even though her motives were pure and there was no doubt that he would be much better off without her, would be the hardest thing she had ever done. It was not so much the promise that she had made to a God who still probably didn't exist that bothered her, but a deep conviction that to put her own dreams and desires first would damage them both; to her they would always be the vicar and the tart.

The tall black policeman drew the meeting to order and invited them all to take seats around a large boardroom table. Simon and Natalie sat beside each other and, as the Commissioner began to speak, Simon reached out and took hold of Natalie's hand under the table.

'Ladies and gentleman,' began Denzel Goodman, 'I think we are all aware of both the facts of the matter before us and the implications of those facts. Before we come to any conclusions, however, I think it would make sense if I summarised the position as I understand it. Please feel free to chip in if you think anything I say is wrong or if you think I haven't understood anything properly.'

He paused and scanned the assembled faces. There was no dissent so he continued.

'It would seem that for more than thirty years the Home Secretary has been involved in serious criminal activity. With the complicity of a number of senior officers of the Metropolitan Police he has sought to conceal evidence of wrongdoing and a number of murders and attempted murders have been committed over a long period of time to this end. I must also report that Inspector Paul Cavendish and Inspector Gerald Jewel, officers seconded to the Independent Criminal Intelligence Service were killed in a road accident in North Yorkshire on Tuesday. Miss. Roberson was shown photographs of these officers yesterday and positively identified them as the men responsible for her abduction. I am now almost certain that ICIS was complicit in Mr. Duggan's illegal activities and we are currently trying to make contact with the officer in charge, but he is neither in his office nor at home. We have also had no success in contacting him on his mobile phone. I am sure that we are all aware of the immense and far-reaching political implications of this situation and, for that reason, I am proposing two things. Firstly I intend to limit knowledge of the full extent of these crimes to those present in this room until I am in a position to decide what action should be taken to detain and question Mr. Duggan. Before doing that I will need to speak to the Prime Minister and my request is that not one of us should leave Scotland Yard until after I have done so. My second proposal is that all material evidence in this case,' he gestured to the papers that Simon had recovered from Terry Clegg's grave and to the hard-backed notebook open on the table, 'including the laptop that Inspector Frith is using to make a record of the meeting is sealed into a secure container and kept under lock and key on the top floor of this building in order to keep it safe from any attempts that might be made to tamper with it or to make it available to the press; any objections?'

'Yes, Sir Denzel,' it was Tim Baxter that interrupted the Commissioner, 'Simon Fenton has been hurt and has received only rudimentary medical attention. I think it should be a priority to get him proper medical care as quickly as possible.'

'Yes, Bishop,' replied the senior officer, 'I apologise, Simon,' he looked at Simon and smiled, 'we really are truly grateful for all you have done; and you too Miss. Robertson, I shall make arrangements for you to be taken to a private clinic for a check up as soon as this first part of the meeting is over.'

Tim Baxter nodded and smiled.

There it was again, thought Natalie, Simon; he had called him Simon while she had been Miss. Robertson. Simon was one of them; he'd been to university, he was sort of in the club and she was not. How could someone like her ever think she could be? She was an uneducated, cheap and common tart with a Yorkshire accent and everyone in the room knew it.

'To tell the story chronologically,' Denzel Goodman was once again in full flow, 'Mr. Duggan first succumbed to greed immediately after leading a successful operation against an IRA drug smuggling operation in Northern Ireland in 1975.' The Commissioner went on to outline Eddie Duggan's early career and how, beginning with the shooting of Simon's father, Duggan and an unknown accomplice had systematically murdered both dissenters and witness of the theft of cash and drugs. He went on to describe the escapes of Tim Ellwood and Terry Clegg and was in the process of outlining Eddie Duggan's involvement in money laundering, fraud and possible connections with drugs and vice rings in east London in the 1980s when a strident bleeping from his pager halted the narrative.

'I'm sorry, 'he said, 'I have to take a very urgent call. Please wait in the room. I will be back as quickly as I can.'

The Commissioner stood up and slipped out of the room leaving his audience in a stunned silence. Upon his return a few minutes later he once again took the chair at the head of the table. 'There has been a development,' he announced, 'the body of Detective Chief Superintendent Bell, the officer in charge of ICIS was found this morning on the cliff top between Dover and Folkestone. It appears that he was killed by a single shot to the head. The investigating officer's preliminary report suggests either suicide or a very clever attempt to make it look like suicide. I'm sorry, but I need to adjourn this meeting. Shall we reconvene at, say five thirty? Thank you. Oh, Simon, Inspector Frith can drive you to the clinic once she has secured all the evidence.' He looked at Natalie and smiled, 'and I'm sure it would do no harm if you had someone take a look at that bruise, Miss Robertson.'

CHAPTER EIGHTY-ONE

The private clinic was south of the Thames; in a side street next to a small square of green space. Alison Frith had missed the turning causing a tortuous circuit of one way streets before she had managed to steer the unfamiliar car through the gated entrance to the car park. They had obviously been expected. A white-clad receptionist ushered Simon straight into an adjacent examination room while Natalie and Alison Frith were directed to sit in comfortable armchairs in a sumptuous reception area. Alison Frith made use of the drinks machine to procure two cappuccinos and the two women leafed through magazines making small talk while Simon was attended to.

He was gone for almost half an hour and Natalie experienced a minor twinge of unease as her imagination began to run riot. Perhaps he was seriously hurt. Perhaps his injuries were much worse than anyone thought. When he eventually reappeared she had to use every ounce of her self-control to avoid leaping to her feet and throwing her arms round him.

'All's well,' Simon reported with a grin, 'I've been poked, prodded and x-rayed and everything's where it should be.' He lifted his shirt to reveal a neat clean dressing.

A buzzing sound from the reception desk signalled that it was Natalie's turn to be examined and she entered the examination room where an earnest-looking young doctor invited her to take a seat on the examination table. The beeper clipped to his waist, however, summoned him elsewhere and after a hurried apology he left her, leaving the door slightly ajar. As Natalie waited his return she could see Simon chatting with Alison Frith in the reception area. She would have to let him down gently, she decided, if she blew a little hot and cold he might realise for himself that she was far from suitable to be a long term girlfriend.

The outside doors of the reception area opened with a loud squeal. Simon looked round to see what had caused the noise and no sooner had he swivelled his head than the familiar face of Kynpham Johal stepped through the doorway. His head swathed in white bandages. Behind him came a medical orderly carrying a suitcase followed in turn by the diminutive form of his twin sister.

'Kynpham!' exclaimed Simon, leaping to his feet.

Kynpham turned towards the sound of his name and broke into a broad grin as he recognised his friend.

'Simon,' he cried, 'what are you doing here? Rebecca has been telling me about finding you half dead in Carlisle only yesterday and now you are here too. What is going on?'

'Never mind all that,' replied Simon, 'how are you? You were badly hurt the last I heard.'

'I'm going to be fine, Simon,' he replied, 'but I have no memory at all of how I was hurt. I have no idea why I was in Carlisle or anything. The last thing I remember is being at the Olympic Stadium. A policeman came to me in hospital this morning and asked if I would mind coming to London to help out the police. Who am I to refuse? I have only been a British citizen for six months.'

'Yes, Simon, what is all this about?' Rebecca had come to stand alongside them.

'I'm not sure that I'm allowed to say,' replied Simon, 'I know it sounds a bit melodramatic, but the police have sworn me to secrecy.'

The receptionist interrupted them. It seemed that a nurse was waiting to take Kynpham to his room. Promising to see him before they left, Simon returned to his seat. Rebecca Johal was rooted to the spot; torn with indecision she chose to leave her brother to his own devices for a few minutes. She walked the short distance to where Simon was sitting and knelt down on the floor facing him. Taking both his hands in hers she looked up into his grey eyes.

'Simon Fenton,' she said, 'I am so happy to see you again. When I left you last night I was so worried that you were badly hurt. If you really cannot tell me exactly what all this is about will you at least let me look after you; and my brother of course. There is a spare bedroom in his flat you know.'

From the treatment room Natalie watched in growing trepidation. The brown girl was kneeling in front of the man she had just vowed to let down gently, but the emotion that rose within her and sent warm blood rushing into her cheeks was pure jealousy. The young doctor returned and closed the door behind him, shutting off Natalie's view of the hiatus in the reception area. As he examined her bruises she knew that she was being brusque and discourteous towards him, but the image of Simon and the Asian girl haunted her memory.

When Natalie returned from her examination with a clean bill of health the girl had gone. Simon and Alison Frith were sitting as they had been before Natalie had left. Simon was quick to tell her of the arrival of Kynpham and his sister. He had already mentioned how Kynpham's sister and her friend had rescued him from the streets of Carlisle, but, she noted, he had not told her just how pretty the Indian girl was or given any hints that they knew each other so well that she had thought nothing of kneeling on the floor directly in front of him and holding both his hands. She declined his invitation to accompany him on a brief visit to seek out Kynpham in his room.

The journey back to Scotland Yard took place in virtual silence. Simon hoped that Natalie was just too tired to make conversation.

CHAPTER EIGHTY-TWO

'I must apologise for the delay,' began Sir Denzel Goodman, 'but there have been a number of developments. First of all Ian Saunders has been to visit the journalist Kynpham Johal who was injured while trying to help Simon Fenton and Natalie Robertson. Mr Johal has been moved at my request to a private hospital close to central London and I was quite prepared to take him fully into our confidence. It seems however that the blow to his head had caused a degree of amnesia and he has no recollection whatsoever of any of the events pertaining to this affair. Ian has cautioned him that should he ever remember even the slightest detail in the future he should not discuss it with anyone at all. I suspect that we may need to talk further with Mr. Johal in a day or two and appeal to his better nature lest his journalistic instincts get the better of him.

Secondly I must report an event of extreme significance. Just before twelve noon today the Home Secretary's motor yacht was in collision with a Panamanian oil tanker. The yacht was completely destroyed and Mr. Duggan's body has been recovered from the sea. We are still, of course, awaiting formal identification but it seems that there can be little doubt that the Home Secretary is dead.'

He paused and the assembled audience glanced at each other around the table. Simon caught Natalie's eye and she smiled weakly. He wondered how the fact that Eddie Duggan was her father might colour her perception of events, but she gave nothing away. The Commissioner took a sip of water and continued.

Troubled Legacy

'Obviously our priority is no longer the apprehension of Mr Duggan. It is quite possible that it was he who shot Chief Superintendent Bell. Strong circumstantial evidence points to the conclusion that he, and all three of his subordinates, were involved in the murders of Terry Clegg and Tim Ellwood; not to mention the attempted murder of Simon Fenton and Natalie Robertson. It seems that the late Home Secretary has taken great pains to tidy up as many loose ends as possible. With all the protagonists dead we may never unravel the full extent of Duggan's web of corruption and deceit.' He went on to outline the plot to murder Simon by forcing Natalie to entice him into her room before she was also to be murdered and how she had overheard the conversation between Wayne Stevens and Andrew Gilroy and had teamed up with Simon to thwart them. At that point he looked directly at Natalie and Simon who were once again sitting close to one other.

'At this point there seems to be a notable discrepancy in the accounts offered by Mr Fenton and Miss Robertson,' he announced, continuing to hold the pair of them in his gaze, 'Both Mr Fenton and Miss Robertson claim to have been grappling with Inspector Gilroy when the fatal shot was fired,' He paused and the silence had its intended effect; both Simon and Natalie looked sheepishly at each other then dropped their eyes. 'I do not suppose,' continued the Commissioner, 'that we shall ever be able to discover which of them is telling the truth.' The faintest trace of a smile was visible at the corners of his mouth, 'And in any case, all the evidence gathered by my colleague's officers,' he gestured at Adam Morgan, 'points towards the guilty party having been Wayne Stevens himself who unfortunately cannot cast any further light upon the matter because he was also murdered by persons unknown shortly afterwards.'

Commissioner Goodman went on to outline the journey that Simon and Natalie had made in fairly general terms, referring to the evidence trail provided firstly by the letters from Michael Duckworth and then by the papers that Simon had exhumed in Hawes to replace those lost to Eddie Duggan. The narrative took the best part of forty minutes before he began to sum up and explain his decisions as to what ought to happen next.

'I have already spoken briefly with the Prime Minister this afternoon', he reported, 'and the political ramifications of this business cannot be ignored. The Prime Minister wishes to consult with the leaders of both main opposition parties and with certain key members of his cabinet. In the meantime, there are certain arrangements that must be made. While I cannot emphasise strongly enough that both Mr Fenton and Miss Robertson are not in any way being detained I must beg their indulgence. Simon, Natalie, are you willing to trust me on this?'

He looked at them and smiled.

'What I am asking is that you stay out of the public eye for the next forty-eight hours or so and keep to yourselves all you know. We have a house available not too far from here which we sometimes use for the protection of witnesses. Will you both wait there until we are in a position to involve you in making the final decision about how we proceed?'

Natalie looked at Simon. After three or four seconds he nodded his head.

'I can't see why not,' he replied.

'Good,' replied the Commissioner, 'I have agreed with Adam Morgan that Inspector Frith will be seconded to my personal staff for the duration of this operation and she will be staying with you and will organise whatever the two of you need in terms of food and clothing. As for the rest of you, are you able to remain close by until Monday morning?'

There was a buzz of conversation as arrangements were agreed and the meeting was dismissed shortly afterwards. Tim Baxter made a particular point of seeking out Simon and Natalie. He slipped Simon a scrap of paper with a telephone number on it.

'I can get a room at Lambeth Palace,' he said, 'but if there's anything at all that either of you are not completely happy with phone me right away.'

Simon nodded his agreement. His mind was already filled with an uncomfortable preoccupation with what the sleeping arrangements at the nearby house might be. He longed for intimacy with Natalie, but was fearful of taking anything for granted. There was also the matter of him hoping above all else to put their relationship on a permanent footing. The last thing he wanted was to spoil things between them, especially as he had detected a distinct coolness in her manner since their return from the hospital.

CHAPTER EIGHTY-THREE

In the event, a call of nature provided Natalie with the solution to her dilemma. While the prospect of forty-eight hours in a safe place with Simon would have been the highly desirable a few days beforehand, the present reality was more perturbing. While her heart and body longed for him in every possible way, her head still cautioned her that a relationship with her would probably not be in his best interests. All this was new territory for her. In the past she had lived life for herself and had made use of other people to fulfil her needs and desires. Now it was all different. The more she thought about it the more difficult it became. There was still a strand of hope that just would not die, yet she was also convinced that even to admit the possibility of hope made her even less worthy of Simon Fenton. More than anything she wanted to make love to him but, at the core of her being, she felt a growing conviction that she must not do so. Upon making use of the toilets outside the meeting room in New Scotland Yard she discovered that her period had started. Natalie had the justification she needed to suggest that they sleep apart.

Alison Frith drove them to the safe house, which transpired to be a Victorian villa in Crouch End. She dropped them off with their meagre possessions and went in search of a supermarket where she said that she would collect food and toiletries. Simon opened the door and they explored their refuge. To Natalie's relief there were three bedrooms.

'Simon,' she began tentatively, 'It's the wrong time of the month... woman's stuff, you know. Would you mind if I had a room of my own for a bit?'

She felt the tears behind her eyes as she tried to paste on a smile.

'No, Nat, that's fine,' he replied torn between relief and disappointment, 'we're both pretty all-in so it might be best...anyway we wouldn't want to upset the Inspector, would we?'

With the delicate matter of sleeping arrangements resolved they occupied comfortable chairs in the lounge and continued to catch up on the details of what had transpired since they had been together in Derby.

'How do you feel, Nat; about Eddie Duggan being killed, I mean?' asked Simon.

'About him being my father?' she asked.

'Mm, I'm sorry if that's not a good question at the moment...'

'No, 'she interrupted, 'I don't mind. After all we've told each other and been through together there's nothing I wouldn't tell you. I don't actually feel anything at all. I just can't come to terms with him being my dad. I'm glad that the killing and stuff's all over, but it doesn't feel like I've lost anyone from my family. I just don't know, Simon. I wanted it to be all over and now it is. How about you? How do you feel about it all?'

'A bit the same, really,' he said thoughtfully, 'I'm relieved that it's all over; not for my dad's sake or anything like that, but because Eddie Duggan and his mob were so evil. I'm not sure that this isn't the best way for it to end actually. I'd hate for us both to have to give evidence against him. His lawyers would probably....' Simon had been going to say that Duggan's defence lawyers would do all they could to discredit Natalie and himself as witnesses, but the implication struck him just in time. 'They'd probably make it last for weeks and weeks and I don't think it would be much fun.'

Natalie began to gently question him about his relationship with Rebecca Johal. She was not sure whether or not she was relieved when he told her that he had only met her two or three times in his life and had not seen her for two years. Throughout the conversation there was a degree of uneasiness and both of them sensed that things left unsaid hung heavily over then like a brooding raincloud.

The return of Alison Frith with her shopping brought their intimate conversation to an end. The bags were unpacked and a rudimentary meal was made and eaten. After the exertions of the last few days all of them were genuinely tired and the three of them sought the solace of their respective rooms before ten o'clock.

CHAPTER EIGHTY-FOUR

Rebecca Johal was perplexed and rather annoyed. The abrupt transfer of her brother from the Cumberland Hospital to the London clinic had left her reeling. The detective had been most insistent, saying that it was a matter of great importance, but no reason had been given. No sooner had Rebecca encountered Simon Fenton and helped him to a place of safety than she found herself caught up in a train of events that she had been unable to escape. With only time for a brief phone call to Sally Chamley she had been sent scurrying back to her hotel to pack her bag and check out before the private ambulance was due to pick them up. The sight of the object of her affection sitting in the reception area of the clinic had been an even more cataclysmic event. With the benefit of hindsight kneeling before him and offering to take care of him caused her to cringe with embarrassment. She was now worried that he might think her behaviour strange. When he had sought out Kynpham, Simon had been polite to her, but had not stayed long enough for her to wriggle out of her impetuous offer or for her to engage him in any more dialogue beyond the exchange of pleasantries. After a restless night in the miniscule spare room in Kynpham's flat she was up and about early. Seeking a distraction she tracked down the reporter's meagre supply of cleaning materials and decided to give the flat a thorough spruce up. As she worked Rebecca could not get Simon Fenton out of her mind. He had been evasive about where he was staying. She wondered if he was in trouble with the police.

Kynpham was also awake early. He was still completely unable to recall the events leading up to his hospitalisation. Recent events were sending his journalistic instincts into overdrive. Rebecca had told him about finding Simon Fenton injured and exhausted lying on the pavement in Carlisle and taking him to the Bishop's house. She had also shown him printouts of internet stories about Simon being mixed up in the murder of a policeman and going on the run with a prostitute. It did not take too much of a leap of imagination to connect his own mysterious presence in Carlisle with Simon Fenton and whatever his friend had become involved in. As yet no coherent explanation had been offered as to exactly why he had been suddenly transferred to London. What he needed, he decided was a computer with internet access and time to talk with Simon alone. There was more than a wiff of a story here, and he was determined to be the one to write it.

Rebecca's arrival at his bedside after lunch gave him the opportunity to quiz her in more detail about the events surrounding Simon turning up in Carlisle, but she paid little attention to his questions. She appeared to be listless and distracted, showing considerably more interest in leafing through an assortment of magazines than in his cross examination. Frustrated and more than a little angry with his sister's lack of cooperation, Kynpham Johal was relieved when the female detective he had noticed with Simon the previous afternoon arrived and asked him if he would mind accompanying her to Scotland Yard.

Rebecca made as if to accompany him, but her offer was firmly and politely rebuffed. Kynpham, the policewoman said, would probably be away for several hours. Piqued, Rebecca announced that she would go back to the flat and carry on with the cleaning as that was obviously her appropriate station in life.

Kynpham was escorted from the car park, through a labyrinth of corridors and into an elevator; which ascended rapidly to the top floor. Detective Inspector Frith took him into an office where a tall black policeman appeared to be waiting for them.

'Good afternoon, Mr Johal, my name is Denzel Goodman,' he said, rising to shake Kynpham's hand, 'please take a seat.'

Kynpham sat in a comfortable chair beside a low table and Alison Frith sat in the chair next to him.

'What I am going to tell you is a matter of the upmost importance,' began the policeman,' I am aware of what you do for a living, Mr Johal and what you are about to find out would undoubtedly enable you to make your name in your chosen profession. I am obliged to explain to you just how you have come to be injured and to fill in some of the gaps in your memory. That is no more than my moral duty, but I also have a pragmatic reason for allowing you access to this story. Together with Simon Fenton and Natalie Robertson you have been caught up in a web of political intrigue, serious corruption and serial wrongdoing spanning more than thirty years. What I am asking you to do, though, is to weigh up the truth in this matter and give some consideration to the implications of the details reaching the public domain. I will be asking you to accompany me to an important meeting later today. All I ask is that you make no hasty decisions or judgements before that meeting. Now, if you are sitting comfortably, I will begin...'

Sir Denzel Goodman told Kynpham the entire sequence of events beginning with the ambush of the IRA drug's landing in 1975 and ending with the apparent suicide of Detective Chief Superintendent Bell and the death of the Home Secretary in a boating accident. He also outlined the part played by Simon Fenton in following the trail bequeathed to him and the efforts of Simon and Natalie in evading both the legitimate police and Eddie Duggan's enforcers for long enough to assimilate the documentary evidence.

'Now, Mr Johal, he concluded, 'Inspector Frith will escort you to the conference room in order to allow you to see the documents concerned. I shall be joining you later as will several other people. When you have heard what we all have to say you may make your decision as to whether this is a story you want to write or otherwise.'

Alison Frith led her perplexed charge back along a corridor and into a corner meeting room where a locked box stood on the table. She took a key from her pocket, unlocked the box and passed a bundle of papers to Kynpham before excusing herself. He was still studying them an hour later when the first of the invited guests arrived.

CHAPTER EIGHTY-FIVE

Simon had not slept well. It was not that the bed was uncomfortable. The safe house was adequately, if basically, furnished and his was the largest bedroom. He was, however, deeply troubled. Things were not quite right between him and Natalie. Although it was pretty clear that their shared adventure was almost over, he had sensed a distinct cooling in their relationship and the resultant uncertainty weighed heavily upon him. He had been foolish, he realised, to think that her affection for him would persist once their shared close proximity spiced with an element of danger had passed. It was becoming apparent to him that the bubble of their love might have developed a slow puncture even if it had not yet burst. Yet her love had changed him; that was true enough. He had no regrets. Meeting Natalie, even if she walked through the bedroom door that very moment and told him that she never wanted to see him again, had been the best thing to have happened to him in years. In spite of his worries hope just would not die completely within him. He would not give up easily, he thought; he would do all he could to win her affections again. There was simply too much at stake to just walk away. She had said that they both needed time to think things over, well that was probably true, but he would find the right time to say his piece. Whatever she decided about her future he wanted her to be absolutely certain that she knew that he was willing to offer her all that he had and all that he was.

Natalie had slept no better than Simon. She realised that he had been sensitive to her swings of mood and sensed his disappointment at the sleeping arrangements. Still, she had to begin sometime; begin the process of letting him go; begin her mission to let him down gently for his own good. With a heavy heart she thrust her feet out of bed. She would cook him breakfast. Although she wanted him to see that the romance between them had to end she could not bear to let him think that she did not care about him. They could still be good friends. They had shared too many secrets and adventures to ever be mere acquaintances.

Simon was sitting up in bed contemplating how he might introduce the idea of marriage to Natalie when she burst through the door carrying a tray. She was wrapped in a white fluffy bathrobe and smiling the smile that threatened to stop his heart from beating.

'Good morning,' she grinned, 'orange juice, coffee and scrambled egg on toast.' Natalie placed the tray on the small bedside table and retreated to sit on the foot of the bed. Simon took a sip of orange juice, uncertain of what his response should be.

'The police lady's still in the land of nod, I think,' commented Natalie, 'and there's a fridge full of food and nothing to do all day but rest.'

'Nat,' began Simon, taking his courage in both hands, 'about you and me...'

'Shh, Simon, not now,' interrupted Natalie, 'we both need time to think. Let's not complicate things just now. All this,' she waved her arm around in an all-encompassing gesture, 'all this is still so false. At least we're safe now. There's a future to look forward to, but we won't know exactly what sort of future it is until we get away from here and start living it. Please, Simon, I don't want to think too much today, let's just chill.'

Simon observed that Natalie's smile had faded. Taking his cue he changed the subject and they chatted aimlessly as he ate his breakfast. Natalie announced that she was heading for the shower and left him alone.

By the time Simon had showered and dressed Natalie and Alison Frith were sitting in front of a computer screen looking at women's clothing.

'Oh, Simon,' Natalie said, 'Alison has been told to go out and get us some clothes and stuff. Come and tell me what you think.'

Drawn into the immediacy of the online shopping experience he pulled up a third chair and made what he hoped were appropriate comments as the two girls noted names and style numbers from Next, Debenhams and Top Shop. Then it was Simon's turn and Natalie took the lead, choosing a selection of trousers and tops for him. Alison Frith was duly despatched to collect the shopping, leaving them alone. Remaining at the computer, Natalie asked Simon about where he lived and looked up his postcode on Google Earth. She zoomed in on his house and began to ask once again about what it was like inside. For almost two hours they planned a makeover for the small terraced house, flitting from website to website to examine home furnishings and colour schemes. It was Natalie's turn next; the block in which her flat was situated was easy to locate on Google and she pointed out where she worked, the gym where she spent an hour three times a week and, eventually, the flying school at Leeds Bradford Airport. As she described the interior and furnishing of her flat the relationship between them had almost returned to the easy-going familiarity they had known before the discovery of copies of her mother's letters. A telephone call from Alison Frith informed them that she had been delayed on police business. Simon cooked lunch and they relaxed in front of daytime TV, but neither of them dared to venture onto the uncertain territory of the future.

Alison Frith's eventual arrival with bags full of shopping prompted Natalie to try on her new clothes and seek affirmation from both Alison Frith and Simon. Simon was then despatched to model some of his new things, but the light-hearted banter was interrupted by a call on the Inspector's mobile. They were all required at Scotland Yard at six thirty, it seemed. Alison Frith disappeared into her room to change leaving Simon and Natalie alone in the lounge. The fragile membrane of their earlier intimacy had burst, however. Natalie slumped in a chair and swore. Simon went over and sat on the chair arm.

'What is it, Nat?' he asked.

'Nothing,' she replied, 'or maybe it's just that I want all this to be over. I just want to go home.'

'Simon laid his hand on her bare arm. 'Do you mean, that, Nat?' he asked quietly, 'are you saying that you don't want us to be together after this?'

'I don't bloody well know what I mean' she said, angrily, shaking his hand from her arm, 'I'm just all bloody mixed up.'

The journey into Westminster took place in a frosty silence. Natalie had taken the initiative to sit in the front seat alongside Alison Frith; relegating Simon to the back of the car. After a few perfunctory attempts to initiate conversation the Inspector picked up on the atmosphere between them and concentrated on her driving. They passed through the security checks and the car pulled into the basement car park. The now familiar trek through corridors and ascent in the elevator followed. They were once again ushered into the upper floor meeting room where, to Simon's astonishment, Kynpham Johal sat at the table in front of several small piles of papers and a laptop computer. Kynpham jumped to his feet and the two men embraced. Kynpham then led Simon to the table and began to cross-examine him, pausing from time to time to pick up one or another of the papers for reference. Natalie moodily stared across the rooftops again, both piqued at being ignored and burdened by the anguish of having to deny her feelings for the only man she had ever truly loved.

CHAPTER EIGHTY-SIX

The presence of Kynpham Johal was not the only unexpected encounter to happen in the meeting room on the top floor of Scotland Yard that Saturday evening. After a wait of around ten minutes, during which Kynpham continued to interrogate his friend, the door opened and a large group of people entered. The two Chief Constables led the way. Sir Denzel Goodman followed with Bishop Tim Baxter, but the surprise guests comprised the familiar faces of the Prime Minister and the leaders of the two main opposition parties.

'If you would all care to take a seat,' Denzel Goodman called the meeting to order. The three politicians sat together on one side of the square table, while the two senior policemen flanked Sir Denzel at the head of the table. Kynpham took his former place beside the piles of papers and Simon sat alongside him. Natalie made as if to sit next to him, but veered off at the last moment and sat on the other side of Kynpham while the Bishop sat with Alison Frith opposite the politicians. The Commissioner began the meeting and the Inspector began to type on the keyboard of the laptop.

'Ladies and gentlemen,' he began, 'every person in this room is now fully conversant with the facts of this case. There is no doubt that the late Home Secretary, with the full complicity of the officers of the Independent Criminal Intelligence Section of the Metropolitan Police had been involved in a long trail of murder, corruption, fraud and other nefarious criminal activities. It is pertinent to note at this early stage that all five protagonists in this sorry tale are now dead and, therefore, there is no possibility of anyone being brought to justice. Justice, however, is not merely a matter of criminal prosecution. There are a number of serious and far-reaching decisions which need to be made as a matter of utmost urgency this evening; decisions which may well have a significant bearing upon the history and future of our nation. We are not here simply to apportion blame to the guilty and to exonerate the innocent.' He turned towards the sombre faced Prime Minister, 'Prime Minister, I believe you wish to address the meeting.'

'To begin with,' the Prime Minister said, looking in the direction of Natalie, Kynpham and Simon, 'I would like to express my heartfelt thanks to you three young people. Through no fault of your own you have been caught up in a series of events which have brought you danger, difficulty and physical harm. All three of you can be assured that, whatever the outcome of this meeting, you will be free to return to your everyday lives exonerated of any minor wrongdoing you may have been involved in as a matter of expediency. Secondly, we are going to ask you to consider a course of action which you may find uncomfortable and to which you may well object. Whatever you decide you can also be assured that all of us here will honour your decision and all that I ask is that the conversation we are about to embark on remains confidential. Are you willing to agree to that?'

Simon looked at Kynpham and tried to catch Natalie's eye, but she continued to concentrate on the Prime Minister. Kynpham gave the briefest of nods and Simon followed suite. The Prime Minister continued his discourse.

'Over the past few months several events have taken place in this nation which have served to undermine two basic tenets of British democracy. The first of these is that the British public have lost a great deal of trust in us; the politicians who they have elected to serve them. This is entirely our own collective fault.' He glanced at the leader of the largest opposition party who nodded encouragingly,' In all three of our parties there have been those who have deliberately sought to fabricate, exaggerate and spread malicious and scurrilous stories about individual political opponents. You may recall the scandal caused by an aide in my own office producing libellous e-mails about senior members of the opposition...'

The leader of the smaller opposition party interrupted.

'It is also true that several members of the party which I lead concocted a sting operation in an attempt to entice ministers into agreeing to accept cash payments in return for commercially sensitive information.'

The other opposition leader took over the baton,

'And you may have heard that one of the potential candidates to replace the Prime Minister had to withdraw his candidacy just over a week ago. What you will almost certainly not know is that the intimate details of the illicit liaison that caused him to withdraw were dredged up as a result of a very expensive investigation by a private detective agency that was commissioned and funded by one of my senior staff.'

The Prime Minister resumed leadership of the proceedings.

'The public outcry when details of the expenses claimed by members of Parliament were made public also severely undermined the credibility of all the mainstream political parties. There is now a deep public scepticism about politicians and politics in this country. I have been meeting with my two colleagues here regularly for the past few weeks. Although we reserve the right to disagree in the strongest possible terms about policy and what is best for our country we have resolved to do our best to rein in the maverick elements amongst our supporters and to attempt to keep an appropriate distance between politics and personalities. That is not to say that we in any way condone wrongdoing on the part of any members of our respective parties. The country has a right to expect the highest standards of conduct and character from its elected leaders, but there is an overriding need to move away from a negative and demeaning policy of attempting to smear and vilify the character of our political opponents and move towards an informed and lively debate about policies and the issues we face as a nation.'

The leader of the main opposition party took over.

'In recent months there has been a significant and alarming swing in the polls. Small and relatively insignificant political groupings representing extremist views are now attracting an increasing level of support; not, we believe, because the electorate actually subscribe to their prejudices and bias, but because ordinary people no longer trust the mainstream parties and wish to register some form of protest. In a recent poll almost fifteen percent of respondents said that they would vote for a party representing the far right and another six percent favoured an extreme left-wing group. With a general election not too far away all three of us are committed to restoring the trust of the people in our democratic system. If we do not take very great care the country might well be held to ransom by those who would wish to undermine the fundamental tenets of democracy...'

The other opposition leader interjected;

'Please don't think this is all about our own self-interest. All three of us truly believe that the threat to the way this country has been governed for many centuries is very real. We also acknowledge that we, the elected politicians, are culpable. It is our intention; the three of us, to appear together on television within the next couple of weeks to make a joint statement to this effect and then to demonstrate our commitment to change at our Autumn Conferences by insisting on a positive agenda focussed entirely upon issues and not on undermining the character and private lives of our opponents.'

The Prime Minister continued.

'The second main area of public concern in the country at the moment is the integrity and conduct of the police service. All too often the police have been drawn into the political arena; often by the rogue elements in all of our parties that had sought to mount personal attacks on their political opponents. Inevitably the police themselves sometimes make mistakes, but the politicisation of this leads increasingly to public mistrust and scepticism. All the way from the individual officers who removed their identification numbers from their uniforms during the policing of the disturbances at the G7 summit in order to evade the consequences of heavy handed tactics to the mid-level and senior officers that have recently been exposed as corrupt, the public have been receiving the message that the police are not to be trusted. Without the trust, respect and even the consent of the public at large, the police cannot effectively enforce the law. All three of us believe that it is imperative to uphold the police in their duties and, so far as is possible, allow them to carry out their legitimate work without undue political interference.'

The room fell silent. Simon turned to look at Kynpham who smiled wryly. There was an unspoken concurrence between them about what was likely to happen next. Natalie detected the nuance and also turned to Simon and smiled. The Prime Minister took a deep breath and resumed his discourse.

'I suspect you will probably have guessed what we are going to ask of you. There is absolutely no doubt that Eddie Duggan was an evil and thoroughly corrupt man. You may feel that it is only right and proper that his misdeeds are made public and that, even though he will never himself face justice, at least justice may be seen to be done. In the same way, it is also abundantly clear that a highly regarded section of the police service, to which much credit had been given for its recent successes, was latterly composed entirely of corrupt officers. You are all aware of the circumstances surrounding the death of Inspector Gilroy. The deaths of Inspectors Cavendish and Jewel were caused by a road traffic accident. The truth, however, is that the accident occurred when they were undoubtedly en-route to support Mr Duggan in his encounter with you, Mr Fenton. Had they not died in the accident I think it is unlikely that we would be sitting around this table today. As for Detective Chief Superintendent Bell, there is little doubt that he was complicit in the nefarious activities of Eddie Duggan since his days as an RAF policeman in Northern Ireland. Although, on the surface, both circumstantial and forensic evidence points towards suicide as the cause of his death, my colleagues,' he indicated the three senior policemen present, 'strongly suspect that he may have been murdered by Eddie Duggan before his attempted escape.

If you are getting the idea that you are about to be asked to condone a cover up of these facts then you are perfectly correct. For the reasons we have pointed out, however, I hope that you will understand that it is the good of the country as a whole that we are seeking to protect, and not the reputations of any individual or political party. Apart from in one instance we are not asking any of you to be actively involved in any deception; it is only your agreement to keep all this strictly confidential that we seek. Apart, that is, from the particular circumstances of the shooting of Andrew Gilroy. Even in that matter, the absolute truth of which we do not actually know, we are asking only for the agreement of you, Mr Fenton, and you, Miss Robertson, that we may issue a statement to the effect that you have been unable to shed any further light on the matter. Evidence already exists which strongly links the killing of Inspector Gilroy to Wayne Stevens, who was himself shot shortly afterwards with the same gun. Inquests into the deaths of both men are due to be held this week and it is our proposal to submit no new evidence.

Our proposal is that, if you agree to our request, you, Mr Johal return to visit your family in India for a week or two while you are on sick leave. Mr Fenton and Miss Robertson, you will be asked to remain in your present accommodation until both inquests are completed. You will then be free to return to your former lives. Your employers will be contacted by the Metropolitan Police who will explain that you have been caught up in a situation beyond your control and have given invaluable assistance to the police in an important matter. Within the next forty eight hours two major police operations are scheduled to take place in various locations and the clear inference will be that you became unwittingly involved in one or the other of these.

Inquests will be held into the deaths of Inspectors Jewel and Cavendish, Detective Chief Superintendent Bell and Eddie Duggan in due course, but there is nothing in the public domain to link any of you to the deaths of these people. All files, computer drives and records pertaining to these matters will be sealed and kept secret for a period of ninety nine years.

On the other hand, should you so wish, the whole affair can be made public. In the event that you choose this course of action, all we would ask is that Mr Johal writes the story and it is first published in his newspaper which is known for its lack of political bias. The choice rests with the three of you. We shall be disappointed should you choose to make these matters public because of the far reaching implications of this course of action, but we will not attempt to persuade you any further. We shall now leave you to talk amongst yourselves. Perhaps, Bishop, you would like to remain also. When you have reached your decision please dial seven three four on the telephone on the wall and we shall all return.'

The Prime Minister stood up and the others followed his example. The politicians and policemen slowly trooped out of the room, leaving Tim Baxter, Simon, Natalie and Kynpham alone. For a while no one spoke. Then Tim Baxter suggested they speak in turn to give their initial responses.

Natalie said that she had been intrigued by the wider issues involved; the politics and the worries about democracy. She also said, however, that she did not really feel it was up to her to decide because she had been the least wronged. She did not share her two most private thoughts: firstly that anonymity was very much the best outcome she could hope for as her past would not stand up well to any public scrutiny and secondly that, because of that, a future with Simon Fenton might no longer be totally incomprehensible. Kynpham said that, attractive though the prospect of making his name and reputation as a journalist by breaking the story might be, he was very much persuaded by the politicians that the consequences for democracy could be serious. He also said that by breaking the story he would be exposing his friend, Simon, to intense media interest and that he thought that Simon would not enjoy the prospect. The main issue, he said, was whether or not the injustice done to Simon's father and the remaining members of the RAF Regiment patrol, together with any other victims drawn into Eddie Duggan's web needed public redress or whether, with the perpetrators all dead, sleeping dogs were better left to lie. It was Simon, he said, who ought to have the final word.

Simon looked at Natalie, acutely aware of their shared secret regarding her biological relationship with Eddie Duggan. She half-smiled at him, but made no comment. After a few moments he began to speak.

'My father,' he said, 'is and always was a hero. Whether he was killed by the IRA or murdered by Eddie Duggan doesn't really make any difference. It's the others that matter; the others that Duggan has killed or ordered to be killed that have no voice. I wonder what they would think if they were here today. I'd like to think that they were all just as brave as my dad. I hope I won't be letting them down by saying that I think they would be brave and honourable enough to do what was right. I don't think making all this public would serve any useful purpose now. It's all over; or it will be in a few weeks. Speaking for myself,' he gave Natalie a sideways look, but she either didn't notice or chose not to respond, 'I've actually had a pretty good time over the past two weeks.' He glanced at Natalie again and was rewarded with a full smile, 'I'm not sorry that the danger is over and I'm not sorry that it's ended the way it has, but I think that the Prime Minister is right. Making it all public won't do an awful lot of good and it could do a lot of harm. Let's just put Eddie Duggan behind us and get on with our lives.' He looked at Natalie again, but she was staring out of the window.

Tim Baxter summed up, stating that there was a unanimous agreement to comply with the Prime Minister's request. Upon receiving the assent of all three of them he walked over to the telephone and dialled the number.

CHAPTER EIGHTY-SEVEN

To say that Rebecca Johal was furious would have been an understatement. As the British Airways Boeing 777 climbed out of Heathrow en-route to Delhi she maintained a frosty silence towards her brother which had been in effect since shortly after he had arrived at his flat where she had been waiting for him the previous evening. He had not arrived until after midnight; having called in at the clinic after his meeting at Scotland Yard to be formally discharged; given a sick note for his employers and to collect his belongings. She had been dozing in an armchair by the fire waiting for him to telephone.

The news that they were booked on the morning flight back home had both startled and upset her. Kynpham, it seemed, had been caught up is some serious security matter about which he refused to tell her anything save that Simon Fenton was also involved. There was, he had told her, a need for him to be away from London for a week or two while the police dealt with some important matters. She would be accompanying him home. Her visit therefore would be cut short. Rebecca was devastated. There would be no opportunity to see Simon Fenton again and the family was most unlikely to subsidise another trip to England in the near future. She had not slept at all, her frustration keeping her awake all night. With bad grace she had packed her bag, thrust her passport and return ticket at Kynpham and accompanied him in a taxi to Heathrow before dawn had broken across the city.

As the aircraft levelled off over the Netherlands Rebecca eventually resigned herself to the inevitable and decided to quiz her brother in another attempt to extract the truth from him. She grabbed the lead of his headphones and jerked the plug out of the socket next to the armrest.

'Right then, brother,' she growled, 'it's about time you told me just what's going on.'

'Sorry,' 'he replied, 'but I really can't tell you. I won't ever be able to Becca, I've given my word and it really is important.'

'Tell me about Simon, then,' she replied, 'did you see him yesterday; was he with that woman?'

'Yes I saw him and yes she was there too, but I don't think you need to worry about her, Becca. There was some sort of bad atmosphere between them, I think. She did not seem to want to have so much to do with him.'

Partially mollified, Rebecca continued to cross-examine Kynpham but had no success in extracting even the most insignificant detail about whatever it was that he had been party to. Her only consolation was to learn that their fares had been paid by the British Government. Her return ticket would still be valid. The cost of a one way ticket to London at the beginning of her long holiday might just be manageable. With the prospect of returning to her pursuit of Simon in the not too distant future and Kynpham's reassurance that he did not seem to have fallen under the spell of the immoral woman things did not seem quite so bad after all. She reclined her seat and drifted off to sleep, planning in her mind how she might engineer to spend some time with Simon Fenton in early December when the school term ended.

CHAPTER EIGHTY-EIGHT

Simon and Natalie were left alone in the conference room after the others had left. Alison Frith promised that she would return to collect them after she had met with the senior officers, while Tim Baxter had taken Kynpham and offered to share a taxi with him to get the reporter back to the clinic where his discharge would be arranged.

'How are you really about all this,' asked Simon, 'about, you know, about Eddie Duggan and your mum?'

'I don't want anyone but us to know about it,' replied Natalie, 'I'll never really think of him as my father, if that's what you mean; and I'm not sorry that he's dead or anything. It's probably all for the best anyway.'

She looked down at her feet. 'Simon, I'm sorry if I seem a bit off, but I really do think we both need a bit of space and time away from each other. I'm not saying that I don't care about you any more. I'm just a bit mixed up. Can you understand that?'

'Not really, Nat,' he replied, 'I'm crazy about you. Nothing else matters. Look, there's something I want to say...'

'No Simon, please, not now. Let's just enjoy being together for a few days. Is that OK? Nobody can ever take away from us what has happened; how we've been there for each other and that, but I don't want to talk about the future; not yet.'

Simon thought for a long time before he replied.

'All right, Nat; no talk about the future for now, but I just want you to know that I really do love you...'

She put her arms around his neck and drew him close, kissing him briefly on the lips.

'I know, Simon, please just let me be for now, I promise you I'll be ready to talk about things soon.' She pulled his head down onto her shoulder and kissed him gently on the cheek. 'Thank you Simon Fenton, thirty four, just hang on in there while I work things out.'

They stood locked in a gentle embrace for a few minutes. Eventually Alison Frith arrived back and Simon reluctantly released Natalie as the door opened. The Inspector drove them back to the safe house where Natalie cooked a quick meal of pasta and fried chicken. Alison Frith explained that she had been given the mission of tying up all conceivable loose ends and they huddled around the computer screen while Simon and Natalie used Google Earth to show her exactly where all the assorted bits and pieces of evidence could be found. The policewoman explained that she would top up the food supplies the following morning before setting off on her round Britain odyssey. She expected to be gone for three or four days.

Natalie lay in bed late the next morning. She could hear Simon and Alison Frith moving about and felt a peculiar reluctance to join them. The sound of the front door opening and closing signified the policewoman's departure on her shopping trip and within a minute or two there was a tentative knock on her door. Simon asked if she would like breakfast in bed, but she declined, saying that she was exhausted and needed to sleep. In reality she was turning the news that there would be no further mention of her past life in the press over and over in her mind. Perhaps Simon's friends might not remember the scandal of her lifestyle for very long. If she and Simon got together in, say six or eight months time there might not be too much fuss. He had told her once again that he loved her and she had no doubt that he was telling the truth. She loved him too; but was that enough? Wearily she concluded that she was in no position to make a decision; only time would tell and for the present she must not encourage him. Presently she actually did fall sleep again. It was after noon when she finally emerged from her room and Alison Frith had returned from the supermarket and left on her mission.

The next three days were an agony of uncertainty for both Simon and Natalie. With both the past and future taboo subjects they existed in a state of uneasy truce. Natalie had discovered a handheld games console in one of the kitchen cupboards and was gradually attempting to solve the puzzles and riddles contained in Professor Leyton's Curious Village. Simon, on the other hand, became increasingly obsessed with breaking news stories. For three days they managed to avoid any mention of the things that really mattered to them.

The deaths of Eddie Duggan and Jimmy Bell had been widely reported, but there had been surprisingly little editorial comment. On Monday morning the news broke that anti-terrorist police had made dawn raids at eleven addresses across the United Kingdom, foiling a terrorist plot to conduct coordinated suicide bombings at major football fixtures the following Saturday. Unlike some previous anti-terrorist operations this one seemed to have been well-handled. Explosive and weapons had been found at nine of the eleven addresses. The media was full of praise for the police. The inquest on the death of Inspector Gilroy took place in Manchester on Tuesday. The verdict was unlawful killing by Wayne Stevens. The news item on the BBC six o'clock bulletin lasted all of thirty seconds and there was little further information posted on the internet news sites. The following day the inquest on the death of Wayne Stevens took place, but there were no reports on national television. An internet report confirmed that a verdict of unlawful killing by persons unknown had been recorded. On Wednesday the lead story in the morning was a report of half a dozen more dawn raids by the police; this time in connection with drug smuggling. Over thirty arrests had been made and drugs worth over four million pounds had been recovered.

CHAPTER EIGHTY-NINE

When Alison Frith set out on her journey on Sunday afternoon her first destination had been Dent railway station. She timed her arrival for just after dark and, with the help of a powerful torch and a sketch map drawn by Simon she recovered both the suitcase full of money from the cleft under the bridge and Simon's camping equipment from the hollow on the hillside. Tired from her journey and exertions she stayed the night in a small private hotel in Sedburgh before setting out on the next part of her journey. Monday morning found her at the main police station in Carlisle where she collected a selection of personal items from the impounded caravan and liaised with the Chief Constables office for the Ford Mondeo to be recovered from the derelict barn at Kilbride. She arranged for the car and caravan to be sold at auction with the proceeds being donated to the Police Benevolent Fund. By late afternoon she was thigh deep in a muddy pond concealed by woodland close to Silverdale station where she eventually located Natalie's discarded bag and its contents under the water. As soon as she regained dry land she stripped off her own wet and mud-streaked clothing and changed into items she had brought with her in a large shoulder bag. She threw both Natalie's bag and her own soiled clothing to a sturdy green bin liner that she had brought for that purpose. From there she drove to a deserted beach on the shores of Morecambe bay and constructed a small fire from driftwood soaked in petrol poured from a two plastic containers that she had brought from the boot of her car. As twilight fell she lit the fire and added more driftwood. Item by item she dropped the contents of the green bin liner into the flames. Occasionally the damp clothing threatened to douse the fire, but each time it happened she stirred the embers into life with a stick and added more wood. Within an hour no evidence remained and she let the fire die out.

Inspector Frith refilled the petrol containers and the tank of her Passat Estate at a nearby garage before she caught the overnight ferry from Heysham to the Isle of Man. After parking at a public car park in Port Erin she trekked over the hill to Fleshwick Bay and located the upturned inflatable boat and outboard motor that Simon and Natalie had hidden amongst the dense undergrowth. Certain that she would be able to find them again after dark, she trudged back over the hill and indulged herself with an extravagant meal in a seafood restaurant. Under the cover of darkness she drove back to Fleshwick Bay, dragged Simon's tent and sleeping bag into the copse then returned to the car for her container of petrol. She liberally doused the accumulated evidence before retreating to a safe distance and tossing lit matches towards it until the petrol caught fire. Before the flames became visible from the road she had driven off.

After spending the night at a cheap hotel in Douglas she drove back to the ferry terminal in time for the morning crossing on Wednesday. As she queued for the ferry, Alison tuned into Manx Radio and was gratified to hear that her handiwork had been discovered. The local radio station was linking the fire to a tobacco smuggling network that had recently flooded the island's shops with counterfeit cigarettes. The police, it was announced, had little to go on as everything but an outboard motor seemed to have been completely destroyed by the fire.

The sun was shining as the ferry approached Heysham Port. Alison Frith confirmed that her mobile phone was in contact with the network and made a call to Sir Denzel Goodman on the private number he had given her. The call took longer than she had anticipated and a small queue of irritated motorists waiting to disembark had formed behind her car when she eventually returned to the vehicle deck. Waving an apology she got into the car and drove off on the next leg of her journey. It was late afternoon when she arrived at the small house in Derby. She was able to unlock the front door with the Yale key that Simon had given her. The back door, however, was showing signs of the forced entry and although it was held closed by a strong bolt, the frame and lock were badly damaged. After she made several telephone calls a local joiner agreed to come out and have a look within the hour. While she waited, the Inspector gathered up yet more items of clothing and packed them into bin liners. The joiner duly arrived and, after measuring up, promised to return with the materials to repair the damage at nine the next morning. Alison Frith booked herself into a local hotel and treated herself to a visit to the cinema and a curry.

True to his word, the joiner arrived promptly the next morning and by eleven thirty she was on the road again. Traffic was light on the M1 and she pulled up outside the safe house in Crouch End in early afternoon.

CHAPTER NINETY

By Wednesday afternoon the tension between Simon and Natalie was almost palpable. Natalie had solved Professor Layton's final puzzle and was no closer to reaching a decision about whether or not the future with Simon that she longed for with all her heart was feasible. The endless prevarication was taking its toll and she knew that her irritability was causing distress to the man she loved. The problem was that she just could not trust herself. If she allowed him the slightest intimacy she knew that she would no longer be able to hold her feelings in check and it would just not be fair to lead him on any further. Instead she had made herself prickly and diffident in his presence and she could sense his unhappiness. The late summer day was warm and humid. She dragged an armchair through the patio doors into the small square of garden, changed into a pair of shorts and a t-shirt and pretended to sleep while her thoughts ran round and round in turmoil.

Simon wracked his brain in an attempt to work out what he had done to upset Natalie. Even allowing for the hormonal effect of her period, he could not comprehend why she continually pushed him away; unless of course it was because his feelings for her were just not reciprocated. Perhaps their brief relationship had been no more than a fling to her, he mused, but the memory of their emotional and intellectual bonding made that hard for him to accept. They had bared their very souls to one another and the prospect of a future without Natalie was almost too much for him to bear. He stood looking at her through the patio doors as she reclined with her eyes closed. He noticed the way her hair framed her picture perfect features. He admired the delicacy of her wrists and hands as she rested them, palms upright on the broad arms of the chair. He gazed at her bare midriff and recalled the softness and scent of her skin. With tears forming in his eyes, Simon turned away. If it really was all over between them there could never be anyone else; of that he was absolutely certain.

As afternoon passed gently into evening Natalie abandoned her self-imposed exile in the garden. Simon had prepared a cold ham salad for them both and they ate sitting opposite each other at the kitchen table in virtual silence. Simon was anxious to avoid provoking Natalie into any further antagonism while, on her part, Natalie could think of no safe topic of conversation. The television failed to engage either of them that evening. Claiming fatigue Natalie informed Simon that she needed an early night and went to her room soon after nine. Half an hour later Simon followed her example. Sleep was elusive for both of them. Natalie lay tossing and turning, her mind filled with the mental image of the man sleeping not five yards away from her. Her period had ended; she contemplated making the short journey to his room and slipping naked into his bed. It was complicated, though. Undoubtedly indulging her deepest desires would re-build the intimacy between them, but there would also be far-reaching implications. It would not be fair to him, however much he might welcome the prospect; she could not convince herself that she could give him all that he deserved. At half past midnight she weakened; throwing off her top and shorts she pulled on a dressing gown and crept out onto the landing. For nearly ten minutes she stood outside his door, daring herself to push it open and make her move. Yet something held her back; something she could neither describe nor comprehend; some inner sense that to make love to Simon would set them both on an irrevocable course that might lead them both to profound unhappiness. Wearily she retreated to her room. It was after two o'clock when sleep finally dried her tears.

Simon sat up in bed making a desultory attempt to read a novel he had found in his room. Although he still clung with his fingertips to his intention of asking Natalie to marry him, he could feel the opportunity slipping through his fingers. Each day the prospect seemed to be a little more remote than the day before. Things were clearly cooling off between them. In all probability, he thought, she had taken a long hard look at the man who was ten years older than her and far from an oil painting and decided that she did not like what she saw. Now that the exhilaration and excitement of their adventure were at an end, it looked increasingly as if she was having regrets about what had taken place between them. He discarded the novel after his fifth attempt at the opening chapter and propped himself up with pillows. It was likely that Alison Frith would return the next day, he thought; and with the inquests into the deaths of Andrew Gilroy and Wayne Stevens over it was also likely that their temporary incarceration would come to an end. He was running out of time. Although he was now very afraid of what her answer might be, Simon Fenton knew that if he did not ask Natalie Robertson to marry him the following day he might have lost his chance for ever. He began rehearsing his lines in his head. At one point he thought he could hear her moving around and almost decided to make his play there and then, but it all went quiet again and he concluded that it had just been wishful thinking that Natalie might be up and about at that time of night.

Simon and Natalie both slept late on Thursday morning. By the time they had both showered and dressed the September sun was high in the sky and the day was pleasantly warm. The relationship between them seemed to have thawed a little overnight and they dragged both armchairs out onto the patio and shared a late alfresco breakfast while talking of matters of little consequence. Their tacit agreement to avoid mention of the future served them well and the morning passed cordially for them both. On two occasions Simon determined to break the taboo and tell her of his love for her and ask her to marry him. Both times his courage failed him.

CHAPTER NINETY-ONE

Alison Frith's arrival put a temporary end to the possibility of Simon fulfilling his mission. The Inspector stumbled in through the door carrying two bin liners full of clothing and, after making two more journeys from the car, four bin liners and a large suitcase stood on the kitchen floor. With a degree of relish Natalie shook the bin liners empty and began sorting clothing into piles on the kitchen floor. Within minutes the washing machine was churning the first load round and round to the accompaniment of the hum from its motor.

'What's in the suitcase?' asked Natalie.

'Have a look,' invited the Inspector, smiling.

Natalie heaved the case onto the kitchen table and began to unzip it.

'Shit!' she exclaimed, 'it's full of money!'

'That's Eddie Duggan's money,' explained Simon, 'it's what I told him I wanted in return for the papers. He must have left without it.'

'It might be Eddie Duggan's, but officially it doesn't exist,' said Alison Frith, 'we can't pay it back to his estate without questions being asked and the Met can't just bank six hundred grand without giving a reason. I've asked Denzel Goodman what to do with it and he says that I've got to give it to you two. Compensation, he called it; compensation for all that's happened to you both and because you won't ever be able to sell your stories to the press or make anything at all out of what you know.'

'But we can't keep all this,' objected Natalie, 'it's not right.'

'Right or not, we don't want it,' replied the policewoman, 'Denzel Goodman says that you probably won't be able to pay it into your bank accounts because of money laundering regulations; we don't want any awkward questions being asked, so he said to tell you that if you give me your bank details and the money he'll see to it that the banks don't query it.'

Natalie looked at Simon, who shrugged.

'I don't suppose we have a choice, Nat,' he said. Looking at Alison Frith he continued, 'Would you just excuse us for a couple of minutes while we have a talk about it?' She nodded in reply and disappeared upstairs.

'Look, Nat, 'said Simon, 'this money is yours really, I mean it's your legacy; from your...'

'No!' interjected Natalie, 'don't ever say it. Whatever the biology of it, Eddie Duggan was not any sort of father to me. If we have to take this money I think we should share it; you me and your friend Kynpham. After all he got hurt more than either of us didn't he?'

'Well, if you're sure, Nat,' Simon replied, 'Kynpham certainly deserves a share. I agree with you there. There's quite a bit left from the stash we took from the hotel as well, I'll go and get that.'

Simon went to get the banknotes from his room, knocking on Alison Frith's door as he passed to tell her that he and Natalie had finished their private conversation. In the kitchen Simon counted out the money on the table while Natalie kept the washing machine and tumble drier in business and Alison Frith produced a beef casserole. The sum of six hundred and seventeen thousand two hundred and ten pounds all but covered the table. They agreed that they would ask Alison to arrange to pay six hundred and fifteen thousand into Simon's account. He would then write cheques in favour of Natalie and Kynpham for two hundred and five thousand each. The remaining cash Simon and Natalie offered to Alison Frith, but she steadfastly refused to take a penny and they eventually decided to share it between them. With the booty stashed in the suitcase they ate their meal and opened a bottle of wine.

Alison Frith announced that it would be their last night in the house. Sir Denzel Goodman intended to pay them a visit at lunchtime the following day and after that they would be free to go. Although not unexpected be either Simon or Natalie, the detective's announcement added a peculiar sense of urgency to the evening.

After the meal Natalie busied herself with ironing and sorting clothing. They had accumulated far too much to take home with them, she decided and took it upon herself to divide Simon's things between those she liked the most, which she told him he would be taking home, and those she did not like so much, which she consigned to a bin liner for a charity shop. As she began to do the same with her own things Simon smiled inwardly. Even though she had consigned the suit he had worn on their "date" to the bag bound for the charity shop he took some hope from the thought that if Natalie was still interested in what he wore, perhaps she had not completely lost interest in him.

Genuinely exhausted by her four days of driving, Alison Frith excused herself and went to her bedroom while Natalie and Simon retired to the lounge. Natalie stood at the patio doors, gazing up at the night sky.

'You know, Simon,' she said, 'three weeks ago I dreamed of having fifty thousand pounds in the bank. I'm going to have four times that. I just can't make sense of anything any more.'

He walked over to stand beside her and took her hand in his.

'Nat,' he said softly, 'I don't know what to make of it either, but there is one thing that I do know,' he turned her gently to face him and held her other hand as he looked into her sparkling blue eyes. 'What I know is that I love you. I love you more that I ever thought it would be possible to love anyone. Natalie Robertson, I have just one question to ask you. Will you marry me?'

For a moment time stood still. Natalie looked up at him, her mind reeling. Had Simon actually asked her to marry him or was she dreaming?

Marriage; that was something she had never thought about since she had been a teenager. Marriage meant a lifelong and total commitment. Marriage was forever, she thought. Sharing a life, a home and a bed with Simon Fenton was one thing, but this was surely something more. Perhaps, she thought, it was the sign she had been hoping for; a sign that things between them actually could work out all right. Yet, even in her euphoria, questions remained unanswered.

Taking her silence for rejection Simon let her hands drop, but she took hold of his again and pulled him gently to the sofa where she sat at one end and manoeuvred him to sit opposite her. Letting go of his hands, she pulled his legs onto the seat and sat facing him, entwining her legs with his.

'Simon,' she said with a catch in her breath, 'I don't know what to say. I do love you, I really truly do, but we need to talk. I know it's my fault we haven't talked about the future, but before we make a decision as big as this we need to talk and think for a bit.'

Simon looked crestfallen, but Natalie reached out and squeezed his hand, 'I'm not saying, no Simon,' she said, 'the way I feel about you, everything within me wants to say yes at the top of my voice, but let's try and work out what being married would mean for us first.'

CHAPTER NINETY-TWO

'What about your friends?' opened Natalie, 'what would they think if you went and told them you were getting married to someone like me?'

'The truth is that I don't actually have a lot of friends,' Simon replied, 'There's Tim Baxter and Kynpham; you've already met both of them. The only other person that's a real friend is Andy Carr; the Vicar of West Wroxham. You'd like him; he's got a great sense of humour. He's married to Jane and they've got two pre-school kids.'

'But how would a vicar take to someone like me?' Natalie asked.

'Look Nat, I won't pretend that I don't know what you're going on about, your past and that, but it really won't be a problem,' Simon countered, 'I'm absolutely certain that Andy and Jane will think you're fantastic. Nobody's perfect and everybody's done stuff in the past that they're not so proud of. It really won't matter, please believe me.'

'But what about the people you work with?' she said, 'wouldn't they know all about me from the papers?'

'What if they do? They won't make things difficult, they're not like that,' he replied, 'they're really nice. Anyway if we got married I probably wouldn't work there any more. We'd be off for a long honeymoon in Miami wouldn't we; for you to get your airliner licence?'

Troubled Legacy

'See, that's just why I can't give you an answer right away, Simon,' she said, squeezing his hand again, 'I know you would give up everything to be with me, but what about me: shouldn't I give up something too?'

'But flying is what you live for,' he said, 'you really come to life when you talk about flying, Nat; and when you flew us over to Northern Ireland I could see that you were literally in your element. Even though it was probably quite dangerous you were so in control. You were born to fly, Nat. You can't give it up.'

'And you are probably a lot more comfortable with your life in Norfolk than you let on,' Natalie said, 'your job seems as if it fits you like a glove and you have friends there. I don't have any friends; not real ones. I could still do my airline training in the UK, or Spain or somewhere. It might cost a bit more, but that's not a problem now, is it? But I am worried about what things would be like for you. I know we'd be really happy at first wherever we ended up, Simon, but what about later on? I want us both to be really sure that we are doing the right thing. I want us to have thought it all out. If you forced me to answer you tonight I'd probably say "yes", Simon, but please don't; make me; answer right away, I mean.'

'So when, then?' asked Simon, 'when will we know do you think?'

'Soon,' she replied, 'but I still think we should both go back to our lives first. Just for a week or two while we think it out. How about if we both went home for a fortnight; then you came to visit me? After that I think we should wait another couple of weeks and I'll come and stay with you. If you still want to marry me after that you can ask me again and I promise you I'll give you my answer. Is that OK?'

'I know you're being sensible about this, Nat, but why do we have to wait? Nothing will ever change the way I feel about you, Natalie Robertson, twenty four. If we got a move on we could have the banns read right away and be married in a month.

'You mean in church,' she asked, 'with a white dress and all that?'

'Only if that's what you want,' he replied, 'I know that you're not so keen on God and stuff, but whatever you want is alright by me.'

'Actually, I don't disbelieve in God quite so much as I used to before I met you,' she replied, 'church would be good, but I don't want to rush into it; for both our sakes. I love you too, Simon Fenton, thirty four. Now I'm tired and it's time for bed.'

Natalie untangled herself from him and stood up. She took both of his hands in hers and pulled him to his feet and into an embrace. Their lips found each other's and time stood still for a while.

'Your room or mine?' whispered Natalie as she came up for breath.

Simon rested his hands gently upon her shoulders and their eyes met.

'Actually, Nat, I don't think we should tonight, make love I mean,' he said, 'even though I really want to. I don't regret what we've done in the past, but I'd quite like us to wait now; until we're married if we're going to be. You're just so special to me. If we wait I think it might just be a bit more special for both of us when we're married; something for us to really look forward to.'

As the implication of what Simon had just said began to sink in Natalie was moved beyond words. She buried her face into his neck as the tears began to flow. In suggesting that they abstain from love making she realised that he was paying her the highest possible compliment; he was in some unfathomable way absolving her from her past. It was as if all that had gone before could somehow be removed and a completely new start made at the point of their marriage. Natalie clung on to Simon for all she was worth. If she had been able to speak at that moment she would have agreed to marry him right away, but the tears just would not stop.

CHAPTER NINETY-THREE

As Natalie Robertson lay in the comfortable twilight between sleep and wakefulness the next morning she shuddered as she recalled the events of the previous evening. Simon had asked her to marry her; more than that he had made sure that she understood that her past life would never be an issue between them. It was as if all her dreams had come true; even dreams that she had never dared to dream. Happier than she could ever remember being, she bounced out of bed and laid claim to the bathroom.

Simon had been up early. Content that Natalie had not dismissed his proposal and more than optimistic about their future together he had woken before dawn and made himself a pot of coffee in the kitchen. In the quiet of the early morning he was already making plans for Natalie's visit in a month's time. Alison Frith disturbed his daydream. She would take the money to Scotland Yard; she announced and would make a final trip to the shops to obtain anything else that they needed. Simon suggested that they could each do with a suitcase for their journeys home. Upon Natalie's arrival in the kitchen twenty minutes later some re-sorting of the bin liners intended for the charity shop was called for. Rummaging in one of the bag she produced Simon's crumpled suit which they had chosen together in Carlisle. She tossed the jacket and trousers to him.

'You'd better get this cleaned and pressed,' she said with a broad grin, 'you never know when a suit will come in handy and I like you in this one.'

Simon's grin was as broad as Natalie's. Inspector Frith took her cue and packed the bin liners into her car before setting out on her last mission.

Natalie and Simon passed the morning in happy contentment; neither of them feeling the need to continue the dialogue of the previous evening. A course had been set with which they were both comfortable and there seemed little point in going over the ground again. Instead they confined their conversation to making plans for the immediate future. They would not, they agreed, spend hours telephoning and e-mailing each other like love-sick teenagers. On Saturday evenings Simon would telephone Natalie and on Wednesdays Natalie would reciprocate. She also suggested that as he obviously had designs on being the world's last true romantic he might consider writing her a letter now and again. Simon agreed, with the proviso that she wrote back. Natalie said that she was worried that if they spent too many nights in each other's homes Simon might waver in his resolve to remain celibate. They agreed that each visit would be for one night only. Using a calendar on the kitchen wall they calculated that it was only thirty days until their potential engagement.

Alison Frith arrived with a matching pair of large fabric suitcases and brought their happy chatter to an end. Packing was a rather more sombre affair as the reality of separation from one another caught up with them. Sir Denzel Goodman eventually turned up wearing civilian clothing and managed to combine his thanks for all they had done with a carefully worded exhortation to keep their silence. He made a particular point about the possibility that the media might become interested in them again and advised them that it would be wise to say nothing at all if that was to happen. Before he left Sir Denzel gave Simon a paying in slip counterfoil from the Westminster branch of his bank showing that six hundred and fifteen thousand pounds in cash had been deposited.

The departure of the Commissioner signalled their own. Alison Frith offered to drive them to their respective stations and, unable to delay things any longer, they both accepted. The drive to Kings Cross passed all too quickly with Simon and Natalie holding hands in the back seat. As the car drew to a halt Simon got out with Natalie and collected her case from the boot. For a few moments they held on to each other, but conscious of the presence of the Inspector, their leave-taking was brief and a little awkward. Simon stood and watched as Natalie trundled her suitcase along the pavement and disappeared into the York Road entrance to the station. Wiping a tear from the corner of his eye he got back into the car for the short journey to Liverpool Street.

CHAPTER NINETY-FOUR

Natalie's journey back to Leeds passed quickly. Although she had bought a couple of magazines her mind was full of Simon Fenton and she did not open either of them. Leeds railway station was thronged with Friday afternoon commuters when the train pulled in and she struggled through the crowds trailing the suitcase behind her out through the concourse and along the familiar route back to her flat. The day, which had begun bright and sunny, had degenerated into a dull drizzle and she was glad to reach the shelter and warmth of her home. There were, however, certain things that had to be done right away. First of all she attacked the fridge, where the remains of the food she had left behind when she set out on her fateful journey to Manchester exactly three weeks ago had started to putrefy. With the rotten food consigned to a bin-liner and the fridge disinfected she began the most important task. From the bottom of her wardrobe she took the large shoulder bag containing the now distasteful accoutrements of her former profession as an escort. To this she added a selection of clothing, shoes and a long auburn wig. These items Natalie bagged up with the rotten food before making a journey to the bins in the basement and consigning her past to landfill. Her next and final task was to log onto the internet and delete Kelly's website and e-mail account. Freed from the last remnants of her former life, Natalie Robertson logged on to the Sainsbury's website and ordered a delivery of shopping.

Later that evening she began a wholesale sort out of her wardrobe; new items picked up in the course of her adventure took their place while other things were relegated to a second bin-liner. Natalie's next move was to begin cleaning throughout. By ten thirty the bathroom and her bedroom were shining like new pins. Utterly exhausted she crawled into bed between clean sheets and was asleep within seconds.

On Saturday, with a telephone call from Simon to look forward to later on, Natalie gave herself time off from cleaning and, with a degree of trepidation, set off in her car for the flying school. Although she had no flight booked she was aware that unless she managed to fly that day her currency as a pilot would lapse necessitating a check flight with an instructor. As she took her place in the Cafe Bar to await the possibility of a cancellation she felt as if everyone was looking at her and thinking about what had been reported in the newspapers, but it was not long before other pilots and students began chatting to her over a latté. Taking strength from the anticipation of Simon's call she gradually felt more and more at ease. If the people at the flying school knew all about her they certainly didn't seem to hold anything against her. There was a blustery wind accompanied by a blanket of cloud at two thousand feet, making conditions difficult for early-solo students and a cancellation duly transpired at lunchtime. Fifty minutes in the Warrior scudding along just below the clouds over the North Yorkshire finally exorcised her remaining demons and she stayed on for a chat with two other aspiring commercial pilots before making her way home.

Despite the joy of aviation, the call from Simon was undoubtedly the highlight of her day. He called just after six and they talked for over an hour about nothing much at all. He still loved her, though; he told her so at least twenty times. It seemed inconceivable that anything would happen to stop them getting married. In a happy daydream, Natalie settled down to watch "Casualty" on the television.

On Sunday the rest of her flat received the same kind of attention that had been lavished on her bathroom and bedroom. With everything in apple pie order she turned her attention to the dilemma of her job. Selling financial products and services no longer seemed to her to be a worthwhile thing to do. In fact the prospect made her feel slightly uneasy. It was something that she wanted to discuss with Simon, but true to their agreement she resisted the temptation to call him.

Monday morning dawned and she was no nearer a decision. She dressed in her work clothes and began the familiar trek through the windy streets to the bank. Instead of making for her desk, however, she sought out her manager. The way he looked at her made the decision for her. He had clearly read all the scandal and appeared ill at ease and embarrassed by her presence. Although he tried to reassure her that the police had been in touch and that he was convinced that she had done no wrong his eyes told her otherwise as he appraised the shape of her breasts beneath her blouse. In the event he seemed to be relieved when she told him she wanted to hand in her notice. In any case her assistant had been holding the fort for the previous three weeks and was doing a good job, he told her. There would be no need for her to work her notice, she was informed; they would pay her until the end of October, but she would not be required to turn up for work. Avoiding any contact with her former colleagues, Natalie left the building a free woman. A new life beckoned and she had no regrets at all about walking away from the old one.

From the following day Natalie adopted a set daily routine. She would get up early and check the weather forecast each morning before spending three quarters of an hour in the gym. Thereafter she would fly the Warrior, which she had managed to book for a two hour slot each afternoon, if the weather permitted as most student pilots only flew at the weekends. In the evenings she would watch TV and daydream about a variety of future possibilities involving Simon Fenton. She had done her research and it was possible for her to do much of her commercial flying training in the UK. One possibility would be to complete her basic Commercial License and build up her hours as a flying instructor. There was a flying school at Norwich Airport. She wondered if they would be in need of an additional instructor the following spring.

On Wednesday a letter from Simon was lying on the doormat when she returned from flying. Enclosed was a cheque for two hundred and five thousand pounds, but the greatest treasures were the words he used to tell her how he felt about her. Natalie Robertson had never received a love letter before and she was thrilled to be able to tell Simon that when she telephoned him that evening. The weekend came and went, each day bringing Simon's visit closer. With growing expectation and a girlish excitement that she had not known for many years she began to count down the days.

CHAPTER NINETY-FIVE

Simon walked down the zig-zag ramp at Wroxham railway station after a heavily delayed journey from Liverpool Street. Instead of crossing the car park and turning right, though, he strode purposefully straight ahead, following the road leading towards the town centre. Ten minutes later he was amidst the Friday teatime chaos of the Carr household. Friday was Andy's designated day off. He and Jane had just returned with two very hungry children from a trip to the park and eggy soldiers were the order of the day. After hugs from both Andy and Jane, Simon was given the task of feeding eighteen month old Megan while the adults exchanged their news. Andy and Jane had read something of Simon's clandestine adventures in the papers, but neither of them pressed him when he explained that he had promised the police that he would not tell a living soul any of the details.

The children's meal over, Andy disappeared with them for bath time while Jane made Simon a mug of tea and began to prepare a meal for the three adults. More than once Jane made openings in the conversation for Simon to talk about his alleged travelling companion, but he refused to rise to the bait. Eventually Andy returned with two clean and pyjama-clad youngsters and goodnights were said before Jane took them up to bed while Andy served out the meal.

'In case you're wondering,' grinned Simon, over coffee, 'I was with the girl in the newspapers for a bit. She's not a bit like that, though; like it says in the papers.'

Andy tilted his head to one side and grinned back at his friend, 'And...'

'And er... and, well actually she's pretty fantastic.'

'Simon Fenton, you dark horse,' interjected Jane.

'So are you two an item?' asked Andy.

'Well, sort of,' admitted Simon, 'I'm going to stay with her in Leeds a week tomorrow and she's coming here a fortnight later. We're going to decide if we're an item or not after that.'

'In that case, so long as you're both prepared to risk Jane's cooking, you'd better bring her for Sunday dinner then,' smiled Andy as Jane threw a cushion at him.

A deep contentment settled over Simon. Some of the things that Natalie had said about her being accepted by his friends had been preying on his mind. The Carr's ready invitation had been no more that he might have expected from them, but their affirmation of Natalie warmed his heart. He stayed chatting for an hour or so before refusing Andy's offer of a lift and trudging home through the fading twilight.

Simon's house smelled fusty as he opened the door. The dated overhead light fitting exposed the threadbare lounge carpet and the shabby chair and sofa that did not match. The makeshift bookshelves bowed under the weight of an ill assorted collection of literature and the faded green curtains were long past their best. As if seeing his home with new eyes, Simon continued his tour of inspection. The large square dining kitchen, with its vinyl flooring and dated units was serviceable enough, but the cooker was too small for the gap in the worktops and the pine table with its two benches gave the impression of an indoor picnic site. He carried on into the small utility room. The elderly washing machine and tumble drier were bridged by a long plank, on which a further assortment of books and magazines were stacked and the solitary former wardrobe next to the back door leant at an unruly angle. He retraced his steps into the kitchen and absent-mindedly emptied the contents of the fridge into a bin bag.

Troubled Legacy

With the domestics seen to, he lugged his suitcase up the steep staircase between the kitchen and the lounge and took stock of the state of the upper storey. His bedroom served its purpose well enough; with two matching wardrobes and a chest of drawers, but the bedding was faded and, again, the ubiquitous books and magazines were piled up everywhere. He noticed that the green carpet clashed with the turquoise curtains. He moved on to the second bedroom; the room that Natalie would be sleeping in. Although book free, apart from the saggy bed there was no furniture save for a beside table and a tall thin chest of drawers. Something would have to be done, he thought, and quickly. His final port of call was the bathroom. The sage green bathroom suite was dated and the shower curtain above the bath was brittle with age. Once again, attention would be needed before Natalie's visit.

Simon unpacked his things while mentally planning just what he could and could not do about his house before Natalie saw it. He recalled them talking about decor on a couple of occasions. He would try and remember what she had said, he thought. By the time she came he would do his best to get all the rooms on the upper floor sorted. He would begin with the spare bedroom. Returning downstairs he decided that he needed to do some shopping. There was a twenty-four hour supermarket on the outskirts of Norwich; a twenty minute drive away. He pulled on a coat and went out to his car. All the response he could get from it, however, was a wheezy groan from the starter. His battery was flat; a not infrequent occurrence of late. Muttering to himself Simon fumbled in the boot and, in the dim glow cast by an adjacent streetlight, he removed the battery and took it into his utility room where he connected up a battery charger and plugged it in. Something would have to be done about the car as well, he thought. Still it wasn't as if he didn't have the money was it?

After a meagre breakfast of black coffee and digestive biscuits, Simon Fenton reunited his Mini with its newly-charged battery. The engine burst into life at the third attempt, sending a cloud of grey-blue smoke spewing from the exhaust pipe. His first call was at the supermarket where he stocked up on everyday essentials. From there he went to a large DIY store where he spent a hundred and twenty pounds and a few coppers on scrapers, brushes, rollers, paint and other decorating accessories. Opposite the store was a Volkswagen main dealer. An hour later he had test driven and paid a deposit on an eighteen month old Golf.

The DIY project in the spare bedroom soon proved to Simon that he was out of his depth. Three hours work had not even seen the old wallpaper stripped from two walls. Instead of the smooth plaster he had expected to find beneath the wallpaper the walls proved to be pitted and uneven. By late afternoon he had trawled the yellow pages and three local decorators had agreed to give him quotes for the whole house on Monday evening. Relieved of his duties he sat down at the kitchen table and wrote a letters to Natalie and Kynpham. For three pages he told Natalie just how much he loved her. On the fourth he told her about his home improvement programme, the new car and the lunch invitation from Andy and Jane Carr. His letter to Kynpham was shorter. He did not mention Natalie, preferring to tell his friend about her face to face when he next had the opportunity. In each envelope he placed a cheque for two hundred and five thousand pounds.

The next morning Simon made one of his occasional visits to church. In truth he had an ulterior motive, but he felt uplifted by the experience nonetheless. Over coffee at the end he sought out Peter Brewer, one of the churchwardens. Peter Brewer made his living as a self-employed plumber and kitchen fitter. Simon managed to extract a promise from the churchwarden that he would pay a call after lunch to give an estimate for fitting a new kitchen and bathroom. In fact the afternoon proved more profitable than Simon had first imagined. Peter Brewer apparently had a cancellation the following week and could fit in Simon's bathroom if he decided what he wanted quickly. After some rapid measuring and sketching the pair of them drove to the same DIY store that Simon had visited the previous day and placed an order for tiles, sanitary ware, a walk-in shower cubicle, a power shower and various fittings. Simon also spotted a living flame gas fire on display and Peter Brewer agreed to fit it in Simon's lounge fireplace, which was currently hidden behind a wall mounted radiant heater.

On Monday Simon set off for work with a degree of trepidation. He had telephoned from Liverpool Street before boarding his train the previous Friday assuring them of his impending return, but remained a little unsure of the reception he would receive. In the event, both of the elderly owners were lying in wait for him when he walked in. He found his hand being pumped like a minor celebrity as he stepped into the office. Apparently someone in the Metropolitan Police had told them the he had been of great help to them and had put himself in some danger on their behalf, but would not be allowed to divulge any details. His employers would hear none of his apologies and strenuously declined his offer to count his nine remaining days of holiday entitlement to cover part of the absence. The arrival of Sharon, however, brought Simon back to earth.

'Oh, so you're back are you? About time!' she said as a greeting, 'I've been keeping the routine stuff ticking over, but there's a whopping pile in your in-tray. How about I keep the customers and suppliers out of your hair while you sort it?'

Simon grinned.

'OK,' he said, 'let's see what kind of mess you've left me with.'

In fact Sharon had dealt effectively with the majority of what had needed to be done and Simon had cleared more than half the backlog by the end of the working day. That evening he engaged one of the decorators to deal with both bedrooms, the staircase and the lounge the week after his visit to Natalie and the remainder of the house later. He also ordered a skip to be delivered and emptied each few days for the next three weeks before visiting his elderly neighbours and arranging with them to keep his spare key to let the assortment of tradesmen in and out. The following evening he took measurements to a carpet warehouse and arranged for new carpets to be fitted the week before Natalie's visit. From there he went to a furniture shop and ordered a number of items from stock for delivery the day before Natalie arrived. His final call was to a well-known chain store where he loaded up a trolley with bedding and soft furnishings. With the exception of the Kitchen and utility room the whole project would be complete in time for her visit.

The frenzy of domesticity made time pass quickly for Simon. Nonetheless he was aware of a number of matters that would have to be dealt with if he was to make the most of his visit to Leeds. Peter Brewer informed him that the bathroom facilities would be out of commission the three days before he was due to travel to Leeds and, with the lure of the new car parked outside, he decided to deal with everything in one go. After asking for and receiving two days leave for the Thursday and Friday he packed a bag on Wednesday morning and set off on his travels immediately after work that evening.

Traffic was light in the early evening and the novelty of the new car buoyed his spirits as he ate up the miles across the flatlands of Eastern England. After a brief stop at a Little Chef near Grantham he pulled up outside the house in Chester Green Lane in Derby a little after ten. He did not linger there, preferring to force the unhappy memories of what had happened to Natalie there from his mind. With a small screwdriver he had brought expressly for that purpose he unscrewed the back of the television set and extracted the photocopied letters that were concealed there. He slipped the copies into a sturdy brown envelope and re-fixed the back to the television before slipping out to his car. From there he drove to the Travelodge at Alfreton where he had booked a room.

The next morning he was on the road before seven, taking the winding route through Matlock and the Peak District to the southern outskirts of Manchester. Despite the heavy traffic in Stockport he was able to secure a space in a multi-storey car park and catch a train into Central Manchester in time for his eleven fifteen appointment with Mr. Baldwin of Green, Arbuthnott and Harris. He reclaimed the unopened envelope containing the copies of Michael Duckworth's letters and informed the solicitor that he wished the property in Derby to be sold, signed some papers and handed over the keys before retracing his steps to Stockport and circumnavigating the M60 ahead of the evening rush. By tea time he was checking in to the small hotel on the outskirts of the small Cumbrian town of Dalton-in-Furness where he regularly stayed when visiting his grandmother. The evening was warm and, having booked a table in the restaurant for later in the evening, he took a walk along the ancient footpath linking the old town with the ruins of the nearby abbey. For a while he stood at the abbey fence, gazing contemplatively at the red sandstone ruins. He felt a deep-rooted contentment; he was on his way to visit the girl that he loved; she had as good as said that she would marry him. Simon Fenton could not remember ever being so happy.

The following morning he checked out after a hurried breakfast and drove up the steep hill beside the cemetery and through a neat council estate to the care home where his grandmother lived. Even though it had been more than a year since he had held a lucid conversation with her, Simon still felt a twinge of disappointment when she failed to recognise him. Seated in a high backed chair beside her bed, she was staring out over the tarn when he entered the room. She turned at the sound of his entry, but looked vacantly through him with no hint of recognition. He pulled over a hard chair and sat opposite her talking gently about everything and nothing, but there was little evidence that she was taking any notice of him at all. Now and again she was gripped by a bout of chesty coughing and after an hour or so she appeared to be on the brink of dozing off. Simon stood up and stooped to kissed her on the forehead before taking his leave. On his way out he stood chatting with one of the care assistants. His grandmother had developed her cough a couple of weeks ago, he discovered. The doctor had visited and prescribed antibiotics, but they did not seem to be doing her much good.

With a mixture of relief and guilt Simon returned to the car and set out on the next leg of his journey. He drove slowly through the traffic-calmed town centre and out into the countryside. Within minutes he was re-tracing the route of the fateful journey he had taken with Natalie after picking her up in Barrow-in-Furness. As the memories flooded back of her unburdening her soul to him his heart was filled once again with his overwhelming feelings for her.

He had plenty of time in hand before the next part of his mission so he parked the car in the small coastal town of Ravenglass and treated himself to a round trip on the miniature railway which ran from the mudflats of the Irish Sea coast into the Lakeland hills. The trip evoked childhood memories of making the journey with his grandfather as a boy. He would bring Natalie one day, he decided.

The warmth of the day dissipated as the sun dipped towards the horizon, turning the banks of cloud in the western sky of a flaming orange. Standing on the beach at Allonby where he had swum and sunbathed with Natalie while they were on the run he took out his digital camera and took a couple of dozen shots at a variety of settings. He would select the best one and have a large canvas print made to hang above the fireplace in his refurbished lounge; that would be a romantic reminder for Natalie when she visited. Conscious that his dalliances had occupied rather too much of the day Simon set out on the penultimate leg of his day's travels.

The village of Hawes was almost deserted under the soft glow of its meagre streetlights when Simon parked on in a virtually empty car park close to the disused railway station. From the boot of his car he took his torch and a large trowel, both of which he slipped into his coat pocket. A short walk took him to the cemetery and he quickly located Terry Clegg's gravestone with the aid of his torch. Sweeping aside the blue pebbles he dug into the soft earth with the trowel and pulled free the plastic wrapped letters which he had returned to their hiding place after exhuming the biscuit tin of documents. It was almost midnight when he reached the Travelodge at Skipton.

CHAPTER NINETY-SIX

Natalie had been awake since well before daylight. She was almost breathless in anticipation of Simon's visit. She had virtually convinced herself that there was no point in procrastinating any longer. She could agree to marry him that very day and then the banns, or whatever he had called them, could be read and they would be husband and wife within a month. Yet underneath her joy was an integrity that was new to her; new and, in its own way, exciting. Just as Simon had surprised her by suggesting they abstain from making love until they were married, so she was beginning to understand that by agreeing to his request their relationship had become elevated to something that was somehow greater than the sum of its parts. For the first time in her life Natalie Robertson caught a glimpse of herself as she realised Simon probably saw her; special, unique, and loved. She would keep to their plan she decided. Anticipation was not un-pleasurable in itself and the secret knowledge that they would almost certainly be engaged within a fortnight and married soon afterwards made her heart flutter within her breast. She checked the clock for the tenth time in half an hour; six thirty. Simon had said he would arrive at eight. It was time to be up and about.

Following the directions Natalie had given him, Simon circumnavigated the Leeds inner ring road and pulled into the designated visitors' parking bay outside Natalie's block of flats a quarter of an hour early. Savouring the moment, he chose to sit in the car for a few minutes before setting out on the short walk that he had been looking forward to so much for the past two weeks. At precisely five minutes to eight he pressed the buzzer and was rewarded immediately with Natalie's joyful shriek.

'Simon,' she squealed, 'come on up, the door's open.'

No sooner had he crossed the threshold than she threw her arms round him. He dropped his bag and took hold of her by the waist, lifting her from her feet and kissing her as she wrapped her legs tightly around him. The kiss was wonderful, the scent of her overwhelming and the entire experience shot through with emotions that defied description.

'You'd better put me down, Simon Fenton, thirty four,' Natalie whispered, breaking off the kiss, 'or that deal we made about not making love could be off.'

Simon gently lowered her to her feet and she closed the still open front door.

'Coffee and croissants all right?' She asked as he took in his surroundings.

'I'd rather have you,' he quipped, instantly regretting his impulse, 'but I can wait a few weeks for that; coffee and croissants will be great.'

Natalie chatted animatedly as she showed him round the small apartment. She insisted that he sleep in the bed while she slept on the couch and would brook no argument. When she showed him the tiny balcony with its panoramic view of the railway station below he told her that he wished he'd brought his anorak so he could sit out there all day, earning him a good natured swipe with a large cushion.

As he sat at the tiny kitchen table watching Natalie prepare the breakfast Simon was once again overcome by her beauty. She had done something with her hair, he noticed; the blonde dye had gone and the lustrous mid-brown colour that it had been when he had first met her was back. The feathering into her neck was also less pronounced. She was wearing tight white jeans and a cornflower blue sweater that matched her eyes. Natalie turned toward him and smiled. She was probably wearing just a trace of make-up he thought.

Troubled Legacy

'Simon,' she began, 'I know we weren't going to talk about the future and stuff today, but I just want to tell you two things that I've made my mind up about. Whatever happens, I don't want to stay here. Leeds and all the places around here hold too many bad memories; it's time for me to move on. The other thing is that I don't think I need to go to America to do my airline training. There are other options. If we did get married I'd want us to be together, not living on opposite sides of the Atlantic...'

'But, Nat,' he stuttered, 'you wouldn't have to give up anything, I'd...'

'No, Simon,' I know what you're going to say; you're going to tell me that you'd go along with anything I wanted to do, but I wouldn't want to ask you to give up everything you care about. Now let's change the subject.' She padded across the wooden floor on bare feet and placed a plate of hot croissants and a coffee pot on the table before sitting down opposite him. 'Now you have to make a hard decision about what we're going to do today. You have three choices; retail, culture or anorak.'

She went on to explain that choosing retail would involve accompanying her to the city centre shops and giving her advice on choosing an outfit suitable for a weekend in rural Norfolk. Culture involved a visit to the David Hockney gallery and museum at Salts Mill and choosing anorak would result in a trip on the Keighley and Worth Valley steam railway. Seeking the safety of a middle course he chose culture.

Before they began to make preparations for the day out, Simon produced the brown envelope from his luggage.

'I've picked up the copies of the letters from your mum to Eddie Duggan,' he announced, 'and I've dug up the originals from Terry Clegg's grave.'

Natalie frowned.

'Do you think anyone else but us knows about them?' she asked.

'I shouldn't thing so, Nat,' he replied, 'there's no one alive who could know, is there?'

Natalie went over to the kitchen area and returned with a large saucepan and a box of matches. She opened the French doors to the balcony.

'Bring them here, then, Simon,' she instructed. She took the first sheet of paper and lit the corner with a match. As the flames took hold she dropped it into the pan and lit the corner of the second sheet. One by one she burnt every trace of the original letters and the brittle faded photocopies, leaving a flaky residue of ash in the saucepan. As the last flames died away Natalie upended the pan over the balcony rail, letting the charred remnants of her paternity fall into the breeze as they dissipated and swirled into the damp atmosphere.

'That's it, then,' she announced, 'now no one else but us will ever know.'

Following her example, Simon took out the copies of Michael Duckworth's letters that he had reclaimed from the solicitor and destroyed them in the same manner.

Natalie packed up some sandwiches and they set out. It felt strange to both of them as they walked through the city streets towards the railway station hand in hand that there was no one looking for them and they were in not in any form of danger. They took an electric train to the small town of Saltaire and spent a happy couple of hours looking at the brightly coloured paintings in the converted mill. The day was overcast with a warm westerly breeze. The decided to brave the elements and located a picnic area for lunch. The breeze ruffled Natalie's hair as they ate. Simon produced his digital camera and proceeded to embarrass her by shooting lots of pictures of her. He needed something to remind him just how beautiful she was, he told her, and for the first time in many years she accepted the compliment unreservedly. In the company of Simon Fenton she really did feel beautiful.

After lunch they explored the small town. Simon spotted a necklace made of metal lozenges in a mixture of shades of blue in a craft shop which he insisting on buying for Natalie. In return, she sought out an antique brass vase which she said would complement the new brass framed living flame fire that would be waiting for him in his lounge. Happy and tired they took the train back to Leeds where Natalie had announced that she would cook them dinner.

After a little awkwardness over getting themselves organised for the night, Natalie lay down to sleep on the sofa while Simon luxuriated in the softness of her double bed. He could smell her scent on the pillow. Utterly content, he determined to stay awake for as long as possible to fix the memory of an amazingly wonderful day firmly into his mind. In fact he was asleep within minutes.

Simon awoke the next morning to the twin sounds of rain beating against the window and Natalie pottering about in the kitchen. Presently she arrived in the bedroom wearing a thin cotton top and a pair of matching shorts carrying a tray with two mugs of tea and hot buttered toast. She set the tray down on the bedside table and curled up on the bed next to him. Simon found her presence and proximity distracting and alluring. He drew her towards him and within an instant they were locked in a passionate embrace. Again it was Natalie who stepped back from the brink.

'Oh, bloody hell, Simon,' she said as she gently unlocked his arms and moved backwards to sit on the edge of the bed, 'I didn't think it would this hard for is to hold ourselves back.'

Simon struggled to sit upright.

'Do you want to change your mind, Nat?' he asked.

'I want to make love to you Simon Fenton; I want that more than anything else right at this moment, but you just don't know how special you wanting to wait has made me feel so I'm going for a cold shower right now. I'll let you know when it's safe to come out.'

Later she asked him if he wanted to go to church. She would be quite happy to go with him if he did, she told him. Simon declined the offer, but Natalie announced that he had better be planning to take her to church when she visited him. After all, she argued, she could hardly turn up at the vicarage for lunch without having seen the vicar in action beforehand, could she? In the event, Simon was treated to a truncated form of the retail option he had declined the previous day. Even though the rain had stopped there was a chill of autumn in the air and Natalie led him on an expedition to the shops where she chose a couple of outfits for her impending trip to Norfolk. Although Simon's opinions were constantly sought, he thought that she looked wonderful in anything she wore and ended up being gently chastised for his total lack of taste. He didn't mind a bit. Burdened with their purchases they had a late lunch in a pizza restaurant before returning to the apartment for a re-run of the fashion parade. As the time of Simon's departure drew closer an air of melancholy began to intrude on their joy and Natalie once again had to resist the overwhelming temptation to tell Simon that she would marry him and offer to accompany him back to his home. Resist she did, however, and she sprung the surprise on him that, unless the weather forecast was poor, she did not intend to drive to Wroxham in a fortnight's time, but to fly. She would arrive; she said, around ten o'clock on the Saturday morning at the general aviation terminal at Norwich Airport and would fly back at three-ish on the Sunday afternoon. Time passed all too quickly and as daylight began to fade they said their goodbyes and Simon drove off into the dusk, leaving Natalie a little tearful at the parting, but more certain than ever that she wanted to spend the rest of her life with Simon Fenton.

CHAPTER NINETY-SEVEN

It was late when Simon got back home. For the first part of his journey the traffic had been heavy, but once he had left the congested motorway stretch behind he had made good progress along the rural single carriageways. Upon entering the house he was immediately thrilled to see the new gas fire in situ and was even more delighted with the bathroom. There was one thing he had to do before going to bed though, he switched on his computer and uploaded the images from his digital camera. He then selected a picture of the sunset over the Irish Sea and sent it by e-mail to an internet company that specialised in canvas prints and ordered a twenty by thirty inch reproduction. From his shots of Natalie he chose one of her laughing with her head tilted on one side and her hair billowing in the breeze. He ordered a twelve inch square canvas of that one. Mission accomplished, Simon climbed the stairs and went to bed. For the second successive night he slept like a log.

In the morning he checked his answering machine before work and found several messages waiting from Kynpham who had returned from India and wanted to know what was behind the cheque he had discovered lying behind his doormat. His latest call, timed at two o'clock on Sunday afternoon informed Simon that Kynpham planned on paying the cheque into his account first thing on Monday morning so it had better not be a wind up. Grinning Simon dialled his friend's number and caught him before he left for work. In guarded terms Simon explained about the money and asked Kynpham about his time in Shillong. Apart from Rebecca's petulance at having her visit to England cut short, the family time had been enjoyed by all concerned and Kynpham was now back at work. He had been placed in the features department to write a series of articles on prominent British Asians who had integrated well into contemporary British society and would be travelling the length and breadth of the nation in the next few weeks to seek them out and persuade them to be interviewed. Kynpham hoped that if he was successful in the task he might be moved from the hurly-burly of the news-desk to the features department on a more permanent basis. In the meantime, he said, the vast fortune that had come his way would enable him to put a substantial deposit down on a new flat and pay very little more each month in mortgage payments that he was currently paying in rent. The unexpected income would also mollify Rebecca, Kynpham announced, as he would be in a position to pay for her long awaited tourist trip to the UK in December after the end of her school term. Simon told Kynpham about his programme of home improvements, but found it strangely difficult to tell him about his blossoming relationship with Natalie. They agreed to meet up in the not too distant future before the pressure of time upon both of them brought the call to an end. By the time they met up, Simon thought, he would probably in a position to introduce Natalie to Kynpham as his fiancée. If Andy Carr agreed to conduct the marriage service he would need a best man; Kynpham would be the ideal candidate.

Although the backlog of work in the office had been cleared up, it was a busy week for Simon at work as Sharon had decided to take a week of her annual leave. Simon was glad of the distraction as time passed rapidly. In the evenings he continued to project manage his schedule of household re-furbishment. The decorator arrived again as promised the following week and made short work of the walls, ceilings and woodwork. On Tuesday evening Peter Brewer called round with plans and drawings for re-fitting the kitchen and utility room. Simon made his choices of units and appliances and arranged to have the work done the second week in November.

By the middle of the week all the carpets and much of the furniture had gone the way of the majority of his accumulated books and magazines and been consigned to one of the succession of skips that came and went from the road outside his house. By the time he spoke to Natalie on the telephone on Wednesday the lounge was ready for the decorators and the

Troubled Legacy

furniture from the guest room had been dismantled and consigned to yet another skip. By the weekend his own bed and bedroom furniture had filled a final skip; leaving him sleeping on a borrowed camp bed above the bare floorboards of his bedroom. On the telephone Natalie told him that she would be disappointed if she had to sleep on the floor when she came and that she hoped all his deliveries arrived on time. She also told him that she loved him and had been flying a "complex single", whatever one of those might be.

The carpet fitter arrived with the carpets on the Monday morning and, by evening, Simon had hung the two canvas prints; the larger one of the sunset above the fireplace in the lounge and the smaller on his bedroom wall. He would tell Natalie about the sunset, but not about the smaller print, he decided. As the days before Natalie's arrival grew fewer Simon's excitement and anticipation rose to a fever pitch. Andy Carr masterminded the furniture deliveries on the Friday morning and stayed to help Simon, who had booked half a day's holiday for the Friday afternoon, with the final assembly of one or two items that arrived in flat packs. Jane, having suborned a younger member of the congregation as baby-sitter, arrived a little later and saw to the hanging of new curtains and adding the final touches. With everything complete Simon thanked his assistants and slumped exhausted on his new leather sofa well content with his lot in life. He had checked the weather forecast and a cool but sunny weekend was expected. Simon had also decided to reciprocate Natalie's idea of offering choices of what to do. He would offer her shopping, steam or seaside. Shopping would involve a visit to Norwich city centre; steam, although he doubted it would be her choice, would be a trip on the nearby Bure Valley Miniature Railway and, seaside, which he thought she would probably opt for, would be crab fishing and fish and chips in Cromer. A few minutes later he sat up with a jolt. There was something he had forgotten! A quick dash to the twenty four hour supermarket put things right though. A voluminous white towelling bath-robe now adorned the hook on the back of the door in Natalie's room; if she wandered round wearing her skimpy night clothes the temptation would be in danger of leading them off the straight and narrow. On the nearby dressing table was a bunch of flowers standing in a new vase. His home was finally ready for its most important visitor ever.

CHAPTER NINETY-EIGHT

Simon's departure from her apartment had left Natalie with a sense of emptiness. All her expectations of his visit had been more than fulfilled. She had no lingering doubts; in less that a fortnight she would agree to marry him and to move to a small town she had not yet visited to be with him. If that meant that she would never fly airliners for a living so be it. It would be quite possible to enjoy working as a flying instructor, or perhaps she would be able to find work spraying fertilizer from the air or something. There was also the possibility of having children she mused; she had never thought of herself as the maternal type, but when you loved someone as much as she loved Simon Fenton old perspectives tended to become a bit wobbly. Twelve days, she counted them off on the calendar in her kitchen, just twelve more days until she would see him again.

The next morning Natalie resumed her daily routine. After a forty minute workout at the gym she showered and changed before setting out for the flying school. Although the weather forecast was not good there was a possibility of an improvement later in the day so she installed herself in the cafe-bar to wait. A little later she encountered the chief flying instructor who was also at a loose end due to the low cloud and rain. He told her that the school had just taken delivery of a Piper Arrow, a single engine monoplane with a more powerful engine that her regular Warrior which also had a retractable undercarriage and a variable pitch propeller. He suggested that with approaching two hundred hours in her log book it would be an ideal next step for her to complete the difference training necessary to fly it. It should only take her three or four hour's instruction,

Troubled Legacy

he told her. The lure of arriving at Norwich Airport in such a machine proved too great to resist and she booked four of his available slots over the next few days. In the event, the weather stayed bad all day and the next day was no better, but she managed her first lesson on the Arrow on the Wednesday, immediately warming to its higher speed and more precise handling.

Speaking to Simon on the 'phone that evening lifted her spirits still further and the following afternoon, after another hour in the Arrow, she dared to stop of at a newsagents on her way home and, feeling a little foolish and self-conscious, bought a couple of bridal magazines. Friday was unfit for flying and Natalie was listless and impatient. Even a second visit to the gym failed to invigorate her and she wandered aimlessly into the city centre after lunch and ended up with a selection of tourist guides to Norfolk. Back in her apartment she once again located Simon's house on Google Earth and, as she slowly zoomed outwards she began to refer to the guides and build up a mental picture of the surrounding area. Apart from speaking to Simon on the telephone and receiving yet another letter from him, the weekend proved uneventful. On Tuesday Natalie was signed off to fly the Arrow solo and immediately booked it for a two hour session on Thursday and for her weekend trip to Norwich. The chief instructor suggested that her logical next step would be to undertake a rating enabling her to fly twin engine aircraft. Wednesday brought another telephone conversation with Simon and news of the impending completion of his home improvements.

She flew the Arrow on a triangular navigation exercise on Thursday morning, making her turns at Pickering and Grimsby before re-entering the Leeds Control Zone via Dewsbury. The long range weather forecast was promising and she decided not to fly again before her trip to Norwich. In the afternoon she returned home via Salts Mill, purchasing a framed Hockney print as a contribution towards Simon's new-look home and a reminder of their shared day out.

Thursday evening passed in a frenzy of anticipation and, after pacing endlessly round and round in her tiny apartment following her regular visit to the gym and breakfast on Friday, Natalie once again sought the distraction of the city centre. After ambling aimlessly for a while she found herself standing outside the brooding grandeur of St. George's

Church. With a frisson of guilt she remembered the anguished prayer she had made, offering to sacrifice her love for Simon in return for her life. She turned away and tried to dismiss the memory from her mind, but it just would not go. She felt herself reluctantly drawn towards the door and pushed at it tentatively. To her surprise it swung open and she stepped hesitantly into the silence of the dark and sombre interior. The building appeared to be deserted. She sat down in a pew at the back and gazed absently at the pale sunlight filtering in through the stained glass windows. In her mind the words began to take form.

'God,' she mouthed, 'if you are there that is, well, what I mean is that on balance I've got to admit that I've changed my mind a bit about that, I guess you are probably more likely to exist than not to exist – I mean if you're good enough for Simon Fenton to believe in, you're good enough for me...only you know what I said about not spoiling his life if you let me live, well I just wanted to say that I don't think I would spoil his life now if I did marry him. I guess what I'm saying is that unless you tell me otherwise I'm going to tell him that I'll marry him tomorrow. Is that all right then, God? Should I call you that or do you prefer Jesus or something? Anyway, I'll be popping in to see you again on Sunday I expect; with Simon, so 'bye until then...' Suddenly she felt stupid and embarrassed. It was true that getting to know Simon had changed the way she thought about God, but she didn't really believe in him, did she? Annoyed with herself, Natalie stood up and walked briskly out through the door and back into the heart of the city. Feeling in need of a caffeine rush she sought out an upmarket coffee shop in the Victoria Quarter where she ordered a large latté and an indulgent slice of cake. As she gazed around the tables she recognised Kynpham Johal sitting two tables away in earnest conversation with a well built young Asian man who was wearing a smart suit and a sporting a red silk bow tie.

CHAPTER NINETY-NINE

Kynpham's assignment was proving more challenging than he had first thought it would. Out of the first twelve potential interviewees on his list of seventeen only five had agreed to be featured in the series. As he sat facing Hardeep Kaur, a second generation Sikh businessman from Huddersfield, the omens were once again not looking good. Hardeep Singh had built up a network of mobile phone outlets across Yorkshire and Humberside since leaving school with hardly any qualifications fifteen years earlier. He was also a director of the local football club and had recently been selected as the Liberal Democratic candidate for Batley North in the General Election that was widely expected the following spring. Mr. Kaur's reservations about being featured in the Independent were not unfamiliar to Kynpham; he had worked hard, he said, to present himself as a successful British businessman and politician – not a successful British Asian businessman and politician. Despite the journalist's best efforts at charm and persuasion Hardeep Kaur drained his coffee mug and stood up, offering Kynpham his hand. Kynpham also rose from his seat and reluctantly shook the proffed hand. He watched in polite exasperation as yet another potential interviewee walked out through the door.

At that moment a pretty brown-haired girl stepped in front of him, blocking his view of the retreating businessman.

'Excuse me she said, but aren't you...'

'I'm sorry, Miss,' Kynpham interrupted brusquely, 'but I'm afraid I'm rather busy at the moment.' Kynpham side-stepped the girl and strode rapidly after his quarry. He would catch up with him and make one last effort, he decided.

Kynpham's persistence paid off. He had caught up with Mr. Kaur on the street and had politely pointed out that the very point of the articles was to present the people concerned as fully integrated and quintessentially British. With the dexterity of a born politician Mr. Kaur had given in graciously, recognising that exposure in the national press would probably do more good than harm to his prospects of being elected to Parliament. He had agreed to spend a couple of hours with Kynpham the following afternoon.

Later on in his hotel room Kynpham's thoughts returned to the girl in the coffee shop. She had seemed familiar to him, but he could just not place her. She had looked a little like the girl that Simon Fenton had been on the run with he thought, but Natalie Robertson's hair had been blonde and her skin bronzed. The girl in the coffee shop had brown hair and a paler skin. Whoever she was he realised that he had been rude to her and felt sorry for cutting her off and walking away. Still there was nothing he could do to put matters right was there? He had absolutely no idea who she had been.

CHAPTER ONE HUNDRED

Being snubbed by Kynpham Johal had disturbed Natalie deeply and pricked the bubble of her euphoria. She returned to her seat and cupped her latté in both hands as she felt the blood rising in her cheeks. Simon had told her that her past would not be an issue with his friends, but Kynpham Johal had not wanted to acknowledge her. Perhaps, she thought, he had not recognised her, but that explanation did not seem very likely as she brooded upon the rebuff. It was more likely that he had recognised her all too well, she concluded, and did not approve of her past life and wanted nothing to do with a woman like her. She sat deep in thought until the coffee became too cold to drink, then ambled wearily back in the direction of her flat. She was so looking forward to meeting Simon again the following day, but the incident in the coffee shop had definitely taken the edge from her excitement.

The second blow came as she crossed the car park towards the entrance to her block. A small wiry man with a mop of curly hair emerged from a parked car and stepped in front of her, blocking her path.

'Natalie Robertson?' he inquired, 'Steve Harrington, Sunday Messenger, how do you fancy making ten grand?'

Natalie made as if to sidestep him but he dodged in front of her.

'Come on Natalie, or should I call you Kelly? Ten grand for a kiss and tell story; the vicar by the tart sort of thing. Just a couple of hours for an interview and a photo shoot; come on, I'll go to fifteen.'

Natalie pushed him aside and carried on walking, but he fell in step beside her.

'What was it like, then, love,' he asked with a leery grin, 'I bet you taught him a thing or two didn't you?'

Natalie speeded up, but he kept pace with her.

'OK, Twenty grand, my final offer. I'll tell you what I'll go to twenty two and a half if you get your tits out and do the pics topless.'

Natalie forced him aside and stormed through the door. Fortunately the lift was on the ground floor with its doors invitingly open. Natalie stepped in, pressed the button for her floor and whirled round, pushing the man violently backwards as the doors began to close.

'How about twenty five?' he shouted as the motor began to whirr the lift jolted into life.

Back in the sanctuary of her apartment Natalie's tears began to flow as the implications of recent events began to dawn upon her. She had reminded God of their bargain and then these two awful things had happened. Was he trying to tell her something, she wondered in the irrationality of her half-belief; was it that God, whoever he might be, was calling her to account? She sat and cried for several minutes before common sense kicked back in. Kynpham could just not have recognised her and Sir Denzel Goodman had warned them that reporters might come sniffing about. The events were probably no more than coincidences. For a moment she considered phoning Simon and telling him all about it; surely he would be able to reassure her that everything was going to be all right? Anyway, if God wanted to tell you anything he said it in three ways didn't he, she thought, dredging her mind for vaguely recalled RE lessons from her school days. Only two bad things had happened so it couldn't be anything to do with God. Reassured, she decided against calling Simon; he would only think she was being silly and he would be looking forward to the next day as much as she was; telling him would only worry him and spoil his enjoyment of the anticipation. She kicked off her shoes and began to lay out her clothes on the bed ready to start her packing.

Preparing and eating a light tea kept her occupied for a while and, when she eventually settled down on the sofa in front of the television, she had all but regained her previous sense of well-being. She was going to see Simon in, what was it, fifteen hours time and she was going to tell him that she would marry him. The television failed to hold her attention and Natalie, who was usually most fastidious about avoiding alcohol for at least twelve hours before flying decided to permit herself just one glass of wine. She opened a bottle of red and poured out a small measure before sitting down once again on the sofa. As she sipped the wine she began to flick through the channels in the hope of finding something to help pass the time.

Two minutes later she knew for certain that she was not going to be able to marry Simon Fenton after all.

A familiar face on one of the satellite news channels had grabbed her attention. It was Bishop Tim Baxter. He had apparently made a speech in the House of Lords condemning the internet sex industry; claiming that the relatively anonymous access permitted by the web was fuelling a boom in prostitution which, in turn, was leading to a worrying increase in people trafficking and the exploitation of women. It was not so much what he was saying that stopped her in her tracks though; it was the image displayed as a backdrop on a large screen in the studio behind where the Bishop was sitting. There, for all the world to see, was the photograph that had once formed the centrepiece on the homepage of Kelly's website. Mercifully a blurred oval concealed her facial features and the bottom of the picture ended at her naval so that the fingers tucked into the top of her pants were not on display. In an instant she knew that she could never be totally free of her past. Whether or not this was a third sign from God was not important. Simon had told her that his three friends would be happy to accept her, yet Kynpham Johal had not wanted to know her and now Tim Baxter was ranting on about prostitution right in front of a lewd and tasteless image of her shameful past. Even if Andy Carr had invited her for Sunday dinner it was probably just because he was a vicar and he thought it was his duty. No, Simon's friends would never accept someone like her; she had been deluding herself. Even though she knew that Simon loved her and would marry her as soon as he could, he would regret it in the long run. What is it that they said; marry in haste, repent at leisure?

If he married her he would lose the respect of all his friends. He would be saddled with an ex-tart and would end up ashamed of her and bitter about all the opportunities and friendships he would lose on her account. She could not bring herself to do that to him. Her love for him was too strong.

Natalie gulped down her wine and went to the kitchen to re-fill her glass. Staring through the television in her misery she realised that she owed it to Simon to tell him to his face that she did not want to marry him any more. As the tears flowed freely once again she finished the whole bottle of wine and eventually tottered into her bedroom, throwing her neatly folded clothing aside and crawling beneath the duvet.

Natalie awoke with a raging thirst and a throbbing head. As consciousness dawned the realisation of what had happened overwhelmed her with misery all over again and she rolled over in bed, pulling the quilt around her in an attempt to hold reality at bay, but the oblivion of sleep would not return. She rolled back over and looked at her alarm clock. It was six thirty, only an hour and a half before her planned take off time. She staggered out of bed and switched the kettle on while she made an attempt to wash away her lethargy in the shower. Half an hour later with two cups of strong coffee and two paracetamol inside her Natalie Robertson set out on what would undoubtedly be the most difficult and anguished mission of her life.

CHAPTER ONE HUNDRED AND ONE

Simon was up before dawn on Saturday morning. He padded from room to room in his house, checking that all was clean and tidy enough to receive the honoured guest. It was a pity, he thought, that the kitchen and utility room had not been modernised, but that would come later. With a start he realised that, if he included the cost of his car, he had already spent almost twenty five thousand pounds in the past month, with another seven thousand being set aside to complete the home improvements. Still, even with that included, it was only a little more than he had recently inherited from Michael Duckworth, he calculated with a smile. With Natalie around his miserly ways would almost certainly have to change in the very near future.

After showering, shaving and dressing Simon drank two mugs of coffee. Too excited to eat he was anxious to be on his way. He pulled into the car park outside the general aviation terminal at Norwich Airport over an hour early. The day was fine with a cool easterly breeze. Some early autumn leaves rattled around the tarmac beneath his feet as he pulled on his coat and walked over to the chain link fence that separated the car park from the airfield itself and stood scanning the northern sky for the first sign of a light aeroplane. The cold had driven him back to the car when Natalie arrived. He spotted the small red and white monoplane as it lined up on its final approach and his eyes followed it until it taxied behind the building in front of him. Simon knew that Natalie would have to deal with paperwork and formalities so he waited with growing anticipation in the car.

He knew that things were not right as soon as he saw her. He had expected her to be dressed in one of the outfits she had chosen when he went shopping with her in Leeds, but she emerged in a baggy sweater, faded jeans and grubby trainers. She was not carrying a bag and, as she crossed the car park towards him he saw that her eyes were red and puffy. Simon got out of the car and made as if to walk towards her, but Natalie held up her hand in front of her.

'What's up, Nat?' he croaked a she approached, 'where's your bag and stuff?'

Natalie gestured for him to get back into the car and Simon complied, in a state of confusion. She slipped into the seat beside him and Simon turned to put his arm around her shoulders and draw her into an embrace, but she pushed his arm away and slid round in her seat so that she her back was against the side window, maintaining as great a distance as was possible between them.

'What is it, Nat?' asked Simon again, 'What's happened?'

'I've got something to tell you, Simon,' she said, looking somewhere over his shoulder, 'please don't interrupt me...'

'But Nat,' he interjected, as solitary rear trickled down her cheek, 'have I done something wrong?'

Natalie pulled a tissue from her sleeve, wiped her face and blew her nose.

'No Simon, you've not done anything wrong, but I've been thinking and I've made my mind up. I don't want to marry you.' she said.

'No!' exclaimed Simon, 'No, tell me it's not true Nat, tell me what I've done wrong and I'll put it right, Oh, Nat I love you, please don't do this.'

Natalie took a deep breath and, looking him in the eye, began her speech.

'I just don't think it would work out for us, Simon. It's nothing you've done, it's just that I think we'll probably both regret it if we get married,' her eyes wandered back to somewhere over Simon's left shoulder as she continued. For all the world she longed to throw herself into his arms and let him tell her again how much he loved her and that everything was going to be all right, but she had to resist the temptation; for his sake. 'I do care about you Simon,' that was the first lie, she thought, she loved him with all her heart, 'but I'm just not ready to settle down and you're the settling down sort. I've decided that I want to fly airliners more than I want to marry you.' That was the second lie. 'I wanted to tell you face to face, but after this I don't ever want to see you again. I think that would be better for both of us,' the third and final lie was out. 'so please don't telephone me because I won't answer, don't e-mail because I'll just delete them and don't write because I'll burn the letters. I want to end it Simon. It was fun while it lasted, but it's over.' The tears were flowing freely down her cheeks.

'I d-don't believe you,' spluttered Simon, 'it c-can't be true. Tell me this is just a bad dream, Nat... you can't mean it, you just can't.'

'I'm sorry, Simon,' she replied, her voice barely audible, 'I'm so sorry. I'm going back now. Please just let me go. Find someone who deserves you and marry her, I'm not the right one for you.'

She turned in her seat, opened the car door and stepped out. Simon opened his door and began to push himself upright, but she waved him away.

'Let me go, Simon, please don't make this any harder than it is,' she said. He slumped back into the seat as she walked slowly back to the terminal building and in through the entrance. As the door closed behind her Simon's tears began to flow in earnest. The pain of his loss pierced him to the very core of his being. A few minutes later the roar of an aeroplane engine starting up penetrated his despair and he shuffled back over to the chain link fence. He watched the red and white aeroplane taxi to the end of the runway. He watched it as it gathered speed and rose unsteadily into the air. He watched as its wheels retracted into the wings and it turned a slow quarter circle towards the north. He watched it until it was a tiny speck in the sky. He stood and watched the spot where it had finally faded from his sight for almost another hour, hoping against hope that it would re-appear and that Natalie would come and tell him that it had all been a big mistake. The cold penetrated Simon to the bone and the wind dried the tears on his cheeks to white streaks, yet he still could not bring himself to abandon his post by the fence. In the end it was an inquisitive security guard checking the perimeter fence from the inside who broke his vigil.

'Are you all right Mate?' the guard asked.

Shaken from his stupor, Simon nodded distractedly and re-traced his steps to the car. He remembered nothing of the journey back to Wroxham. Back in the house, Simon slumped down on the sofa clutching the brass vase that Natalie had given him, staring sightlessly ahead. Wracked with despondency and dismay he wept for his lost love until fatigue and exhaustion overcame him and the blessing of sleep brought temporary refuge. It was dark when he awoke. The pain and distress returned unabated. Apart from responding to calls of nature, Simon spent the hours of darkness and most of the next morning alternately sleeping and staring vacantly at nothing in particular.

It was not until late on Sunday afternoon the Andy Carr found him. The vicar had not been surprised when Simon and Natalie did not appear at the morning service; he had not really expected them to. As the time for lunch came and went however Andy and Jane became increasingly anxious. Forty minutes after the agreed time the family had eaten alone and immediately afterwards Andy was dispatched to investigate. Simon's car was parked in its usual place outside, but there was no reply to the doorbell. Andy moved over to look through the front window and saw Simon, apparently wide awake, sitting in a trance-like state on the sofa. Persistent knocking on the window eventually gained Simon's attention and he shuffled stiffly across the room and opened the door. With gentle questioning Andy established what had occurred and, after telephoning his wife to let her know the situation, persuaded Simon into the kitchen where Andy made tea and managed to get Simon to eat a sandwich. Reluctant to abandon his friend, Andy remained with Simon for the rest of the day, only leaving when Simon promised to have a shower and go to bed.

The vicar was still concerned about Simon's wellbeing the next morning and made a point of calling into Simon's office on the pretext of needing to ask his advice over a church matter. He was relieved to find that, although pale and drawn, his friend had at least partly re-entered some vestige of his of normal life.

For the rest of the week Simon functioned as an automaton. He was glad that he had not told his work colleagues about Natalie, and they in turn, recognising that all was not well with him, offered him a gentle and supportive care that did not intrude upon his privacy. In the evenings he did all of the things that Natalie had asked him not to do. He tried repeatedly to call both her landline and mobile, but the calls went unanswered. He emailed impassioned pleas for her to get in touch but to no avail and he wrote two letters to her telling her how much he loved her. On the following Saturday morning he topped up his car with fuel and set out for Leeds. He got as far as Sutton Bridge before the futility of what he was attempting overcame him. If she would not answer his calls or e-mails she was not likely to answer her door to him either. With the return of a modicum of rationality the finality of his predicament overwhelmed him. She had obviously meant what she had said. It was over. She did not want to be with him. Filled with misery, he sat in his parked car for over an hour before driving slowly home.

Upon his return to Wroxhan he immediately went to apologise to Andy and Jane Carr for what he referred to as his "temporary aberration" and began the process of coming to terms with a future that did not involve Natalie Robertson. Accepting the reality of the situation, however, did nothing to dull the pain, but at least, he persuaded himself, he had made the step from denial into mourning. At work the following week both colleagues and customers commented privately that Simon was more like his old self and the old adage "least said, soonest mended" was used more than once behind his back as those who knew and respected him sensed that whatever had been bothering him seemed to be over. In reality, however, it was far from over. In private, Simon was still behaving in a number of bizarre and illogical ways; he had not entered the spare bedroom since that fateful morning, he had taken to keeping a brass vase on the table beside his bed and he rarely slept for more than three or four hours a night.

It was the call from the care home that marked the beginning of his slow climb from the depths of despair. It was thirteen days since Natalie Robertson had told him that she never wanted to see him again; a Friday. He had been cashing up in the office and entering the takings on his computer when the telephone rang. His grandmother, it seemed, had never recovered from her cough and had been diagnosed with pneumonia that afternoon. She was eating little and was breathing with the help of oxygen. The care home supervisor was guarded about the prognosis and suggeted the Simon might want to visit sooner rather than later. It was already too late to make the journey by train that evening and Simon, having realistically acknowledged the consequences of his recent lack of sleep, decided against attempting the long drive after work. He decided to drive into Norwich the following morning and catch the first train of the day.

He found the train journey therapeutic. He had enjoyed train travel since his grandfather had introduced him to it as a toddler and, with the real possibility that he might be on his way to see his grandmother alive for the last time, the flood of childhood memories helped to push the heartache of his parting with Natalie to the back of his mind. Changing trains in Manchester brought a fresh pang of sadness, but he felt his spirit strangely lifted as the train took him closer to his destination. He walked straight from the shabby little station up the steep hill to the nursing home, having booked his hotel room by telephone the previous evening. It was mid afternoon when he arrived in the old lady's room and the long shadows darkened the view over the tarn. His grandmother was awake when he walked in and he thought he spotted a flash of recognition in her rheumy eyes as she smiled at him; it was the first time in more than a year, he thought, that there had been any real connection between them. She was sitting upright in her customary chair wearing a nightdress and dressing gown. The sight of the oxygen tubes running under her nose distressed Simon, but he pulled up his usual chair and began to chat. His grandmother did not speak but, unusually, she seemed to be paying some attention to what he was saying. At first he kept to the safe ground of banal platitudes. He told her about the weather, his train journey and a little about the recent improvements he had made to his little house. For some of the time she seemed to be paying attention to what he was saying, but at others her eyes were closed and he had no idea if she was awake or asleep. A care assistant interrupted his flow, bringing tea and biscuits for him and a bowl of soup for his grandmother. The care assistant helped her into bed while Simon made a call of nature. Back in the room, he picked up the bowl and gently fed the soup to the old lady with a spoon very aware of the fact that it might prove to be the last thing he would ever be able to do for her. It was dark by the time she had eaten her fill and Simon switched on the bedside lamp. She smiled at him again in the dim light and he felt tears begin to well up. After wiping his eyes and blowing his nose, Simon took hold of her wrinkled hand and began to talk one again. Despite the promise he had made to the Prime Minister, he began by telling his grandmother all about how his father had been killed. He told her how Eddie Duggan had then set out to systematically wipe out all the witnesses and about the bravery of the two men who had lived long enough to acquire the evidence needed to fight back. He told her of his peculiar legacy and about the most wonderful girl that had been drawn into the unpleasant business and how they had fallen in love with each other while they were on the run. He told her all about how things had worked out in the end and that the man who had killed his father was now also dead. He told her about how he had asked Natalie Robertson to marry him and, with tears streaming down his face, how she had told him four weeks later that she didn't want to. As he sobbed he distinctly felt his grandmother squeeze his hand, which caused the tears to flow even more freely. When he had regained his composure the old lady was asleep. Her eyes were firmly closed and she was snoring gently. Simon slipped quietly out of the room, acknowledged the smile of the duty care worker as he passed the office and walked out into the night.

He returned the next morning to find the doctor in his grandmother's room. She was awake, but showed no sign whatsoever of recognising her grandson. Outside in the corridor the doctor confirmed that the outlook was not good; it might be a few days or a few weeks. He had seen similar cases before, he said, and surmised that after a certain point old people simply chose to not to fight any longer. Simon stayed a while with her before kissing her on the forehead, telling her that he loved her and walking back down the hill to the station.

It was late when Simon arrived back home, but there were things that he had to do. He took the brass vase from his bedside table and replaced it beside the lounge fireplace. Together with the print of the sun setting over the Irish Sea it would always remind him of the goodness and joy of his all too brief relationship with Natalie Robertson. He still loved her more than life itself, but he would not see her again and there was nothing he could do but accept the fact. Returning upstairs he went into the spare bedroom and removed the dead flowers and the vase that contained them; the remains of the flowers he disposed of in the kitchen bin and the vase he put away in a cupboard under the kitchen sink. He climbed the stairs once again and returned to his room. His last act before bedtime was to take down the canvas print of the laughing blue-eyed girl from the wall opposite his bed. He placed it face upwards in the bottom drawer of his bedside cabinet with the four letters that Natalie had written to him. It was time to let go; there would never be anyone else in his life, but he would not spend the rest of his life feeling sorry for himself.

For the first time in over a fortnight Simon Fenton slept for a full eight hours.

CHAPTER ONE HUNDRED AND TWO

Natalie's take off from Norwich Airport had almost been her last. She had been able to hold herself together only long enough to book out with Air Traffic Control and walk across the apron to her aircraft. As soon as she closed the door behind her the tears began to flow in great wracking sobs. Through a mist of grief she performed a bare minimum of pre-flight checks and had to make three attempts before she could make herself understood over the radio to request clearance to taxi. After performing the power checks at the end of the runway she forgot to reset the carburettor heat to cold, unnecessarily limiting the power output of the engine and, through her veil of tears she misread the airspeed indicator and hauled the Arrow into the air at ten knots below its designed take-off speed. The aeroplane lurched and wobbled alarmingly before she instinctively levelled off a few feet off the ground to allow proper flying speed to be built up. Natalie rubbed the moisture from her eyes, retracted the undercarriage and set course for home, but every few minutes the tears returned. Normally flying was the one activity that could completely engage a hundred percent of her attention and cause her to leave behind her earth-bound troubles but that was not the case on that fateful day. On the flight south she had managed to keep her composure. The demands of piloting a faster and more complicated aircraft, the gentle throbbing in her head and the constant rehearsal of her deceitful but necessary duty had held the tears in check, but now that the deed was done and she had made the final and irrevocable break with Simon her world was in tatters and she knew that she was not fit to be flying. After a fraught and stressful hour and twenty minutes in the air, during which she had lost her track three times and had ended up navigating from her handheld GPS rather than using a map and dead reckoning as she had been taught, Natalie Robertson made an inelegant and bumpy landing at Leeds Bradford Airport. She taxied in, completed the post-flight paperwork, paid for the hire of the aircraft and drove home.

In the sanctity of her apartment Natalie finally permitted herself the complete breakdown that had been inevitable for the past twenty four hours. As the door swung closed behind her she let out a keening wail and threw herself onto the sofa, burying her head in the softness of a cushion and lay alternately sobbing and groaning for more than two hours. In her pain and anger, she tried to lay the blame on a vindictive god, but the truth of the matter continually reasserted itself. adding injury to anguish and fracturing the last remnants of her self-esteem. It was simply that she didn't deserve Simon, she concluded. Because of all that she had done in the past; the selfish greed, her amoral and uncaring approach to both customers and colleagues at work and most of all the willing and premeditated sale of her body for sex. If there was a god, he was giving her exactly what she deserved and if there wasn't a god what was happening to her was no more than natural justice. Exhausted with grief she eventually roused herself from the sofa and emptied another bottle of her dwindling stock of wine.

During the next two days Natalie finished off her remaining four bottles of wine, ate little and slept even less. On the third day she awoke with a raging thirst, a thumping head and the realisation that she could not remain wallowing in self recrimination forever, if only because she had no wine left and little food in the flat. She had not switched her mobile phone on since her fateful flight on Saturday and she had been ignoring the intermittent ringing from her landline. With growing resolve she decided that she must avoid contact with Simon at all costs. Even the sound of his voice might be enough to send her back into his arms and consequently set him on the path to long term misery and unhappiness. She broke up the SIM card from her mobile and made one last call on her landline to cancel her telephone, broadband and satellite TV service.

A small and vulnerable figure, almost lost amongst the vastness of the cityscape within which she found herself, Natalie once more ventured out into the world. She felt ill. Logic told her that her physical condition was a consequence of excess alcohol, little food and lack of sleep, but there was also a deeper malady; some kind of illness of the soul. With no Simon, no job and no clear idea of what she actually wanted from life, Natalie felt adrift and desperately lonely. The fair weather of the weekend had degenerated into a typical late October day of windswept showers and a growing accumulation of damp leaves littered the canal-side as she trudged towards the city centre. A brief foray into the shopping centre resulted in a new pay as you go mobile phone, an internet dongle to connect her laptop to the web for three months and a few essential foodstuffs. She had prevaricated over whether or not to buy some more wine, but decided against it. If she was ever going to rebuild her life now was as good as anytime to begin again.

Late that afternoon Natalie paid her first visit to the gym since the previous Friday. She worked out for almost three hours with only a few short breaks. When she returned home she was physically exhausted and the prospect of a reasonable night's sleep drew her into its arms and provided her with a measure of respite from her torment.

The next morning Natalie woke up stiff and sore from her exertions in the gym. The physical pain was a welcome distraction from her troubled mental state and she forced herself to endure yet another hour of strenuous exercise before breakfast. Upon her return she found a letter with her address written in the familiar handwriting of Simon Fenton. She crumpled it her hand unopened and consigned it to the rubbish bin as a fresh bout of tearfulness threatened to overcome her. It was time for her to get a grip on herself and face whatever the future might hold. She had told Simon that she wanted to be an airline pilot more than she wanted to marry him; a shamefaced lie, but not altogether without some basis in truth. Her driving ambition before she met and fell in love with Simon Fenton had been to become a commercial pilot. She had the money and had not completely lost her motivation. Natalie logged onto the internet and worked out her options. There were three possible flight schools in Florida offering flight training for the commercial pilot's licence and instrument rating. All three, it transpired, had vacancies on courses starting the following January. Reluctant to commit herself without first hand knowledge, she decided against making a firm booking and decided to follow her flying instructor's advice and travel to Florida, hire a car and have a look for herself. In the meantime she would need to qualify to fly twin engine aircraft and pass her remaining exams. A telephone call confirmed that the distance-learning college she was enrolled with could fit her into a brush-up course at Bristol Airport beginning the last week in November and enter her for the remaining examinations in early December. She had done no studying for nearly six weeks, though; it would be a hard slog to complete all the modules before the residential fortnight. With her diary open in front of her, Natalie began to plan out her future. The six hours required for twin engine conversion training would depend on the availability of the aircraft, an instructor and the weather, say six half days in total. That would leave her twenty eight days to complete around a hundred and eighty hours of studying using books and computer-based material. If she split each day into two sessions of three hours that would make a total of a hundred and sixty eight; only eighteen short. It would be hard going, but it was just possible. She booked her place on the residential course and downloaded an application form for a US Student Visa. In the afternoon she booked a seat on a charter flight to Orlando leaving from Manchester on Saturday January 2nd. On her way home she visited a branch of the Halifax and paid off the balance of her mortgage. Another hour in the gym after tea helped exorcise the depth of her sadness and she slept reasonably well for the second night in a row.

For the next four weeks, Natalie imposed a regime of iron discipline on herself seven days a week. Starting with an hour in the gym before a breakfast of fruit and cereals, she would then fly if she was able and if not she would sit down and study for three hours, breaking only for a ten minute coffee break. Lunch would be a sandwich or bowl of soup and then another three hours of study. Her main meal would emerge from the microwave after minimal preparation and then, just before bedtime she would visit the gym again for an hour to help her to disengage herself from the rigours of aviation theory and help her sleep. After a week she had completed three hours flying and rarely thought about Simon Fenton more than twenty five or thirty times a day.

CHAPTER ONE HUNDRED AND THREE

After his visit to Cumbria, Simon slowly began to accept the reality of a future in which Natalie Robertson would have no part to play. Things were no different, he reasoned, than they had been the day before he first met her. Well, apart from the fact that he now knew all the circumstances surrounding his father's death and that he had played a part in significant events in the secret history of his country. The familiar routine of the steady life he had chosen for himself after leaving the ministry gave him comfort and he resumed his round of occasional visits to the pub and attended church on the following Sunday morning.

Early the following week Kynpham telephoned in a state of giddy excitement. The ruling party had elected a new leader several weeks earlier and she had been invited by the Queen to form a government. Kynpham had been offered the chance of a one to one interview with the United Kingdom's second female Prime Minister the day before the State Opening of Parliament. As Kynpham waxed lyrically about his permanent transfer to the features department of his newspaper Simon was glad that he had not confided in his friend about Natalie. It was good, he decided, to have a close friend to talk to who did not feel sorry for him. Kynpham had several exciting assignments in prospect and had also been given the services of a young photographer straight out of Art College who was working for the newspaper for six months for a nominal wage in order to gain experience. Kynpham had also secured a brand new two-bedroomed flat on a development in Haringey. His mortgage was in place and he hoped to be moving in within a few days.

Although they were both keen to meet up, much of Kynpham's work was scheduled to take place at weekends and they could not find a suitable date until the last weekend in November. Rebecca would be flying in for a couple of week's holiday on Friday 27th. Kynpham proposed that Simon join them in London for the weekend. He would have to work from Monday, though. Perhaps Simon might like to stay on for a couple of days to show his sister the sights, Kynpham suggested.

Glad of the offer of a distraction Simon agreed. He liked Rebecca well enough; she had been kind to him after Sophie had died and she had very probably saved his life in Carlisle a few weeks ago. Showing her London while her brother was out at work all day might be a welcome distraction from his lingering unhappiness. He had annual leave owing, so he agreed to his friend's suggestion.

As soon as the call ended, Kynpham e-mailed his sister in Shillong, telling her that he had done exactly what she had asked of him and that he had succeeded in his mission.

Kynpham's call had reawakened Simon's interest in the events surrounding the death of Eddie Duggan and he began to use the internet to catch up with developments. A joint inquest into the deaths of Inspectors Jewel and Cavendish had recorded verdicts of accidental death. Both funerals had taken place immediately afterwards. In the case of Detective Chief Superintendent Jimmy Bell a coroner's jury decided that he had committed suicide as a consequence of the stress of losing three of his junior officers at a time when he was also undergoing severe personal difficulties. He was buried with full Police Honours and the coroner suggested that the Metropolitan Police review their welfare arrangements for officers experiencing family break ups. Sir Denzel Goodman went on the record as agreeing to order such a review right away. As for Eddie Duggan himself, the verdict was accidental death. His funeral was a private family affair; but several photographs of his grieving widow wearing fashionable black outfits subsequently appeared in Hello Magazine. A memorial service held at St. Margaret's Westminster, just outside the Houses of Parliament, was reported as being not particularly well attended. The three party leaders had appeared together on television calling for a cleaner and more honourable approach to politics and their unity of purpose had been well received. The proof of the pudding though, commented several political pundits, would be in the campaign for the General Election due the following year.

Regular calls to his grandmother's care home kept him abreast of her progress. She seemed to have rallied a bit the week following his last visit and had been taking solid food, but her breathing remained a problem and the long-term prognosis was unchanged. He repeated his visit the weekend after Kynpham's call and found the old lady significantly worse than she had been just a fortnight previously. She had not been out of bed for several days, was eating and drinking very little and was fast asleep for virtually all the time he was with her. The doctor called in again while he was there and suggested that he prepare himself for the worst. His journey home was not a happy one; he strongly suspected that he had seen his grandmother alive for the last time. Discovering the newly upgraded kitchen and utility room that Peter Brewer had completed installing while he was away did nothing to lift his spirits.

In fact the old lady died eleven days later; late in the evening on Wednesday 25th November. By the time he should have been starting work the next morning, Simon was driving along the A17 past Kings Lynn. He pulled into a lay-by a few minutes later and telephoned his employers who expressed their sincere condolence and immediately agreed to him taking the balance of his leave entitlement so that he could take care of all the necessary arrangements. It was not until he had almost arrived at his destination that he realised he would be unable to keep his promise to Kynpham and Rebecca Johal. He telephoned the journalist that evening to apologise and received another expression of sympathy.

Simon's grandmother's funeral took place at Barrow-in–Furness Crematorium at nine thirty the following Tuesday morning. Although quite used to death from his time in ordained ministry and secure in the knowledge that his grandmother had held a deep, but private Christian faith, Simon was nonetheless moved and upset as the curtain closed; concealing the coffin from view. Apart from some of the care home staff and three former neighbours there were no other mourners. For a moment he longed for Natalie's embrace; she would understand, he felt; she would hold him and make him feel that life was worth living. But

Natalie Robertson was not there. She had chosen not to be with him and he would not see her again. Grieving and lonely, Simon got into his car and began the gruelling drive back to Norfolk. He would be back at his desk the following morning.

CHAPTER ONE HUNDRED AND FOUR

Natalie was signed off to fly a twin engine aircraft after her sixth hour of dual instruction and immediately booked the aircraft out again for a forty minute solo over the Vale of York. For the first time in many days she felt that she had achieved something that she could be proud of. As she taxied the aircraft back to the flying school she felt an urge to telephone Simon Fenton and tell him all about it. He would be so pleased for her, she thought. Then the awful truth re-asserted itself. It was over between them; over for all time. There would be no telling him of her success; no prospect of hearing his voice; no possibility of experiencing the taste of his lips on hers and no absolution for her lies and for her past. The realisation took the edge off her achievement and she meekly paid for her flying and set off home. She would not fly in the UK again, she decided, until after her course in the USA was complete. She would have to concentrate hard on her studies if she was to pass her examinations in time to start flight training in January.

She lost a further day's study time in mid November as she had to travel to the US Embassy in London to be interviewed as part of her visa application process. The visa duly arrived a week before she was due to attend the residential ground school and Natalie placed the letting of her apartment with a city centre agency, leaving a key and telling them she would be prepared to move out at the beginning of the new year and that she was looking for a six month initial tenancy. On the eve of driving to Bristol for the last part of her theory course Natalie had managed to complete all but six sessions of study.

The ground school took place in a building at the airport, but students were responsible for arranging their own accommodation. Natalie had booked a room in a guest house for the duration of the course and travelled down late on the Sunday afternoon. She discovered that of the eighteen other students who arrived at the airport the following morning only two others were female. Over coffee she joined the other two girls, hoping that some form of friendship might be established through their common bond as women seeking to succeed in a man's world, but the pair of them seemed to be far more interested in the male talent which might become available to them than in the technical aspects of aviation and Natalie went into the first session disappointed. The study was challenging and intensive. By the end of the day they were all pretty much exhausted and the suggestion of a drink in a nearby pub was received with enthusiasm. Several of the men offered to buy Natalie's first drink, but she tactfully refused the offers. Although it was not an uncommon occurrence, the antics of a group of males vying for her attention irritated her immensely. After an hour or so one of the bolder ones sidled up to her and whispered an indecent proposal into her ear; she could save a lot of money, he told her, if she checked out of where she was staying and moved in with him. He had a king size bed and a mini bar, he told her; what more could a girl wish for? Natalie calmly picked up his almost full pint glass from the table, upended it over his head and walked slowly out of the pub. Sitting in her car afterwards the tears began to flow again; how dare the young upstart dare to think he could compete with Simon Fenton, she thought; there could never be anyone else for her.

From then onwards Natalie was regarded with a degree of awe and a grudging respect by her fellow course members. She did not join them in the pub again, but applied herself to her work and tried to make up for the modules she had failed to complete. At the end of the two week course she drove to Oxford where she sat the examinations. The computerised marking system generated the results almost immediately and by the time she drove back to Leeds on the Thursday evening Natalie Roberson needed only to complete her flight training to become a qualified commercial pilot.

Troubled Legacy

Awaiting her at her apartment was a letter from the lettings agent. A young couple who were getting married on Christmas Eve had viewed her apartment while she had been away. They wanted to take it at the asking rent, but only on condition that they could move their things in before the wedding. The offer was too tempting to miss. The next morning Natalie agreed on the Friday before Christmas as the handover date and contacted her travel agent to try and rearrange her flight. The best that they could offer was a seat on the Manchester – Orlando flight on Wednesday 23rd. They could also offer her a room at an airport hotel in Orlando over the festive period at a reasonable rate. Natalie accepted. The die was cast; she would be leaving the country before Christmas. That evening she treated herself to a bottle of wine, but not as a celebration; it was more of a wake for her lost love and the life that might have been.

CHAPTER ONE HUNDRED AND FIVE

Kynpham Johal avoided telling his sister about the death of Simon's grandmother and his friend's inability to spend time with them in London until after he had met her at Heathrow and they had found seats together on the Tube train. Although Rebecca was not without compassion for the man she had adored from afar for so long, when she heard the news of his grandmother's death the girl could not hide the bitterness of her disappointment. She had anticipated being in the company of Simon Fenton within twenty four hours and now it seemed probable that she might not see him at all. Booking a return flight in time for her to spend Christmas with her family had proved difficult and she had been forced to limit her stay to less than three weeks. She was due to fly back early on the morning of Wednesday 16th.

Rebecca had arranged to spend the second weekend of her visit with Sally Chamley and her family in Carlisle. Her school had a twinning link with the Church of England Primary School in Dove Holes in Derbyshire and she had also arranged to spend a few days there staying with one of the teachers and her family while learning about the modern style of teaching that she had been told was in use in the UK and which was very different from the overtly didactic approach that she was used to in India. She knew that Simon worked from Monday to Friday and Kynpham had explained that taking time off to attend to his grandmother's affairs had robbed him of his remaining leave entitlement. For some time after they reached

Kynpham's flat she sat silently in thought, oblivions to her brother's attempts to cheer her up with anecdotes about his work. Eventually her good nature won out and she tried her best to respond to his attentions. His new home, she told him, was very impressive; far better than she had been expecting. For a while she was distracted by the novelty of British television but, as bedtime approached, she could hold her disappointment in check no longer and, comforted by her twin brother, Rebecca Johal shed a few tears.

The next morning Kynpham made a special effort to lift Rebecca's spirits. He had managed to book a trip on the London Eye and had used one of his contacts from the newspaper to secure two returned tickets for a West End musical. On her part, Rebecca did her best to show her appreciation, but there was little joy in the excursions for her. The ingredient of the trip that she had been most looking forward to was missing. It was no one's fault, but that did little to mollify her. Sunday brought a church service in the morning and lunch at a local Chinese restaurant, but not even Kynpham's unexpected early Christmas gift to her of five hundred pounds spending money for her holiday could draw Rebecca out of her unhappiness. Throughout the weekend she felt a keen compassion for Simon, persuading herself that he had been just as disappointed as she was at the cancelled get-together and that coupled with his grief at the loss of the woman who had been virtually mother as well as grandmother to him he would be even more upset than she was. Sitting in front of the television that evening, Rebecca turned things over and over in her mind. While she did not want to inappropriately intrude on Simon's grief she had the glimmerings of a plan. All she needed to do was to persuade her brother to play along.

In the event, Kynpham was given a new assignment the following day. Together with the young photographer he had been tasked with visiting a selection of the most deprived and most prosperous town and cities in Britain during the run up to the coming festivities with a view to producing a set of features comparing and contrasting places of a similar size from each end of the spectrum for inclusion in the paper in the week before Christmas. It had been Kynpham's idea to match them by alliterating their names; Burnley and Basingstoke, Skelmersdale and Surbiton and so on. He was pleased and proud to be given the job, but after a couple of days doing research and making appointments he and his colleague would be away for most of Rebecca's time in England. She was travelling to Carlisle on the Friday so there would only be a day or so between Kynpham leaving and her departure for the North, but Kynpham feared that she would be returning from the school at Dove Holes to an empty flat. Rebecca, however, was not at the least disappointed to hear the news; events were playing right into her hands. If Simon Fenton could not fit in a visit to London then Rebecca Johal could certainly pay a visit to Wroxham on her way back south.

At first Kynpham was reluctant to make the call, but Rebecca's insistence and his own instinct that Rebecca and Simon might actually be good for each other eventually persuaded him. He left a message on Simon's landline voicemail asking him to call as soon as he returned home.

CHAPTER ONE HUNDRED AND SIX

Simon arrived home late on the Wednesday afternoon. He returned Kynpham's call later that evening. After once again expressing his condolences, Kynpham announced that Rebecca was with him and would like a word. Mildly perplexed, Simon agreed to the request.

'Simon, it's Rebecca,' she said, 'I'm so sorry to hear the bad news about your grandmother.'

They went on to talk in general terms for a minute or two about Simon's loss and Rebecca's time in London before she made her pitch.

'Simon,' she said, 'you are probably going to think that I am being very rude, but I have something to ask you.'

'Ask away then,' Simon replied with absolutely no inkling of what was about to follow.

'First I have to tell you some things about my brother,' she began, 'Now that he is an important feature writer he has been given a very important job and he is in danger of neglecting his dear twin sister.'

'And...'

'And he is not altogether unhappy at the prospect. He is to go on a tour of Britain to write articles about how rich and poor placed are preparing themselves to celebrate Christmas. And he is to take with him a photographer; a lady photographer. Her name is Katie Brookfield and she is just twenty one years old and, he tells me she is very pretty. He has now told me that she too is a Christian and lives in Croydon with her parents. I do not think that Kynpham is altogether troubled by the fact that he will not be at home to look after his poor sister.'

Rebecca went on to outline her plans to visit Sally Chamley in Carlisle and the school at Dove Holes before getting to the main point of the call.

'You see, Simon, I will be quite alone over the weekend of eleventh to fourteenth December and I was thinking that I might be very presumptuous and visit your home on my way back from the north. It is sad that we could not meet in London, but perhaps we could meet in Norfolk to make up for it?'

There was a long pause in the conversation. Simon could hear Rebecca breathing rapidly.

'I suppose you could come for a day or two,' he replied.

'Oh Simon, that would be excellent,' she replied. Simon, taken rather by surprise, floundered for words. Rebecca continued; she had thought it all through in advance.

'Would it be possible for me to arrive after you finish work on the eleventh?' she asked, 'and then I could take the train back to London on Monday morning when you go back to work; that would give us three nights and two days together..' Fearing that she had seemed too pushy, Rebecca paused, '...if you think that will be OK.'

Once again Simon agreed. They chatted briefly about the arrangements before Rebecca put Kynpham back on the line for a final chat with his friend. Kynpham apologised for his sister's poor manners, but thanked Simon for his offer to entertain Rebecca during his assignment. Simon asked about Katie Brookfield, but Kynpham became rather coy and evasive so Simon did not press the matter. After the call Simon sat at the kitchen table with a coffee.

Spending time with Rebecca Johal would not be an altogether unpleasant experience, he thought. He remembered her as a lively and inquisitive girl, if a little immature. Showing her the sights of rural Norfolk in mid-winter might be a welcome distraction to his recent unhappiness. It was not until he was getting ready for bed that the full implications of her visit struck him. The Indian girl would be sleeping in the room he had prepared for Natalie; Rebecca would be the first visitor in his newly refurbished home. For a moment he contemplating contacting Rebecca and telling her that he had changed his mind. Good manners and gratitude for the time in Carlisle when she had almost certainly saved his life prevailed however and he resigned himself to dealing with whatever wounds Rebecca's visit might open in him. It was hardy her fault that things had not worked out between him and Natalie; he would just try to make sure he made Rebecca's visit as different as possible from the one he had planned for Natalie.

CHAPTER ONE HUNDRED AND SEVEN

When Kynpham Johal left his flat on the morning of Thursday 3rd. December for his ten day odyssey around Britain Rebecca was in a state of near euphoria. In only nine days time she would be alone in the company of the man she had admired from afar for so long. With her brother's Christmas gift burning a hole in her pocket she set out to make her preparations.

Later that afternoon she laid out her purchases on the bed; a light green woollen coat, two pairs of jeans, tops in a variety of colours, a thick woollen sweater, some cotton pyjamas, a pair of fur-lined boots, and several items of underwear. Still in its bag was the rather daring item that she had impulsively bought for use if all else failed. Although there had been sexual encounters in her distant past, Rebecca had remained chaste since her conversion to Christianity and the purchase had not been made without a twinge of guilt. There would, however, only be the one opportunity for Simon Fenton to fall in love with her and drastic measures might be called for. She hoped that God would forgive her if needed to resort to them. Rebecca tried on her various outfits in front of the dressing table mirror and was not displeased with what she saw. She put the clothes that she had tried on neatly away in the wardrobe and turned her attention to the blue carrier bag on her bed. A not unpleasant shudder of anticipation ran through her body as she stripped off her underwear and wriggled into the dark red, low cut silk nightgown. The feel of the material on her naked skin was sensual and she thought that the colour complemented her brown skin perfectly. Deep within her a battle raged between her sincere desire to behave as a good Christian should and the mental image that was forming in her mind of Simon Fenton sliding the nightgown slowly down her slim body, exposing her most private and intimate secrets to his eyes and touch. Rebecca shivered at the thought and quickly slipped off the nightgown, covering herself up in her brother's fleecy dressing gown. She ran a bath and pushed the troubling daydream from her mind. Her rendezvous with the man of her dreams was over a week away; before then there were other things that she must do.

Sally Chamley met Rebecca's train at Carlisle station and the visitor from India quickly found herself swept up into the bosom of Sally's family. A hot meal of Cumberland sausage and mashed potatoes was served up within minutes of her arrival and Sally's two teenage brothers were obviously on their best behaviour. All five Chamleys were fascinated by Rebecca's tales of living and teaching in India and the evening passed quickly. The two girls shared a room; Sally had given up her bed to Rebecca and was sleeping on an inflatable mattress on the floor. Snuggled beneath the bedclothes in the cool darkness, Rebecca told her friend about her disappointment when Simon Fenton had been unable to visit her and Kynpham in London because of his grandmother's death and how she had taken the bull by the horns and invited herself to his home for the following weekend. The next day Sally drove Rebecca into the midst of the Lake District. Despite the overcast skies and cold wind Rebecca told her friend that she had never seen anything as beautiful as majestic hills rising above the still blue waters flanked by skeletal trees and quaint little houses. They had a late lunch at a pub in Ambleside before returning to Carlisle in time for the evening meal. Sunday brought a visit to the church which Sally, her mother and her younger brother attended. Once again a great fuss was made of the visitor from India. After Sally had dropped off to sleep that night Rebecca lay in her bed contentedly, listening to the distant sound of traffic on the motorway. She could not remember ever being so happy in her life.

Rebecca had agreed to visit the school at Dove Holes more out of a sense of duty than as a highlight to her trip to England. A teacher from Dove Holes had visited the Bishop's School in Shillong before Rebecca had started teaching there; introducing the staff and pupils to the idea of thematic rather than single-subject teaching. The visit had not been long enough, however, to make much of an impact on the curriculum and the Bishop's School still maintained the traditional approach favoured by the Indian Government. Another party of teachers from Derbyshire had paid a flying visit the previous year, although none of them came from the school at Dove Holes. Rebecca had been astonished at the easy familiarity with which the British teachers had treated the children; playing games with them and teaching then songs and rhymes. One of the visiting teachers had brought a glove puppet in the form of a large black bird with him and had chased the squealing pupils around the playground with it. A further visit to Shillong by a teacher from Dove Holes was scheduled for the following April and Rebecca felt an obligation to make a reciprocal visit. Although her professional curiosity had been aroused by the prospect of spending time in the English school, her attitude to the stay in Derbyshire was coloured by her impatience to get to see Simon again.

The headmaster was waiting at the station with two of the older pupils when her train pulled in. The two eleven year olds were introduced as Alice and Lauren. With the headmaster carrying Rebecca's bag the four of them braved the drizzle and made the short journey to the school which was housed in a Victorian building alongside a busy road. The afternoon session was underway when they arrived, but the head had arranged for tea and sandwiches and the four of them sat in the lemon-painted staffroom for a late lunch. Rebecca was surprised when the head delegated the task of showing the important visitor from India around the school to the two eleven year olds; such a thing would have been unthinkable in India. Here, it seemed, things were different and Rebecca marvelled at the interactive electronic whiteboards, the brightly coloured displays and the inquisitive and active learning style of the English children. At break time she was introduced to her host; Mary Sheldrake, a teacher in her mid forties. After school ended Mary drove Rebecca to her home in nearby Buxton, which she shared with her husband Tom and her teenage daughter Emma. At first Rebecca felt awkward in the company of strangers, but after a meal she and Mary sat down together at the kitchen table while the English teacher showed her Indian colleague how lessons were planned, progress assessed and how the complicated English curriculum was being structured around themes to help pupils make sense of their world as well as accumulate knowledge about individual subjects. Rebecca was truly fascinated and the rest of the week passed quickly as she was thrust in at the deep end in Mary's class and, by Thursday, the Indian teacher was delivering interactive and differentiated lessons that she had planned herself under her mentor's watchful guidance. Whenever possible, Rebecca chose to spend break times with the pupils in the damp and windy playground. Alice and Lauren became her constant companions and with one of them on each arm she learned much about childhood in Britain and the interests, hopes and aspirations of eleven year old girls. When she awoke on Friday morning, Rebecca could hardy comprehend that she would be meeting Simon within a matter of hours. Throwing back her bedroom curtains, she received another tingle of excitement. In the first light of dawn it was evident that the grey skies had gone. In their place the eastern sky was painted in a deep shade of azure and the surrounding hills were coated in a powdery coat of white snow. Apart from a distant glimpse of the Himalayas from aeroplanes she had never seen snow before in her life. She had timed her arrival in Wroxham to coincide with the end of Simon's working day. The first part of the morning, therefore, would be spent in school. She had been particularly looking forward to it as there was to be a Christmas Service rehearsal in St. Paul's Church which was adjacent to the school. Flanked by the inevitable Alice and Lauren, Rebecca sang her heart out as the familiar words of Christmas carols acquired new poignancy in the Christmas card church set in a Christmas card landscape. A few of the older children were tasked with collecting the hymn sheets and tidying up after the rehearsal. Standing in the church porch afterwards Alice asked Rebecca what she would be doing at the weekend.

'Visiting my boyfriend,' replied Rebecca, hoping for all she was worth that her answer would prove to be the truth.

The train left Dove Holes a little after the school's morning break. The headmaster, accompanied once again by Alice and Lauren, escorted her to the station. Just as Rebecca was about to step onto the train Alice squeezed her arm gently.

'Have a good time with your boyfriend, Miss,' she said and Rebecca's heart missed a beat.

The snow had all disappeared by the time Rebecca changed trains at Stockport, but the cold blue skies remained. Although she attempted to pass the time by reading a magazine, she could not concentrate on it and as each mile passed by her anticipation heightened. It was dark when she changed trains again at Norwich, and bitterly cold. The train from Manchester had been running ten minutes late, leaving only five minutes for her to make the connection. Rebecca dashed through the station concourse and along the platform, stepping through the train door with only a minute to spare. Her first port of call was the toilet cubicle where she washed her hands and face, combed her hair, applied just a trace of make-up and applied a dab of perfume to her neck and each of her wrists. By the time she found a seat the train was only five minutes away from its first stop and her destination. As the squeal of brakes announced its imminent arrival at Wroxhan station Rebecca stood up, her heart was fluttering and her breathing was rapid and shallow. She was utterly convinced that her life was about to change for ever.

The train drew to a halt and the door slid open. Rebecca stepped down onto the platform amongst a small crowd of homecoming commuters. She stepped aside to let them pass, unsure of her surroundings. As the platform cleared she saw him. Simon Fenton was standing under a lamppost, his hands thrust deep into the pockets of a long overcoat with his breath condensing into a cloud under the glare of the lamp. He looked at her and smiled. Rebecca's heart stood still and it was several seconds before she regained the power of movement.

Simon had been looking forward to Rebecca's visit with mixed emotions. His innate good manners and sense of hospitality convinced him that he should make a real effort to make sure that she enjoyed herself, but his underlying sadness and the uncanny congruence with the weekend he had hoped to spend with Natalie before she had walked out of his life sapped his energy and enthusiasm. He had managed to acquire a pair of tickets for the Thursford Collection Christmas Spectacular for the Saturday night. Thursford was a living museum of Victorian fairground rides and steam traction engines. In the weeks leading up to Christmas it also staged an elaborate variety show with a seasonal theme. Sunday would, of course, involve church and Andy and Jane Carr had insisted on entertaining them for Sunday lunch. At first Simon had refused but, unwilling to divulge his true feelings, he had eventually given in graciously. As he stood waiting for Rebecca's train in the freezing darkness he was not sure at all that he was looking forward to the next couple of days.

The train pulled in and for a moment he could not see her, but as the crowd thinned he spotted her standing quite still towards to rear of the train. He smiled and began to walk towards her. How should he greet her, he wondered, a handshake seemed too formal and a kiss too forward. In turn Rebecca started to walk in his direction trailing a suitcase behind her. He embraced her in an awkward hug and asked her about her journey as he picked up the suitcase and led the way down the zig-zag ramp towards the subway. Simon asked if she liked Chinese food. Rebecca nodded and he suggested they call at a take-away on the way to his house. The girl was quiet in the car and Simon worried that the weekend might prove difficult, but she seemed to perk up a bit in the take-away as they waited for their order sitting side by side on a vinyl covered bench. By the time they arrived at his house, Simon realised that his fears had been unfounded. Rebecca was chatting happily to him about her tour of the Lake District and her friend Sally Chamley. Simon showed her to the spare room and told her to make herself at home while he served up the food. A few minutes later she appeared downstairs wearing jeans and a sweater and they sat down to eat. Rebecca spoke with great enthusiasm about her time in the Derbyshire school. There was so much that teachers in India could learn from their colleagues in England, she told him; it was not really a matter of technology and equipment – more to do with engaging children in their own learning and matching what was taught to each child's needs and abilities. Simon noticed that Rebecca's eyes sparkled when she talked about her vocation. It was disturbingly reminiscent of how Natalie had looked when she told him about learning to fly the first time they met. With her dark hair and lively brown eyes, Rebecca Johal drew the lonely man slowly out of his recent episode of self-imposed exile as she projected her vivacious and effervescent personality into the sterility of his home. With the meal long finished Rebecca insisted on washing the pots while Simon dried. He then suggested that they retire to the lounge with hot chocolate. Rebecca said that she would need to slip upstairs for a moment first. Simon made the drinks and carried the two mugs into the lounge, setting them down on the fireplace before settling into the fireside chair. After a while the girl returned. She was wearing the white towelling dressing gown that he had bought for Natalie over a pair of white cotton pyjamas. Rebecca picked up her drink and curled up on the sofa. For a moment Simon felt an irrational anger; in his mind the girl was wearing Natalie's clothes. Rebecca appeared not to notice anything untoward and began asking him about his plans for the weekend. The anger slowly evaporated as the smiling Indian girl once again brought her warmth and energy into his living room. As he lay in bed that night Simon decided that the weekend might possibly be more enjoyable than he had anticipated; Rebecca was proving to be good company after all.

CHAPTER ONE HUNDRED AND EIGHT

Rebecca was up and dressed early the next morning and cooked Simon a large omelette for breakfast as soon as he came downstairs. Over coffee she gently but persistently interrogated him about the circumstances that had led to him being on the run from the police, the manner in which Kynpham had received his injury, the source of the huge amount of money her brother had received in compensation and the serious affairs that had kept Kynpham from telling her anything at all about any of it. She was no more successful with Simon and he attempted to dissuade her from pursuing the matter any further by suggesting a walk into town. There had been a sharp frost and the ice on the puddles crackled as they made the short journey. The Broads and moorings in Wroxham were coated in a thin crust of ice and they laughed at the antics of a number of water birds which were skating giddily across the frozen surface. Simon bought a few items from a supermarket while Rebecca picked up a selection of souvenirs for her family at home. The biting cold soon drove them back to Simon's house and tea and crumpets warmed them through as they sat at the kitchen table.

In spite of his reservations, Simon decided to take Rebecca to the seaside on the way to Thursford. After de-icing the car he drove them to the little seaside town of Wells-next-the-Sea. They parked in the town centre and Simon insisted that they walk out to the beach along the long spit of land that formed the harbour wall, Muffled by hats scarves and gloves they braved the elements and stood together on the beach watching noisy seagulls wheeling and diving out in the estuary. On the walk back Rebecca plucked up courage and linked arms with Simon. He did not object and she shuddered with happiness and excitement. Things seemed as if they were going to plan.

They ate in a harbour side pub, looking out through the window at a fishing boat being unloaded by two very cold looking fishermen. As the sun sank in the western sky the temperature dipped even further and they set off on the next leg of their journey.

To Rebecca Thursford was like some sort of English fairyland. The Victorian fairground rides and side-shows were festooned with coloured lights and the barrel organs pumped out an endless stream of festive music. Rebecca managed to persuade Simon to take her on the several rides, the most enjoyable of which was the waltzer which squashed them together from thigh to shoulder as it performed its dizzy gyrations. They sat close together in the show and once again Rebecca was enchanted by the singing and dancing. All her life she had lived with images of Christmastime in England from storybooks and films. Now she was experiencing it for herself; and in the company of the man of her dreams. When the show was over they walked slowly back to the car arm in arm, their breath condensing into mist in the freezing air. For Rebecca it had been by far the best day of her life. She glanced up at the man beside her. If only he would stop, turn towards her, take her in his arms and kiss her, Rebecca thought the day would become absolutely perfect.

Mildly disappointed to reach the car without the romantic encounter she longed for, Rebecca was nevertheless content with her lot. She was having the time of her life and there was still another day for the romance to blossom. As she lay awake that night she convinced herself that she could hear Simon's rhythmic breathing in the room next door. She toyed with the idea of "sleepwalking" into his room wearing her red silk nightgown, but quickly dismissed the thought as wicked. She would wait and see what the next day brought, she decided.

Simon was up first the next morning. He had enjoyed Rebecca's company the day before and was glad that he had agreed to her visit. She was like her brother in many ways, he thought, slightly impetuous with an

Troubled Legacy

impish sense of humour. She was also proving to be a good friend. He was grateful to her for breaking through his shell of isolation and forcing him to re-engage with life, but he did not know how to express his thanks in words. Rebecca slept late and had to rush to get ready for church. She and Simon sat together on a pew near the back and, to his surprise, Simon felt uplifted and inspired by the service. Lunch at the vicarage was a chaotic affair with the two children continually competing for attention while Jane attempted to serve up the food. Rebecca found herself drawn into the children's games and enjoyed herself immensely. Over the meal she was once again the centre of the conversation; Andy and Jane asked her about life, church and her work in India. Coffee followed, then another bout of children's games and before Rebecca realised what time it was. Darkness had fallen and she had spent virtually no time alone with Simon Fenton. It would be their last evening together and the romance was no further forward than it had been at the end of the previous day. With growing frustration, Rebecca waited as Andy and Simon debated the best method of fixing small candles to oranges in order to produce Christingles for the Christmas Eve Service and it was after six when they eventually arrived back at Simon's house. He insisted on cooking their supper and left Rebecca nursing her growing, but well-hidden irritation in front of the television. The meal seemed to take an age to prepare but eventually Simon called Rebecca through into the kitchen. Her heart leapt as she saw two steaming plates of beef stew and dumplings and an open bottle of red wine standing on the table, illuminated only by the light of two candles.

As they ate, Simon thanked Rebecca for her company, but made no move towards the intimacy that she longed for. They washed up together afterwards, then Simon pleaded fatigue and the prospect of a hard day at work and told her that he was going to get an early night. They agreed the arrangements for him to drop her off at the station on his way to work and he kissed her chastely on the cheek and retired upstairs. After he had gone Rebecca slumped back into her chair, buried her head in her hands and her eyes were moist with tears. After such a promising start things had not proceeded as she had hoped and expected. Time was running out rapidly; there was just the one course left open to her, but she baulked at the prospect. She lay in bed until almost midnight before finally making up her mind. She switched on the bedside light, got out of bed and with shaking hands peeled off her white pyjamas. From her suitcase she took the long red silk nightgown and slid it over her head. The central heating had been turned off by its timer and she could not tell whether her shaking was caused by the cold, her fear or a frisson of sexual anticipation. Rebecca opened the door of her room and ran water noisily into the bath for a few minutes before flushing the lavatory and closing the door with a thud. She stood on the landing for a while hoping that Simon would emerge from his room; if he did she would throw her arms around him; kiss him and take it from there. Nothing happened. She waited for what seemed to be an eternity but there was no sound of movement from Simon's room. Rebecca was freezing cold. She gave Simon's bedroom door a tentative push and it swung gently open. In the diffused glow of the orange street lamp that penetrated through the curtains she could see him. He appeared to be fast asleep with his back to her. Gathering her courage in both hands, Rebecca gently shook him by the shoulder. Simon groaned a little, but did not wake up. With no further options remaining Rebecca slipped the thin straps off the nightgown from her shoulders and let it fall around her ankles. As naked as the day she was born and trembling with cold and apprehension Rebecca Johal gently pulled back the quilt and slid into bed beside Simon Fenton.

CHAPTER ONE HUNDRED AND NINE

It was a cruel dream. Simon knew it was a dream because he was in bed with Natalie, but Natalie has spurned his offer of marriage and told him that she never wanted to see him again. He could feel the heat of Natalie's body close to his. He reached out a hand and felt the silky smooth skin of her back. He moved his hand slowly around to cup her breast and kneaded her nipple between his finger and thumb, feeling it become engorged as she began to become aroused. Between his legs his own arousal was also making itself known. He wriggled towards her and let his erection nestle between the mounds of her buttocks through the thin cotton of his boxer shorts. He began to slide his hand from her breast downwards towards her groin. She emitted a low groan.

'Simon,' she said, 'oh, Simon.' But it was not Natalie's voice. He sat up with a start. He had not been dreaming after all. In panic, Simon pulled the quilt around him and reached out to switch on the bedside light. When turned back he was greeted by the sight of Rebecca Johal struggling with the remnants of the quilt in a futile attempt to cover her nakedness as she pushed herself into a sitting position. Simon let go of his end of the quilt, but not quickly enough; and the image of her pert breasts, the nipples still standing erect, burned itself into his mind as he climbed out of his bed and shuffled towards the window taking care to shield the bulge in his boxer shorts from his guest.

'What the hell are you doing, Rebecca?' he snapped, not daring to look back over his shoulder, 'Go and put some clothes on and go downstairs will you. I think you owe me some sort of explanation.' Simon kept his eyes averted as he heard his bedroom door open and close.

For several minutes he stood in front of the window, willing his erection to subside. The mental image of the naked Indian girl though continued to torment him. He wondered if he had given her the wrong impression somehow. If he had it had certainly not been his intention, but the memory of what had almost happened in his bed was strong. Rebecca had certainly made it clear that she was available to him and for a long moment he wrestled with temptation. Torn between flesh and spirit, Simon tried to make sense of what was happening to him. With no warning a peculiar sense of calm descended and he walked back towards the bed as his erection subsided. From the bottom drawer of his bedside cabinet he extracted the canvas print of Natalie Roberson laughing with the wind blowing through her hair from the bottom drawer. He hung it back on the hook on the wall opposite his bed, pulled on his trousers and a sweatshirt and went downstairs.

Rebecca was sitting on the living room sofa wearing her pyjamas and dressing gown. In the glow cast by the wall lamps he could see that she had been crying. He turned on the gas fire.

'I'll make us some hot chocolate,' he said. Rebecca made no reply, but continued to sniffle as she wiped her nose with a tissue. Simon busied himself in the kitchen and when he returned the girl was sitting staring into the fire.

'Simon, I'm so sorry,' she sobbed.

'And I'm sorry if I led you on,' he said, 'and I'm even sorrier for what I was doing when I realised it was you I was doing it to.'

'No, Simon, it was all my fault,' replied Rebecca, 'you see I've been in love with you for ages and you didn't seem as if you loved me back so I thought that if I could get you to make love to me you might change your mind and...' Rebecca subsided into sobbing once again and Simon waited patiently for her to stop.

'Listen Rebecca, I think you're a great girl, but I'm not in love with you.' Simon said softly, 'you can't choose who to fall in love with. I know that from experience, but you can't make someone who isn't in love with you fall in love with you either.'

'But I was so sure,' she sniffled, 'ever since I was in England after your wife died. I didn't want to say anything then because you were still grieving for her. I didn't want to be pushy or anything, but I think you're fantastic, Simon. Are you sure we couldn't ever be together?'

'I'm really sorry, Rebecca,' he answered, 'but the answer is no. I won't say that I don't find you attractive,' he coloured up, 'but you probably know that already. I'll be absolutely honest with you; I think you deserve that. I can't ever be in love with you Rebecca, because I love someone else.'

Rebecca started crying again. Simon resisted an impulse to sit beside her and put his arm around her shoulders.

'B.b.but, who?' she stammered through her tears, 'is it the woman you were with when the police were after you?'

Simon sighed.

'Wipe your eyes and drink your chocolate,' he said, 'and I'll tell you about her.'

Without going into specifics about the exact circumstances in which they had met began to tell Rebecca about how he and Natalie had fallen in love and how he had asked her to marry him and how Natalie had turned him down and told him that she did not want to see him again. He told the story with a frankness and honesty that surprised him and, from time to time the flow was interrupted by his own emotions. Rebecca listened with growing attentiveness, interjecting the occasional question. The tale took almost an hour in its telling and Simon was physically and emotionally wrung out by the end of it.

'Thank you for telling me this,' said Rebecca, 'I have behaved like a silly girl, Simon. Please forgive me. While I was thinking that you had just broken my heart it was your heart that was broken and compared to the great love you have told me about I can see that what I felt for you was just a pale shadow of the love you have for this Natalie Robertson. While you have been talking I have been listening and thinking and I think that by telling myself I was in love with you I was maybe somehow avoiding my calling. It is glamorous and attractive to believe you love a man who lives thousands of miles away in another country, but I think now that Shillong is the place I must be in and not this Wroxham.'

Simon looked up at her and smiled.

'Now don't you go smiling at me, Simon Fenton,' she ordered, 'It is hard enough for me to accept what has happened and if I am not careful it will be possible for me to persuade myself that perhaps I have some hope of winning your heart after all. I am going to bed now, my own bed, I will not sleep well and I will cry a little; but I know now that I must let go of this love I have carried for you and I must go back to my school and teach others how the children of England learn. Who knows, perhaps there in India there might be someone who will love me like you love your Natalie one day. I will pray for you Simon; I will pray for you and Natalie that God will bring you back together,'

Rebecca stood up.

'I'm not sorry you came this weekend,' Simon said, 'Whatever the rights and wrongs of what happened in my bedroom I'm not sorry that we have had this talk. You have helped me more than you will ever know Rebecca; you have helped me to put into words what I feel about Natalie; and even if I never see her again, I know now that there can never be anyone else for me.'

Rebecca smiled.

'Let us not talk of what happened or did not happen here tonight ever again. Perhaps even after all that has passed between us we might one day be good friends.'

She turned and climbed slowly up the stairs leaving Simon staring at the flickering flames of the fire. It was as if speaking of his love for Natalie had somehow set his heart aflame for her all over again. In a bittersweet moment he realised that what he had told Rebecca was the absolute and irrefutable truth. He would love Natalie Robertson until the day he died. He walked back up the stairs to his bedroom. He did not take the portrait of Natalie down from the wall.

CHAPTER ONE HUNDRED AND TEN

Freed from the twin rigours of keeping up her flying hours and study, time hung heavily on Natalie's hands. All around her images and music proclaimed the approach of Christmas, but Natalie considered the festivities a double hypocrisy. The superficial bonhomie and the giving and receiving of presents meant little to her. As a child there had been presents and the occasional treat, but her abiding memory of Christmas past was of her mother lying drunk on the sofa after an argument with whoever had been living with them at the time. Even during her time with Matt the festive season had been little more than an excuse for another round of parties. As for the religious element, she could not comprehend how anyone could want to celebrate the birth of the son of a cruel and vindictive god. There was not even any real respite from the frenetic hubbub in the gym, as a medley of festive hits and Christmas carols blared out over the music channels on the large screen televisions.

During the last few days in her flat Natalie busied herself in packing up boxes and taking them a few at a time to a self-storage unit she had hired on the outskirts of the city. By Wednesday afternoon all that remained were the few clothes she had decided to take with her to Florida and a large suitcase. On Thursday morning she drove her car round a collection of used car dealers and parted with it in return for a cash offer amounting to less than half its market value. It was a long walk back to her apartment, but she welcomed the distraction of having something to do. Her television and radio had both gone into storage. After a final clean round, Natalie Robertson spent the evening looking out over the city listening to her i-pod and trying to figure out why, if she was on the very verge of achieving her dream, she was so unhappy.

First thing on Friday morning Natalie packed her few remaining possessions into her suitcase. Mindful of the warm climate of her destination she had chosen mostly lightweight clothing. She would be wearing her only warm clothes when she was outside over the weekend and for her journey to the airport. She locked her apartment door behind her, descended in the lift and, trailing her suitcase behind her, took her keys through the rainy streets to the lettings agency on her way to the budget class hotel where she had booked a room until the day of her departure. The room was not ready when she arrived and she spent an hour sitting in the rudimentary reception area while the domestic staff completed their duties. The newly cleaned room was spartan; containing only a bed, chair, dressing table, open plan wardrobe and an elderly television set. The adjoining en-suite shower room was clean, but basic. Natalie was bored to the point of distraction within an hour. The mediocre banality of daytime TV failed to attract her attention and the novel she had bought from the city centre branch of Borders lay discarded on the bed after her third attempt at starting it had lasted no more than ten minutes. Natalie pulled on her short woollen coat and ventured out into the chaos that was Leeds city centre the week before Christmas.

The morning's rain had faded to a light drizzle as she sidestepped and swerved to avoid the burgeoning crowds seeking bargains amongst the garishly festooned stores. It was almost dark and clusters of coloured lights winked and flashed from lampposts and in banners stretching across the streets. Natalie searched for a coffee shop with a vacant table, but could not find one. A brass band was playing Christmas carols on Lands Lane and she ducked into WH Smiths to avoid the gathering crowd of onlookers. Browsing the shelves, Natalie selected a few magazines and a couple more novels; perhaps one of them might prove to be more engaging than the book which was lying on her bed, she thought. The queue at the checkout was moving slowly and she almost gave up waiting, but her turn eventually came.

'Twenty six pounds, forty five, please,' the shop assistant announced, paying little attention to her customer, 'oh and there's a free pack of Christmas cards if you spend over twenty pounds tonight.'

'No thanks,' said Natalie as she held out three ten pound notes. The shop assistant was having a side conversation with her colleague on the next till and slipped the thin plastic pack into the bag with Natalie's purchases. Natalie took her change, shrugged her shoulders and fought her way back into the street.

One of the new novels did the trick. All evening Natalie read, losing herself in the plot to the extent that she looked around in surprise when she put the half read book down having almost forgotten where she was. As she got ready for bed, Natalie cleared the accumulation of books and magazines from the quilt. Amongst them was the pack of Christmas cards. The front card showed a simple Nativity scene; mother father and baby amongst the clutter of a stable. For some reason the serenity of the scene reminder her of Simon Fenton. She had not thought of him since she had returned from her shopping trip. Natalie wondered what he was doing at that very moment. Perhaps he would be involved in churchy things, she thought, or maybe he was curled up in front of the new gas fire, that she had heard about but never seen, with a magazine. She opened the pack of cards; all five of them were identical. Impulsively she pulled her chair up to the tiny dressing table. She would send him a card, she decided, and a brief note just to let him know her plans; after all, no one else in the world was interested in where she went or what she did. She opened the card and smoothed it out before beginning to write.

Dear Simon,

I hope that you are well and happy. I just thought I'd write you a note to let you know that I've passed my Commercial Pilot's exams and I'm off to Florida to start my flight training now. My flight from Manchester is on Wednesday afternoon. I've let out my flat so I'm staying in a hotel until then.

I know that I've hurt you and I'm sorry, but I hope that you will realise one day that us not being together is the best thing for us both.

Take care of yourself and have a good Christmas.

Nat x

Troubled Legacy

As she wrote she had to blink back the tears from her eyes. With a flash of anger she tossed the card into the bin. It would probably just open up old wounds if she sent it; it was far better not to have any contact at all with him. In her lonely room Natalie crept into bed and switched off the light. Sleep, however, was elusive. At ten past midnight she sat up, switched the light back on and read her novel for a while, but the longed for fatigue remained at bay. At two thirty she got up and rooted around in the flap of her purse. Yes, she had been right; there was a first class stamp there. She retrieved the card from the bin, put it in an envelope, wrote Simon's address on the front and affixed the stamp. Dressed again in the clothes she had left on the bedroom chair, Natalie Robertson crept past the woman dozing at the reception desk and out into the night. She posted the card in a pillar box and returned to the hotel. Within minutes of getting back into bed she was fast asleep.

The next few days passed tolerably quickly with the help of magazines, novels and some old films shown on television. Each morning and evening Natalie crossed the city for her habitual workouts on the gym and at lunchtime she resigned herself to queuing for a table in the Pizza Hut across the road from her hotel. Wednesday morning eventually arrived and, after consigning her grubby sports clothing to the bin and checking her travel documents for the last time Natalie checked out of the hotel. It had turned colder overnight and a thin covering of snow masked the pavements and open spaces as she trudged towards the railway station pulling her case along in her wake. Although check in for her flight would not be open until after lunch Natalie had nowhere else to go. She bought her ticket and ordered a large latté from the Starbuck's kiosk on the wide bridge above the tracks. Although there was no table vacant she managed to find a seat nearby and sat down with her coffee. Her short coat, jeans and leather ankle boots were scant protection against the biting cold. Natalie contemplated buying a hat, scarf and gloves from the outlet on the station concourse, but decided that the airport would be warmer. After swallowing the last of her rapidly cooling coffee she descended the steps onto the far platform where she had a short wait for the Airport train. It began to snow again as the train pulled out of Leeds; by Huddersfield blizzard condition completely obscured the view from the window and things did not improve as the train neared its destination.

By the time the passengers had been disgorged into the airport complex chaos had come to reign. Apparently heavy snow had been falling over much of northern Europe all night. Many airports were closed and virtually all flights were delayed or cancelled. Natalie's own flight was showing as "delayed" on the screens. The airport brought memories of that first night with Simon flooding back and, lost in thought, Natalie wandered slowly through the corridors and terminals that had been almost deserted on that August evening, but were now filled by a milling throng of irritated passengers. Almost without realising it she found herself at the foot of the escalator facing the Mancunian Restaurant. The smell of food reminded her that she had not eaten for almost twenty four hours and she joined the slowly moving queue. After a long wait she bought a hot bacon and brie baguette and a soft drink. To her surprise she immediately found a seat at a cluttered and soiled but vacant table. As she looked around she realised that it was exactly the same table at which she and Simon had sat that fateful night. With her eyes moist and her heart heavy, Natalie munched her way slowly through her baguette. As she took the last sip of her drink she became aware of an elderly couple hovering at her side, obviously waiting for the table. Natalie stood up and collected her belongings. Almost straight ahead of her a large sign over a door proclaimed it to be the entrance to the airport's Prayer Room. Natalie shuffled over to the door and pushed it gently. Inside there was only one other person; a woman not much older than herself who was wearing a clerical collar and sat hunched over a laptop computer in a corner. The room had an air of peace about it. Natalie sat down in the almost silent stillness. She wondered if Simon had received his card; and if he had what he thought about it. Did he still think of her, she wondered; and would the knowledge that she had left the country help him to get over her or make his pain worse? She tried to convince herself that he had probably found someone much better than her to love by now, but the thought caused her more distress than comfort. Oblivious to the figure sitting behind her Natalie Robertson began to cry again. She had cried almost every day since telling Simon Fenton that she did not want to see him again.

CHAPTER ONE HUNDRED AND ELEVEN

The morning after his close encounter with Rebecca Johal Simon had expected things to be awkward between them. He had got up and dressed early planning to leave Rebecca free access to the bathroom but she had been downstairs, fully dressed and cooking omelettes, when he arrived in the kitchen.

In the event, Rebecca went out of her way to make him feel at ease. Her smile reached into the corners of her still puffy eyes and their last hour together passed pleasantly as the girl enthused once again about the English education system and how she was going to try and make use of what she had learned in her own practice.

They continued to chat about safe matters as they ate breakfast and then Simon drove her to the station.

'Do not come onto the platform with me,' Rebecca said softly, 'I still cannot properly trust my emotions. Be happy, Simon Fenton, and thank you for being kind to a young Indian girl who has behaved very badly.'

Moved by Rebecca's sincerity, Simon leant across the car and kissed her on the forehead.

'Goodbye Rebecca,' he said, 'now I have the good fortune to count both of the Johal twins as my good friends,' He watched her walk up the ramp towards the platform, but it was a mental image of Natalie Robertson that occupied his mind. The events of the previous evening had brought the pain of their separation once again into sharp focus and the heartache was back with renewed intensity.

Kynpham telephoned him two days later.

'I did not call before, the journalist said, 'because my sister has told me that she has made a fool of herself over you and she is embarrassed for me to talk to you while she is England, but now she will be half-way back to India and we can speak.'

Simon baulked at the prospect of telling Kynpham the details of what had passed between him and Rebecca.

'Well, let's just say that she made her feelings for me pretty clear and I had to disappoint her,' Simon replied, unsure of what Rebecca would have told her brother.

'I am relieved, 'commented Kynpham, 'for many months she has harboured a deep affection for you and I have been torn by my loyalty to you both. Rebecca will be sad for a while, I think, but it is better that she knows how things stand. She will get over it.'

'I'm sorry she had to get hurt,' said Simon, 'but whatever she felt for me, I just didn't feel the same way about her.'

'No, she had told me that' was the reply, 'and she has also told me about your love for the girl that I met briefly at Scotland Yard. I thought that there was not much evidence of love between you then, but obviously I was wrong. Rebecca says that this girl has ended things between you, Simon, and this has hurt you very much.'

'Well it's not exactly like that,' replied Simon, 'look, I'll tell you all about it when we meet up. Now what's all this I hear about you and a young lady photographer?'

Kynpham acknowledged that his friendship with Katie Brookfield was developing, but was just as reticent as Simon to discuss his love life over the telephone, prompting a shared bout of laughter as Simon suggested that if they had both been female they would have known each other's intimate secrets long ago. Simon asked Kynpham what he would be doing over Christmas with a mind to invite his friend to come and stay for a few days, but Kynpham, it appeared, had agreed to spend Christmas day with Katie and her family. They agreed that Simon would visit Kynpham for the New Year bank holiday weekend.

Almost as soon as he had put down the telephone Andy Carr arrived at Simon's house. He had been sent by Jane, he admitted with a broad grin, on a fishing expedition to find out how things stood between Simon and Rebecca. Caroline, it seemed, claimed to have detected some chemistry between them the previous afternoon. Simon quickly put matters right, confiding in Andy that the chemistry had been in one direction only and that he and Rebecca were no more than friends. Andy stayed for a while and by the time he left Simon had surprised himself by agreeing to read one of the lessons at the Carol Service and to help out at the Christmas Eve Christingle. Andy also invited his friend to join the family for Christmas lunch and refused to leave until Simon had accepted the invitation. Simon gave in with good grace; the company of the Carrs, he thought, would be infinitely better than brooding alone in front of the television.

The card from Natalie was waiting for Simon when he got home from work on the Tuesday before Christmas. He did not notice the handwriting at first and placed the card on the kitchen worktop with the assortment of other items that had dropped through the letterbox while he went upstairs to change. It was only when he sat down to his evening meal the Simon retrieved the letters and recognised the writing on the envelope. Oblivious to the cooling meat pie in front of him, Simon tore open the envelope and, with trembling hands opened the card. He read the note several times, searching each time for nuances of meaning. She had made contact with him; that was enough to stir up a tumult of emotions. There was, however no invitation to respond - she had given him no return address; and she was about to fly to the USA to continue her flight training. Simon took a deep breath and tried to make sense of what was happening to him. Natalie had not completely forgotten him, but the card seemed to be more of a goodbye than something the held out any prospect of reconciliation between them. It did not mean that she had changed her mind in any way, she realised, but the fact that she cared presented him with both comfort and renewed anguish. He checked the date and realised that her flight was due to leave the next day. A quick check on the internet narrowed the possibilities; there were just two flights from Manchester to Orlando indicated; a scheduled Virgin service in the morning and a Thomas Cook charter in the afternoon. If he set off right away he would be able to intercept her on her way to check in. His imagination ran away with him as he mentally reviewed all the possibilities, then he picked up the card and read it again. However hard he tried he could find nothing to fuel his fantasies; there was no hint that the card was anything more than an expression of seasonal goodwill containing the briefest of updates on what she was up to. It was not an invitation for any sort of knight in shining armour to pole up at the airport and sweep her off her feet.

Simon sat at the kitchen table for a long time as the food congealed before him but the glimmer of hope that the card's arrival had fanned into life faded slowly into oblivion. He took the card into the living room and gave it pride of place upon the mantelpiece among the scattering of other festive greetings. It was good that Natalie had not forgotten him, he thought, but the blessing of receiving her card was most certainly mixed.

The snow began to fall the day before Christmas Eve and promised that rarest of British phenomena: a white Christmas. The firm that Simon worked for closed down for the holiday at lunchtime on Christmas Eve. A buffet for staff and a few selected customers and suppliers was provided by the owners and Simon had to rush through the snowy streets to church in order to be on hand to help with the three o'clock Christingle Service. Simon's role was to help Andy and the churchwardens distribute the decorated oranges in time for the lighting of the candles on top of each orange, the dimming of the church lights and the singing of "Away in a Manger" in the semi darkness. For the first time since Sophie had died he found himself moved almost to tears by the simplicity of the age-old story that was being told in words, music and drama. Natalie Robertson, he reflected as he walked homewards through the white covered streets with large snowflakes falling softly all around him, had certainly changed his life. Through her he had been able to reconnect with reality; his sterile emotions had been stirred back into life through meeting her and falling in love with her. He wondered what she would have made of the smiling faces of the excited children as they received their Christingle oranges as precursors of the gifts that would surely follow the next morning. But

Natalie was on the other side of the Atlantic, following her dream. He missed her so much.

CHAPTER ONE HUNDRED AND TWELVE

Karen Black was having a bad day. She was in the sixth month of her curacy in the Glossop Team Ministry and not particularly enjoying it. The Team Rector had given her the responsibility for preaching the sermon at the Midnight Communion Service on Christmas Eve at St. Catherine's. With less than thirty six hours to go she had not written a single word of it. If only she hadn't offered to meet John at the airport, she thought. Her husband was a geologist who worked for a charity which dug wells in rural parts of the developing world. Between leaving her job in the city and her ordination Karen had worked briefly as a volunteer for the same charity and she knew all about the primitive conditions and hardships that John would have endured during his three weeks in The Gambia and she had wanted to be on hand to welcome him. To save the charity's money he had booked himself a seat on a holiday charter flight and, because of the severe weather conditions affecting most of northern Europe, the flight had already been delayed twice. Karen muttered to herself as she sat before the blank screen of her laptop in the Prayer Room at Manchester Airport. If the flight had been on time she and John would have been at home by then.

The arrival of a slim brown-haired girl distracted her. Karen watched as the girl walked dejectedly across the room trailing a large suitcase behind her and slumped into chair. Karen looked back at the blank screen and typed a couple of tentative phrases on the theme of God's gift being for life and not for Christmas, but before she was able to develop the idea she was once again distracted; the brown-haired girl seemed to be crying. With an inner sigh, Karen clipped her laptop closed, stood up and went over the where the girl was sitting.

'Excuse me,' said Karen softly, 'but are you all right?'

Natalie looked up.

'No, not really,' she sniffled, 'it's just that I'm going away to do what I've wanted to do for ages, but now that I'm doing it I'm not sure that it is what I want to do after all.'

'Do you want to talk about it?' asked the Curate, my name's Karen.'

Natalie took in her clerical collar.

'Are you a vicar or something,' she asked, 'because if you are I don't thing you'll be able to help. You see I think I've upset God.'

'Why don't you tell me all about it,' suggested Karen, 'and we'll see how we go...'

'But you wouldn't want to help me if you knew what I used to do,' interrupted Natalie, 'I know all this is my own fault. Please, just leave me, I'll be OK soon.'

Karen was tempted to take the girl at her word and return to her sermon, but a mix of duty and interest held her in her seat.

'What's your name?' she asked.

Natalie paused before replying. Taking her courage in both hands she decided to put the vicar lady to the test,

'I'm Natalie and I'm a prostitute,' she said.

Prompted by Karen, Natalie began to talk about her life before Simon and how she had chosen to trade her body for the money to finance her dream of becoming an airline pilot. Taking pains to explain that she had not met Simon Fenton in the capacity of a client, and keeping broadly to an edited version of the truth that gave nothing away about their involvement with either policeman, crooks or politicians she described how she had fallen in love with a wonderful man who had been a vicar himself until his wife had cheated on him and got herself killed in the process. She made no bones about having slept with Simon and was relieved to notice that Karen's facial expression remained open and affirming.

'It all went bad after I was in a bit of trouble,' Natalie explained, 'Things were looking bad and I thought that God was angry with me for making someone as good as Simon fall in love with me. I did a bargain with God. I told him that if he got me out of the trouble I was in I'd give up on Simon. I mean I'm not a believer or anything, not really, but since then I think God's been on my case. I was going to break it off, and then Simon asked me to marry him. I was going to accept; I really loved him and I wanted to marry him more than anything, but I made the mistake of reminding God about my deal and when I told him I was going to break it he gave me the three signs and it all went bloody rotten. Anyway, Simon is so good, so wonderful that someone like me would only mess things up for him and his friends would know what I used to be and think he was doing the wrong thing and he'd never be able to be a vicar or anything 'cos people would call us the vicar and the tart...'

'And how does this Simon feel about it all?' asked Karen, interrupting Natalie's anguished flow.

'Oh he loved me as much as I love him, I think. He always sort of gave the impression that it didn't matter what anyone had done because nobody's perfect. Simon would have married me like a shot, but I know I would just have spoiled everything for him. And now I've broken his heart, but it was for his own good – I did it because I really loved him. It isn't Simon that's the problem, it's God. He's just so cruel and spiteful and I don't really believe in him anyway'

Karen allowed Natalie to sniffle for a few moments as her emotion subsided.

'I don't know if you want to listen,' she said, 'but there are a couple of things I'd like to give you to think about, Natalie; before you get on that aeroplane. Can I carry on?'

Natalie nodded.

'First of all I don't recognise the cruel and spiteful god that you seem to half believe in. The God I know is a lot more like the way you describe Simon Fenton. He's quick to forgive, good through and through and packed full of love. Don't try and judge God by what you call signs. Shit happens, Natalie; to all of us. Don't ask me why a loving God lets bad stuff happen 'cos I can't answer that one, but a lot of bad stuff happens because people make it happen; that's not God's doing. He gives us all freedom; freedom to believe or not to believe and freedom to do good or bad. If I told you that prostitutes are amongst God's favourite people would that make any difference?'

Natalie gave a wry smile.

'But they're not are they. God doesn't like girls who sell themselves for sex.'

'Actually,' countered Karen, 'it's what people do that gets to God, not the people themselves. Christians believe that he created us all and he loves us all to bits. It's just what we sometimes do that upsets him and as your Simon says, nobody's perfect. Just let me get my Bible.'

Karen sat close to Natalie and showed her a story in which a prostitute called Rahab had played a key role in the rescue of some of God' people who were in a fix. Karen went on to point out passages that showed that Jesus himself had often been criticised for spending his time talking with prostitutes and how it was more than likely the Mary Magdalene, one if the first witnesses to Jesus' resurrection had also been a prostitute. Natalie was astonished. All this was new to her.

'And last of all,' continued Karen, 'whatever you might think of God, stop blaming yourself and stop running. Have a long think about what you really want from life; you, not what other people tell you that you ought to want. Stop worrying about what you think that others might think about you, do what your heart tells you. Before I started dressing up in funny clothes,' she touched her collar, 'I used to work in the city. I was on more than a quarter of a million a year. When I got engaged to a geologist who's fifteen years older than me, bald, overweight and lucky if he earns a tenth of what I was on, a lot of my friends and colleagues told me I could have done a lot better for myself, but I loved him and he loved me. In the end, that's all that matters.' Karen glanced up at the arrivals screen. 'Oh shit, his flight landed ten minutes ago. Listen Natalie, I've got to go. Take care of yourself. I hope talking has helped.' She squeezed Natalie's shoulder. 'God bless,' she whispered and, with a last smile, Karen Black scooped her laptop and Bible into a shoulder bag and left.

Natalie sat deep in thought for a while before re-emerging into the chaos of the airport. Flights seemed to be arriving and departing, but there were still many delays and a number of cancellations. She noticed the message "contact airline" showing against the number of her own flight. Tugging her luggage in her wake, Natalie queued at the information desk. She was told that the flight crew had used up all their allotted work hours and the aircraft was stranded in Florida. The flight had been postponed until the following afternoon. The airline was struggling to arrange overnight accommodation for its passengers and the best they could offer Natalie was a night in a hotel in Manchester city centre. Natalie accepted the offer. She wondered if the delay to her flight might be a sign from God, but dismissed the thought immediately in the light of her conversation with the lady vicar.

Natalie retraced her steps to the railway station and caught a train to Piccadilly, from where she walked through the slushy streets, illuminated by myriad coloured lights as twilight turned to darkness across the city and found her hotel overlooking Piccadilly Gardens. By the time she reached her room Natalie was very tired. The delays and frustrations of the day had taken their toll. Then there had been the deeply unsettling conversation with the lady vicar. Dragging her suitcase through the slush had also sapped her energy. With her mind and heart in turmoil, exhaustion drew her remorselessly into slumber. Lying fully clothed on top of the bed Natalie Robertson slept.

Her watch told her that it was half past one in the morning when she awoke. Natalie stretched and yawned as she pushed herself to her feet and shuffled over to the window. It was snowing again. There were a few late night revellers about in the streets below, but no vehicles appeared to be moving and the roadways were coated in a new white blanket. Natalie closed the curtains, threw off her clothes and crawled into bed. Lying in the darkness she reflected on the advice that Karen Black had given her.

'If you're there God,' she whispered, 'I'm sorry if I stuffed up. Could you please help me because I'm feeling a bit lost at the moment.'

CHAPTER ONE HUNDRED AND THIRTEEN

It was daylight when Natalie Robertson woke up the next morning. Her mind was clear and she knew exactly what she had to do. She took her time getting up, thinking through every step of the course of action that suddenly seemed so obvious. After a long hot shower she dressed in the same clothes she had worn the previous day and set out on her mission. Although there had been a fresh snowfall the trams were running and after a cold wait at the tram stop Natalie was whisked directly to the undercroft of Piccadilly railway station. At the top of the escalator she walked straight out into a scene of disorganised mayhem. Many trains had been cancelled and most others were late. Throngs of angry Christmas Eve passengers were milling about aimlessly. Natalie navigated her way through the masses and joined the queue at the ticket office. By the time she had purchased her ticket the crowds were beginning to thin a little. She had not eaten breakfast and was hungry. In the still crowded concourse she managed to get a large latté and a pastry from a Costa Coffee outlet and she stood below the constantly changing electronic departure boards awaiting information on her train; the ten forty two to Norwich was cancelled, but the eleven forty three was shown as running on time. Natalie finished her makeshift meal and made her way to platform thirteen. Despite the milling crowds and air of uncertainty she felt strangely calm. Her mind was made up; it was all or nothing now and nothing was going to stop her. The waiting room on the island platform was bursting at the seams. Natalie shivered with cold as she stood waiting on the exposed platform. It had stopped snowing, but there was a bitter wind blowing. She wished she had followed her instinct and bought a hat, scarf and gloves before leaving Leeds the day before. She had noticed a stall near the booking office with similar items on display and contemplated returning to it, but the train was due in twenty minutes by then and she decided not to bother. Spot on time the Norwich train pulled in, disgorging a frenetic horde of passengers. Natalie slipped quickly through the door, stowed her case and found an empty seat near the vestibule. The die was cast and there would be no turning back.

Natalie was almost warm by the time the train reached Sheffield. She took off her coat and put it on the overhead rack. As the train sped through the East Midlands it began to snow again and the first seeds of uncertainty penetrated Natalie's defences. Perhaps she should have telephoned first, she thought, if things did not turn out well she would end up stranded in the snow. She could always stop off somewhere and find a hotel; that might be safer. That way she could continue her journey in a couple of day's time and insure herself against the consequences of rejection. The snow became heavier and the train slowed perceptibly after Nottingham. Second thoughts began to overwhelm Natalie and she had almost decided to get off at Ely when the snow stopped to reveal a beautiful orange sunset. That reminded her of the photograph that Simon had told her that he had taken of the sun setting from where they had first made love and the thought gave her courage. She bought a sandwich and a drink from the refreshment trolley and tried to hold onto the memory of the blissful few days in the caravan. The on-board announcements apologised for train to being ten minutes late at Grantham twenty two minutes late at Peterborough, forty five minutes late at Ely and fifty one at Thetford. It arrived in Norwich at a quarter past five, over an hour after it had been due, and it was once again snowing heavily. The station was almost deserted, but a short train for all stations to Sheringham stood idling in a platform. Natalie checked the display screen and noted with relief that the first stop was at Wroxham. She boarded the train, took a deep breath and began to rehearse her speech again.

All too quickly the train set off and fifteen minutes later she stepped down into ankle deep snow on the Wroxham platform. She was the only passenger to alight. Although she had never been to Simon's house she had studied its location on Google Earth with him. She was fairly confident that she could find it. Natalie pulled the collar of her short coat up around her neck and dragged her suitcase behind her down the ramp into the subway. The swirling snow made it difficult to see where the pavements ended and the roads started as she stood on the station forecourt trying anxiously to orientate herself with her memory of the birds' eye view on Google Earth. Turning to the right she began to follow what she was fairly certain was Norwich Road. The wind was blowing snow directly into her face, her feet and legs were soaking wet and the wheels on her suitcase were clogged up and useless. Dragging the case behind her like a sledge, Natalie plodded slowly through the blizzard.

In a rising tide of panic her anxieties returned. What if she was making a complete fool of herself, she thought; what if Simon had found someone else and another woman answered the door? Might she have hurt him so badly that he wouldn't want to talk things through with her? He might even not be in; he might have gone on holiday somewhere. All day she had been rehearsing then changing, then re-rehearsing, then changing again what she would say when Simon answered the door, but suddenly it all seemed totally inadequate. If she had known where to look for a hotel she would have turned tail there and then, but it was a day for burning all the bridges behind her; it was still all or nothing.

Almost without realising it she had reached the block of houses where Simon lived. With eyes screwed up against the snow Natalie peered at the house numbers under the muted orange glow of the streetlights. Her stomach churned; she had reached her destination. She stood on his doorstep and pushed the wet hair away from her face. With a racing pulse and butterflies fluttering in her stomach Natalie Robertson reached out and rang the doorbell. In a moment of sheer terror she realised that she had absolutely no idea what she was going to say.

Simon had been sitting in the living room nursing a mug of hot chocolate when the doorbell rang. His first thought was that some brave and hardy carol singers were outside so he returned to the kitchen in search of a two pound coin. As he walked back towards the door the bell rang for a second time. Simon could detect no sound of singing. Puzzled he unlocked the door and pulled it slowly open.

There, right in front of him was an apparition. For all the world he was convinced that Natalie Roberson was standing only inches away from him. He rubbed his eyes but the bedraggled figure did not disappear. His heart leapt for joy.

'Nat!' he shouted, 'is it really you? Come on in out of the snow, Oh, Nat it really is you isn't it?'

She reached out and placed a freezing finger over his lips.

'Shh, Simon, she said, 'before I do anything there's something I want to say. After that you can decide whether you really want me to; come in I mean...Its just that...It's just that I love you, Simon, I really, really do love you and I'm so sorry for all that I've put you through...and if you still want to marry me after all that then...er...then the answer is definitely yes.'

THE END